Lord Of Mists

ISBN 0-9677336-3-4
First Printing/Trade Paperback Edition: December, 2002

LINDSEY BOOKS are published by
Lindsey Publications
P.O. Box 1022
Berthoud, CO 80513
1-800-464-6311
E-mail: Lindseydes@aol.com
Web site: www.lindseypublications.com

This is a work of fiction. Names, characters, places, and incidents either are the
product of the author's imagination or are used fictitiously. Any resemblance to
actual events, locales, organizations, or persons names, living or dead, is entirely
coincidental and beyond the intent of either the author or the publisher.

Printed in the United States of America
10 9 8 7 6 5 4 3 2 1

Lindsey Publications is a member of:
Small Publishers Association of North America / www.SPANnet.org

Lord Of Mists
A NOVEL

Desirée Lindsey

www.lindseypublications.com
2002

Lord Of Mists

**DESIRÉE LINDSEY goes straight for the heart
Her tales will transform your world!**

Raves for *LORD OF MISTS*:
"A compelling story of dark and dangerous passion with intricately-developed characters and sizzling dialogue!"

—*Lily Stevens, author of Keeping Faith*

"Wonderful...very beautiful, emotional story...readers will love it!"

—*From a pool of Editor Comments*

Praise for *PRISONER OF PASSION*:
"Get ready to sizzle and burn. *Prisoner of Passion* will leave you breathless!"

—*Kathleen Harrington, National Bestselling Author*

"Lindsey has done it again! A novel full of passion, heartache, tenderness...love. All the more powerful for its thought-provoking portrayal of the truth. Bravo Desirée Lindsey!"

—*Amy Sandrin, author of Snow Kiss*

"Lindsey is wonderfully talented and has evoked some of the most sensuous images I've read in years! Everything about this story, from the beginning twist...keeps you riveted. Engaging style...an excellent story!"

—*From a pool of Editor Comments*

"Spicy...highly erotic...those who want hot, hot sex will enjoy this new addition!"

—*Romantic Times*

Books by Desirée Lindsey

ENSLAVED (novella)
www.redsagepub.com / Secrets vol. IV /
ISBN: 0-9648942-4-6
He awakened her passion, captured her tender heart, then silently stepped aside to let his best friend marry her. Years of frustration spent failing to give her husband an heir have taken their toll—now a childless Lady Crystal Halverton turns in desperation to friend and libertine, Nicholas Summer to ask the unthinkable.

PRISONER OF PASSION
www.lindseypublications.com / booksurge.com /
amazon.com / ISBN: 0-9677336-1-8
ebook / dload / www.hardshell.com /
ISBN: 1-58200-138-3
Circumstances have forced Sarah Gray into a life of debauchery to protect her daughter. A highly acclaimed courtesan, she is accused of poisoning one of her patrons and now his brother, the virile and handsome Stephen Rathburn, Duke of Whitbury, is determined to see her suffer as he has suffered.

LORD OF MISTS
www.lindseypublications.com / booksurge.com /
amazon.com / ISBN: 0-9677336-3-4
ebook / dload / www.newconceptspublishing.com /
ISBN: 1-58606-221-3

Acknowledgements

Many thanks to those whom have made this story possible—

Lois Crisler and Farley Mowat for your wonderful stories about our four-legged friends, the *bledig*, and an enlightened understanding and appreciation of wolves.

Love to my daughter for her beautiful poem on wolves.

Susun Weed for your invaluable input on plants and herbs.

Norma at the library for your help in tracking down my extraneous list of references.

My thanks to Charlie, Lee's favorite guide in Wales, for your searching variations in Welsh for me.

A great big hug for Sandi and Nick whose hearts are in every cover—for seeing my vision the way only you can—and for your extra care in crafting a beautiful piece of artwork for my stories.

To Zayne, cover model extraordinaire, who makes the perfect hero for this story—you have my deep gratitude for being so charming while on the photo shoot—only you make Ifan come visually alive for thousands of readers. To JRPdenver.com for the best professional models.

Let me not forget, my cohorts behind the scenes who tirelessly poured over each page at least a handful of times—Amy and Jane, Maggi, Terri, Lynda and Anita.

To my agent and editor for believing in me—I only perform great feats with your support—the best of karma to you.

And heartfelt gratitude to those who were there for me through the many months spent on this story, my husband

and children, my friends and my patient readers—bless you—who never tired of waiting for this one.

To everyone, I hope you enjoy—

Author's Note

Dear Reader,

In the land of wild Welsh marches, a fertile and lush place beckons...the home of my ancestors and setting for the annual *Eisteddfod* where seer and bard meet for a timeless celebration of feats. It is here, I give you my hero and the lady who will either be his cross to bear or his eternal mate for life—you can decide. His is a life riddled by sorrow, for the ways of old cannot be thwarted. Man cannot change the course of his destiny any more than he can choose his parentage. Where I found the blight on happiness for the *Cymry*, my ancestors, my faraway home in the midst of a wild Wales setting, was in the uprising against humanity. It was not a time of romance and love, but a struggle for survival. Oft times against one's own blood kin.

Into this foray of survival I abandoned a man, a healer, to his fate...not a bad fate necessarily, for merciful I am to give him a burr under his blanket. Her name, this sweet burr, one he would come to both curse and hold dear to his heart. For his life he felt over, his sorrows deep and painful, his gift for healing sadly, too, forsaking him when all else has been taken from him.

I've spent a good number of years following his journey through the many vistas of healing, although I never knew I would one day be writing his story, researching the uncharted, the unknown, and always with great awe and respect for the powers of the mind. Those powers which we are mysteriously born with and somehow forget in the early processes of maturity. Today, healing is more vastly accepted, each culture with their own techniques. Those born and cultivated by each generation. Today, we pin fancy names to unknown phenomenon, like metaphysical energies, alternative healing, kirlin auras, Tai Chi and the like. And a wide variety of medicinal plants figure into these multifaceted arenas, as well. What have I found in my quest, I have found the more I learn, the less I really know...the world out there is a vast plane of wisdom. If we all had enough time in this lifetime to tap into every wisdom, we might begin to touch on the wondrous thing we call a mind...on the subtle and not so neatly explained powers, and we might all begin to heal one another.

Love of course, nicely figures into the realm of these less easily explained vistas.

Love moves mountains, transforms our lives, brings us closer to that within us we share by touch...by a simple smile of kindness. Dance was born rich in these qualities, his special gift making him both an oddity and a marvel. Certainly, in his time he could be viewed as a threat to some, his power used against him. As man will sometimes do to man. The sadness of his story is perhaps a particularly harsh reality of that time, but if he were born today, I would wish him a more forgiving life, and I would wish him kindness and compassion. And I would lead into his path a bearer of hope and a burr under his blanket to remind him life is good, it's worth living, and love always works its magic when we least expect it.

Best wishes,
Desirée Lindsey

"Unless we learn to understand this metaphorical or hieroglyphic language of the ancient world, we shall look upon the Upanishads and on most of the Sacred Book of the East as mere childish twaddle."— Max Müeller

—From the Ancient Symbols of Scriptures and Myths—

ARCHETYPAL MAN

To understand the pilgrimage of healing powers as my hero experiences them, it is my belief you need to look deeper into the man and to probe the potential Evolutionary Scheme of Divine manifestation in the universe. The method I used is called the Archetypal Man. Whereby man's unique constitution makes him a measure of the universe, for he subtends, latently and actively, the whole of the five planes of manifestation. And because as man is thus the microcosm of the macrocosm, his totality on the higher planes is identical with the Archetypal Man, while on the lower planes he is active as a natural man. There is a chart in the Dictionary of Scriptures and Myths that explains this pictorially if you can get ahold of a copy of the book. It explains the five planes in the world systems.

It says, the Archetypal Man, or World-soul, is to be regarded as the Divine Life of the solar universe, visible and invisible, and also of the human soul both as to formative idea and phenomenal action. According to Myths and Scriptures of old, Divine Life became organized for phenomenal activity in time and space, by means of the process of spiritual Involution whereby mental, astral and physical matter became endowed with all the qualities needed for Evolution. Qualities which we observe today in all natural conditions and growth of forms. The Sacred Books teach us that the Archetypal Man became complete in plenitude at the close of the cycle of Involution; whereupon there was a period of rest before renewal of activity in the present cycle of Evolution.

The supreme intelligence of the Archetypal Man proceeds from the higher mental plane and is manifest throughout all nature. On this plane are the *directive causes* of all phenomena, while on the physical plane are the *directed forces* producing the effects which we perceive by means of our five senses. The laws of physics and chemistry are expressed by science in mental terms, thus proving that the causation of the phenomena investigated is mental and not physical. The causative intelligence from within is very obvious in the building up of plant and animal organisms. In their growth these are constructed molecule by molecule; each molecule being directed in purposeful accordance with a fixed scheme or plan of the growth and maturity of each particular species of organism.

I easily see healing powers capable of the same growth dependent upon a man's experiences or evolution. I have given you a brief summary of the Evolutionary Scheme of Divine manifestation. Or a parallel way to introduce you to the phenomena of my hero's gift.

MIDNIGHT WOLF

Purple sunsets in your eyes,
ashy hopes that make us cry
My dreams and wishes fill your hand,
you walk along moonstruck sand
The land that cries your warm name,
you held my hand it made me weep
Deep into the moonlight pool of the
shallow bark of the midnight wolf.

Creepy looks from those within,
who yell those things you dare not think
You wish and hope he does not follow,
the wolf in him that makes you crawl,
from wet dark grasses to soft full moons.
With shooting stars that pierce his lips,
in the winters that become so crisp
That man is nothing, nothing more but
a child. But at night he is him,
he is the shallow bark of the midnight wolf.

By D. N. Moore

ARENA OF LIFE:—
A symbol of the lower quaternary, or the mental, astral and
physical planes on which the Soul expresses itself under the
aspects of Will, Wisdom and Love.

I.

Midlands, Wales 1815

Madeline Carlton looked up from her father's frail body, her heart filled with anguish. His blood speckled the front of her fashionable traveling gown, her hands smeared with more. Somewhere outside, the dull toll of a church bell clanged loudly, yet she hardly heard a sound. The few shopkeepers hailed passersby as shutters were latched against the growing cold, the village folk scurrying home before dark, all going on as if in an oblivious dream, while she struggled with numbing fear.

Opposite her, her adored brother Philip wore a grim face cast in early evening shadows, his worried gaze lowered to the unconscious figure lying atop a scarred table in the barren sick room.

"Whoever this mysterious healer is who can help papa, I'm going to find him," she announced softly, her gray eyes swimming with unshed tears. Exhaustion pinched together her brows. A wet copper curl clung to her cheek. All the way from Aberystwyth's bustling quay to Llandeglay by oxen cart they traveled through the night with their cargo in the rain. To look at her now, one wouldn't know her as the toast of genteel Boston society.

Philip was opening his mouth to forbid her, but he didn't get the chance.

"Please, Philip, we don't have time to argue." Madeline's gaze held her brother's, his pained expression echoing her own. Philip was the youngest of five brothers—what she was contemplating put him in grave danger of inviting their wrath. Worse than that, though, this was the first time in all of her twenty years she'd be leaving him behind. "Now don't be looking at me like that—it's long past time you and the others got it through your thick skulls I've grown up and you can no longer treat me like a child."

Philip stood there looking down on her from an imposing height, arms crossed over his chest, and glowering. "Maddie, we know you're no longer a child. In fact, we've been noticing it for months now and it scares the hell out of us. What worries me this time is we know nothing about this healer," he said in all seriousness, his darker auburn hair dripping in his eyes. "I do know our elders will beat me senseless if I let you go off alone."

"That's just it—I won't be alone," she assured him, her eyes pleading. "Llwyd has agreed to escort me into the woods." More desperate than ever to make him understand, she swallowed against the thick lump choking her. "What happened back there, there was nothing you could have done any different to protect me from that man's insults at the tavern...nor chances are, anyone else could have stopped him...look what happened to papa..." Her voice trailed off, her lip quivering as she lowered her gaze to keep Philip from seeing the guilty tears blinding her. Keep him from seeing how truly helpless she'd felt when the masked stranger accosted her, her father's anger in her defense, the terror when the stranger's pistol discharged. The horror she felt the instant the bullet found its mark, shattering her father's collarbone, leaving a fleshy hole.

She could still taste the acrid bite of gunpowder, hear the ring throbbing in her ears. With Philip's help, she'd worked quickly to apply a makeshift bandage, which was already soaked with blood. They had done their best, after finding the village *meddyg,* or physic, had been called away to save a child burned when a cottage in a neighboring village caught fire. No one knew how bad the child's injuries might be, nor did they know how long before the doctor would return.

This healer, however, could be reached in a matter of hours. "This was all my fault," she finished hoarsely, "and I will be the one to go for help."

"For God's sake, Maddie, at least let me ride along with you," Philip appealed, his hand shooting out to steady her as she swayed on her feet.

Madeline stiffened her back, slowly shook her head. "You can't leave papa alone here. Besides, you heard what Llwyd said—you wouldn't stand a chance of making it beyond the forest without being turned away. He thinks, however, a woman might succeed." Scared as she was and consumed by apprehension, she had to prevail—she couldn't fail when her father's life rested in her hands. Her voice dropped to a quavering whisper, "Don't you see, Papa's only hope lies with me?"

In the damp hovel of a room devoid of baser comforts, her words hung in the air like the heavy mists hovering over the small village.

Philip moved to her side and gently pulled her close for a hug. His gesture of solace was meant to comfort her, yet only made her feel more wretched. Her father lay dying of a bullet wound. Because he had been trying to shield her from the vile wild man who, to Madeline's horror and her brothers' surprised outrage, appeared out of nowhere to grab her. Before she'd been able to scream, he had shoved his beefy paw down her bodice and squeezed her breast—in plain view of her family. The unprovoked insult to her person had happened so quickly. What followed was still a blur in her mind. Vaguely she remembered her assailant escaped in the turmoil. His identity hidden behind a crudely-fashioned helmet. Her brothers were tracking him on foot this moment.

Pushing the scene from her mind, knowing her father was usually a strong man—yet pressed by a sense of urgency nonetheless—she hugged Philip tight. This was the brother with whom she shared all her childhood secrets. The one who took the blame—she'd found out—when her outrageous escapades went awry. Philip had never been able to deny his little sister anything.

Knowing any minute her guide could return with the horses, Madeline looked up with teary eyes at her brother. "I'm dreadfully sorry I have to leave you behind to face Leroy alone—maybe they won't beat us so badly." Her lips thinned faintly in a grimace, while in truth, no matter how furious, her siblings never laid a hand on her. Philip would be the one to suffer the brunt of their anger. "I'll have to find some way to make it up to you."

She stroked his stubbled jaw, penance in her gesture as she continued, "You know it will be up to you to sway Leroy and Adam from trying to come after me. It'll be up to you to remind them how papa warned us there are those who might take issue with a Boston merchant peddling steam-winding engines, even if we're also bringing relief in corn. Remind them if you have to, we are strangers here, we know no one. Whatever you do, while I'm gone, don't let them do anything rash. And I promise I'll hurry back as soon as I can."

Philip hugged her fiercely one last time and would have said more were they not interrupted just then by Llwyd who came hobbling through the door. Madeline moved out of Philip's arms to stand at her father's side.

"We best be hurryin'," Llwyd said pointedly, "if we are to be reachin' the forest `afore it grows dark."

Giving her brother a look that said "don't worry," Madeline turned back to Llwyd. Her squat little escort wore a drab brown tunic that looked centuries old. He went by his Christian name, the Welsh way of address. A quiet sort, her brother remarked in private, not an overly friendly man. But then her guide didn't have to be especially pleasant, he only had to know his way around the forest. Besides being first on the scene to rush to their aide, Llwyd had been there to clear a path from the Castell Dyffryn Inn to the doctor's cottage.

"Ole Bones is saddled and awaitin' for ye out front," Llwyd urged, breaking in on her thoughts, his expression devoid of emotion. "Jus' like ya asked."

It was too late for a change of heart even should her siblings return in the next few minutes. "Thank you, Llwyd."

Wishing to be away quickly now that her horse arrived, Madeline glanced back to Philip to find him peering at her with eyes suspiciously bright.

Madeline's throat clogged with fresh tears. She turned harrowed eyes back to her father. Her fingers gently clasped his to find them cold, frightfully limp. Fear near suffocating her, she bent to lightly kiss his leathery cheek, while as carefully as possible she tucked the red woolen blanket tighter around his narrow shoulders. She tried not to let his death-like pallor scare her.

A single tear ran down her face.

Please, oh please, papa, wait for me...

Perched atop her borrowed steed, Madeline took one last glimpse of the village over her shoulder. All was quiet now that evening was upon them. The last few stragglers, with baskets in hand, were womenfolk wearing odd-shaped hats which had intrigued Madeline as soon as she stepped foot on Welsh soil. They wore wool and flannels, their bright red and blue stripped petticoats showing beneath a white apron and blue *betgwyn*. Fringed shawls were used to keep the dampness from penetrating. Had she found time, Madeline would have purchased something more suitable for the climate.

Her gaze landed on Philip. Hardest of all was saying good-bye to the brother she adored. The brother who stood on the threshold to see her off. Torment twisting his features, he still made an impressive picture. Strong, proud, devilishly handsome in his blue frock coat. So different were his looks from the dark-headed Welshmen.

Putting on a brave face, Madeline turned back around in the saddle. She was anxious to find this healer and get back. Assured she would encounter no obstacles she couldn't overcome, she nudged her heels into her mount to catch up to Llwyd whose shaggy palfrey trudged up the road. They trotted the horses along a lush field, called a sheep walk, where the herder sat on a rocky outcropping watching over his flock. Newborn lambs scurried after their mothers. Others stood bleating, their cries carrying over the far away chirp of a lark settling in the treetops. Choked by yew trees, the road ahead of her wound through the *glyn* like a ribbon leading the way. She could have been looking at a medieval landscape where once upon a dreary day, a crusade of brave knights rode in perfect columns.

The people or *Cymry* as they called themselves, were simple folk, an ancient culture. They were also unlike anyone she was accustomed to in Boston. Actually, nothing in Boston could have prepared her for what she saw here. This strange land of bards, their hard-to-pronounce language, their infertile mountain ranges. The Welshman's ability to thrive where Englishmen would starve. She admired how they had survived centuries, with their crude weapons, the siege of their Norse foe. Silently awed, she had been equally shocked by the stories her father told her as they waited to dock in Cardigan Bay. The stories of treachery where not so long ago one Welsh ruler usurped another by joining an alliance with a Dane or Saxon enemy. The Welshman's determination to overcome his own flesh and blood kin had opened her eyes to how naïve her views of life. These men were not simple peasants by birth. They were noblemen, some of them titled. Men in position of great power. Their forefathers princely warriors. Chieftains. Their greed dividing families in the bloody struggle to conquer all of Wales for oneself.

The viciousness of that betrayal appalled Madeline whose life evolved around a family who loved one another. Protected one another.

Her perception of these people she found altered even further after the first hour on the road with Llwyd. As brave and warm-hearted as most the Welsh she encountered, others were just as unpredictable and austere as the weather. After trying unsuccessfully to engage him in conversation, her guide was, she decided, a man of few words. Her oldest brother, Leroy, was like that.

Finding Llwyd's manner somewhat disconcerting, wishing only to hurry, she too lapsed into silence.

It wasn't long before Madeline realized how ill-prepared she was for the harsher mountain climate. In the higher grasslands, already the sheep were growing thick woolly coats for the coming winter. Stiff from the cold, balancing in the saddle, she carefully pulled her silk-lined cloak tighter about her shoulders and was glad she'd changed into breeches. Dusk had descended, bringing with it a bone-deep shiver. Rain-sodden marshes filled her nostrils with a pungent earthiness.

And here she was headed for God-only-knew-where. Could it have been just three short days ago her family had been docking *The Boston Lady* in Aberystwyth?

Her silent guide, she noticed, had been making a steady eastward climb since leaving Llandeglay. The weaving path they were on had parted from the main road over two hours ago. They left behind the rolling green hills — civilized man. Ahead of her now, all around her in every direction she turned, a dense tangle of gorse choked the forest. The air grew colder as well. A heavy dampness had already penetrated both her cloak and linen shirtwaist. Her clothes clung to her skin. The weight hung about her shoulders as though she was carrying the horse on her back instead of the other way around.

True to his word, Llwyd had found her a worthy steed. He appeared to be a huge war horse, black as midnight and twice as tall as he was wide. She looked down at the ground swaying past her vision. A view not unlike how it must feel peering from a castle wall-walk upon a valley below. Until now she hadn't thought about how she was going to dismount and mount without Llwyd's help.

Actually, aside from that one small oversight, ole Bones couldn't have been better suited to her needs. Certainly an improvement over traveling by oxen cart. He was gentle, sure-footed, and remarkably responsive when she'd expected a horse with a name like his to have a mouth as tough as an old shoe. Nagged by a sense of urgency, she nudged him into a lively gait.

An hour later, the path they were on grew considerably narrower. The denseness of the thick foliage closed in around the horses as if the mighty jaws of the forest were swallowing them whole. Wishing she were already headed back with help, Madeline tried not to think about the sounds around her. The snap of a twig under ole Bones' massive hooves. The scutter of a winged-shadow swooping overhead. There was no telling what kind of wild creatures lurked beyond in the cover of darkness. Everything in her screamed that she turn back.

She desperately needed a distraction from the path of her thoughts.

Heart pounding, praying fervently that their destination was just up ahead, she kept her gaze trained forward, her teeth clenched to keep them from clattering. Cringing at every little sound heralding intruders to the forest, she tried focusing on the moon above. A brilliant silvery orb in a surprisingly clear black sky. `Twas the kind of moon that reminded her of stolen kisses. A garden party, a secluded alcove and Robert Dunbury, who had been most eager to show her something that couldn't be seen from the ballroom. She'd been anticipating her first kiss with relish, and then she'd learned exactly what a man of his caliber intended.

His kisses had drugged her mind, there was no other explanation for her reaction nor his behavior when he'd pushed up her skirt, his whispered words strangely compelling and strained. She could feel him shaking, hear his low voice pleading she trust him, while his hands moved like warm silk drawing nearer the beat of her heart. Only her heart was beating lower, lower in a place she'd never dreamed a heartbeat throbbed. His hand moved to her heartbeat, melting her insides...then came the slow penetration of his finger and in an instant she was jerked back to reality. She hadn't understood until then, how once passion was stroked to a full blaze and left quivering on a precipice, how devastating the descent back to earth.

Rubbing his stinging cheek, anger just barely contained, Robert insisted he couldn't marry her unless she assigned him complete control of her inheritance. His anger was nothing compared to hers, her mortification, the feeling of betrayal when she'd nearly blurted out she loved him.

It had been Philip who had found her crying that night. Dear, outraged Philip. She had learned Robert had left Boston rather quickly. Bodily escorted by the Carlton brothers, aboard a departing cargo ship bound for the other side of the world. It was from Mimmie, their kitchen maid, that she'd learned the cad had narrowly escaped a lynching.

The very next day she set sail for Wales with her brothers and father. And it was the last time Madeline had gone for a walk in a garden on a moonlit night.

Her distraction only provided a momentary reprieve from what lurked in the dark of the forest.

More precisely what kind of creatures roamed about.

Only desperation for her father kept her on course. She was safe. Her horse sturdy.

He wouldn't be so easily dragged to the ground. Not like her pretty gray mare had been dragged to the ground by a snarling pack of feral dogs.

Shuddering at the memory, sick with remembered sorrow, Madeline shied away from the heartache those thoughts brought her.

Impelled by renewed purpose, she turned her thoughts to the mysterious healer of which Llwyd spoke of in hushed tones. What was he like? Why did he live all alone in this forest? Very briefly, it had occurred to her to ask for proof this healer of Llwyd's had indeed saved someone's life. She should have thought of it sooner. She thought about asking him now. What if his answer only frightened her worse?

A gurgling stream meandered its way along their left flank. They were following an elm-lined path crowded by broken branches, a denser woodland area. Strange silver mists spiraled down like serpents, wisps swirling around the forest as if moving by some magic. Dew collected on her lashes. The heavy mist felt cold on her skin. Her view ahead was limited. Cavorting shadows played over the forest floor, prickling her nape. Llwyd rode ahead of her, his hunkered shape a darker blur leading her farther and farther into uncertain territory.

She could stand it no longer. "How much farther do you think it is?"

"Not long now," her companion replied in hush tones, his back slumped with fatigue. By his tone he didn't care whether she collapsed or not. They had been riding, she estimated, three—maybe four hours. His answer, of course, did nothing to calm her frayed nerves. Exactly what did he mean by "not long now?"

She had only a moment to ponder that question when the horses came to a halt in a clearing at what appeared to be a riverbank.

"The River Edwy," he informed her as if anticipating her question. "Ye'll be going on from here alone."

Alone? Shocked out of exhaustion, Madeline's head snapped around to pin him with frantic eyes. "What do you mean 'alone'? You can't just leave me here to wander about on my own!" Her voice came out a high-pitched accusation. "I thought you were going with me?"

"As far as this here river."

"But—"

"There's naught much good I am to ya beyond this point. Jus' follow the moon," he said, pointing skyward. "Keep it in front of ya, the mountains on yer left and right, and ye'll be there by dawn."

Her growing apprehension quickly turned to full-blown panic. "But I have no weapon, nothing to protect myself—"

He just chuckled. "Ye'll not be in danger."

Not in danger! Her breath left her, her fear giving way to outrage. Why the irksome man was actually going to abandon her in the middle of nowhere.

"All right," she muttered, glowering at him, glad now Philip had the foresight to think ahead. "With or without you, I'll find this Castle Wolfglyn. But you'll not get a single farthing when you get back, for my brother will not pay you without knowing I made it safely." She gave him a triumphant look. "We agreed upon a code word."

Her companion's shrewd little eyes narrowed for a moment, then he sneered. "I'll tell yer brother ya forgot yer code."

Her fingers clenched tighter to the reins in dismay. "He won't believe you."

The odious man chuckled. "He'll pay all right. If he wants ta know which way ya rode into the woods."

Seething with outrage, Madeline furiously turned her attention to the obscured path leading into the forest from the opposite bank. That way was the direction she needed to go to save her father. If she turned back now, he would surely die. How much farther could the healer's lair be, anyway?

Angry as she was, a moment's queasiness knotted Madeline's stomach as her gaze dropped to the river. Sinister-looking in the moonlight, the shiny surface undulated like a sea of slithering vipers. Its depths looked bottomless and black, looming before her as if the mouth of a great beast waited for her horse to venture in for its feasting.

Her ignoble companion turned his horse around. "Once ya enter the heart of yonder woods, `tis the Lord o' Mists ya will be looking for. Just stay on that path."

Madeline swung around in the saddle. "Lord of Mists?"

"Aye, laird of this *glyn*. Powerful healer of Castle Wolfglyn."

It might have been the shadows playing with her imagination, but her guide's twisted smile grew almost demonic, as if deriving some secret satisfaction from her dilemma. Ignoring the shiver racing down her spine, she knew she was on her own. Her father needed her to be strong. It was up to her to overcome whatever awaited her on the other side of the river. Philip, Leroy, the others, they would not have hesitated one minute. Nor would she, she decided bravely, swallowing the heartbeat rising in her throat.

Without another word to her, Llwyd nudged his palfrey

into a walk. Madeline watched in numb silence as man and horse disappeared beyond the shadows from which they'd just emerged.

So be it. She didn't need a bloody guide. She knew the name of the healer. She'd ride to the nearest village and simply inquire around. If the man lived in this forest and was as skilled as Llwyd claimed, it stood to reason someone had to have heard of him, knew where to find him. A description, she realized, would have been helpful.

Madeline sat up straight in the saddle as a slower realization dawned.

Until now she hadn't thought of her healer in terms of a flesh and blood man. Until now he'd seemed more a mystical wizard in her mind, a pagan Druid with a long flowing white beard calling himself Merlin or some other fanciful name.

Please God, whatever happens, let him be the powerful healer Llwyd claimed!

Sitting there on her faithful steed and watching the spot where her guide vanished, Madeline felt the grips of panic recede as the first stirring of despair hit her—a great weight bearing down on her heart. Finding this healer was only half the challenge. It was after she found him that worried her. A recluse who hid in the forest? What would he say when she told him she wanted him to come with her back to Llandeglay? More to the point, *how* was she going to convince him to return with her?

Lord of Castle Wolfglyn...

God help her, this healer better know something about healing.

An hour later, Madeline found herself in a tiny clearing,

staring at a dead-end. The forest closed off to her except for the path back the way she'd just come.

Of all the worst possible outcomes...this last one she never expected.

She tried not to grow alarmed, tried to stay calm and not give in to hysteria, but her mind refused to heed.

Tears of defeat sprang to her eyes and lumped in her throat with the painful certainty she was doomed. Why would Llwyd deliberately mislead her? How could anyone be that cruel?

A painful sob burst from her throat as her mind tumbled with frightening possibilities. A vision flashed through her brain. One of her father dying...fading away before she could get back.

Llwyd expressly told her to take this path, knowing she'd not find her healer, curse his black heart. Did he think he'd actually be able to escape unscathed once her brothers learned of his treachery?

Then came a distressing thought—maybe he didn't expect her to make it.

To believe that, though, would be admitting all this had been planned with some diabolical purpose in mind. That would mean he'd lied about everything—

No—there had to be a healer!

Madeline's mount waited patiently, his ears alert to the sounds around them. Those silent, eerie sounds that, now she found herself alone and betrayed, seemed magnified in the dark.

"I'm sorry, Bones." She sleeved tears away. "I don't even know where we are."

Since she had no guide to consult, she had no idea what her next course should be.

Llwyd, if that were indeed the weasel's name, had

tricked her. He'd led her into the forest to lose her way. That much was apparent, even if she didn't yet know why. One thing she did know—when she got back she'd skin him alive.

If she got back....

Madeline's stomach growled, reminding her she hadn't eaten since evening last. The emptiness felt like a festering hole in her gut. More hungry than she realized, too tired to go on, slowly the exhaustion she fought to keep at bay seeped into her soul. It vanquished her confidence — wanted her to fail.

Terribly despondent, more scared than ever for her father, Madeline gave into a rare moment of self-pity, and huddling over her horse's broad neck, gave into heart-sick tears. Tears of despair for her father. For herself. For every failure she could remember.

Her every muscle aching to the ends of her limbs, she slipped from the saddle to the soft cushion of leaves blanketing the forest floor. The moment her feet touched the ground, her legs buckled. She fell to her knees in the bramble next to her horse, her long braid tumbling free of her hood. She wavered on hands and knees. Bits of branches poked through her breeches and jabbed into her knees, cut into the soft flesh of her palms. Madeline hardly felt anything for the misery engulfing her....

A woman's mournful sobs reverberated through the damp winter's night, stopping human and animal alike. Sheva circled her master's legs, and yapping softly in response, she lifted her muzzle to the great white moon. She howled her own piercing answer...before she loped away on the jagged deer trail into the thickest cover of trees.

ARCHANGELS:—
A symbol of primordial Divine Powers on
the highest planes of manifestations. Its messengers
of exalted intelligence who introduce the spiritual
life-element in the forms fully prepared and
awaiting its reception.

2.

No longer able to feel her legs, Madeline numbly pulled her horse's muzzle into her lap, her fingers absently stroking his soft nose. She had no idea how long she'd knelt there sobbing, her teeth chattering from the cold shuddering through her body. One small thanksgiving, whatever else had happened today, blessedly ole Bones hadn't abandoned her.

A teary hiccup escaped. "I—I hope you remember the way home," she sniffled, leaning closer to press a trembling kiss to the placid face so near her own.

Her mount's reaction caught her totally unexpected. Before she could move, anticipate his sudden alarm, he snorted and backed away. Branches crunched under his large hooves. The reins pulled from her grasp. Madeline frantically scrambled to retrieve them while Bones backed farther from her outstretched hand. He was getting away when she made a lunge for the reins. Spooked, his eyes wild and terrified now, he shied far enough from her reach she had to stretch.

If she could just reach him....

That's when a prickling of something tingled down her spine. It came with a warning as sheer panic pushed up her throat. The next breath dove into her heart.

From the corner of her eye she saw a blur. Shoulder height and staring back at her, not five feet from where she cringed in breath-held fright, a silver-white wolf with glowing amber eyes stood motionless...watching her every move.

Madeline couldn't breathe. She couldn't move. She felt the wild creature's breath on her skin, saw its sharp teeth bared. Shards of white death smiling at her. Predatory. Telling her she was going to die. She imagined them tearing into her, the dull thud of her lifeless body being dragged off. The trail of blood.

She heard herself panting. The pathetic sound of sheer terror.

From somewhere nearby a branch snapped...and at the same instant the wolf moved, Madeline closed her eyes. All she could do was wait to die.

"Where did you come from?"

Jumping out of her skin, Madeline swallowed the shriek rising up her throat. That deep male voice registering on her mind was a wondrous sound—had to be part of her imagination. Her head felt light from fear, her senses disoriented.

The voice of her imagination came again, "Are you mute, woman?"

Not her imagination.

"Where's the wolf?" she managed in a tiny voice, still refusing to look, certain if she was going to die she didn't want to watch.

"She's waiting to eat you. Answer my question."

Her eyes still closed, Madeline flinched at the animosity in his voice. "I—I can't!" She covered her face with trembling hands and shook her head. "I just can't—" she cried helplessly.

Her inane reply provoked a growl of frustration. "Come, *bledig*"—he whistled softly—"you're frightening her."

Holding her breath, still afraid he might vanish, that she was dreaming, Madeline heard the animal's low whimper circling before it skulked away. Still, she didn't believe she was alive. Her heart slamming madly against her ribs made it impossible to think. It took her a moment more to gather courage enough to peek between her fingers.

When she did, Madeline's throat constricted around a soft gasp.

The wolf forgotten, it was her savior with a deceptively soft voice standing above her bathed in moonlight. A divine guardian of all creatures. She was already dead, she was certain of it. Her deathbed hell.

Her hell came with an unholy dark angel, his blue-black hair falling wildly around his broad shoulders, disheveled as though he'd tumbled from bed to race to her rescue. In a glimpse—a man too beautiful to be of this world.

Certainly, this had to be a dream.

Her fleeting perusal came to rest on the rich, sable cape wrapping his powerful body and his question was forgotten entirely. Sparkling in the moonlight under his chin, a glittering jewel clasp held his finely-sewn mantle in place. The clasp a huge topaz. A vivid purple lined his ebony mantle—a color usually reserved for royalty.

Madeline knew she was staring, but she couldn't help herself. She'd never seen anyone like him.

He broke the spell when he whispered something in a soft fluent tongue.

He was talking to the wolf, she realized incredulously. More incredible yet, the animal waiting a few short yards away seemed to be listening. It was a fascinating notion, but

Madeline was almost certain the wolf understood him—a revelation totally beyond her realm of comprehension.

But before she could ask the question springing to her lips, the stranger turned back to her.

Madeline's startled gaze met his for the first time.

Glorious eyes the color of amber jewels surveyed her with mesmerizing intelligence. In their depths a hint of some other-worldly mystery. Eyes that held a dark silence. Brilliantly keen like those of his wolf.

Her errant heart tripped over.

He was looking down at her as if she were a bothersome nuisance while at the same time his intimate scrutiny touched her every feature. As if he'd just awakened from some spell to behold his first glimpse of a woman.

Madeline's throat closed around a soft moan before she knew she'd made a sound.

His full mouth hinted at a smile. His caressing gaze grew intent, moving over her body in a slow sweep, while he just stood there, seeming oddly hesitant to venture any closer.

She sensed he resented her being there. She noted too, he spoke flawless English.

Knowing some sort of response was expected, Madeline tried to rise. Her legs cramped beneath her. Of a sudden, she found herself sprawled flat on her belly starring at the toes of his boots. Hot patches of mortification flooded her cheeks.

He abruptly turned away. She tried again to find her legs.

"Wait—" Madeline crawled after him before she made it to her knees. She didn't get far for a feral snarl instantly stopped her advance. Her gaze swung to the shadows beyond the tree-line. Fierce looking and deadly, his silver wolf gave clear warning.

"Who sent you?" he demanded as he signaled his wolf with some indecipherable gesture.

"No one sent me." Madeline looked up to the breadth of his broad back. "In truth, I came here on my own."

He turned to stare at her with those intense topaz eyes as if to proclaim her a fool. "You lie. Someone had to lead you here—you wouldn't have found this place on your own."

His accusation as much as his tone rankled. "Well, maybe you're wrong, too." One raven-black brow raked up telling her what he thought of that. "All right—maybe someone did guide me here. I can't see how it matters—"

"Whoever led you to the river, he left you at my mercy."

Her startled eyes blinked up at him as she sat back on folded legs. "At *your* mercy?"

"Did no one tell you what happens to strays wandering into this forest?"

She shook her head, her braid swinging as her hand went to her throat. "Really, I intended no harm." Drawing on what strength she had left, Madeline pushed to her feet to face him unflinching. She wasn't about to let him out of her sight. "All right, so I wandered off the trail by mistake. Before I got lost I was looking for—"

"I doubt it was by mistake."

Her temper flared. "And how would you know that?"

"I live here."

As sluggish as her weary mind worked, it didn't take her a heartbeat to seize upon that knowledge. "If you live here, then maybe you have heard of this Lord of Mists and you could lead me to his castle?" she said, brushing her hood out of her face at the same moment the mists parted to a brilliant full moon.

What he saw seemed to startle him for an instant before he averted his gaze. Madeline was used to men's reactions. In her experience, beauty was more a curse than a blessing. Certainly it did nothing but bring her heartache and cause her family grief.

Whatever this man's reaction, Madeline wasn't going to let it distract her. "Do you know of him?" Hope reflected in her expression, lifted her flagging spirits. "If you know of him, then maybe you can take me to him."

Instead of answering her, he started to walk away.

Her brows drew into a frown. "Wait—I can afford to make it worth your time."

"I've no use for your coin."

Madeline's brain scrambled for a new approach. "All right. If a small fortune doesn't interest you," she added carefully, willing to offer him most anything, "I'm prepared to trade information for a fully-manned merchant ship."

He didn't even break stride.

"Then name your price."

That stopped him, but only for a moment before he swung to face her, his cape swirling. The fierceness in his gaze this time was enough to send her running. Her throat tightened in the face of uncertainty. A wrathful force, he came within a foot of her before stopping. Close enough to touch him if she but reached out. She could feel his anger, smell his wild male essence. The smell of clover assailed her senses.

"Leave here, fool girl," he growled between even-white teeth, "before you get hurt."

His broad frame swallowed her in shadows. "I want you gone from here tonight."

She blinked. "But I can't leave," she whispered hoarsely, her valiant effort at bravery crumbling. Embarrassing tears stung her eyes. "I can't go back until I speak to this healer."

For a flashing instant, he looked as if she had struck him. A paleness leached color from his face. When that instant passed his savage expression returned. "You will leave! Or rot in my dungeon!"

Not letting herself flinch, Madeline swallowed her tears. After all, she had grown up with five overbearing brothers. "You don't scare me," she said rashly, wondering oddly why. "If `tis your dungeon in which I must wait until my brothers come pounding on your door, then fine, let us not tarry. Just be warned they will come. And when they do they will be looking for blood."

He gave an exasperated sigh. "Your healer has lost his powers." Turning from her to collect her skittish mount, he finished, "He can't help you. Whoever you talked to lied."

Madeline stood there mute, her suspicions about Llwyd taking on new meaning. "And maybe someone just doesn't want me to find him," she rasped thickly, her throat convulsing as her heart refused to let go of hope.

A rustle of branches drew her attention.

Her horse had his reins tangled around a branch. Poor Bones dragged a rotted stump around behind him and was trying to get away from it. The faster he fled, the faster the stump followed.

The stranger moved from her side, speaking to the wolf, his tone gentle in what sounded like a command to stay put. He moved toward her mount.

She noticed his hands, the softer voice he used to gentle ole Bones, his words sounding like some magic incantation she couldn't discern. Madeline stood rooted, unable to think beyond the awful crushing weight sitting upon her heart, should he be telling her the truth.

If it were a lie, why had that weasel Llwyd encouraged her to go in search of a healer? Why if only to fail? After traveling all this way, now she was being told to go back to the village, the healer had lost his powers. Confusing as it all was, she'd managed to hold onto one scrap of knowledge. They both knew of this healer...that much was clear.

If she could just talk to him....

It couldn't have been a handful of minutes passed and he had her mount calmed. In short order, he untangled the reins.

She tried again. "I'll talk to this healer myself. If you won't take me to him, then I'll just ask someone else to take me to him."

He continued to speak unintelligible words to the frightened animal as he tightened the cinch. "I told you he can't help you. And you are leaving."

After all she'd been through to get this far—to be repeatedly told with unyielding conviction the healer in which she'd put her every hope couldn't help her.

Pain lanced through her heart.

Had she wasted precious time coming all this way for nothing?

He turned from his task of adjusting her stirrup to catch her with tears streaking down her cheeks. His scowl softened. "Listen—I know how you must feel," he said in a surprisingly tender tone, "but whatever you were told, the Lord of Wolfglyn is no longer a healer." His gaze lingered on her quivering chin as he brought the horse to a halt beside her. "As much as anyone might wish otherwise, nothing will change that fact." His voice held a touch of sadness.

Forced to accept what she didn't want to proved brutally painful.

The enormity of defeat blurred her vision....

She swayed on her feet, the forest all at once swirling around her....

Then just as the ground rose up to swallow her, she was being gathered up by strong arms. It came to her through a fog of blackness. The vague awareness of a warm breath whispering against her ear, a softer demand she breathe deeply. A compelling sense of something deeper move through her...something warm and alive. Almost tender and careful and solicitous, and arousing her slumberous senses. An aura wrapping itself around her, making her feel at once safe and protected. The alluring force, she weakly conceded, was coming from the man supporting her. The creature whose tawny eyes had both devoured and avoided her. His clover scent filled her lungs. She buried her face into the warmth of his body, seeking his scent, the comfort of something elusive.

Held intimately against his hard male body made it hard to breathe. Harder yet to assimilate the unexpected sensations stirred to life by his nearness.

The tenderness in the way his fingers brushed away her tears touched a place in her heart.

It was several more long minutes before her head started to clear. Bringing back more than sensory perceptions.

Her lashes fluttered for a moment....

Senses sluggish, she peered up at the harsh beauty of the face so close to hers. His gaze sparkled topaz fire. Concern for her drew his brows together. Then like a mask drawn over his features, whatever he was feeling pulled back.

"Are you all right?" Once again his harsh beauty was chiseled in cold stone.

Madeline wasn't capable of more than nodding.

"I'll take you back to the river." Not waiting for her to fully recover, he carefully lifted her atop her horse and leapt up behind her. The weight of her body melted against him. Supporting arms, warm against her ribs and wrapped protectively around her, guided her horse back down the path on which she'd lost her way. She was shaking, the events of the day beyond mortal bearing.

One tear fell, then another....

Dance knew she was crying, he felt it in the deep shudders resting against his chest. While he held himself distant as best he could, he couldn't stop what was happening to his body. Her softness was seducing his senses—to hold a woman after all these years felt like heaven. Her lavender-scented sweetness made him painfully aware of that which was absent in his life.

The gentle sway of her backside brushing his thighs made his groin burn, his blood race rapidly to those areas awakening to her touch. Each lush shift of subtle movement, the innocence in the accidental contact, made his body respond in ways he knew were forbidden to him. The simplest contact as her fingers brushing the backs of his hands brought him agony, like a blade nicking open old wounds. He didn't care what she wanted from him. He didn't ask. He needed to quickly get her off his land—away from the forest and its many eyes. Away from certain death.

The heavy mists were already swallowing them in a blanket of fog by the time he approached the perimeter of the forest's dense cover. The mists were growing heavier. Before long they'd be surrounded by a haze that would make it impossible to discern direction. He called it his world removed from reality. A woman, however brave, could easily become disoriented in his world. However she had accomplished it, this was not the first time someone had lost their way in his forest. Once in a great while, even he lost his way and he knew every stone, every gnarled tree trunk, the tiny paths left by wild squirrels. He knew this land intimately, he'd lived in the castle the whole of twenty-eight winters amidst the marsh's untamed *glyns*.

He couldn't let himself care why she'd come to seek him out. He wouldn't let himself show the least concern. For to do so would invite irreversible repercussions. The first and last time he'd taken a risk he'd near lost his mind. In the end he'd lost his *powers*. The latter had deserted him, along with his will to live.

They emerged from the forest at the spot where she'd crossed the narrowest part of the River Edwy. The exact spot where the earth had been churned up by two sets of hoof prints.

"From here your horse should find its way back to the village. Sheva will follow a short distance to make sure you reach your destination safely." The lavender-scented woman in his arms was trembling, but he was forbidden by his own device to let himself comfort her. Indeed, `twas more merciful she be trembling now than needlessly destroyed later.

Though she showed great courage in coming this far on her own, she possessed an extraordinary fortitude that could be disastrous if not discouraged.

At least her bravado had its limits. He'd seen her initial reaction to Sheva, the suffocating fear evident in her panicked gaze. Mirroring her every emotion, her eyes were the soft gray of a winter storm. Expressive eyes of a child, innocent yet of man's cruelty. He couldn't imagine her being terrified like she was of wild animals and yet willing to enter the forest. He could have told her Sheva was one of the more docile females among the pack back at Wolfglyn, but it didn't matter since the woman was leaving. Besides, that fear just might keep her alive.

"I trust Sheva with my life," he murmured against her hair, "if you should run into any trouble, she's capable of taking down a grown man." Another shiver from the curvaceous maiden. His arms gathered her more closely. He pitied the girl the cruel deception his nemesis played on her. No one else could have led her here besides Llwyd...or there was one other. One whose name Dance never spoke.

"Do not despair, *Arddun*"—the endearment came natural for she was 'beautiful'—"Whatever you want from the healer, I'm certain you will succeed in finding elsewhere."

Still locked within his embrace, she sniffled.

His grip tightened reflexively around the pommel, a strange hesitancy in him, his concentration divided. He wished he could forget how it was to crave a woman in bed—to mold her pliant warmth to his own aroused body. Forget how it had once felt to have a hot, tight sheath locked around him...instead of relieving himself now when his body ached with suppressed longing.

Numb with long-suffered self-loathing, inviting the bitter cold, he edged the horse around a huge flat stone; a landmark unnoticed except to the watchful eye of a guide. With his knees, he encouraged the beast down the bank and into the knee high water. The river this time of year was icy cold and shallow. They wouldn't have been able to cross here in the spring after the rains swelled over the banks.

Dance held the slender woman in his arms as if afraid

she might slip into the churning river as her sure-footed charger waded across. His great hooves clamored for purchase in the mud on the opposite bank, splashing them both with numbing cold water. Then the beast was standing on the other side, flanks heaving.

Dance swiftly dismounted and stood there looking up at the woman whose pain he could feel whether he wanted to or not. They were completely alone—if he weren't certain she'd suffer death, he might have lifted her down, pulled her into his arms...soothed her tears away. He might have—if he were one of the Norse beserker's of older times—dragged her from her mount to do other things to her. Like relieve himself in her young body there on a bed of damp leaves.

All he had to do was imagine her on her back, her hair unplaited and all that fiery glory tousled upon the ground and he'd be back to his old pastime—spending his nights pacing the great room. Better that he try to curb useless thoughts, those that would certainly start haunting him again after tonight, than try to ignore what was humanly impossible. From what he could remember, he hadn't seen breeches on women in Llandeglay. He liked breeches on this one. How they molded her slender backside in a way that enhanced his torment.

It had been so damn long....

"Back that way will take you directly to Llandeglay." Ignoring the growing ache in his groin, he nodded toward the path leading back to the village.

Madeline was too drained at the moment to argue.

In his native tongue he spoke quietly to his *bledig*, using the Welsh name for 'wolf'. A word she fleetingly recognized from the list her brother quizzed her on during the Atlantic crossing. The wolf he called Sheva stood a short distance away shaking her wet fur. It was clear the bond between this man and his companion seemed one of mutual affection. A bond Madeline scarcely comprehended, nor tried. The wolf slithered up to her master who had dropped to one knee, his dark fingers stroking the scruffy silver coat as the animal listened to him as if understanding.

Now—this she could tell was a fierce man. Put her in his dungeon, indeed.

And what—feed her to his pet dragons?

With a slanted look in her direction, the starkly beautiful creature rose to his feet. Topaz eyes met hers with a stark intensity that sent her heart tipping over itself. They neither said a word. Then while a dreadful weight settled in her stomach, he bid her farewell. Vanished from sight as mysteriously as he appeared—blending with the shadows as if part of the forest. Madeline scarce believed he had been of flesh and blood a mere moment later, that she'd actually had a conversation with a heathen creature in the forest. She might have considered it all a terrible dream, were it not for the chilling silver reminder licking herself dry.

Madeline's gaze strayed to the opposite bank, then back to the spot where he vanished and lastly settling on Sheva before the impact hit her. Now that he was gone, the eeriness once again enveloped her, the sounds of the night forest skittering down her spine. Gooseflesh danced upon her skin. That's when she realized she was cold, the water splashed by the horse's great hooves had wet the hem of her cloak, sprayed her face and clothes. Her teeth were chattering.

He thought to send her back to Llandeglay. A worse ultimatum he couldn't have given her should he have ordered her locked in the stocks to die a slow death.

How did she go on living without her father? How could she bear to learn he'd died, while she wasted precious time getting nowhere?

Locked in a dungeon, even fed to dragons seemed more merciful.

Madeline really tried to find his trail in the forest, but in the fog blanketing the valley, all the paths seemed interconnected as if some mischief-maker intended trespassers to wander aimlessly through the woods until they were either driven insane or eaten alive.

Fear and frustration were goading her and had done so now for the better part of the night. All of it came to a head when her horse stumbled upon a familiar clearing.

"I thought you knew the way out of here," she tearfully accused her silent steed, her limbs so cold she couldn't feel her feet nor fingers anymore. Her head hung as she stared down at the muddy bank where a huge set of hooves left imprints in the mossy clearing. She'd been going in circles for the last two hours.

Slowly, she turned in the saddle to glare at the outline of fur bringing up the rear. "Well? Don't let me stop you—go on. Go home. I'll just camp out right here on the bank and wait for your friends to come along and eat me." Madeline didn't dismount though. "Go on, get out of here." Her throat convulsed on tears, her voice sounded strangled as self-derision overwhelmed her. "Go on, damn you."

The wolf just stood where she was a dozen feet away.

Angry with herself, not thinking clearly, and too numb to realize the foolishness of her actions, Madeline slipped from her horse. Instantly, she felt unsteady and her hand snaked out to clutch the stirrup. In her other fist, she clenched the reins in stiff fingers. All around her branches poked through the fog like wispy arms reaching for her. It was then the first fat raindrop splattered against her cheek.

Blinking through the drizzle, stooping to snatch a handful of earth and brambles, she straightened and hurled them at the wolf. "Damn you and damn your master to freezing hell!" she shouted. Her horse jumped but blessedly didn't bolt.

Sheva paced the perimeter of the clearing, her keen eyes watchful of horse and angry rider, staying just out of reach of the next handful of flying missiles. She stopped to sniff the ground, dart a look at Madeline, and then reversed her pacing as the clouds rumbled above the treetops.

ALCHEMY:—
The production, by unperceived processes, of
the higher qualities from the lower; that is, from the
baser metals, or lower mental qualities, the precious
metals, or higher mental (silver) and buddhic (gold)
qualities, are by transmutation produced.

3.

Morning was a glimmer on the distant horizon when Dance entered Wolfglyn's gray stone walls, his strides taking him over the sturdy-hewn planks of the drawbridge. The first of the angry storm clouds waited until he reached the gatehouse before they cracked open. In a matter of seconds, a torrential downpour let loose. Icy daggers poured from the sky, stinging his face, the raging winds whipping his cloak about his legs. Gusts whirled across the mossy moat engorged with dense cattails waving in the storm's wrath. Rain slid into Dance's eyes and down his neck.

Amidst the thunderous downpour stood the limestone walls of the castle's keep, rising like towering sentinels topped with tattered banners of doom. Wolfglyn's soggy wet standards flapped in the wind amid the conical peaks, their fierce red dragons standing out like splashes of blood against an ebony field. Among the crimson slashes were more of solid black, bearing the mark of mourning—their grimness heralding the young master's approach.

As was his habit, Dance raised harrowed eyes to them—

as if he expected to find his soul among the remnants. He stood there squinting in the rain, welcoming the bitter bite of *mother nature's* cold onslaught and the passing of another season. Each season putting distance between him and the pain roused by memories.

Memories of not so long ago when the castle's vassals called Dance, *Ifan Gwyalt. God's favored wild one.* Ifan Gwyalt ab Owain D'epanier of Mynydd Castell. Son of a wellborn lord, so named by the sire who had once inhabited this great mountain castle. A castle where once vast happiness reigned...until tragedy befell its lords.

The now reigning heir was simply referred to as Master of Wolves and Wizardry. His closest and sole companion an old man. For reasons he never spoke of, Dance lived alone. His soul stripped from him as was his given name, Ifan Gwyalt, stricken from usage by the same Owain of Mynydd Castell. The inscribed stones of Dance's birth, now cursed, lay buried below ground where they remained after grief seized the souls of Mynydd Castell.

Dance preferred no connection with that past. Thus, Mynydd became Wolfglyn. What remained of the place was hardly more than a shell of a once great stronghold.

From the bowels of Wolfglyn's keep, a hunkered figure draped in a muddy wool robe ambled into the barren courtyard to greet Dance and save him the bleakness of his despairing memories.

"*Bore da,* good morning, mi lord. I see ya brought us a fat hare," remarked Hywel over the noise of the storm as they quickly sought shelter in the foyer from the downpour. "How be the hunt today?" the older man inquired as Dance removed his sodden mantle to toss it over a stag's antler to dry.

Joining the wet cloak just inside the door, Dance hung

his bow and quiver in its rack before placing his catch in the outstretched hand of the old man. "Has Sheva returned?" he asked, concern tingeing his voice.

"*Ydw*, master. Shortly after dawn. Though when I saw that one come back without ya, I worried something happened." He followed Dance into the great hall off the foyer where the deep-hood fireplace glowed with a welcome warmth. "Ya gave me quite a scare, mi lord. How did ya two get separated?"

Hair dripping wet, Dance warmed his hands over the flames, his gaze through the window scanning the *glyn* beyond the gates. "I sent her on an errand."

Hywel blinked in bewilderment. "Errand, mi lord?"

Ignoring the question, Dance asked patiently, "Did Sheva return alone, old man?" In his tone was a deep-felt respect and affection. The mutual kind felt by two lost souls.

Hywel's bushy brows grew together, his confusion apparent. "*Ydw*, mi lord. Is something amiss?"

Dance chose his words carefully. "I saw tracks again—hoof-prints of a mountain pony leading across the river. The snares I found were baited with venison. Whoever our poacher, he has strayed onto Wolfglyn and protected land."

Hywel shuffled about the room and returned to hand Dance a dry length of linen. "Do ya think `tis *him*, master?"

Scowling, Dance dried his hair and gritted out harshly, "You mean Owain?"

Hywel's dark thoughts were written across his wrinkled features, his silence bemoaning grave discord. With Dance's sire. The one who sought to destroy his own son.

"I heard in the village he has been seen around. Ye think `tis him laying the traps? Ye know how he hates yer wolves."

"If Owain is back, he rode an unshod horse." Dance stared with unseeing eyes beyond the bailey. "If it is an unwary poacher, I'll soon put a stop to his raids. Whoever it is, I don't want you venturing far unless accompanied by Druidh."

As if just discovering his master returned, Druidh, hearing his name, bound from the shadows of the dais and barreled up to Dance. His coat black as coal, and near twice the size of Sheva, the rangy male wolf impacted Dance's thigh with bone-jarring playfulness as Wolfglyn's seasoned menace welcomed his master with wet licks.

Druidh's daughter was not far behind. Sheva circled, looking for her opening. Always jealous of the attention Druidh received, Sheva nipped at her father's heels.

Giving Sheva his full attention at last, Dance squatted to bestow his favorite girl a bearhug. He had worried unnecessarily, it seemed. After the welcoming party was contented, Dance rose and shed his wet tunic.

In their usual aggressive play, daughter and father frolicked about Dance's feet before racing toward the impressive winding stairwell leading to the upper chambers. At the foot of those stairs, they turned as if waiting for their master, tongues hanging, keen eyes alight with eagerness.

Hywel pinned a stern look upon the master's loyal shadows and followed Dance up the massive stone stairway that dominated the ancient beauty of Wolfglyn's grand keep. "As I didn't know when ye would be back, mi lord, I hope it doesn't displease ye, but I had ta lock the unruly bunch in the study while ye were gone." Of the six wolves, Sheva's sisters were the most destructive.

At the top of the landing, Dance glanced over his shoulder at his solemn retainer before halting outside his bedchamber. Hywel stood back, not wanting to be knocked from his feet while Sheva and Druidh pushed past his legs as the door was opened.

The master's chamber was elegantly appointed, the charred remains of a mysterious fire no longer noticeable. All that remained was the lingering smell of smoke. The walls had been scrubbed clean with lye, the ruined furniture, all of it, dragged from the chamber and tossed out. Most of what had been destroyed had never been replaced, except for one elaborately carved wardrobe of Roman origin. The only other pieces of furniture in the room were a dressing table near the cheval mirror and the master's state bed. The bed dominated the west wall with its heavily embroidered, gold privacy curtains against the austere background of ebony velvet. Aside from the gnawed bedposts, the master's bed looked as lavish as anyone might expect to find in the Prince of Wales' own residence.

The old man lowered his gaze to his hands. "I fear the destruction this time is worse than before. I fear they are punishing ye, mi lord, for leaving them behind."

Dance next shed his wet breeches. "It's for their own safety."

"*Ydw*, I know that—but they do not."

"Too bad the stories Llwyd has spread around the lowlands aren't as effective as they used to be. Especially now that our poacher has resurfaced."

"That traitor Llwyd consorts with the devil. Knife his own flesh and blood in the back were they not already rotting in their graves. Ye speak too kind of him, mi lord."

"I've been fortunate the trespassers have stayed away

this long." Keeping in mind his companion felt responsible for every mishap that befell the castle in his absence, Dance asked again, "So what have those unruly bandits chewed this time?"

Gnarled fingers clasped together, reluctantly Hywel admitted, "Forgive me, mi lord, I left the barn door ajar for but a moment while I went ta see if I could spot ya from the battlement. Ya know that new leather bridle ye tooled for Lucifer?" Hywel cast a dark look at Druidh who lay negligently sprawled in front of the fire. "Well, `tis shredded beyond repair."

Dance's gaze followed that of his friend's to the culprit warming himself on the rug. Druidh was left behind more and more these days because his moods had become unpredictable. Before his brutal encounter with poachers, the wolf had been friendly and loving and playful. Whatever cruelty Druidh had suffered, it had ruined him. The scars left behind had affected the mind — the animal couldn't be trusted. Which on occasion made him dangerous.

Dance and his unpredictable shadow shared similar tragic pasts. Which was why he felt a compassion for Druidh.

So considering the last raid of his belongings had cost him a new pair of boots and a handsome leather saddle, Dance thought the loss this day minimal. A bridle could be replaced. At least Hywel hadn't locked the bandits, with their leader, in his bedchamber this time where they could get at the already suffering bedposts.

"If ye won't be needing me, master," Hywel put in, hefting the hare above his head to keep Sheva from latching onto it, "I'll just go put this carcass on ta boil. Give me half an hour and I'll have yer *brecwast* ready."

"I'll be down shortly to help with chores."

Dance preferred hard work to that of leisure. Hard work helped keep him occupied when he would have otherwise gone mad.

Hywel turned to leave, then paused as if he thought of something else. "`Twill be winter a comin' by the looks of it outside. My bones are telling me we will want ta be setting the hearth ablaze in the other rooms `afore the dampness sets in. If ye be goin' back out in the storm, we could use more firewood."

Telling himself the girl would be all right, that by now she was in her warm bed back in Llandeglay, Dance donned a dry tunic of deep blue with fine gold threads painstakingly stitched around the seams. "I'll take care of it." He reached for his breeches next. "Anything else you need done?"

Hywel smiled. "With the rain blowing like `tis, I don't know that ye wanna be riding out in it. But that beast in the barn has been raising cane again, an' he won't be letting me near him when he's in one of 'is moods."

"Unhappy, is he?"

Hywel snorted. "Spoiled, I'd say—like the rest of 'em." He chuckled softly. "I be thinkin' that devil's waiting for ya. An' he's gonna be a mite sore at ya for keepin' 'im penned up with the woollies."

Dance's unruly black stallion had his own ideas about station. Sharing the barn with the sheep was below him and he made it known.

Dance sat by the fire, rubbing feeling back into his cold limbs before donning clean breeches. "I'll see to Lucifer, as well," he said.

"*Ydw*, ya take care o' 'im, an' mind ya stay outta the way o' his hooves. That one is a menace." Though he was smiling, Hywel's wizened features held a seriousness, the gaps in his smile caused by age—signs of youth, long past, twinkling in his eyes. Perhaps it was those same signs of mortality that now made him seem older in the filtered light shining through the west wing's stained-glass panes. The travesty of mortality was watching one's youth slip away. Indeed, how long before Dance would find himself completely alone? Without even an old man's company to ease the darker spells of loneliness?

Dance refused to worry about the girl, whether she made it back to Llandeglay before it started raining.

He stared down at his hands, his hair shielding his expression from Hywel. "Some day you will want for more than an empty castle and a cold bed. At least there's work in the village. There you could spend your days living comfortably."

"*Na*, mi lord. My place is with ye. I've no want that cannot be found right here at Wolfglyn. `Tis here I will stay."

Dance shoved his feet into dry boots. "But you don't have to live like this...like I do. I want you to think about my offer of the cottage in the village."

Turning a deaf ear, Hywel met his master's gaze head on. "Twill be a blustery night, mi lord. We best get it warm in here or we both'll be curled up this night with yer wolves." Sheva circled his legs. "Off with ye, thief, `tis not for ya, but yer master." He shot Dance a hurried look. "I'll be taking myself downstairs `afore she steals yer meal, mi lord."

Nodding, Dance let him go.

In truth, he wholeheartedly dreaded the thought of being alone. But then he hated worse seeing the old man suffer the long lonely winter ahead. When the rains would keep them confined to the keep. It was Hywel who worked by his side in the alchemy chamber, one of the many cold drafty rooms of the main floor. During the coldest months,

Dance spent his time divided between distilling herbs and delving into the ancient mysteries of the *philosopher's stone*. He spent hours on end studying dusty volumes by noted seers. He spent the long winter days deciphering the veiled writings layered with wisdom from the *Wordless Book*. Pouring over metaphors, symbols, and allusions intended to conceal hard-won knowledge from all but the most persistent pupil.

Somewhere, in there, amidst the teachings of the *philosophers' stone* in the *Mutus Liber*, or the *Wordless Book,* lay the answer. To why he must continue to live when there was nothing to live for.

Tomorrow, after being away from his books through summer, Dance would lock himself in his quiet chamber and attempt again to unravel the rhyme of life, the *arcanum*, or the secret of another alchemical process. This time he just might try the mercury he'd distilled to transform and expand on his recipe for metals of wealth. This winter, if his findings bore fruit, Hywel would have gold enough to buy the village itself should he change his mind.

What stores of gold Dance set aside for himself, he would trade part of it for precious stones. *Michael the Wise*, a trusted friend and fellow bard, claimed his crystals were givers of life and harmony. Other more rare crystals wielded elusive healing properties.

If only there were such a crystal to ward off memories....

After Dance gently reprimanded the wolves—with a soft verbal rebuke—he turned them out into the courtyard. The storm had spent its fury. A light drizzle scented the air. And the wolves enjoyed romping through the puddles.

As much as the wolf was feared, Dance knew only the very few who kept to the wilds survived.

Liebault's French Folk beliefs claimed a wolf's tooth worn by a child protected that child from night fears, and wolf-skin shoes made children strong and brave. To a sheepherder they were a menace, while the *Ojibwa* claimed the wolf represented fidelity, while still others poached for the fur.

Dance saw the wolves not as pelts to keep one warm, but as highly intelligent animals, wild and graceful, using instinct and cunning to survive. At Wolfglyn, their presence helped relieve the loneliness. Fiercely protective and faithful, they looked after one another as they looked after the castle.

In all, there were five females and one male. Of the former group, was Druidh's mate, and Sheva's mother, Roannan, and Sheva's three sisters. While her sisters were unmanageable, Sheva herself was sweet and well-behaved. She had been born a runt and immediately captured his favor by following him around like a shadow. She had become his constant companion.

Wordlessly, Dance watched the wolves lope around the perimeter of the courtyard before he shut the door and retraced his steps into the hall. Only instead of taking the hallway leading to the east wing where he'd find the woodshed and barn, he climbed the stairs as if drawn by the vital presence of his memories.

The worst of his past had been locked away on the upper level. All the rooms sealed shut, save for two. Every room but his bedchamber and the room he couldn't bear to shut off. The chamber he avoided. The chamber where he lost his heart along with his soul. Ultimately the chamber of profound despair.

Later `twas the dank chamber below ground, forbidden and dark, which took from him what he cherished beyond this world. His penance for the gravest mistake of betrayal. For his foolish loss of honor. For falling in love.

Compelled by the overwhelming sense of loss roused by those memories, Dance reached the hallway just outside his dead wife's empty room. What brought him to her door, he didn't question, but he was here and his hand was already raised to the dusty latch before he stopped himself. What did he expect to find? Comfort? How many times had he come here looking for her? Knelt by her bed and wept?

His heart ached for her. At times he ached so fiercely in other places, he would dive naked into the icy river to alleviate the torment. And the torment would surely plague him again with renewed vengeance. He shouldn't have allowed himself near the woman he encountered in the forest. Lord knew, coming in contact with her supple curves did nothing but call forth long-suppressed desire. Surely, he hadn't expected to feel any of the fire his beloved mate had possessed. The rapture he'd shared with Aneira bespoke a passion beyond bearing, undaunted, fearless, and sadly forbidden.

It had cost his beloved her life.

If he helped the young woman, her death, too, would be of his making...senseless and brutal. Yet his life, he feared, was already touched. Finding the girl looking so forlorn had already moved something in him. Something about her had rekindled all the pain buried with Aneira. Buried with his infant son.

"Pardon me, mi lord," came the nervous voice approaching from the hallway, intruding upon the private moment, "but I think ye should come right away."

Dance looked over his shoulder, a dull glaze haunting his amber eyes as the spell was broken and his hand lowered to his side.

Hywel rushed toward him in the corridor. "The wolves are raising a ruckus in the bailey or I'd not have bothered ya. Mi' eyesight `tis not what it used ta be, but it looks ta be a great black devil grazing in yonder field."

ARCHED GATEWAYS:—
A symbol of mental qualities which open the way to
knowledge.

4.

Dance strode across the inner bailey toward the castle's gates, calling a gentle command to the wolves. Their yapping ceased as they gathered around as escort, following him to the portcullis. Hywel was raising the great iron grate. Chains squealed as the pulley hefted its weight. The drizzle had lessened. Dodging puddles, at the gate Dance gestured the wolves to wait, his gaze trained on the clearing beyond the drawbridge.

Wolfglyn sat in the heart of a well-concealed *glyn* surrounded on all sides by Radnor forest. On occasion, deer wandered onto the verdant grazing field bracketed by thick oak, yew and elm trees. This time it wasn't a deer. Hywel's description of a 'great black devil' turned out to be a big clod of a beast. The very one Dance had ridden to the edge of the river to see the woman on her way home.

The big clod appeared completely at home. Standing alone in the drizzling rain where the lush green field split down the middle by an overgrown path, the black charger was looking Dance's way.

Dance quickly scanned the copse of trees for the rider, thinking if the animal's mistress were watching, she'd now make her move. No one emerged. Certainly, if she survived the night, whatever her reason for defying him, she'd not convince him a second time that she'd lost her way. Whatever her game, she had just forfeited her horse.

Dance made it within five feet of the animal before it jerked its head higher, eyes flashing, watching him warily as if ready to bolt. Dance came to a halt before he noticed the blood trickling down the black hide washed slick in the rain. "Easy, boy. I mean you no harm." Her black beast was injured, though Dance couldn't yet tell how bad. Wicked looking thorns tangled his mane as if he'd run through the brier wall before realizing the danger. The same brier patch that had been planted to thwart trespassers.

Hywel finally caught up. "Looks like the poor beast needs doctorin'," he commented, standing back so as to not further scare the animal.

Dance averted his gaze, soothing the dumb beast with soft words in his native tongue as his hand slowly reached out, his steps taking him closer, his fingers finding the reins. Sides quivering, but sensing no danger, the distraught animal lowered his huge head and heaved as if giving a great sigh of relief.

"Where ya think he come from, mi lord?" Hywel asked as Dance gave the worst wounds a cursory look.

"Llandeglay."

Hywel's brown eyes twinkled. "Aye, he told ya that, did he?"

Dance's lips drew into a mocking curl. "His mistress told me."

Ignoring Hywel's astonished look, he led the horse back to the castle as he provided an abbreviated version of his encounter evening last with a young woman. Dance explained how she claimed she'd been told that she'd find a healer in the forest. She'd known him by name, but she had not suspected for one minute the man she spoke to was the healer for whom she was searching.

They reached the drawbridge before Hywel put a hand out to detain him. "What about the woman?" He looked back at the forest. "She'll be out there, mi lord. Mayhap hurt."

"She could be laying in ambush, too."

Hywel's expression disapproving, he looked downright obstinate, his mop of hair slicked to his head, rain dripping into his eyes. "Ye can'a leave the girl out in this storm—"

"She deliberately ignored my warning." Dance's teeth clenched as an icy tremor slid through him; he remembered his cloak was hanging back in the hall. "Whatever has befallen the unfortunate chit is none of my concern."

Again, he started forward, but Hywel was there in his path, shaking his head. "Ye cannot mean that, mi lord? She'll die out there."

Dance's brows raked together harshly. They were both now soaked to the bone and the man had to pick this moment to bedevil him. "Even if she survived a broken neck from the fall, the way she was dressed, she wouldn't have survived the night on foot. Forget her, she won't be alive." Hating that thought as much as anyone else, he brushed past Hywel and proceeded toward the bailey with her mount in tow.

Clearly disgruntled, Hywel took himself off toward the keep, grumbling under his breath as Dance settled the horse in the barn.

Dance first tended to the animal's injuries with a poultice of pudre ruge, a red powder for healing wounds. Lucifer snorted his disdain, watching the intruder across the companionway, his teeth bared as if he'd dearly like to lay into the big clod of an animal in the stall opposite him.

Dance calmed Lucifer, giving him his favorite treat, a juicy red apple. When the apple was gone, he fed both horses and poured fresh water from the water casks into separate troughs. The sheep were similarly fed and watered.

A half-hour later, when Dance emerged from the woodshed with his arms loaded, it was to find Hywel dragging a crudely-fashioned litter behind him across the bailey.

Their gazes clashed when the old man spotted him, Hywel's face set in grim lines. "I'll not be leavin' her out there."

His surprise shuttered, Dance glowered darkly. "Bring her back here and she's as good as dead anyway." To Sheva who was wagging about, he turned grave eyes. "You," he accused softly, "led her to my door. Go with Hywel—see he doesn't get lost."

Sheva gave him her toothy smile then bound after the retreating figure.

It was growing late. Already the shadows of dusk were stretching their arms over the valley below where Dance reclined his back against the window's ledge high in the face of the tower. Lilting tunes drifted from his flute, each woven with heartrending emotion. When restless as he was, he sought the solitude of the watchtower. He would come here and lose himself for a time, and grieve through his song.

And on very lonely nights when he couldn't sleep, he would imagine his son playing in the moat as had Dance once played as a child. If he looked toward the north he could almost see Aneira. It was from this same perch he would sometimes imagine her like he remembered her.

A slender figure draped in flowing white silk, dancing in the *glyn* of verdant wet grass. His wife would lift her soft eyes to him—because she knew he was watching from the tower—and he would feel her love move through him.

His family lived with him still, though Dance could never hold them, nor comfort them, nor grow old with them as he so craved with every breath. Separated by whatever barrier he could not breach, they were forced to live apart. His family held just out of reach. When the winds were quiet, like they were now, the soft whisper of dew misting his face, he could speak to them with song wrenching from the depths of his soul.

A soul that prayed for death....

Had Aneira not made him promise that he would live for her and his child, he'd have taken his life that day alongside them.

How he wished to God he hadn't made that vow.

As if listening to the tunes carried on the wind above the bailey, Druidh raised his head to the fissure in the face of ancient stones.

From where Dance stood leaning against the sill, shutters thrown wide, he could hear the wolf's mournful chorus join that of the flute.

Druidh always sulked below, as if he too felt the sorrow that could not be shaken. As guardian of the bailey, the wolf saw and heard things long before Dance could. It came as no surprise when Druidh's attention shifted to a spot beyond the bailey. Dance lifted his gaze likewise. A matter of heartbeats passed and then he, too, saw what Druidh had.

Hywel making his way across the field with his burden.

It wasn't yet dark and already the raw chill promising a cold winter seeped through Dance's shirt, prickling the hairs on his arms and chest as he emerged from the keep. The rain still drizzled. In another hour the harsh elements of the mountain regions would send creature and man alike seeking cover.

Dance met Hywel at the gatehouse as he was coming in, dragging the litter, Sheva at his side. The old man hesitated, his face drawn, his expression solemn as if unsure where he would put his burden as he looked around the bailey.

Dance raised a hand to halt Hywel's progress before he looked down on the unmoving shape bundled like a swaddling babe...and his soul cringed from the sight. In broad daylight her beauty wasn't only staggering, it called forth images he'd not thought to behold again. His young wife. All it took was one glimpse and he knew why he had avoided looking at her more closely last evening. The innocence he'd detected was even more startling than he cared to admit. She had skin like pale silk, enticing a man to touch. Exquisite even by the most jaded standards, she would no doubt have a good many admirers wanting to fill her every wish. Her hair, he recalled, fell well past her waist in a braid. In the light of day the color could only be described as the vibrant fire of autumn.

On purpose, he hadn't wanted to see her clearly last evening nor have this vision to dwell on. The sweet musical voice she'd used on him in the forest was haunting enough.

And Hywel, curse his soft heart, had dragged her home.

Over his initial shock, his attention instantly shifted to more alarming observations. The bluish cast to her skin and lips portended death. If she wasn't already past help, she would be in a matter of hours. Her hair lay pasted to her skin, sharply contrasting her paleness. In her sleep-like repose, she looked younger than he'd first thought. Forlorn and in need of protection. He suddenly felt a maddening need to fall to his knees in the mud beside the litter and draw her into his own warmth.

Only cruel reality kept him from acting on impulse.

"You know what will happen now," he told Hywel, his voice softly tortured, "why didn't you leave her out there?"

"Because, mi lord, the lady shouldn't be left ta die alone."

"So you brought her back here among strangers to die in a cold bed. That is merciful for certain." A dark brow lifted. "So where, I want to know, are you going to put her?"

Hywel shrugged his bowed shoulders, his burden weighing down his small frame, but he didn't proceed, he just stood right where he'd halted in the courtyard. "I think, mayhap, the chapel, mi lord. There be no drafts there. She would not be disturbing ya in the chapel."

She'd need out of her soaked clothes, Dance thought pragmatically. "I won't help her."

Hywel nodded. "*Ydw*, master, I know. I understand I'll be taking care of her miself—that is, of course, by yer consent, if ya see clear ta grant mi' permission."

Glowering, Dance grumbled a curse, but gestured as he did so toward the small round chapel that hadn't suffered too great a damage from neglect. Then he abruptly turned away and stalked back into the keep.

Hywel had the fire blazing and the girl settled where he'd fashioned her a straw pallet close enough to the hearth to do her the most good. The chapel was indeed, the best place for her. It was quiet and warm, centered in the middle of the bailey where it was protected on all sides by a sturdy curtain wall of stone and mortar some three feet thick. In the days of Dance's grandsire, the castle had withstood bombardment by catapult, sappers, scaling ladders and the like. The castle, however neglected and perishing now, had never once fallen to siege.

The small antechamber at the heart of the chapel had suffered the least ruin. The fire stoked in a deeply inset fireplace soon had the tiny room sweltering. Beads of sweat snaked down Hywel's neck. Yet when he felt the girl's forehead, her skin was like ice to the touch.

No matter how large a fire he built through the long night, he could not bring the color back into her face. Disrobing her might have helped. Left to his own meager skills, however, Hywel hadn't been able to bring himself to breech her modesty. But then, he was not a great healer. He was a simple vassal.

The one who could help her wouldn't. The master, in his day, would not have hesitated a blink to deposit her, naked as a lark, into a steaming bath. He'd have known exactly what oils to rub into her skin to bring back circulation. In everything, Dance had been wise and caring and he had been loved by cotter and villein alike. He'd been blessed with the *touch*. He'd been revered and besieged by visitors flocking daily to the gates of Mynydd Castell, seeking the all-powerful force of his healing strength. No magician nor seer could compete with young Ifan Gwyalt's magic.

Then Aneira ferch Meurig, daughter of the powerful Meruig, a lord of great wealth, come to Mynydd from the sea. `Twas a tragic day to be sure, the day the fair Aneira arrived to meet her betrothed. `Twas a worse tragedy she revile him. `Twas that which was destined to bring trouble, for Aneira's beauty blinded mortals, her sweetness a tempting potion none could resist. And when she chanced to meet Owain's beloved son, the powerful healer Ifan Gwyalt, it was understandable she would find him as irresistible as had all the unmarried young maidens.

All it had taken was one woman to destroy what mighty armies couldn't lay siege to.

Blinking heavy eyelids, Hywel rubbed the girl's slender fingers between his own, his grueling vigil by her side tiring. Several times he almost nodded off sitting cross-legged next to her pallet. He was a pitiful substitute for a great healer. The one who could save her was being an obstinate mule.

`Twas a shame her fate. Fragile peerin' as a wood sprite this faerie-child dropped from the sky at his master's door. To be sure, `twas her looks bedeviling the master. For were she ugly with warts on her nose, Dance would not have turned her away.

With her face clean, she was rather comely in a pathetic sort of way. Bits of leaves and earth tangled in her pretty hair.

"Were my master here," he murmured to the poor mite frozen stiff on the pallet, "he'd have ya taken care of. I'm a poor substitute ta be sure." His gnarled finger brushed a damp tendril from her brow. "But `tis best I know ta do for ya." All he could do now was make sure she was not alone when she passed over to that golden kingdom of everlasting sleep.

Having done what he could for her, Hywel prayed most fervently for her soul...

Some hours later, Dance entered the chapel without making a sound and found Hywel curled up on the floor, softly snoring. The old man and his lovely patient looked like two puppies snuggled together on a narrow straw pallet. Hywel's hand held a paler, slender one. To one side of the pallet on clean rushes, lay a vat used for drawing steam into the lungs. Kneeling, he dipped his fingers into the smelly water, brought it to his nose. Boiled bark, mint leaves and lung oil. The very same combination of herbs Dance would have used. It momentarily surprised him that Hywel remembered which of those lining the shelves of his apothecary to add to boiling water.

But then Hywel had often been in attendance when Dance had used his magic. The two of them had worked side by side. Their work endless, every hour of the day and night beleaguered by those set upon by illness. Those were the days when he might be beckoned forth in the middle of the night by a midwife whose patient could not be soothed. Nights he worked through dawn while half asleep on his feet. He'd been there for the birth of tiny Thomas who came into the world with his cord tangled about his neck. He'd been roused from sleep that night, after one of the rare occasions he'd actually made it to his bed and fallen asleep before the summon from the gatehouse watch.

There had been countless limbs to set, wounds to mend, ailments so numerous he'd wondered if a few poor souls weren't being plagued by their imagination. Other ailments were nothing more than active imaginations of those chaste young maidens growing into womanhood—those insisting they were bleeding to death from their nether region. All a harmless ruse, Dance was well aware, to engage his attention. Get him alone where he'd be forced to notice them. In those cases, it was not what ailed the body, but often what ailed the heart.

Never had he turned a soul away.

Then he'd lost his gift and all that had changed.

He hadn't tried to summon *the powers*, since.

The girl's color was only slightly improved, he noticed grimly. Or perhaps it was just that Hywel had her somewhat cleaned up. No doubt, she still wore—under that mound of wool blankets—the same damp shirtwaist and breeches as she had evening last. Hywel wouldn't have disrobed her. The sight of a naked woman always sent him running off to fetch from the adjoining kitchen, some implement he'd forgotten to retrieve from the boiling vat. Always, the task of removing the barriers of modesty had fallen to Dance.

His gaze scrutinized Hywel's patient. The signs weren't in her favor. He didn't need to examine her to confirm them. He'd seen it before. When the body's core could not be roused.

It unexpectedly saddened him. Such vital youth wasted. Surely she would have been wiser to go home. There was no honor in dying needlessly.

He reached to tuck her hand under the blanket. Against the warmth of his own skin, her slender fingers felt cold and stiff. He found himself wondering what fool had left this precious prize unguarded. Why the hell was she wandering around alone in the forest looking for a healer?

Shut off from the world in his empty castle—a prison cleverly devised for his own punishment—he hadn't thought it possible he could still find purity in this world.

Nor had he thought to behold beauty again such as Aneira's. So child-like his bride had been when she'd come to his bed, so pure of heart, full of laughter, wise beyond her years. Aneira—the naked fire in his veins. She alone had been worthy of his fall from grace. She alone had braved death for him.

Shaking with the force of emotion that memory roused,

Dance focused on the girl's death-blue pallor. She had no way of knowing what she'd done by coming here. She couldn't know the torture it would cause him to have a woman in the castle again, even brief as her stay would be.

Unfortunately, she wouldn't make it the night...unless he acted.

HEALING:—
A symbol of a spiritual process by means of which
qualities are energized, harmonized, and purified.
Evolution is often irregular and unbalanced
through the vacillations of the egos; and spiritual
adjustments are made according to an ideal pattern,
as the souls become prepared for them.

5.

The great black wolf with snarling fangs held Madeline by the throat, taking her down, pain puncturing her body where jaws of death ripped open her flesh. Fear seized her soul while she clung to life, her screams filling the air with suffocating terror, her whole body jerking and flailing against the beast who held her pinned to the ground. The beast's fierce face was there above hers, unrelenting in death...then it was contorting, shifting shape to reveal long white fangs protruding beneath a great helmet battered with age, smeared with crimson streaks...streaks of blood....

Her throat now was convulsing with each breath, her screams lessening...and her body was slowing its valiant fight....

Her eyes were shutting just as she saw a figure take form out of the mists, the darkness emitting a darker shadow. Then someone was there, enfolding his arms around her...some presence beyond her vision, reaching for her...fending off with his bare hands that snarling image.... The ferocious beast with fangs buried in her throat released her, sulked away under the stronger force protecting her and she was left alone on the grassy bank with a shape-shifting shadow.

She lay dying, her blood flowing from the gaping wound...and she was fading...sinking into darkness.

Then he was gently raising her shoulders, peering into her face and something vital and warm reached around her; bright rings of vibrant light moving through her...bringing a sense of peace so sweet it hurt, and yet she snuggled into it. Let its warmth envelop her...a warmth that was insistent, a breath near her ear soothing her and telling her she was no longer alone.

The voice moved through her like the mist embracing her... coming from the dark angel holding her protectively within his arms...a strange blue light emanating from him as he carried her safely home....

In her fitful delirium Madeline thought she heard an angel's deep voice whispering sweet words in her ear, but then the fires of hell were once again scorching her, burning her skin...and for all her thrashing about she could not escape that dark hole sucking at her feet...reaching to her beyond the fire engulfing her....

The calming deep voice in her dream, however, wouldn't let her drift far from reach...for whenever her restlessness grew worse, there was a murmur in her ear quieting her fears. Through it all, at the heart of her frantic dreams was an urgency pressing upon her heart, one that kept her holding on...*Papa, I'm coming...wait for me...don't give up.*

For the next twenty-four hours, Dance painstakingly supervised the care of the old man's patient. He bathed her fever, bathed her perfect young body with cold water Hywel carried from the well-house. He dribbled barley water and chinchona between her lips to sooth her fever. When he'd gotten her out of immediate danger, he stood back and watched as the old man wrapped her in a sweat poultice of mustard and moss. When she thrashed madly about in her nightmares, Dance pinned her to the pallet with his own body as Hywel looked on with a pitiful expression.

Neither Dance or Hywel slept much during the following two days, nor had they taken time to eat more than a bite of whatever was put before them by the one whose turn it was to take a break. Hywel dribbled sugared-onion *cawl* between her lips for nourishment as Dance instructed, then with Dance's help, they would carry her to the bath where she was repeatedly deposited in cold water to bring her fever down. Hywel worked mindlessly round the clock, his concern never ceasing.

Still, Dance hadn't used more than his potions.

After they got her settled that night, Dance relieved Hywel who looked dead on his feet. The night air was calm, the weather peaceful and he propped himself in a great leather chair in the antechamber's doorway to play a haunting tune on his flute. A beautiful full moon lumbered above a far off mountain ridge. Sheva came by to nuzzle his leg and say goodnight before she joined Druidh. Druidh remained restless as if sensing a stranger amidst them, and he hung back with leery eyes peering into the chapel as if both curious and resentful of the girl inside.

That night Druidh joined Dance in song, his lonely howl followed by Sheva's sisters and mother. The same pattern followed the next night. On the fourth night, however, a storm rolling in sent everyone for cover.

Dance had gone to check on the horses, gather more wood for the fire, and then, because he hadn't had time to track down their dinner in the forest, he'd simply returned to the barn. That evening they feasted on mutton. Hanging upon a large three-legged stand, a black kettle of mutton stew simmered over the fire in the kitchen, the smell drifting deep inside the keep to reach Dance in another chamber off the kitchen. It was the first time in the four days since Hywel brought the girl to Wolfglyn that Dance had left the chapel to see to his own bath, a shave and to change his soiled clothes.

He sat at his worktable in his medicine chamber, head lowered over a cluttered surface, a mug of mead clasped between his palms, his forehead resting on his forearms, the musty smells of damp stone and herbs a welcome change from the stifling air in the cramped chapel bower.

But Dance's brief respite was to be short lived.

The girl was carrying on as if set upon by demons, Hywel quickly explained as he begged Dance to do something for her.

"Please, mi lord," he persevered, his robe dripping puddles on the rushes of the medicine chamber where Dance had been distilling a stronger liquorice draught. "Come look for yerself—she's worse than before. Crying, she is, for someone and I can'a do anything ta quiet her."

That night Dance sat on the floor of the chapel's anteroom with Hywel, bloody slashes marring the side of his face where her flailing claws left scratches.

"Ye have a way with her, mi lord," Hywel said in reverent awe, his own bloodshot eyes holding great esteem, his expression these days one of pride for his master whose subtle magic, if not restored to its full potency, still worked miracles with the fairer sex. "She sleeps like a babe when ya hold her. Her color is better, too, don't ya think?"

Dance sat with his back braced against the wall closest to the hearth and warmth. Across from Hywel on the floor, Dance said nothing as he cradled the sleeping girl against his chest, her head snuggled under his chin. It hadn't escaped his notice that all along Hywel had been trying to find a way to get him involved every time something came up.

"Ye think `tis her papa dying, which brought her here?" Hywel reflected as he cleared the cluttered area around them. Vials of herb and oil remedies were knocked over on their sides, scattered over the floor. A large copper tub of frigid water sat in a puddle splashed onto the rushes when her foot had caught it and sent it sloshing.

"It isn't my concern. Nor do I want to hear about it."

"Oh, aye, I forgot ye won't be helping her." A hint of cynicism tinged Hywel's words.

Dance cast him a withering glare before he gently lowered the now exhausted girl onto the pallet. He drew the thick marten coverlet, taken from his own bed, over her. Then with her quieted, he wordlessly left Hywel and his patient to themselves as he went back to the keep to shut himself in the watchtower.

It wasn't until the following night Wolfglyn's guest finally roused from her death sleep to stare up at him with blinking eyes.

Madeline's sluggish brain came alert, her breath stifled as she looked into the face peering down at her with kind brown eyes. "Where am I?" she asked hoarsely, swallowing around the dry lump in her raspy throat.

The man merely peered at her as if mute.

She'd spoken English on impulse before it occurred to her he might not know her language. "Where am I?" she repeated, mangling what little Welsh she learned on the voyage.

The man smiled warily, giving her a grin full of gaps.

"Why ye are at Wolfglyn, young lady," he replied in his own tongue, reserved in using what English he knew. In Welsh, he explained in great detail with gesture and words, how he found her in the forest near dead.

'Wolfglyn'. She understood that much. She caught other snatches, 'forest' and 'dead', but what he meant beyond that she couldn't comprehend. The name, Wolfglyn, sparked some kind of recollection, though what it meant stayed just out of reach as she gave him a weak smile. She thought back. Yes, she did remember now her horse bolting as the thunder started. She remembered clearly thinking she was going to die alone in the forest before she would be found. And she remembered vividly the freezing cold rain slicing through her.

Her gaze moved past the man hovering over her to the slate ceiling above his head, the stone walls crumbling with age, the kind of walls that formed either a crude dwelling... or castle perhaps.

Castle Wolfglyn?

Her eyes rounded as suddenly a murky cloud lifted. "This is Castle Wolfglyn?" she asked, even knowing he couldn't understand, her heart swelling with elation. Thinking to get to her feet, Madeline half raised herself off the pallet before the movement brought her up short. Dizziness swam over her, bringing a flush to her cheeks. She pressed a hand to her swimming head, breathing deeply, blinking away black dots and afraid she was going to swoon. Something soft brushed her fingers and she looked down at the coverlet which drifted to her lap. The softness she'd felt was a rich pelt of thick fur. Obviously a fur worth a great fortune; at the very least a small one. Not a coverlet of a pauper or beggar.

She glanced up at the man who must have found her. How long, she wondered, had she been unconscious? Near death, he said. Indeed, she felt weaker than a newborn babe.

Her gaze took in the sparsely furnished room, the odd array of bottles littering a small scarred table, the fire blazing in the hearth making the air crackle with heat. She was assailed by an odd feeling as if a great portal had sucked her in and thrust her back in time. To awaken, disoriented, in some medieval hovel and conversing with some misbegotten wanderer wearing sackcloth. A repugnant odor wafted through the air, something boiling in a kettle over the fire. What looked like some sort of bark or root lay on the hearth to one side of the kettle.

Madeline wrinkled her nose at the offending smells made worse in the overheated room.

"So this is Wolfglyn?" she repeated to herself, the reason she'd been searching for Castle Wolfglyn coming back to her now. Her hopeful gaze swung back to the form kneeling before her. Though he looked an ordinary man, could in fact be a beggar, he had likely saved her life. He had to be her healer!

Here she'd been searching for him and he'd been the one to find her. As if fated.

So he didn't have the long white beard she envisioned. All that mattered was this man had

nursed her back from the grave. Any doubts raised about his healing gift were instantly put to rest.

"I need you to come back to Llandeglay with me," she said earnestly, forgetting he wouldn't understand.

He looked at her blankly again, and she opened her mouth to try once more to explain, but just the effort needed to concentrate had already started to drain her. In the next breath, she found herself swaying. A gentle hand was there in an instant to hold her upright. "Maybe

I should try sitting here for a bit," she remarked to herself, trying to convey her message with a smile.

Joy and relief infused her heart and nothing could dim it now. She'd found her healer!

Fie on the surly beast in the forest, she didn't need him after all.

She tried again, "I need healer," she pronounced more slowly, not about to let the barrier of language stop her now. Thrusting her finger at his chest and nodding, she hoped he would nod too, but her fragile strength, so recently restored, was waning.

A smile crinkled around his gentle eyes as he helped her settle back against the wall. "*Ydw*, great healer," he told her, gesturing with his hands something of which she was helpless to decipher.

Madeline took a deep breath, beset by frustration and too weak yet to get to her feet. It was unbearably warm in the room and much as she hated showing weakness, she was growing increasingly drowsy. The heat was stifling. Making her sleepy. Sweat dotted her brow.

She watched her silent companion get to his feet and dip a ladle into a huge, black pot she hoped held something nourishing. As weak as she was, she was more famished. By the time her healer returned to her side, her eyelids were drooping shut. Seeing she was near sleep, he smiled patiently and instead handed her what looked like a chalice of solid gold. An ancient and lavish piece set with amethyst and rubies. Hesitantly she drew the heavy goblet to her lips, smelling the contents, and glad to discover it was water and harmless. She was truly thirsty. The chalice was heavy. Almost more than she could manage with shaky hands. The water tasted better than any she could remember.

The little man peering at her was already reaching for the goblet to help her steady it as it left her lips.

"It's my father," she went on in broken Welsh, "he has been wounded." Her hand reached to clasp his in appeal, but she was already slipping helplessly to the floor even as the last words tumbled from her mouth, "I need a healer."

It was the first night Hywel felt comfortable enough leaving her alone to go see to his chores that had been sadly neglected for five days now. He was confident she wouldn't harm herself this night, for in fact, when he left the chapel bower, she had looked most peaceful in her sleep.

Hywel found Dance in the watchtower where the master was spending more and more of his time these last few days. The reason had started to worry him.

His approach was heard because Hywel was gasping for breath when he finally reached the last stair leading to the top of the watchtower. His wide back to Hywel, the master's gaze remained unfocused on the horizon. "She's awake, is she?"

Hywel blinked in bewilderment as he always did when Dance knew things before being told. "*Ydw*, she's awake."

"Well, that's encouraging. Because as soon as she is strong enough to ride out of here, I want her gone." He turned from the window with haunted eyes. "Take her back to Llandeglay yourself—I don't care. I don't want her here."

"I understand, mi lord." A look of resignation on his face, Hywel drew a steady breath. "From the sound of it, her father is dying—"

"The village has a *meddyg*, she doesn't need me."

"Bah, that one is no healer." Hywel waited just inside the door. "Mayhap Llwyd knew it too, and that's why he led her here. Mayhap there's nothin' the *meddyg* could do ta help her father."

"Nor is there anything I can do."

"*Ydw*, ye think not, but ya just saved the poor mite from a cold grave." When he got no response, Hywel straightened his hunkered shoulders. "I know ya could help her. She'd never 'ave ta know ya went into the village—"

Dance's patience after five days snapped. His face a visage of anger, his boot struck the footstool, sent it crashing into the wall and shattering it. "Leave it be. For Christ's sake take yourself on back to the chapel and leave me alone," he growled, turning his back on Hywel to glare unseeing at the valley far below.

Saying no more, Hywel did as he was instructed and left.

Long after he finished castigating himself for being short with the old man, Dance paced the tower room and thought about the girl. About her sudden appearance in his life. All that she'd said in the forest that first night. How brave and noble her quest. How unnerved he'd been to find a woman so close to Wolfglyn. Later the shock of discovering just how beautiful she was and vulnerable.

Surely, if she weren't in need of a healer, he'd have been convinced she'd been sent to Wolfglyn to torture him....

FRUIT:—
A symbol of results of action—good and bad.
Effect of the operation of the law of karma—moral
causation—in the soul's progress.

6.

The ale Dance consumed that night before he'd reached the state of oblivion only served to sharpen the edge of his restlessness. Frustration stalked his every step as he paced about like a caged predator in his chamber. The images were upon him, more powerful than before, those he'd subdued. Christ—he could still feel her naked flesh under his hands. The texture of her skin like liquid silk. Every curve delicate perfection. He'd tried telling himself the girl was a patient. He'd never been so long without a woman. He hadn't known what celibacy did to a man. Remembering back to the girl's luscious bottom shifting over his groin as he rode with her across the river had been his first mistake. Seeing her unclothed was another.

That he kept telling himself...while he'd felt through his clothes her lushly-naked and slender body thrashing against him. The whole time she'd squirmed about on the pallet under his weight, her warmth seeped into him... igniting something infinitely more painful for having been too long contained.

His groin was on fire...the heavy throbbing distracting him for the better part of two days. He was swollen so hard every move made the pain keener. At times it was almost agony and yet tantalizing in a way that made him almost relish the pain. Hell—being castrated would have been easier to live with.

The reality was a torture like he'd never expected.

For he didn't dare, for one second, allow himself to relax his iron control.

When he fell asleep that night it was from sheer exhaustion; the physical body simply could take no more strain—and shedding his clothes, he passed out cold atop his bed.

It wasn't much later when the dreams came to haunt his sleep. Unrelenting. Sweet living hell mingled with heartache.

From the depths of the castle, an animalistic cry echoed through the dead of night so poignant with suffering its message couldn't be mistaken. One woman's name. The guttural sound of anguish that quieted all creatures.

Dance's body was drenched with sweat, his back arched off the bed where he lay rigid, blue veins in his neck popping out, his whole body taut...his hand shamelessly moving....

He startled himself awake. Like a splash of cold water came the instantaneous wretchedness washing over him. The rhythm stroking him lessened as desolation took over. His hand fell limp at his side.

His eyes were squeezed tightly shut for that fleeting interval when he fought the spasms wracking his loins, clenching his fists as if by will alone he might keep the indisputable truth from intruding. That he would be reduced to servicing himself for the rest of his life...

When all he ever wanted was to be able to hold Aneira for a while longer, feel her sweet sheath clenched around him as he spilled all his love against her womb. In the aftermath of orgasm, that's when he could almost feel her again, beside him, her scent lingering, her loving kisses whispering through him...before illusion faded and self-disgust returned to mock him.

The vision in his dream always felt so real, tangible...and then as all dreams did, the sweet residual started fading.

He opened his eyes to the intensity of loneliness...the room dark, cold. Useless seed trickled down his thigh.

He lay there, heart pounding hard in his chest, his gaze fixed on the ceiling going blurry as the totality of profound emptiness assailed him.

As she always did, upon waking him during his fitful dreams, Aneira vanished.

Cursing his life without her, his ceaseless weakness, his foolish determination to hold onto her forever, Dance swung his feet to the floor and sat on the edge of the bed. His hands cradled his dark head.

Silent tears burned his eyes.

Once awakened from his dream Dance couldn't go back to sleep. He didn't even try, for he knew from experience how useless to go through the motion. The end result was always the same. Wide awake, he'd stare in the dark at the walls and contemplate ways to devise his own end. Useless, that was. When he exhausted every conceivable means to an end, when accidental death—the one greatest possibility of being shot by poachers—was clearly not going to happen, he'd given up his reckless course. Even the sleeping draughts, Hywel had locked away at Dance's own request. Where temptation wouldn't become lethal.

Resigned to living like a monk, Dance found sleep

worked better if he paced the room in circles until he finally wore himself out.

Foregoing another attempt at sleep, Dance hastily dressed himself, then wandered down the stairs. He moved noiselessly through the dark foyer and into a shadow-enshrouded bailey. It was quiet, Hywel had made sure Druidh and the girls were settled down for the night.

The air was crisp. The temperature chilly. The moon overhead obscured by a heavy haze of clouds.

Before he knew where he was headed, he was standing in the barn watching Lucifer. His faithful steed greeted him with weary regard.

A ride. A long hard one. They both had been confined to the castle for six days.

Lucifer needed to stretch his legs. Dance needed to get away from Wolfglyn.

He saddled and led a prancing Lucifer into the dark courtyard when Hywel's words came back to him. Dance shrugged them off. He had one foot in the stirrup when, at the last moment, he cursed a vivid streak.

Grumbling under his breath, Dance left Lucifer to cool his heels while he re-entered the keep. Hardly cognizant of his decision, in his alchemy chamber he found the cache of medicinal vials and expediently secured them in a leather pouch full of compartments to keep them from shattering.

He returned to the bailey to find Lucifer grazing on a small shock of grass. The pouch was placed in the bag draped over the rear of the saddle. "I'm only going to Llandeglay to assuage my curiosity about something," he muttered convincingly to his attentive mount.

Had Hywel been there to see the medicinal pouch Dance carried in his saddlebag, he'd have suspected something more at the heart than mere curiosity. But since Hywel wasn't around to see his master off, Dance escaped an interrogation.

That night, master and beast took the lesser traveled path through the forest to Llandeglay.

While Dance was making his way through the forest, already a posse was rousing from their beds in Llandeglay to once again take up the search for the missing girl from Boston. By now everyone in the village had heard of her and had been appraised of what happened. There was a bounty on Llwyd's head. A hefty reward offered by the Carlton's who had not seen hide nor hair of the man named Llwyd since Philip watched the man ride out over five days ago with his sister.

By a stroke of luck, their father was alive. The village physic had returned. Unfortunately, by the time he'd gotten back, gangrene had started in and Mr. Carlton was hanging on by a thin line. Leroy, the eldest, refused still to give consent to have the arm removed.

The doctor peered at the infected area before glancing up from his patient to meet Leroy's hard blue eyes. "Yer father is a strong man," he said, resorting to his rusty version of English to converse. "In good health aside from his injury. I understand yer hesitation. At this point he's not any worse, but he won't last if the arm doesn't come off. Sorry."

"I need another few days," Leroy murmured, giving the man no recourse but to hold off on sawing, which no doubt the doctor thought was lunacy even if he didn't come right out and say it.

While the hunchback man wearing a black woolen

robe inspected their father, Philip hung back from the family group cloistered around the table, his expression torn. His gaze held the despondent look of a man filled with unimaginable remorse. He'd been beating himself up, which was why Leroy and Adam hadn't lashed into him. They hadn't needed to. Philip was doing a good job of that all by himself.

The physic busied himself redressing the putrid wound. "Women folk these days, runnin' off." He shook his head. "First yer sister, then Gwehydd the weaver. That one, fell she did, on her head and not been right since. Wanders off all the time. I hear she dinna' come back this time. Been gone two days, her ma says. May just be yer sister an' her are out there together somewhere—"

Adam burst into the room, sending the candle flames stuttering. It was still dark, but it didn't matter to the Carlton's.

"We're ready," he said from the doorway. Next oldest, Adam was taller than his brothers, a formidable force, well-built and equally intimidating. He'd taken after their mother, their Celtic blood evident in his pale auburn hair. Like Leroy, he was the serious brother. He wore now a perpetual scowl on his face that had taken on a dark determination following the turn of events surrounding the disappearance of their adored little sister.

The search party was gathered outside the physic's office, the dark sky lit with blazing torches held by a dozen men. Good men who'd come forward to help. Eight villagers and four Carlton's in all. They were rested, stomachs fed and ready to set out once more with fresh horses. Yesterday they had covered most the wooded area off the main road. It wouldn't be dawn for another three hours, but it didn't matter. This morning they were going deeper into the forest.

Leroy was to lead one search party and Adam the other. The two groups were to meet back in two hours at the point where their paths separated at the edge of the forest.

Philip was standing in the circle of torchlight looking up at Leroy, his lips compressed in obvious despair. Torchlight flickered over his hair, burnishing it red, darkening bluer shadows under his eyes. Hemp dipped in whale oil sputtered flames from the many torches. Smoke stung their throats, teared their eyes. Leroy bent from the saddle and clasped his little brother's shoulder. "Whatever you do, don't let that doctor start cutting before I get back. And stop worrying, we'll tear this place apart to find Maddie if we have to."

Philip swiped a sleeve over his eyes. "It's been six damn days," he rasped in a raw voice.

"I know." Leroy straightened in the saddle as those waiting a discreet distance away held tight to their horses as the beasts pulled on their bits in a hurry to be off.

Leroy, Adam, Wesley, Theodore—they all knew how close their two youngest siblings were, how hard Philip would take it if something happened to their little sister. Maddie was too young, too beautiful to die, Leroy told himself. His sister was a Carlton, by God. She was tougher than she looked. In spite of her delicate appearance, she was a fighter.

Still, one incessant thought prevailed. Leroy refrained from voicing what they all feared. That Madeline's attacker had resurfaced. Too, it was starting to look like her guide, who hadn't returned either, had something to do with her disappearance. She could have ridden into most anything. Abducted. And God only knew what else, in these last six days, someone might have done to her. It had them all out of their minds. For Phil's sake they each contained their fears.

Leroy turned in the saddle to nod to Adam, then they were turning their horses toward the east in the direction Philip last saw their sister ride off.

It was still dark when Dance approached a copse of yews on the outskirts of Llandeglay. From his vantage everything looked peaceful. The small village was divided down the center by a single road cut through town. Cottages lined each side of the road. For no bigger than it was, Llandeglay had two inns, a general store and a doctor whose job it was to also tend to the ill of neighboring villages. Dance had tended to many a patient the *meddyg* said couldn't be helped. In a word, the *meddyg* of Llandeglay was lazy. He simply found it easier to turn people away than to admit to a lack of skill needed to treat them properly. It was one of Dance's greatest regrets that those ill and dying had stopped coming to him for help after word had been spread of the horrors at Wolfglyn.

Dance left Lucifer tied to a tree where he wouldn't be spotted.

He knew the village like the halls of his own keep, and crouching close to the shadows of the buildings, he crept his way around to the alley. No one locked their doors in the village. Everyone knew their neighbors, and the Welsh, though they fought against each other for centuries, were trusting souls at heart.

All appeared quiet to him, yet Dance stayed to the shadows for a moment longer.

He didn't have to wait long for the door to creak open to

the doctor's cottage. Dim light briefly limned the shadow on the threshold. Then whoever the occupant was heaved a sigh as he shut the door behind him and made his way to the tavern.

Dance listened for sound outside the door where he stood, making sure that before he entered he wouldn't find any unexpected stragglers. Hearing nothing, he slipped inside. The sick room was in shadows, a single taper in a pewter stand casting a dim glow from a three-legged table. Dance had, on his one visit to the *meddyg* all those years ago, thought the room resembled a cold crypt. Sparse and uninhabitable. No sign of cheerfulness present, no color save that of somber brown coverings that still draped the one drafty window. Nothing had changed in the room's appearance. This time, though, there was a putrid stench to the air. That of rotting flesh.

On the larger table in the center of the room lay the body of a man enfolded in a red wool blanket. His auburn hair stood out against ashen features grooved by time.

If the pain twisted upon the man's face hadn't indicated a problem, his senseless muttering would have immediately alerted Dance. Incoherent words of a man in the grips of delirium. Muttered in the same language spoken by the girl now recuperating back at Wolfglyn. The man looked to be well past his prime. Handsome by a woman's standards. He could see where the girl got her wavy tresses from, though her hair was thicker and more the vibrant hue of gold set afire. The inflection in the man's voice carried the same accent. No mistake—the unconscious man and the girl Hywel rescued were kin.

Not wishing to tarry longer than absolutely necessary, Dance withdrew the pouch from the deep pocket of his cloak.

A half-hour went by, and he was at last satisfied he'd done

all he possibly could to reverse the effects of infection. The smell coming from the wound was gone, the skin lanced and cleaned and re-dressed. He could do nothing more for the man—he would have to trust the honey and basilicum beeswax to work its magic. Before he departed, though, Dance carefully lifted the senseless man's head and poured a vial of bitter tonic—a mix of licorice root, poppy and cinchona—through his lips then watched him swallow.

Dance got him settled again, when he was unnerved to find the man awake.

Tired, sightless eyes stared up at Dance as if thanking him. Eyes trying to discern the face obscured within the dark hood hiding Dance's features. The man murmured something too softly for Dance to hear. Then a great sigh heaved from his chest, and he drowsily closed his eyes to slip into a deep sleep. On the rickety table, Dance left a small jar with enough of the healing mixture for three more dressing changes. He left a small vial of opium laced with fever water. The *meddyg* would know what to do with them.

Dance left as silently as he had arrived, a lone shadow moving stealthily toward the forest to find his horse in the dark and leave behind the village before it grew light. Indeed, Hywel could no longer nag him about her father's condition. In truth, were Dance ready to admit as much, the time briefly spent in the village that night brought back to him some of what he had missed and so long denied himself. Contact with the world beyond Wolfglyn.

The first fissure of change. The first time he'd done something worthwhile in a long, long time. A tiny taste of normalcy that, now experienced, would surely make the return to an empty castle all the more keener.

In another part of the forest, hidden well from sight, all tracks leading in and out of the camp were carefully concealed. Two men of indiscernible features sat hunkered over a small fire discussing their clever plan.

"I saw the ole man disappear with the girl inside the castle. Been near a week. Ye haven't said what yer waiting for...what yer gonna do."

Sparks hissed above the flames as fat dripped from the roasting carcass.

The big nobleman seated on the same stump, pinned his cohort with a lethal look of disdain and retribution. "I want her alive, of course." His fingers stroked the new growth of hair on his face that would help conceal his identity. "I don't want anything to befall her just yet."

"But his powers are gone, he can't help her."

"Oh, he'll help her"—a caustic tone full of bitterness—"it's a weakness in his blood."

The crusty little man, jabbing at the fire with a twig, snickered. "Aye, and ye `ave him right where ye want him."

"True, and easier than I expected." A diabolical glint darkened his eyes. "Now we watch her break him."

Another snicker from his partner. "Once he cracks"—he snapped the twig in half for emphasis—"then ye'll make yer move."

"Then I'll watch him squirm, right before I make him beg for her life."

"Jus' like last time," the snide little man chuckled, his squinty eyes dancing with mirthful anticipation. A toothy grin appeared. "Ye think he's swiving her—?"

The blade of a dagger came out of nowhere. Cold steel glinted under the little man's nose, making him flinch, the lethal point nicking him as he scuttled back. Eyes bulged in fright, he yelped, grabbing his nose as blood trickled between his stubby fingers into his gaping mouth. Opposite the fire pit, the witless girl staked to a short tether scrambled behind a downed log, her dark eyes tearful, her tattered gown filthy. She was paid no notice.

The master's fierce eyes glowed at Llwyd with the same deadly intent as did the sharp blade. "Like he did my faithless bride!"

"I didna mean anything by it—honest," his cohort muttered behind his hand, all mirth wiped from his expression. Two heartbeats passed before the blade was lowered and only then did the bleeding man heave a great sigh. Caution in his voice, he asked, "Ye wanting him to fall in love with the girl...`tis a clever plan. But just supposin' he don't? What then?"

The bigger man grunted as he severed a leg from the sizzling carcass. Fat dripped from the leg of mutton in his fist, his eyes glowing with an unnatural light. "Oh, he will, make no mistake. With that wench lookin' the way she does. I know Ifan—he's been living like a caged monk." His barrel-chest expanded as he laughed harshly, his thin lips twisted into a cruel curl. "No woman in all this time...hell, he'll be sealing her fate in no time." He envisioned the whole scene, relished the day of reckoning. For the girl was a beauty all right. Tempting enough to make a man lose his mind. And he'd waited a long time for another one like Aneira to come along....

GEMS, STRINGS OF:—
Symbols of virtues and high qualities of mind
and emotion.

7.

Hywel awoke to the sound of squawking chickens. The sounds that heralded morning and a new day. He blinked his eyes in the pale light of dawn blinding him through the chapel's one small oval window. Something, his brain told him, was after the chickens again. The sheep joined the chorus, bellowing to be turned out to graze. He didn't immediately notice in his groggy state, however, where he was nor how he came to be so stiff and cold. What did register on his dull senses was that something wasn't quite right. His hand cramped from stiffness as he felt for that something he remembered he'd been next to on the pallet last evening.

The woman he'd fallen asleep next to. His hand met air.

Instantly awake, Hywel scrambled into sitting position. Heart stopping, he stared aghast at the empty spot where she'd been on the mend the night before. The blankets this morning were thrown aside. The brazier cold. A quick visual search of the chamber procured nothing of the girl he recalled.

Trouble was afoot and he'd overslept!

In another part of the castle, in the private chamber overlooking the storm-washed newness of Wolfglyn's sleepy valley, dawn's pale light radiated warmth upon the startled features of one breathless woman.

Heart pounding, Madeline could do nothing but remain completely still. To move would be perilous. To rouse the darkly beautiful man she was snuggled against was the *last* thing she wanted.

Especially since she could feel, dear god, the heat between their naked bodies...her every nerve tingling where she lay pressed intimately against him.

Saints help her, she was abed—he'd taken her clothes!

A quick glance affirmed the culprit was still asleep.

How long that might be, though, she didn't know with the commotion going on somewhere outside. Chickens were squawking loud enough to startle the dead from their graves.

The noise was the least of her concern. For as shocked as her discovery upon wakening, it was something else altogether that drew her gaze, held her spellbound. Her head was cocked to one side, her rapt attention riveted on his gloriously proud lance.

She had five brothers—as kids she'd once stumbled upon them bathing. She had not seen what the big fuss was over, but they forbid her near the lake after that. Little wonder why, she thought now.

So this is what a grown man looks like!

Mouth gaping—knowing someday she'd become acquainted with such a sight—she hadn't actually thought it would be so soon, nor that a man's lance would look quite so wicked and splendid all at the same time. `Struth, it was more magnificent than anything she'd expected. Swollen as if bruised...his arousal was jutting up from a nest of glossy black curls. At the base, she spied two perfectly formed globes covered in the same curls. Fleetingly, she decided, her lessons in anatomy—Philip's crude drawing in the dirt behind the barn—had been sorely lacking. "When a man is aroused," Philip had explained, "he will want to put this inside you. Until you are married, you aren't going to let him...." Her lesson had ended with that curt order and her brother had stalked off before she could ask any more questions.

This morning 'twas her first look at the real thing.

Her fingers itched to explore the satiny crown to see if it felt as hot as it looked.

Profoundly intrigued if not astonished by what she saw, she became vaguely aware of the room beyond her focus. The expansive bedchamber, ebony and gold privacy drapes enveloping the bed, the soft down mattress dipping under their weight. The sweet smell of clover, and some vague dream of wallowing in it. More immediate, the weight of his head pinning her arm. Under her cheek warm skin; his broad chest, rising with each slumberous breath.

She was intensely aware of warm hard muscle under her fingertips where her other hand lay splayed over his taut stomach. She discovered how different from her own, the texture of a man's skin. How crisp the hair covering his body. Her senses picked up other mundane perceptions. The cooler temperature in the room, a cold hearth though it smelled as if a fire had burned through the night. Filtered sunlight poured through the window dappling their skin.

All were perceptions independent of conscious thought.

And she'd just been compromised her brain rationalized. Though to what extent the damage, she was completely ignorant, since Philip had refused to elaborate on such things.

Secretly mortified she'd slept though it all, growing increasingly apprehensive as the seriousness of her predicament became clearer, she decided upon further reflection, his rod was far too enormous anyway, to go... well...go where her brother explained that such a thing—

"You were restless in your sleep," the soft male voice in her hair explained. Then instantly and before she could move, strong hands set her away. The mattress dipped, his warmth retreated and the beautiful creature she'd met in the forest was tumbling out of bed. "My intent was to calm you, keep you warm, nothing more."

Abruptly returned to the present, Madeline's bemused senses registered panic as her hands scrambled for the bedclothes to draw them up around her neck. Swoon or scream, she knew not which to do first. Sin of all sins, her gaze was already straying. Even as she fought it. He was naked. Her eyes following him of their own will as he walked the short distance to the wardrobe.

Ogling his body while he slept was one thing. Having him awake....

Dear God! her thoughts gasped.

Disbelief etching her face, she sat in his bed awed, watching with no small amount of trepidation as his glorious manhood grew larger still before her eyes. The transformation looked painful. Indeed, his fists were clenched as if it hurt.

Something about the way he was hurting triggered an awakening in her body. Madeline bit down on her bottom lip to hold back an involuntary moan as sensation spread out like tiny fissures pulsing straight to her core, leaving her shaken, stealing her breath.

She was aching in a way that Robert Dunbury had

started her aching that long ago night. Only this time the aching was different—somehow more fierce.

Sweet Mary and Joseph was he wanting to put his lance...inside her?

And what if he did? her wicked thoughts echoed back. What then?

He was searching through the wardrobe, his profile to her. She could do little else but stare. Her perusal moving over the muscled contours of his perfectly-formed buttocks. Powerful thighs and long muscular legs were perfect foil to his beauty. His raven mane fanned broad shoulders, a shorter lock falling rakishly over one dark brow. The first time she'd laid eyes on him she'd thought him some guardian creature of the forest. In the full light of day, she could see he was very much a man. Seemingly born a virile pagan all splendidly in rut as if dropped to earth with but the single purpose of mating fertile maidens.

What, dear God, would she do if he wasn't yet finished with her? If he pinned her to the bed...slipped his hand between her thighs to lovingly massage her heartbeat? What would she do—or rather—what could she do if he decided to press those fingers deep inside her?

Her heart was pounding a rapid beat....

Dunbury, rot his despicable soul, was responsible for awakening her wanton needs. How many times had she dreamed the same wicked dream, shaking with desire and yearning for some way to satisfy that mysterious craving he'd stirred to life? It shamed her to think she might have let this stranger push himself inside her as she dreamed her wanton dreams.

While Madeline turned a mortifying red, the man standing but a handful of feet away behaved as if his nakedness were completely natural. As if impervious to her scrutiny.

Then again, was he impervious? He *was* wanting her. That much she knew even if she didn't understand why he wasn't forcing himself upon her.

But then maybe he yet intended to....

Ready to spring from the bed if need be, Madeline sat perched upon his pillow and still hadn't said one word, for they were all stuck in her throat.

He broke the silence first. "Hywel found you near death. You wouldn't have lived if we hadn't—" His words broke off as her gaze caressed his groin...his blood raging, his body throbbing.

"Then he...then you...." She'd found her voice only to fall silent as he caught the direction of her gaze.

"We kept you alive," he rasped into the stammering lull, her maidenly interest enflaming his senses.

Madeline quickly glanced away, her face burning anew, her thoughts at last forming a coherent sentence. "I'm sorry. I don't remember any of it," she said in all honestly, not knowing what to do about the man in whose bed she had obviously slept the night. "If you don't mind, I would have my clothes back now—if you have finished saving my life."

A sensible, if not an entirely grateful woman, Dance noted with a faint grin.

With or without clothes mattered not. She was every bit exactly the way he remembered her the times he held her pinned to the pallet with his body to keep her from hurting herself. Every sweet inch of womanhood pressed against him, while he both relished the contact and held his emotions distant. He still wasn't sure what had prompted his actions this morning near dawn. Whatever the excuse, he'd dreamed the worst kind of dream imaginable. He could still feel her feverish and damp body thrashing beneath him in the dream, her heat tantalizing, teasing...consuming him mind and soul....

Here he found himself awakened to reality and experiencing a paralyzing sense of regret—the unforgivable foolishness that faced him right now.

For the briefest of moments, the dream yet lingering around, he let himself imagine her tossing aside the coverlet, seeing her skin flushed with arousal. In her dove gray eyes an invitation instead of innocent dismay.

His fists clenched painfully—his body throbbing, memories surfaced. Any other man would have, by now, availed himself of her charms. Virgin or not, she'd be given no choice. He'd seen the vile act borne. The broken spirit, the battered body left by the thoughtless bastards who vented their lust on an unwilling woman. A lifeless child who'd been brought to him in the night. No power Dance wielded could heal that kind of brutality. Sadly, brutality thrived—rape forced on unwilling women since before the first invasion on these shores left bellies swollen with Norse bastards. Used to inflict suffering, terrorize—enact revenge.

Appalling him, a bride's maidenhead was commonly viewed as property. Belonging to her father to be given to his rival in securing peace between opposing powers.

Through a haze of pain, Dance looked at the *engyl* in his bed. What would she have done, he wondered, had she awakened to find him lying between her pale thighs? Would she still be looking at him with trusting interest?

All a man had to do was imagine her...lying beneath him....

Blood pounded in his ears. "Your clothes are over there."

Dance nodded to the chair over which he had carelessly

tossed her badly wrinkled shirtwaist and breeches in his haste to get her into bed earlier this morning. He gave her his back so she could scramble from bed. When a second later he heard no movement, he glanced over his shoulder to find she still hadn't moved. Indecision pinched her lovely features.

Growling a curse under his breath, he snatched her clothes from the chair and tossed them at the bed. She gave him a guarded smile before he turned back to slip on his own breeches.

Good thing she didn't ask, because Dance didn't care to explain how she ended up in his bed. His decision last night, or rather this morning before daybreak, had come natural as it had back when tending the ill came second nature to him. He had heard her crying out in her sleep as he'd ridden into the bailey. He'd found Hywel dead to the world, and frankly he'd had his fill of sitting on the hard stone floor in an overheated chapel watching over her. The natural course, having been to calm her—get her fever down and out of her damp clothing—was done so without thought of maidenly embarrassment. All he had wanted this morning upon his return was to crawl into bed and let exhaustion take over. He had done nothing to be ashamed of.

Or so he told himself. Until one look at her this morning all flushed and deliciously naked with her hair unbound and sleep-tousled, had him weighing the odds against tempting fate. Clearly she was worthy of the punishment he would endure. Death was certainly a consideration with heaven sitting in his bed. He could almost taste the shafting sensation pulsing through his blood...her sweet body sheathing him...that first deep thrust against her womb....

The way her eyes were fixed on his groin at the moment near had him going down on his knees.

Dammit—he was supposed to have risen before she awakened. It would have saved him this torment, saved the awkward platitudes to get her through the next few minutes.

"If you're going to become hysterical, I'll have to lock you in the dungeon," he told her over his shoulder, the teasing in his voice meant to put her at ease. Then more seriously, he finished, "Just so you know. In case you haven't noticed the absence of blood on the bedding, I've left you a virgin."

She blinked at him in stunned silence. Then her head dipped below the coverlet.

Dance could easily imagine the look of disbelief on her face and was hard-pressed to suppress a grin.

When her head came back up, her lips were compressed. "I suppose you think I should thank you for that?" she muttered ungraciously, all her scorn infused into that single statement. "As I recall, it was you who also claimed there was no healer. What are *you*, his retainer? A guard perhaps? Nothing so noble as a knight for sure," she said scathingly, "that would require a code of honor—a different century altogether. And I want the truth this time—just what are you to this healer who supposedly doesn't exist?"

He sighed. "Guardian of the castle." A truthful answer. "And it is you trespassing on private land."

She blinked in astonishment. "Am I? Well that didn't seem to matter while I lay unconscious in your bed."

"Don't worry, you're leaving here today." He picked up the boar-bristle brush and made a couple passes through his hair. "If you wish for privacy, the water closet is that way"—he gestured to a closed door in the north wall—"if not, I suggest you dress and do it quickly, while your meal is being prepared. We leave within the hour."

Her eyes narrowed. "And who decided I was leaving? Not you surely?"

He didn't answer her question.

"That's what I thought. Well, if you insist on bullying me, I'll report your behavior to...to...." Her brow wrinkled as she pondered the answer.

"Hywel," he supplied, smiling darkly to himself.

Her fingers holding the coverlet under her chin were fisted, knuckles white. "Indeed, I'll report you to your Lord Hywel. I'm sure he won't approve of your outrageous behavior to a lady."

He set the brush aside. "Hywel can't save your father."

Blood drained from her face. "How do you know about my father?"

There was nothing he could do about the obvious bulge in his breeches as he buttoned them, so he didn't try. "You talk in your sleep."

If possible, she turned even paler.

He stomped a foot to the bottom of one boot. "While we're on the subject of courtesy, you might wish to thank Hywel for putting up with you as long as he has."

"Putting up with me," she repeated faintly, then stopped cold. "Heavens, how long *has* it been?"

He pulled the other boot on and straightened up to give her a measuring look. "Long enough to wear out your welcome."

That had her tumbling off the bed, dragging the ermine-trimmed coverlet with her. "Please," she said breathlessly, her gray eyes suddenly pleading as she rushed to lay a hand on his arm in earnest appeal. "How long has it been? I must know." She looked up at him with large, anguished eyes feathered with sooty lashes. Her bottom lip trembled.

He could have withstood the assault were it not for the sadness in her voice. He could have drawn her into his arms, he could have kissed her fears away...if he were another man...if he weren't putting her in peril by simply being in the same room with her.

His voice gentled. "It's been six days since Hywel brought you in out of the rain."

Her hand on his arm reflexively tightened. "Papa," she whispered, wretchedly. "You're right, I must leave immediately." Clearly distressed, not thinking now about her state of undress, she was a frightened damsel in need of his help.

The next moment, she caught her reflection in the mirror behind him and moaned aloud. "A brush. May I..." she went on as if he were her personal maid as she reached for his brush. "Can your lord meet me downstairs, you think, in half an hour?"

"And who shall I say requests an audience with him?" His tone subtle mockery.

"Tell him, Lady Madeline Carlton. Of the Boston Carltons"—distracted, she grimaced at her reflection—the modest black coverlet draping her body. "And I believe I'll need something appropriate to wear. Can you help me?"

That she thought of him as a mere servant should have insulted him. It seemed appropriate to let her assume whatever she wanted. "Anything you want is yours"—he reached out to steady her on her feet—"so long as you leave here within the hour." Smiling, she looked up at him with her heart in her eyes, unaware how near her breasts came to grazing his chest...how the heat rising off her body provided a potent lure.

"Oh, dear." Her brows suddenly drew together in concern. Before he could retreat, she reached up impulsively with her fingers. He flinched as she lightly traced the red slashes left by her claws.

"Did I do this?" she murmured apologetically.

He held himself rigid, his hand coming up to clasp her wrist. Halt her tender exploration.

"Hywel was worried you would injure yourself while thrashing about in a fever," he said simply. "All I did was help him quiet you."

In her gaze was a tender realization. "It *was* you then who talked to me," she murmured to herself, "I remember now. The dream." Her gaze scrutinized the claw marks, her voice going soft, "I'm terribly sorry if I hurt you."

Her breathy apology threatened to undo him completely. Her tentative touch left him weak, shaken. The feel of her fingers on his skin a fleeting caress that would haunt him now long after she was gone. He couldn't let himself, however brief, entertain the foolish notion that came to mind.

You can't protect her! She'll be destroyed!

Relinquishing her hand, already feeling the loss of her nearness, he slowly let go of her.

"I want you away from here within the hour." His shield erected once again against temptation. "I suggest you hurry and dress."

Those soft gray eyes that had been regarding him with tenderness now held the keen pain of rejection, a sadness he purposely put there.

He wouldn't comfort her. Nor would he let himself soften.

She still looked pale, came the misplaced thought.

He scrutinized her carefully, knew she wasn't as strong

as he would have liked, yet he had no choice but send her on her way as quickly as possible.

In short order, Dance found her a suitable gown to borrow. When she asked for a quick bath, he carried hot water upstairs to the water-closet he'd enclosed with a screen in a corner of his bedchamber.

Downstairs, Dance nearly collided with Hywel who burst through the kitchen door.

"The lady—" Hywel gasped in alarm as he near toppled.

Dance's hand shot out to steady his old friend. "She's safe and right now upstairs bathing." Hywel raised an arched brow. "And I don't have time to explain...."

With no time to spare, Hywel was quickly informed of the switch in their stations as master and manservant while Dance helped him off with his peasant robe and on with one of Dance's tunics. While Miss Carlton took her bath, mutton stew was served with laver bread for *brecwast* on Glamorgan plates decorated with the 'Ladies of Llangollen'. Dance carried out the duty of footman as well, content to let Hywel pose in his place. In consideration of their guest, Dance turned the wolves out into the courtyard. Sheva, in particular, hadn't wanted to budge from her spot under the dining table. So Dance had to coax her in very much the same way he might have coaxed a patient to take a nasty serum. He felt bad about Sheva. She didn't understand why she was being shut outside when she normally joined him under the table.

Impersonating his master, Hywel was sitting at the head of the table on a raised dais, Dance standing at attention behind him when their guest paused underneath the arched portal of the great dining hall.

Both men stopped breathing at the same time upon

seeing her. Dance's reaction was for a reason quite apart from Hywel's.

His first thought—her tentative smile could bring the fiercest dragon to his knees. Have every knight eating out of her hand.

He liked the gown on her. He'd found the elegant sapphire brocade lying in the bottom of the *cistiau styffylog*, or great oatmeal chest, where Dance also found a tiny swaddling gown. His swaddling gown. Carefully preserved for him by his mother years before she would pass and leave destruction to follow in her wake.

Dressed in the height of French elegance, if somewhat dated, it was apparent his guest was a gentle born woman of consequence. If he hadn't already arrived at that observation upon his encounter with her in the forest, it was evident now in the way she carried herself.

He remembered how the first night he'd found her, she'd offered to pay him in exchange for his help. When that hadn't worked she'd offered him a merchant ship.

A smile curling his mouth, he found himself wondering now just how wealthy her family and just how far she might have gone to enlist his help had he given her half a chance.

Hywel cleared his throat and motioned their lovely guest to join them, while he slid Dance a speculative look to find the girl wearing the very gown belonging to the late Princess Tolstaya. Dance's mother had had the gown special sewn for the festival of bards—and her son's first performance at the annual *Eisteddfod*. No one knew then that the Princess would perish from consumption that same winter. It was the last festival for young Dance. His hopes of becoming a great bard were buried along with his poems in his mother's grave.

Though his guest approached the dais in a self-composed manner, Dance couldn't help but feel her nervousness. *Brecwast*, he decided, should be interesting.

Her tentative gaze searched out his. Like a dolt, Dance found himself smiling back as he thought about what it would be like after she was gone. The relief in knowing she'd soon be out of harm's way. The thought brought him none of the solace he'd hoped for. In fact, were he willing to look deeper, he would have wondered at his sudden lack of appetite.

"Come in, my dear," Hywel greeted in his best authoritative Welsh. The ten minutes of formal tutoring Dance gave Hywel on lordly manners was hardly adequate for such an occasion as a meal with a well-born lady, but it was the best they could do in so short a time. He gestured for her to join him at the table.

"My lord," Madeline replied, her cheeks glowing with warmth, and hoping her response appropriate to whatever greeting her host just used. She was nervous, her palms damp. It didn't help that she'd had to struggle with the closure on her borrowed gown. To make up for the delay, she'd had to make a hasty descent down the stairs — practically at a run — while mindful of tripping over the voluminous skirt.

Though she was pressed by an urgency to get back to her father, Madeline schooled her features to be patient and approached the elegantly set table. If enlisting this man's help required she bathe with the barn animals, Madeline had decided she would find a way to do it with dignity.

So to say she found comfort in her host's approving look was an understatement. Indeed, she was most thankful for the loan. The color she knew was perfect contrast to her fiery hair. With a matching ribbon, she'd made a makeshift chignon. She too, was aware that what she wore was more apt to be seen at a formal dinner soiree, but right now she wouldn't have changed a thing about her appearance.

It was one man's gaze she sought and held. He was standing guard near her host, his appraisal reticent, yet she detected a glint of something bordering on desire....

Heavens, could it be he found her desirable? After he'd given her little more than a moment's notice? She'd seen that sort of look before, she knew what it hinted at.

But then it had *never* made her tingle all the way down to her toes.

When his gaze moved over her it felt like a thousand tiny torches licking her nerves.

He was using his torch on her this very minute, making her feel giddy, breathless.

She didn't know why she would think such a thing, but she hoped he felt just as breathless. That, he at least, wasn't completely immune to her charms.

Because if he felt nothing, she'd be mortally humiliated after what had transpired earlier in his bedchamber.

She had to pass him to get to the dais. He was wearing a faint grin on his lips that dared her to voice what she was thinking. Secretly she divined, he had to be the most alarmingly potent man she'd ever laid eyes on. Hot patches of color bloomed in her face at the memory of just how potent a man.

When she reached his side, she felt a moment's raw need in his perusal and faltered in her step. Her silly heart started fluttering. The next thing she knew he was inches away and whatever she thought she saw was quickly masked, his lips twitching into a devilishly sinful smile. A smile that knew her intimately.

The room suddenly felt confining....

Manners impeccable, he politely inclined his head.

She was standing much too close to him....

Heat from his body seared through her, melting her insides and she only just managed to swallow the moan pushing up her throat. A haunting essence of something enveloped her. She remembered somewhere wallowing in it. Burrowing into his warmth. His clover.

"Your breakfast, my lady."

This side of him, this attentive and charming side was not what she expected. Of course it was obvious with his lord present, he was having to put himself out. Obviously, he couldn't get rid of her fast enough.

She didn't know why. What he feared. So she chose to ignore the fact he resented her being there. Smiling back, she inclined her head, was in fact marshalling strength enough to step away when she changed her mind. Rather, she leaned close to him—"After this morning," she whispered so only he could hear, "I wouldn't think we need be so formal. Why not call me Madeline?"

Tight little lines of amusement graced his mouth. "I'm sure I'm enchanted."

So that was the way of it? She might have guessed he was going to pretend as if nothing happened between them, as if they hadn't been lying abed together not a stitch on, his body aroused and wanting her. She didn't know why that thought should bother her so much, but suddenly she could not help the impulse goading her.

"You were enchanted earlier, remember, I saw you." Brazen, she dared provoke the beautiful pagan. "So...my lord 'enchanted'," she murmured, smiling warmly, "is that what you prefer I call you? Maybe you have other equally fascinating names to go with lunch and supper?" A burnished brow lifted. "Shall I guess what they are?"

He looked momentarily taken aback, then his lips twitched.

All at once he tossed back his head and laughed.

Madeline felt his laughter move through her like heated silk. When he laughed it was as if sunshine rained from the sky, filling the dining hall with a poignant sweetness. She marveled that she could bring about the transformation in him. Give this beautiful pagan something to laugh about.

The sound had also startled Hywel, who watched with mouth gaping during the whole curious exchange. Before his sense of duty returned to him and he cleared his throat.

"My food will grow cold," Hywel interjected in his best haughty Welsh, "while you stand there wooing my guest." He didn't care to see revealed what he witnessed in the girl's expression. For Dance had suffered enough. "Do be a good man and help *my* guest ta her chair." Playing his part to the fullest, he clapped his hands for effect.

Smile gone, Dance shot him a sober glare. The sadness reflected back at him was sufficient reminder of the danger in letting down one's defenses.

"Miss Carlton is in a hurry, don't forget," Dance reminded Hywel, sliding him a warning glance that said "let's just hurry up and get this over with."

Dance gestured for her to precede him to the table.

"You still haven't told me your name?" she remarked brightly, moving to the chair he indicated. She was ahead of him and didn't see his cordial façade replaced with a scowl.

He quietly seated her next to Hywel as was arranged. "I was christened, Ifan."

She glanced up at him thoughtfully. "Ifan? Doesn't that mean in your language, *God has favored?* A name given to a chosen one?" she asked, clearly intrigued.

His thoughts turning inward, he said, "Around here a learned woman is a rarity. One who knows how to manage her curiosity is even a rarer find. Notice, Miss Carlton," he said, peering down at her gravely, "we have no women at the castle."

Instantly seeing her mistake, she wished she knew what she said to bring that scowl back. Wishing to restore peace between them, her interest fully engaged, now, she asked more carefully, "Do you not also have a nickname? The Welsh, I hear are famous for bestowing nicknames."

Scowl still in place, he started to turn away when she touched his arm to halt him.

He glanced back, looking down at the hand detaining him as if he preferred she not touch him. As if being in close proximity was somehow distressing. "My nickname is Maddie," she offered softly, withdrawing her hand.

He gave her a strained smile. "Dance."

"Dance?" Truly captivated now, she turned to Hywel for confirmation. "Really?"

Hywel smiled expectantly as if, too, waiting for an explanation. Dance was forced to translate. Which brought a wide grin to the old man's lips, in his eye a sparkle of some secret amusement. "Did ya tell her how ya got the name?" Hywel asked his now glowering master. "Naked and dancing in the moonlight. Howling like one of yer wolves. Pretending ta be—"

"You've got exactly five minutes to finish your stew and convince her to leave." The look Dance gave booked no arguments.

Madeline looked between the two, aware of some current underlying their words, wishing she understood their language better. Wishing that she had time to learn Welsh.

Dance rounded the table to take his place at Hywel's side, where he served first Madeline, then his lord. She thought him rather competent for a man whom she'd thought would be awkward serving others. But then her perceptions had undergone many changes since her arrival. And so would she gracefully contain her impatience while making some observations.

Her impression of Wolfglyn that first fated night of the storm, was to behold a spectacular vision in white stone, the castle's glistening towers set amidst an enchanted valley. Rain slashing down like spikes hurled to earth. The surrounding forest cut away in a sweeping circle. That particular night she'd stood there mystified by the ghostly mist swirling like ribbon through the emerald valley, hugging the keep like fingers of pale smoke. From far away, she'd thought it the most breathtaking of any place she could imagine, in awe to be gazing upon a mystical setting so real she could almost see in her imagination the fairies at mischief. Right up until Bones bolted.

How sad it must be for Hywel to idly watch each decade chip away at his enchanted home, the decaying myth crumble stone by ancient stone. What stories the rooms of such a castle could tell. Its character chiseled into each fissure by the gnarled hands of her villeins. The generations of great lords and ladies residing in a mystic world created within these ancient stone walls.

To be inside was like stepping back in time.

Her gaze took a cursory sweep of the sparse, but elegant dining hall, the lighter spots on the walls where fine tapestries must have hung. She made particular note of the precious jewels embedded in the heavy gold chalice setting before her on pristine linen, the bread served on a gold platter, the fine wine to drink in place of ale. She had noticed, too, the various swords displayed in a solid mahogany rack just inside the arched entry to the spacious foyer. The foyer where she recognized Dance's cloak suspended from a branch of antlers. She'd taken in every detail of the hallway, the loose stones under her feet as she'd descended the grand stairs to join the Lord of Wolfglyn at his table.

All the while she perused her surroundings and rehearsed her appeal, self-doubt kept coming back to mock her. What if she couldn't get the Lord of Wolfglyn to cooperate? What then? Perhaps he'd quietly accede to her wishes and she was just worry for nothing. *Still*, asking for a favor, asking Hywel to come to the village for the purpose of healing her father required a certain tact. Perhaps even groveling. Most definitely groveling if his beautiful guard had anything to say about it.

As it turned out, the stew was delicious, what broken conversation there was, at least pleasant. She had noticed during the course of their meal, Hywel preferred to call him by his nickname. Which should have come as no surprise, since they appeared to be good friends.

But there was something else nagging her.

Dance was quite a wonderful tactician as it turned out. When he didn't like the path the conversation was going, he would change it, almost always cutting off what little Hywel might have said. Dance was protective of his lord. It was apparent he cared a great deal for the older man. At this point, she didn't care one way or the other if Dance came with them to Llandeglay, since she rather suspected he'd want to tag along to guard over the frailer man.

Now guarding a healer, what of that? Exactly how many enemies could the kind old man have?

Her gaze shifted between them. Dance—now he would be the more likely one to have crossed someone with his overbearing manner. And yet, she also glimpsed in him a caring compassion. The opposing facets reminded her of her brothers. Exactly what it was about Dance that puzzled her, she couldn't say. Perhaps it was more something she sensed...like an intangible mystery...illusive and compelling and unnerving at the same time.

Madeline pondered that while she ate her breakfast, curbed her impatience, and made herself endure each passing minute—during which her gaze kept straying—to the man who was fast becoming an enigma. Not only had he surprised her by joining them at the same table, she'd found it equally disconcerting to have him seated opposite her.

It was apparent Dance was well educated. Well versed in at least two languages that she knew of. Qualities all that she curiously found absent in her host.

Then she discovered, rather remarkably, something else. She hadn't at first noticed the manner in which both men dressed for breakfast. Here she had worried that her gown was overly grand for the breakfast table. Of which fact, she was quickly disabused. For Dance was attired as handsomely as was Hywel. A curious find among even the most casual of households. This morning both of them were wearing identical royal blue tunics stitched heavily around the hem in gold thread. Boots of the same hand-tooled leather.

By the time she was halfway through her second chalice of wine, and her breakfast companions had polished off a second helping of stew, she'd catalogued several more oddities. Like how her host looked as though he were swimming in his clothes, while on Dance the same tunic looked as if tailored to the exact width of his broad shoulders.

And why had she seen no other servants? Where was everyone else?

It appeared to be just the two of them running the castle. A truly barren castle.

Dance, she recalled, had brought her bath water. But he couldn't have cooked this delicious mutton stew while lying abed with her this morning.

The roles minion and master shared seemed to blend more and more as breakfast wore on.

Really, she had to wonder—what did it matter what they each did or didn't do when all she really wanted was to return posthaste to Llandeglay?

When Madeline simply could not wait a moment longer...when her host had at last finished his own meal, she likewise pushed her plate to the side and politely thanked him for his hospitality.

"My lord, I owe you a great debt of gratitude for all you've done for me." She looked down at her hands now clasped in her lap. "Actually...I was hoping to speak to you frankly, if I may. On a private matter." She cast Dance a meaningful look, saw he was watching her closely. She deliberately turned back to her host. "What I have to ask, I would prefer you hear in private." She let out a sigh. "But then I suppose it is allowable for your guard to stay." She smiled nervously. "After all, someone is needed to translate."

She'd as much as hinted at dismissing Dance. A hint he probably took issue with. The fact was, she had no more than a slim grasp of their language. She needed an interpreter, so she had no other choice.

"What I was hoping," she went on, appealing her cause to Hywel, whose kind face she'd come to hold a fondness for. "I was hoping, you could come with me back to Llandeglay." Before he could answer, she rushed on, "As you've probably already guessed, my father has been injured. You're the only healer whom, I understand, can help us." Madeline's voice, in spite of her efforts otherwise, was shaking. Truthfully she didn't know what she'd do if she got back and found her father already laid to rest. "Please, I'll do anything for my father. Anything you ask, if you will just come back with me."

She was leaning forward in her chair, her gaze beseeching, each beat of her heart slamming madly against her ribs. What could she really offer him of value equal to that of her father's life?

Hywel turned his brown eyes to his guard. Madeline's gaze followed Hywel's.

"Well?" she ask breathlessly, looking directly at Dance, "can you remember all I just said, translate everything for your lord without leaving anything out? Or do I need to repeat it?"

He gave her a deceptively wicked grin. She knew she'd clearly issued a challenge and he could do nothing about it with Hywel present. After a very long time, he finally translated for Hywel what she wanted.

Madeline sat in breath-held expectation, not daring to move, her hands in her lap where they couldn't see her bloodless fingers twisted together.

There was a very long discussion, during which her interpreter scowled several times, even raised his fist, but always the rage in his voice was controlled. What did it matter to him so much that Hywel helped her? What was it he seemed to fear? That she would put Hywel in peril? Well, she wouldn't.

"Please," she said in the lull of a heated debate, getting to her feet, her bloodless fingers clutching the side of the table for support. "Dance—please. I don't mean any harm to come to your lord. I beg you let him come with me." Mortifying tears stung her eyes.

Leveled on her, Dance's amber gaze pinned her where she stood, bore into her with a finality that told her he'd already decided for Hywel.

Was he going to force her to use her one last appeal? One she'd saved for the starkly beautiful man opposite her. "My virtue is yours, Dance," she bravely murmured, a breathy resignation in her voice, her heart thundering. "I will willingly serve you, should it help in deciding you."

They, neither one, seemed to breathe....

Her gaze drank in his full sensual mouth. That wild heathen mane as black as soot. She felt her pulse pounding. Her memory of him this morning permanently seared upon her mind not so very frightening as it would have been before her brush with death.

For a moment it felt as if he were looking straight into her heart. As if he would relish the thought of her staying.

Dance knew what that kind of desperation felt like. She'd just offered him her precious innocence, and it painfully knotted his insides. "You win. Hywel will take you to Llandeglay."

A pulse-beat passed before the words registered.

When they did, tears poured down her lovely face—and Dance found himself very close to taking her in his arms, comforting her.

His heart was pounding in his chest, his hands shaking as he clutched the arms of the chair against temptation. She was so beautiful, trying so hard to be brave, and she was looking at him with a tender regard potent enough to unman him—as if he'd just given her the moon and stars on a silver platter.

"Hywel will see that you make it safely," Dance rasped

softly, hardening himself to the assault she dealt his senses. "In return you must never speak of what you have seen here, never try to return for any reason. Is that understood?"

Tears streaking her face, she nodded.

His grateful guest rose to her feet then and did the unexpected. She came around the table and knelt at his side—and before he knew what she intended, she demurely bowed her head. The kiss she pressed to his hand was a mere gesture of gratitude. Yet Dance felt it all the way to his core...and the softer regions of his soul recoiled in pain....

DARKNESS — LOWER ASPECT: —
Symbolic of ignorance which is absence of the light of
truth.

8.

Dance grumbled under his breath as he prepared her black beast for departure in the barn. He checked the harness, making sure it was secure, the leathers buckled and reins untwisted going back to the hay cart that would carry Hywel and Madeline back to Llandeglay.

Dammit — he was determined not to let loneliness assail him. More determined than ever to put her from his mind.

He thought back over the past week. Thought about the brief respite Madeline's presence brought against a lifetime of solitude...and facing the bleakness once she left was almost more than he was humanly capable of.

In the dining hall, one kiss had rendered him speechless.

A mere kiss had branded his soul.

It wasn't just the kiss though. It was something inexplicably more compelling. He could still feel it...the warmth of her mouth moving through him, the searing contact making him want things he couldn't have. He'd spent the last few days wishing like hell he could allow himself to feel. Allow himself the simplest of human contact. Take comfort where he could. To look beyond that, he knew was pointless.

Christ—how he wanted fiercely to drag her into his arms...he craved it so badly the shame of it was nearly overwhelming.

What he'd caught himself wishing for appalled him.

God Almighty—could he be so shallow as to besmirch a sacred memory? When Aneira gave her life....

His shoulders sagged under the weight of guilt.

Had the woman he loved...the wife who gave him a beautiful son...been faithless in facing death for him?

Cut out his own heart, he should, for forsaking the memory for even one moment.

Yet it was upon him, the gnawing voice of temptation coming back to haunt him.

How could he be expected to withstand the utter solitude of his long lonely vigil without ever once giving in to human emotion? Had he not already weakened in the flesh? Had he not already let loneliness turn him into little more than an animal?

Bitterness twisted into a mocking curl on his lips.

There had been endless days—so many he'd given up counting—where he didn't want to go on living. When despair struck so intensely he couldn't breathe. When the last of his self-respect deserted him, and the only relief from it he saw was a coward's way out.

He could either fight to the end for whatever scrap of honor was left him or wallow in self-pity. The honorable path grew exhausting.

So what had he just done? He'd quit the dining hall like a coward—leaving Hywel to contend with the girl. Both of them staring after him. It was the tenderness on Madeline's face that stayed with him as he'd wordlessly stalked away.

Damn Hywel's hide, anyway, for bringing her home.

Thank God she was leaving.

Midmorning brought angry black clouds that threatened to let loose with a storm. Fitting weather to go with his darker thoughts, Dance reflected grimly as he led the horse and cart across the quiet bailey and halted at the foot of the steps.

For a fraction of a second, he wondered if he might still slip away before she came out, take himself off in the opposite direction through the forest. His gaze swung past the gatehouse in contemplation of an expedient getaway. He had an excuse ready.

He couldn't keep killing off the sheep or they'd soon have no flock at all. Dance would hunt the thicket for their evening meal. If nothing else, it gave him something useful to do with his time each day.

Lifting them over his shoulder, Dance removed his longbow and quiver to set them against the step. Were he a true coward he could easily make a run for it. Not have to face the next few minutes seeing Madeline was comfortable for her journey.

The woman costing him precious sleep emerged from the keep just then and Dance's attention was drawn to her. Damn if she didn't look enchanting as hell in those breeches.

Assisting her into the cart, he knew, required he put his hands around her waist long enough to lift her.

She made it all the way down the steps before he decided to recheck the harness. The girl's stride hesitated, a frown furrowing her brows as if she suspected he did as much to deliberately avoid her.

He saw in her expressive gray eyes an anxiousness — the eyes of a child, openly trusting.

But she wasn't the child he'd first thought he'd stumbled upon in the forest.

Rather the woman he found possessed a rare and fragile beauty. Every flawless curve testament to that fact, should he care to reflect on the times he'd carried her naked between the cold baths and the bed. More recently the way she looked—like a lush offering—in his bed this morning.

She had made life a sweet hell for a good week. She'd distracted him briefly from his melancholy, he further reflected, and he hadn't given it much thought, oddly enough, until now.

He reminded himself, the woman bedeviling his thoughts had a family waiting for her. Her father would be on the mend unless the town *meddyg* had somehow neglected to give the man the contents in the vial Dance had left evening last.

Dance gestured to the step. "You should find it easier to climb in from here."

She approached the cart as if torn by conflicting thoughts of leaving—seeming both reluctant and impatient at the same time. He watched her glance around for another mount for himself. When she didn't find one, she looked to him for a hesitant moment as if perplexed he wasn't going.

Wanting her out of harm's way, Dance stiffened his spine, set his face to give nothing away. She lowered her gaze to the last step. Her sleeve brushed his when she halted at his side, and he felt a tangible glimmer of awareness move through him. The gaze she kept trained on her conveyance shimmered with tears, her chin trembling.

Jesus—why did she have to look so forlorn and vulnerable?

At the last minute when she reached for the ermine coverlet nestled on the seat, she turned huge bleak eyes to him. Her fingers absently stroked the fur he'd provided for her comfort.

The mix of apprehension and confusion revealed in her expression did strange things to his aloofness.

He barely resisted the urge to touch the silken tendril lying against her creamy throat. He resisted the urge to tell her what she needed to hear—that her father would live. "Remember, you can't come back here for any reason."

A tear slid down her cheek. "Then this is good-bye, isn't it?" Her fingers clenched in the fur, she took a tremulous breath. "You won't change your mind and go with us?"

Wanting nothing so badly, he shuttered his gaze and gave her his shoulder as he adjusted yet another buckle that didn't need adjusting. It was his only defense against the temptation to do something rash like touch her. It helped to remind himself she was distressed, not about leaving, but about what awaited her back at Llandeglay.

He moved behind the cart, going through the senseless motion of adjusting some buckle on the opposite side. "Sheva will follow you and Hywel as far as the village."

A gasp of fear coming from her brought him to a halt. Because she was following on his heels, she slammed into his back. All at once he felt her pressing herself against him, her hands clutching to his cloak as if to use him as a shield. Sheva stayed her distance, patiently awaiting his next command.

"Remember Sheva, Madeline? She won't hurt you. She'd not attack unless you make a move that threatens me."

"Oh God," came the muffled sob against his back.

Fearing her nails were going to leave permanent holes in his hide, he sighed and reached behind him for her hand to gently loosen her fingers. If she could have managed it, he imagined she'd have climbed upon his shoulders.

If she'd let him, he could help her with her fear.

"See there," he soothed, "nothing to fear. Sheva is well-behaved." The sleek gray wolf advanced as Dance gestured her to. "Come, Sheva."

"Please don't—" Madeline begged, burrowing her face into his spine, shaking her head.

What happened, he wondered, to the girl who not minutes ago, bravely offered to sacrifice her maidenhead to him?

Hywel chose that very moment to emerge from the barn carrying a burlap bag of supplies for the half-day journey, Druidh and the pack following. "I brought us a blanket—"

Dance shook his head; a silent command for Hywel to stop where he was. But Druidh had already seen his master and was barreling toward Dance in greeting....

"Madeline, don't move," he murmured softly in warning, his body shielding her against possible danger.

Druidh caught her scent at the same time Dance heard the voice behind him ask "why?"

The black male wolf slid to a halt a few feet away, his lips curled menacingly in response, the hair on his back standing straight up.

Hywel, recognizing the danger, held his breath as Dance readied himself to take on Druidh should he suddenly lunge for Madeline.

It was Sheva who surprised them all by growling, inching herself between Dance and Druidh. Dance held tight to Madeline's hand. Sheva's sisters and mother stayed their distance, hanging back in confusion. It was the first time Dance had seen Sheva take a stand against the dominant male.

"She's protecting me," came the soft whisper of astonishment at his side.

Dance looked down to find Madeline peering around

his arm. Her face, what he could see of her expression, was pale, her gray eyes wide with fear. But she stood her ground.

He gave her trembling hand a reassuring squeeze. "Actually, she's protecting us both."

Druidh was snarling at Sheva now, his intent clear to Dance who knew this rogue wolf better than anyone.

Blessedly Hywel was thinking quick and disappeared inside the barn. When he came back out a second later, he was dangling a dead chicken in the air to get Druidh's attention.

It worked. Druidh's favorite treat presented too strong a lure to resist.

"Go with the ole man, Druidh," Dance said gently. "That a boy."

Druidh sidled away. Sheva relaxed as Dance reached down to stroke her ear, thanking her for her unexpected bravery.

Because her gaze was following Druidh, Madeline hadn't realized in those first tense moments that the softness she felt between her fingers was wolf fur. When she did, she gasped in alarm and tried to pull her hand back. But Dance held tight.

He'd been holding her hand, using both their hands to stroke Sheva's ear.

Pulse skittering, Madeline glanced up questioningly to find him watching her, those intense amber eyes looking down at her with a mix of admiration and encouragement that warmed her inside, waylaid her first panicked reaction.

Dance gave her a knowing wink. "Still afraid?"

She paused to think about it, then gave him a weak smile. "Maybe not so much now."

A mutual understanding passed between them as Sheva

basked in the attention. The wolf didn't seem to mind who was petting her so long at they worked her favorite spot.

"She's really gentle, you know?" His smile for her was a lavish reward. "I raised her from a pup." Because wolves had evoked fear in the hearts of mankind for centuries, Dance understood how it took time getting used to accepting that which caused one great distress.

A patch of sunshine decided to break through the clouds for the intimate celebration.

The girl's delicately arched brow was creased with perspiration. The puddles that had dotted the courtyard this morning were dry. A gentle breeze rustled through the bailey. Warmth from the sun radiated through his cloak... through their bodies, and Dance took what immense pleasure he dared in being the one to ease some of her fear.

Madeline, too, was pleasantly amazed to find herself petting a wild animal. Maybe it was the hypnotic softness in Dance's voice that dazzled her senses, maybe the reassurance in his nearness.

Whatever it was, facing her fear head on was a heady experience. Her teacher patient, understanding, his silent presence making her feel protected in an oddly familiar way. A way she'd never expected from anyone other than her family. In the space of a few minutes he'd accomplished what no amount of talking to herself over the years had done.

As startled as she was by that revelation, she was more startled to feel a keen sense of despondency in leaving. As if she were leaving behind some part of herself.

Then there was reality. A cold hand squeezing her heart. She didn't dare linger any longer. Her father needed her, he needed Hywel's help. Philip and the others would be waiting, likely worried sick. For the first time in her life, she felt a blossoming sense of accomplishment for having not failed them.

She'd say good-bye and be on her way. She'd see her father soon, her heart prayed.

She found herself wishing quite earnestly that Dance was going with them.

Get over it Maddie. He clearly doesn't want you here, nor does he want you returning.

He'd been nothing if not brutally honest about that. So why did that thought hurt so much?

So much had happened since she'd awakened to find Hywel nursing her back to health.

Madeline sighed. Her gaze dropped to Sheva and a little tremor of apprehension snaked through her still. She had come here in search of a healer and in the process learned so much more than she ever imagined possible. Learned things about herself. About the man in whose bed she'd discovered for herself the beauty of male anatomy. She'd learned not all men were as dishonorable as her experience with Dunbury. Not all were insensitive and ruthless. It was understandable she'd feel a certain despondency.

Her gaze lifted to the mysterious and beautiful man at her side and strangely she couldn't stop the tears choking her. "Thank you," she rasped softly, "for what you did just now."

He looked down at her for a long moment with stark warmth in his topaz eyes. Then as if just remembering she was pressed intimately against him, he released her hand. This time though he didn't move to put distance between them, and Madeline felt her foolish heart give an unexpected tug. He wasn't pushing her away.

They were still standing far too close together, the

heat between their bodies tangible, the shared silence passing between them poignant with unspoken feeling. Condemning them both in the eyes of Wolfglyn's approaching visitor.

As always, Dance felt the intruder's presence before he saw him.

Under his breath, he let go a growled curse as he swung around to greet the lone rider. Just as swiftly and none too gently, he pushed Madeline behind him to once again shield her with his body. This time from a danger more sinister for the malicious intent in those black eyes peering at them through the hideous mask covering the man's head—obscuring his face.

The headdress his archenemy wore was the skin of a wolf, with fangs protruding from the open jaws resting atop his head. A sight meant to strike terror. Contrived specifically for that purpose.

It was apparent the rider approaching the cozy little scene from the drawbridge had already drawn his own conclusion about the intimate display between the two. A cruel twist of retribution cracked his face.

The thunder of hooves clattered over the heavy timber drawbridge.

The air stilled as if making ready for a fierce confrontation.

Dance held his tongue. His rage, just barely controlled, was compounded by a gut-wrenching realization that he was too damn late in getting her away.

With that realization came the memories rushing back to claw at his insides. Bile churned in his gut. He knew in a heartbeat what this visitor's presence meant. What unspeakable sentence Dance had just brought down upon their heads. It wouldn't matter to the bastard that

Madeline was an innocent victim. Because they were found together, her fate was sealed.

"What's the matter, boy, no greeting for your sire?" the huge man mocked in Welsh as he drew his mount to a halt a dozen feet away.

No one had noticed Hywel had emerged from the barn.

It was all the old man could do to hold a snarling Druidh by the scruff of his neck and not be dragged forward as the wolf repeatedly lunged for the rider. Sheva's sisters and mother had vanished. Dance felt Sheva ready for attack and likewise held tight to her, his fingers fisted in her fur to keep her still. That didn't stop her from snarling.

Owain spat on the ground, his obsidian eyes glinting with hatred for the black wolf, before he turned back to sneer down at Dance from his superior perch.

"Who is it?" came Madeline's soft whisper.

Just as quietly he replied, "Stay where you are and be still."

"So, boy, I gather you know what you've done," Owain growled. "Such a waste, don't you think, to die so young? And this one so beautiful."

A muscle ticked in Dance's jaw, his body rigid, his own gaze fierce. "Leave her go. She's innocent of your wrath."

The man's cruel laughter sang out in the deserted courtyard.

Dance felt Madeline jump and he quickly sent up silent thanks she knew when to keep quiet. He was prepared to barter his soul for her life. To use every skill at his disposal. He'd need complete concentration if he was going to have any chance of getting her away from Wolfglyn unscathed.

"Let her go," he repeated quietly. "Chain me to the walls to rot. Just let her go in peace."

Those black eyes glittered back at him with menace. "You think a simple visit to the dungeon will do it, do you?" A contemptuous snort. "I told you five years ago to heed well your precious Aneira's fate for the same end would befall the next woman you touched. What—you think I've forgotten your treachery? That my faithless bride preferred your bed over mine? You knew then, you would live alone the rest of your days...or watch each ladylove die. Perhaps if you beg well enough, I might just let this one die mercifully. Why don't you get on your knees and we'll see?"

When Owain didn't get a response, he laughed bitterly. "I rather thought this pretty piece was worth begging for. But then you've done that, haven't you? What a shame it didn't help. Poor faithless Aneira, she actually thought your pitiful powers would save your son." Words dripping with scathing hatred, he said, "Well praying doesn't work, does it? Nothing will ever bring back what you took from me."

Goaded into defending her memory, Dance snarled back, "Aneira was forced into that betrothal. You would have made her miserable, but that didn't matter to you." His voice held all the pain the memories roused. "All that mattered was we had wronged you by falling in love—and for that you had her destroyed." His vision blurred. "While the woman you claimed to hold a fondness for begged you for mercy—you made her watch as you dropped our son from the tower." He was shaking, his voice raw, his eyes glittering. "For that you can fucking rot in hell!"

Owain tsked. "A shame you feel that way. I'll have to make certain now you are blamed with this girl's unfortunate death. Oh, don't look so surprised, boy. You didn't think I would let you bed her and merely send her on her way—"

"I told you she's innocent, damn you!"

"Ah, what a pity it is you have denied yourself these years only to let this one die a virgin. What are you waiting for, you have my consent this time? Take her right here. Or stand by and watch me break her in. Oh, yes, I do recall you watched the last time. Sad how they cry, isn't it?" He chuckled. "Tell me, how does it feel when your loins grow heavy with seed? Still pacing the halls all hours of the night? How's your hand feel when you tire of swimming in a cold river?" A demonic sneer on his lips, he went for blood. "How are the sheep looking to you these days? No—well it will only be a matter of time. How about it? I could still have Hywel castrate you if you'd rather."

Raging hatred roiled inside Dance, silent as death stalking its prey, so powerful in magnitude it was almost overwhelming. He fought down bile with every tortured breath, mentally pulling himself back from the edge over which there would be no return. "Get the hell off my land," he ordered in a strained voice.

Dance's challenge brought a smile of triumph to the other man's face. "Ah, yes, I did relinquish the castle when I sentenced you to a life of solitude. Here there are no temptations. No serving wenches to warm your bed, no tenants to plow the fields. Only a useless old caretaker for company. I wonder if you still think our sweet little Aneira was worth it. Tell me, did she spread her pretty legs when she asked your forgiveness as you turned your back on your people?"

Dance started forward, his fists clenched, when the hand tangled in his cloak halted him.

"You've got exactly five minutes to get off my land—then I turn the wolves loose."

Owain chuckled harshly under his breath as he slanted a look at the girl whom he'd sent here for one purpose. Her fearless expression couldn't hide the fact she was shaking.

Giving her a thick smile, he peered back at her with lusty intent. Her time was up, she'd served her usefulness, what did it matter now if he used her before breaking her lovely neck. Actually, the prospect would be all the more sweeter if Ifan just so happened to be watching.

Having served his sentence, he grew bored with the game. "Remember, boy, you can't protect her from the many eyes of the forest. No matter how careful your steps, sooner or later I will snare the little beauty. Then I'll give her a day or two in my bed and see if she doesn't wish she were dead—"

Dance cut him off. "Hywel?"

Hywel waited for Dance's next command.

Owain shrugged his broad shoulders. "Don't forget, boy, I will be watching you." Then with his mission fulfilled, he leered at the girl for a fleeting moment longer and turned his steed to ride out of the bailey.

It was some long, intensely silent moments later—after Owain rode out of sight—that Dance felt his ungovernable fury begin to recede enough he could breathe.

There was no other way, he told himself as he prayed for God's forgiveness.

Before he could talk himself out of it, he turned to Madeline, who stood as if rooted in place, her dove soft eyes wide in dismay. The pulse in her creamy throat beat as rapidly as his own.

"I'm sorry," was all he said as he bent and swept her off her feet.

Madeline was so shocked by his move she didn't at first realize he was carrying her back inside the castle until the door slammed shut with a kick behind them.

"What are you doing," she gasped as alarm spiked through her. "Where are you taking me!"

He said not one word as he headed for the dark stairway opening in the stone wall. Her mind was still digesting bits and pieces of what just occurred outside and so it was a bit slow to register on her reeling senses just what he intended. Until he started down the dark hole with her.

His dungeon!

Dawning horror slithered over her skin as she struggled then in his arms. Lashing out with her fists, she fought the fear rising up to choke off her cries of protest, she fought and squirmed to gain her freedom. He held her effortlessly—his strength superior.

"No—you can't do this!" she wailed as he didn't even break stride to drag the lantern off the wall to light the way. Twisting orange flames danced over the shadows of the narrow passageway. Down they spiraled, down deeper still he carried her into the bowels of the castle, his intent scaring her. His reasoning evading her.

She was out of breath, the insults hurled at him turning to raspy whimpers of defeat as he came to the end of the dark corridor where a great oak door stood barring the way. Her gaze locked on the heavy iron latch securing the portal....

Dear God, no!

The dungeon. The very one he'd spoken of when she'd run into him the first night in the forest. The dungeon he was going to toss her into if she didn't leave.

A sick dread tightened her chest.

Madeline's gaze flew to his face. The serious slant of his

jaw told her this was no jest, the resolve in those ruthless amber eyes making her heart bolt in fear. While her struggles momentarily ceased, he shifted her in one arm to hold her around the waist. That arm felt like a band of steel cutting off her air. In short order, she found herself dangling in his arm, her back pressed against his chest, her feet flailing the air. He fumbled with the latch.

With an indignant curse, she started kicking like a mad woman, trying desperately to do him grave harm, trying with what strength she had left to break free of the steel band.

Her boot heel connected sharply with his shin making him hesitate only long enough to mutter a dark curse. He didn't, however, loosen his hold as she hoped, nor was he giving her a chance to get away.

Mounting fear assailed her as the door scraped open on screaming hinges. Then he stepped over the threshold, and she was deposited unceremoniously in a squirming heap. Cold, hard stone broke her fall. She yelped as her backside took the worst of it. Her outraged panting filled the musty chamber as she lifted her chin to glare up at the face hidden in shadows. The face of the man she had inexplicably started to trust.

All her anger infused her voice. "So you've changed your mind?"

He looked down on her a moment in silent regard as he set the lantern down beside her on the crude stone floor. "Hywel will bring your dinner."

Then he whirled on his heel and soundly shut the door on her shriek of outrage.

Dance stood in the passageway and felt her fear slicing into his heart as her fists pummeled the door at his back.

He deserved each insult, he deserved every vile name she called him, every furious curse.

He didn't leave her immediately, though.

He'd offered no explanation. Not so much as one word in answer to her frantic pleas. How the hell could be begin to explain all that had happened out there in the courtyard? The shame in admitting how close the bastard had come to the truth?

How could he bring himself to explain all that had transpired the day he buried his wife and son?

Instead, Dance turned to the door Madeline clawed and rested his forehead against the rough wood. If she had to endure a cold dungeon he would endure it with her in silence from the other side. Where she couldn't see his hands shaking, nor see how devastated the encounter in the courtyard had left him.

For the next grueling hour he suffered each of her angry slurs upon his head, those he deserved as well as those he didn't.

It wasn't until her voice grew hoarse that she finally lapsed into tears.

Her despair tore at his heart.

Her muffled sobs cut through him, lancing him open as surely as if she wielded a blade. She was hurting. Furious. And muttering how her brothers were going to rip him apart. Blood-thirsty little baggage, she described vividly how they would gladly sever the limbs from his body with agonizing slowness as she watched. He invited her anger. As long as she stayed angry, she'd fight back.

When she'd exhausted every slur, her vengeful tirade turned once more to keening cries. The kind of mournful sobbing that she wouldn't want him to hear. And it was all Dance could do not to throw wide the door and give her the dagger to carve out his heart.

He fought against the moisture gathering in his own eyes. He fought the visions he'd hoped never to see again when he'd opened this door. All the pain shut inside. The suffering he'd been forced to witness while chained to the walls. His mind and heart shrank away from the misery that vision recalled....

God forgive me, Madeline, I can't let you die the same vile death.

His fists clenched at his sides, his eyes closed, he leaned against the door as if he could somehow absorb Madeline's pain. Each minute he spent there with her, he willed her to forgive him. God help him, the brutal truth was he'd let his resolve weaken. As surely as if he'd plunged the blade into her breast, he'd committed her to death.

Sickened by his weakness, he waited for the fading sound of her hiccups, the punctuated sniffles for another half-hour. Not long did he have to wait before she fell into exhausted silence. Still he waited until he heard her breathing turn shallow through the door.

Only then did he leave her, turning soundlessly away to retrace his steps along the cold corridor below ground.

CAPTIVES:—
Symbolic of the spiritual egos confined to the
lower planes, and held in fetters of the lower desires
and the attractions of the objects of sense.

9.

Her throat raw, Madeline sank to the cold floor and faced the lantern. One tiny flame flickered orange shadows upon the stone floor. One tiny flame saving her from overwhelming panic. Bleakly, she looked around her in numb disbelief.

This couldn't be happening.

She breathed in the distinct odor of decay and damp earth and felt a suffocating weight envelop her. Spine-tingling eeriness crept over her. There was no window for escape. No glimpse of sky nor any chance of contact with the outside world. Just intense solitude and gray stone walls.

Her teeth chattering as much from shock as from chill, Madeline dared look beyond the immediate ring of light.

Her gaze fluttered to the far wall and a shudder went through her. With her vision adjusted to the shadows, she could see rather clearly the hideous device of long ago tortures.

A ghastly image to behold.

Black dots swimming before her eyes threatened to swamp her again. And she'd just momentarily recovered from the dizziness, when in her frantic search for some possible escape, her fingers brushed thick shanks of iron secured to hooks high in the wall.

Repulsed by what her imagination conjured up, she couldn't ignore it either, and she stared aghast at the chains and shackles draping the walls like great black webs. Glad to be sitting down, she felt a sick revulsion. All the pain represented by those chains was blatantly apparent, even if the need for torture in a dungeon evaded her.

And here she sat, not knowing why she was imprisoned like a wretched criminal.

Heart thumping against her ribs, she forced herself not to cringe while she took quiet inventory of her surroundings — the limestone walls crumbling with age, yet looking impregnable for a decaying castle. Down this deep in the belly of the castle, she imagined the foundation was several feet thick. So even were she given a knife with dinner, she knew it would take more time than she had to dig her way out. She mentally counted the number of stairs they must have descended. Her cell, she figured, had to be several score below the bailey. She vaguely remembered in her struggling, a fleeting glance of another passageway branching off opposite her chamber. She considered the possibility of an access to the outside, but then it did her no good if it should turn out to be just another dungeon.

This deep in the earth the air around her hardly seemed to stir.

No sound from above could be heard.

She could be kept down here indefinitely.

Her trust in Dance was slain like her fragile belief in what she foolishly thought genuine and honorable intentions.

Surely her return to Llandeglay would only be delayed as long as it took for Hywel to berate his demented guard?

Indeed, she hoped he was punished severely.

Sitting up straighter, she knew better than to hold much stock in a Welshman's honor. Better that she devise her own plan. But what? If she should be presented an opportunity of escape, she couldn't afford to trust that this was all some temporary misunderstanding. Or lose time wandering aimlessly through the underground passages that may lead nowhere.

She grimaced. Her beautiful captor with his stealth and grace and unquestionable strength had easily overpowered her.

Hywel, on the other hand, was more her match, with none of the warrior instincts his guard possessed. She was younger and could quickly dart out of his reach before he knew what she was about. Though her risk of running into Dance would be greater, she decided a more likely escape would be back up the same stairway by which she'd arrived.

Once she made it to the bailey, a bigger problem on her mind was Sheva.

The wolf presented a terrifying obstacle.

Whatever her opportunity, Madeline didn't care to spend any longer than need be confined to a dungeon haunted by ghosts of torture.

As if luring her, her gaze once more shifted.

Between herself and the wall rested a crude stone altar. Large enough to lay upon. What manner of punishment required an altar, Madeline could scarcely conceive. Shuddering at an image coming to mind of a man staked to the slab, she anxiously looked to the narrow mattress. She'd already tested it and found it inexplicably comfortable. Resting upon the sturdy, if narrow, bed sat a pristine pillow and two colorful blankets of woven wool.

No hairbrush. No mirror. No water for bathing. Nothing but a chamber pot and bed.

For all the longer she was staying, Madeline told herself she would need nothing else.

Thank heaven she was already dressed for riding. Heartened by that blessing, she stared thoughtfully at her boots. She might be able to run faster barefooted. Like the times she raced her brother about the garden at home, only to lose him by hiding herself in the sprawling hedgerows. Though she would be hampered by boots, she was heartily glad for something to wear for the long haul back to Llandeglay. Especially if she must travel by foot.

Foolish as it was, Madeline stared unseeing at her riding boots and thought about the beautiful gown she'd borrowed this morning for her breakfast with Hywel. Satin slippers that she'd discarded in her hurry to dress and be gone. The gown she'd been so pleased to borrow for this morning's appearance would have been a definite hindrance in escape. Her shirtwaist, she saw, had a fresh tear at the sleeve from her struggles. Nothing so serious it couldn't be repaired.

But the injustice done her at the hands of Dance *was* irreparable.

He knew her father was dying. He knew how dire it was that she return to Llandeglay posthaste. How could he begin to justify detaining her?

For that matter, Hywel had had plenty of time by now to make his way down to the dungeon and demand of his guard that she be set free. So why hadn't he?

Until her meal was delivered, she could do nothing but sit it out. Sit it out while consumed by nagging doubts, apprehension, fear and simmering anger. All during which she marshaled her courage to make a run for it. It was long after dinnertime must have come and gone, she muttered furiously to herself, still resigned to maintain her silent vigil huddling by the door. That's where she spent her evening—between fervent prayers for her father's life—cursing Dance to the foulest depths of hell. All during which time, it never occurred to her that they might not come at all.

It wasn't but a handful of minutes later, thoughts of her father brought on a fresh wave of despondency. Set upon by desperation, she shifted positions. Her balance wavered for a heartbeat. Her hand shot out to steady herself before she hit a hollowed out hole. Gingerly, she felt around in the dirt. Her future bleak, she cared not that she was reduced to crawling on hands and knees. Her hands skimmed over the uneven features between stone and ground. Blood pounded in her ears. Her thoughts jumped ahead to escape as hope soared. Grateful tears stung her eyes as she saw in the flickering light where a large stone must have once filled the void. In the stone's place was bare ground.

If she could dig....

Madeline ran her fingers along the bottom of the door's rough edge.

Still angry, she slowly clawed the unprotected earth with her nails. Heedless of the unyielding soil, the lack of gloves, and the bits of grit scraping her palms, she worked with mindless purpose. Tears strangled her, but she pushed on. Her arms ached. Her breathing grew harsh. And she retreated into her anger hoping to ignore the excruciating pain. But her hands were those of a gentle-born lady. She had no calluses for protection.

Fitful sobs shaking her, Madeline dropped her gaze to her palms. She glared back at the pitiful hole. For all her effort it was no bigger than a man's fist. Disappointment lanced her heart. Her raw fingers trembled. Dirt and blood streaked her hands.

Jagged nails and torn skin met her gaze. These were not the hands of a lady.

An insidious reflection in retrospect to her life in Boston. She could scarcely believe how, not that many months ago, she'd been seated around one of several elegant dining tables, a dozen resplendent guests all watching from their chairs for a lull in conversation in which to press their opinion on the end of the Corsican's terror on Europe. That same night she'd been dazzled by what then seemed like a horde of suitors clamoring over themselves to sign her dance card. She'd looked on with faint amusement, with nothing more perplexing on her mind than deciding which attentive young gentleman to treat to the first quadrille of the evening. Her life before the Atlantic crossing felt displaced here in the bleakness of a cold dungeon.

Nothing more than a fading memory of a naïve young girl.

She'd struck out on a hapless mission, her mind set from the beginning on what she knew now was at best a perilous course. All intent on proving her worth. Dear Philip—her brother had had no such illusions about life. She realized that now. The helplessness she'd seen in his eyes as she rode away, she'd thought for her father. But his fear had been for her as well. Because he was acquainted with unpleasantness founded in reality. A reality that Madeline had been otherwise sheltered from all her life.

Raw fingers...kneeling in dirt...cold dungeon stones— this was reality.

Being bodily assaulted in a tavern wasn't just something that happened to someone else, it had happened to

Madeline Carlton. Bullet wounds and blood and death were realities that her brothers had tried to keep from her. The beautiful sapphire gown she came down to breakfast in was part of her dream world, the same part of some grand plan to find her father a healer. While reality was a very real fear of being forgotten in the healer's cold dungeon.

Foolish in the extreme, she'd given her trust into the wrong hands...she'd trusted Hywel. She'd been lured into confiding in Dance. Into thinking he wished to aid her, but what she found instead was bitter disappointment.

Well, she'd not be so trusting a second time.

She may not understand anything else, but the seriousness of the confrontation this afternoon in the courtyard was obvious. Something was happening here of which she had little knowledge. It wasn't a dream. The threat of the danger she felt was serious. And preoccupied with her own problems, she had been oblivious to whatever danger was fast closing in around her. She'd left Philip struggling with the truth that he couldn't protect her, while she'd tossed aside his each objection.

She understood now. How helpless and frustrated he must have felt.

How stupid it was to have gone off alone....

Castigating herself, Madeline swallowed hard against tears. The thought of never seeing her father again bitterly clenched her heart.

She could no longer withstand the weary truth crashing down upon her, swamping her frail courage. Overwhelmed by grief, she curled into a ball on the floor. Uncontrollable tremors shook her body as she slowly rocked herself, her guilt silent and condemning, her unfocused gaze fixed upon the dancing flame. A certainty enveloping her in cold misery, her loss suffocating, for she knew in her heart she'd been gone too long....

It had to be some time after midnight when Madeline slowly roused from her dozing slump to the faint sound of shuffling footsteps approaching her dungeon from outside.

Sluggish as her movements, hampered by the uselessness of her hands, she gritted her teeth against the prickling pain and struggled to sit upright.

She held her breath...waiting.

Instead of the door opening, it was the heavy latch at the bottom being shoved open. The portal was no bigger than the width of a serving tray. Metal squealed, grinding against hinges. Then the small panel slid aside.

Her heart started pounding hard. "Hywel, is that you?" she asked urgently, holding her breath, oblivious to the tray inching its way through the narrow portal at the floor. "Hywel, please...let me out!"

No reply came to her plea, no other sound except that of her stomach growling in response to the smell of mutton. She gave no notice to hunger pangs. Instead, she was shoving the tray aside to reach her hand out, frantic to clasp hold of whoever it was on the other side.

The speechless entity stood back, she couldn't reach him. Nor could she see, unless she laid flat on her stomach. The impulse was resisted with superhuman effort.

She sensed a slight hesitation from the other side and then the portal was being slid back slowly into place. "Please, I beg you don't go," she pleaded in a teary rasp, fear prevalent in her tone, her desperation humiliating when she'd never have otherwise begged for compassion from her captor.

Madeline's plea turned into choking sobs. She wept aloud while the portal closed on her hand. A wet tongue licked her raw fingers—making her heart jolt. An involuntary shriek burst from her lips, filling the noiseless chamber. Sheva!

She swiftly snatched her hand back.

The portal closed shut, blocking out what light had briefly illuminated the small opening. A chilling loneliness paralyzed her where she sat, her legs folded under her as she waited for the retreating sound of footsteps.

More fervently, she quickly implored, "I can't stay here. Please. Dance? Hywel? Don't leave me alone down here. Please stay for a minute. Just a minute. I beg you...."

There was no answer, but neither did she hear the dreaded sound of retreat.

"Hywel?" she asked, faint with hope. "Is that you? Won't you talk to me?"

But it seemed all her pleading was falling on deaf ears.

An ungovernable fury welled up inside her to replace prudence. Wailing angry curses, she gave vent to tremulous emotion. Wincing, she snatched up the tray with her bowl of stew and hurled it against the door. It slammed with a loud clatter. The tray clanged to the floor. Veering in the opposite direction, the bowl ricocheted, spewing mutton chunks over the wall, on her face and clothing, before it rolled under the bed. Her fork flipped in air to clatter atop the stone altar before falling to the ground. Her heart was hammering fierce blows against her ribs, her breathing erratic and punctuated by sobs of despair and indignation and condemnation.

Hywel didn't care for playing the role of master at all, and he told Ifan so that next morning. He had to speak up, however, as he was talking through the door. Because Ifan had not emerged from the forbidden chamber since he returned from the dungeon last afternoon. "I don't like it. Pretending ta be ya," Hywel objected through the door. "It na right. She's a proper lady, she is. Our guest. Na a prisoner." Hywel raked his hand through thinning hair. "Ye hear me—she didn't eat, master. Make herself sick, our Maddie girl will. Then what am I ta do with her?"

No answer.

"Master?" Hywel inquired, equally worried about Ifan though he was young and strong enough to endure starvation. It wasn't as if Ifan hadn't gone without before. In fact, when melancholy struck its worst, he'd gone days at a time. But then his master hadn't been visited upon by the evil one since Aneira's death, and never had he shut himself in her bedchamber where the memories would eat at him.

Hywel pounded his fist on the door. He pounded until his fists hurt.

Faintly aware of some droning noise, Dance held his son's swaddling cloth to his nose, its softness against his cheek as he breathed in the lingering scent of his flesh and blood. Hot tears welled in his vacant gaze. Five damnable lonely years. And he could still remember the way his son smelled. The soft down of Iolo's curly black hair. His slight weight nestled in Dance's arms. At the heart of the memory, the aching that grew beyond human bearing.

At the time, he hadn't known how swiftly the precious moments would perish.

He'd had no warning of disaster. For if there had been warning, he would have gotten his wife and son away from danger. Hid them away on a whaling ship sailing far away from Wolfglyn.

The yearning to hold his family to his heart never lessened.

All too keenly, he remembered vividly their last night together. Aneira resting content in his arms, a charming smile on her lips as they laid abed, Iolo's tiny form warm between them. The exact image of himself suckling greedily at her breast as Aneira drifted off to sleep, like she sometimes did while nursing. The memory remained with Dance through time...the unmitigated pleasure he'd taken in watching his wife and son during those rare and intimate hours of peaceful reflection....

If he hadn't thought he could protect them, they would still be alive.

Ironic how time had come round full circle to test what was left of his strength.

It seemed a lifetime since he'd held a woman. Yet he'd fallen asleep this morning holding Madeline in his arms. He damn well knew better. The mistake would be costly and grave and unforgivable. He should have tried harder to avoid her. Why hadn't he left her care to Hywel? Let Hywel bathe her fever?

And if his foolishness wasn't bad enough...now it would seem his memory of Aneira was fast becoming clouded by frequent images of Madeline's face. He'd resisted. Fought it.

As it happened, the image couldn't be evaded.

Her smell was everywhere. It was in his bedchamber. It was on him, on his clothes, on his skin. Her body's heat where he'd lain against her evening last, aroused by sensations he'd near forgotten.

He could feel her. As if she were standing beside him,

her body heat tangible, her scent uniquely compelling. He'd never expected to be able to *feel* another woman besides his wife. It was damnable and unsettling and...unwelcome. And he couldn't displace her.

Truth of it was, if he were honest with himself, he had lost the battle the very morning Hywel carried her in on the litter. Like the mists over the glyn, Madeline had invaded his fragile guard, his mind and his senses.

In these last few days, he knew now what he feared more than losing her. He feared Madeline, because she had little by little become as much a part of his solitude as the young bride who had come here to take a husband six long years ago.

Only this time Dance was certain to die. Because he would not be caught off guard. Nor chained to the wall to bear witness. He would not be forced to go on living when he had nothing left to live for.

When the master's sad little *engyl*, angel, made no sound the next time Hywel came around, he was hesitant to leave without checking on her.

At first glance as he entered, he feared she had passed on, her shadowed eyes staring and glassy, his candle casting the dungeon in muted gold light—not a muscle did she move.

She stared sightless as Hywel looked down at her with woeful expression, in his hand a candle branch, her breakfast tray in the other, his lips pressed together as if disapproving of her treatment.

The smell of burning beeswax reached her nose, but Madeline didn't care to rouse herself.

He was standing upon the threshold surveying her, still

wearing the same tunic from breakfast last, and holding what she presumed was her meal.

Why the Lord of the manor would trouble himself to serve her, she didn't know, nor at this point did she care. Escape was her one salvation.

Unfortunately, in the next breath her chance of escape dissolved. A fleeting silver form darted past her line of vision in the outer corridor. That brief sight of Sheva made her heart sink. Hywel shuffled past her as he set her tray upon the edge of the bed, obviously unconcerned about pulling the door shut behind him.

Curse it all—she hadn't anticipated her flight to freedom thwarted before she reached the courtyard.

"Ye need eat, Miss."

As if coming out of a sleep, Madeline blinked. Thinking she was hearing things, his words so startled her, she forgot all about her plan to escape as her gaze swung around to meet Hywel's.

"You speak English!" Abbreviated as his speech was, he'd spoke her language and she understood him.

To her look of astonishment, he merely raised his brow.

"You pretended not to understand me," she bluntly accused in the next breath, affront in her tone. "Why?"

"*Ydw, Siarad tipyn bach Saesneg*, I understand some Saesneg."

"Saesneg—you mean English?"

"*Ydw*—English. Ifan teach Hywel English." There was apology in his tone.

Hearing him speak of Dance brought an immediate scowl to her brow. She'd just as soon never lay eyes on that beast again. "Wolf," she said pointing to the open portal behind him. "Your *bledig*? Send her away—I want to leave."

"*Ydw, bledig*. Sheva keep ya safe."

Madeline softly snorted. Only Hywel would believe that. While Dance, it would seem, had anticipated her attempt at escape and knew precisely how to discourage her. "Dance coward! Blackguard. Brute."

His look vacant, Hywel shrugged. She'd spoken too fast.

"Did you punish Dance?"

By the appalled look he gave her, Hywel understood this time. Instantly grave, he mutely shook his head. "Na."

"*Ydw*, punish! Dance cold-hearted. He put me in here." Chaffing at captivity, she uncurled herself to stand facing him. "Now I go home."

With her temper restored full force, she had again spoken too swiftly. His kind gaze held hers.

"Me"—she clenched her fists in frustration and instantly smothered a gasp of pain—"why in dungeon?"

Instead of answering her right away, his eyes followed her movement as if keen to discern her injury. "Keep ya safe," he muttered, his focus distracted as he reached into his tunic pocket. He withdrew a soft strip of linen while Madeline struggled to keep her fury in check.

When he tried to take her hand for a look at her injury, she pulled away. "I don't believe you."

Hywel looked at a loss for words for a brief moment, her rejection wounding him. "Ifan not want ya hurt. He not tell ya he worry after ya." Again, he held out his hand to her. "Come—let Hywel tend ya."

She bit her lip to stem unwanted emotions. "I don't need your tending. I want to leave." Regardless how she fought them, she felt embarrassing tears welling and wished only to be on her way. "Hywel, help me, please...my father," she softly extolled, anguish mirrored in her eyes. "My father," she repeated, entreaty in her rasp, but her voice wavered and she couldn't go on.

"Not safe up there," Hywel insisted, flicking his gaze upward to convey the danger she faced outside the castle walls.

And a dungeon was, she supposed! "Not safe from what?" she asked disgruntled, her tears checked somewhat by a stab of apprehension.

"Owain's curse."

"Curse?" she croaked in a tiny voice.

"Evil curse over castle. Curse bring ya here."

All her suspicions from days ago resurfaced. "Evil curse? You mean the weasel who abandoned me in the forest?"

He shrugged. "Your *tad*, father, he wounded, *ydw?* Mayhap ta bring ya here," Hywel carefully pointed out as if she was the only one unaware of evil doing.

Madeline blanched, her gaze lowering against a fresh threat of emotion. Why would Hywel make that up when he had nothing to gain—unless he meant to play on her sympathy to justify his actions?

When she looked into his craggy face creased with concern and saw in his eyes only frank honesty staring back at her, her apprehension grew twofold.

Ever so gentle, Hywel took one dirty, raw hand in his to carefully wipe away the dried blood. She stood silent while she bit her lip to refrain from crying out. He must have sensed how precarious was her emotional state, for he said nothing for a long time. Strangely, he was trying in his own way to comfort her. And she was too despondent and confused to protest this time.

"Ifan"—he sighed heavily and went on—"Ifan, make Owain leave." He shook his head sadly, his gaze raising to hers. "But not for long. Evil one will be back for ya."

Back for her! Momentarily jarred out of her thoughts,

she wasn't sure she heard correctly. "Surely you jest?" He
wasn't smiling. "Well, I don't know what *Ifan* has told you,
but he's obviously lost his mind! I just arrived here a little
over two weeks ago. No one could have known my family
was traveling to Llandeglay. The shooting at the Tavern
was a...an accident. I've never set eyes on this Owain,
so he couldn't be after me. You tell *Ifan* I don't need *his*
protection, he's imagining the whole thing."

Her voice took on a harsh edge, conveying her utter
contempt for her captor. "Actually—better yet, you bring
him down here and I'll tell him!"

He regarded her solemnly as if she were sadly ignorant
of the danger. "Ye eat—I return with salve." A weary
resignation in his tone, he let go her hand.

Madeline instantly wished she had been more prudent.
"Wait—"

The discussion was abruptly over as Hywel ambled
toward the door, leaving Madeline dismayed and wavering
on her feet. At the threshold he paused only long enough
to kick dirt back into the hole she'd been digging. Then
he tapped on the mound with his boot to pack it down as
if covering up her deed. Saying nothing about it, saying
nothing more to her, he soundlessly withdrew and pushed
the great oak door shut behind him.

BITTER :—
A symbol of suffering undergone in the process
of the purification of the soul-qualities.

10.

Hywel loudly protested to his master through the door to Aneira's bedchamber, "She not be eating, master." He waited for instruction, again, to no avail. "I take *cinio*, lunch, down now." Under his breath, Hywel grumbled about stubborn masters and forlorn ladies.

Ifan, if he could hear, wasn't responding, so Hywel took himself back down to the dungeon to see how the wee sad *fach*, girl, was feeling about lunch. He had her salve and clean dressing balanced on the tray with her lunch. He was winded by the time he descended the stairwell. His steps slowed as he reached the bottom, and he had to rest a spell before ambling across the spacious corridor.

When he entered the cell, his first glimpse was of an empty dungeon. "Maddie, where be ya, *fach*?"

Silence.

He was certain she hadn't unlocked the door from the inside, so unless a wandering spirit had assisted her, she had to be hidden.

He found her on the far side of the altar, crouched against it with her legs drawn up under her chin, her gaze stony—lost in thought.

Despair. Bleakness. All reflected themselves on her features. "Ye look like death, mi *fach*. Shame on ya. A *pert* thing like ya, wasting herself away." He knew what was wrong with her. "What will your *tad*, say when he sees ya?"

A fleeting flicker of interest crossed her vision and was gone just as quickly. Suffering she was, just like the young master. Both of them grieving to no good.

Chunks of dried mutton stuck to her autumn tresses, stained the white of her shirtwaist. Poor frail mite, she was fast languishing away. How could a soul not feel pity for her?

He set her lunch tray at her feet. "Did ya hear me, Maddie *fach*, ya *tad* is alive."

"If he lives, you will let me go." The simple whispered statement bore no outward emotion, her tone lifeless, her hopes seemingly abandoned. She didn't believe him. He knew she thought it all trickery. Yet, Hywel heard in those words the merest hint of hope just the same and was heartened to find her responding.

"I tell ya true." Selecting the jar of salve from the platter, Hywel prayed the lie wouldn't come back 'round to beat him. He had been praying to the Gods with everything he had in him, that her appearance at Wolfglyn would turn things to rights. Then Owain showed up to work his evil.

He squatted level with her, his fingers removing mutton with painstaking care from her long burnished tresses. "I tell ya true, *fach*. Your *tad* not be gone from this world. Because I go miself ta tend him." A small fabrication befitting his new status. When in truth, Ifan would be furious if he learned that Hywel had been relieving himself in the shadows of the barn when he recognized the leather pouch the young master tied to Lucifer's saddle night before last.

"I want to go to my father." A tear trickled from the corner of her eye.

His feeble heart bled for her. "Ya eat yer *cinio* and Hywel will talk ta Ifan."

She *was* hungry. And he was, she allowed resentfully, trying in his own way to help her. Hope wanted to bubble up inside her, but she instantly squashed it. It was all a ruse to start her hoping again when she knew better.

"Give Hywel yer hands now—I will mend."

Slowly, Madeline gave him one scraped palm. "Teach me your *Cymraeg*," she appealed, wanting to be prepared for whatever lay ahead. It was a long way back to Llandeglay and she may need shelter before reaching the village. In which case she might need to speak their tongue. As for Dance, blister his ears she would in his own language, if he thought to interfere with her escape.

Her dungeon companion brushed a deeper gasp and she winced, effectively snatching her attention back to the matter at hand.

Hywel proceeded more carefully. "Sorry, mi *fach*." He gently finished one hand. "Now the other one."

She gave him her other palm. "Do you always defer to his wishes?"

Though she sensed he got her meaning, he said nothing. Instead, he worked intently on doctoring her.

She would need a different approach, she surmised. "I'm probably not going to get out of here, am I?" He said nothing, his work absorbing every bit of his concentration, or so she suspected he wanted her to believe. "What am I supposed to do with my time, if not plague you for answers? What say you to a truce? How about it? You entertain me with a story while I eat my lunch."

"*Cinio*," Hywel corrected softly, putting his salve aside. "Lunch."

"*Cinio*," she repeated awkwardly, as he gently wrapped her palms in strips of gossamer linen. "Lunch."

A faint grin of approval turned up the corners of his mouth. He was done, his handwork finished and with a minimum of discomfort.

"Thank you," she murmured with sincere gratitude, for the pain had already lessened. With his task now completed he would leave. She didn't want to be left alone. "So tell me about your cowardly guard."

He slanted her a disapproving look and she didn't think he was going to answer, for he started to get to his feet. "Forgive me, I know you hold him in high regard." Her bandaged hand shot out to stay him. "Please—keep me company. I'll try harder to guard my tongue."

She swallowed hard. "So why did this evil one pick me?" Her tone was conciliatory, soft with appeal and fear. "Won't you help me understand?" The remonstrance stuck in her throat, but she wanted more powerfully to hear what he might reveal about the mysterious confrontation in the bailey. She wanted to know particularly why Dance reviled the hideous visitor so vehemently. Especially since her detainment seemed linked somehow to both. If she could find a way out of this mess, she still might return unscathed—to what family she had left.

And she desperately wanted to go home. She desperately wanted to believe what Hywel said about her father.

So Madeline listened quietly for the next half-hour while eating her *cinio*. She drank from a Cambrian jug, a sweet tasting wine she found surprisingly palatable. She ate a raisin and currant bread with cherries and cinnamon that Hywel called *barmbrack*. She probably shouldn't have had the wine, but it warmed her bones and settled her nerves. She had devoured the salmon and settled into her oxtail soup as Hywel relayed in broken English, bits and pieces of appalling truths and the identity of Wolfglyn's unwelcome visitor.

Near the end of his story, he told her of the old master's grief upon losing his first wife. How Owain slipped into exhaustive bouts of melancholy. How on occasion, Owain's melancholy turned to longer bouts of senseless violence and how unmanageable he could be. Then all was saved, or so the people of Mynydd Castle thought when talk of a new bride seemed to cheer him. Her name was Aneira. Her calming affect on the master was miraculous and all believed it a blessed union. But the bride held her own sorrow, for she did not come to the marriage willing. It was learned later her father was a harsh ruler, that he had forbid her out of her bedchamber unless she bend to his command. She spoke not to him for two months. Servants who were caught befriending her were dismissed. Daily she was forced into reciting passages from the holy book on obeying her *tad*. The lady Aneira, she possessed an unusual penchant for cleanliness. So bathing, as well, was denied her. Anyone in her father's service giving her more than a saucer of water to soak her bread in was horsewhipped. She faired admirably for another month, but by summer's end, it was loneliness that broke her.

"Understandably, Owain's bride arrived here unhappy, but nonetheless obedient. The wedding was postponed ta give her time—but she felt no tendre for him, we all could see that. So ta help her ease into her intended position as beloved mistress of Mynydd Castle, Ifan was given the task of directing her as ta her role at Mynydd. Many a time, Ifan argued the wisdom of providing her daily instruction; he objected ta Owain's every order. He resisted contact with the desolate young beauty."

He sighed heavily. "Owain ignored every attempt Ifan

made ta appeal...." Hywel's voice trailed off as he recalled what happened next. "Ye see, he knew the folly in Owain's plan. He tried ta reason with Owain, but the master's mind hadn't been right for many months and he just laughed Ifan's concerns away...."

After a moment, when he didn't go on, Madeline prompted. "And his concerns were?"

Hywel looked up blankly, his thoughts engrossed in the awful past. "He worried that the sweet Aneira would do something foolhardy out of desperation."

Madeline sat with her empty bowl in bandaged hand, her spoon poised in mid-air, her rapt attention engaged. "And did she?" she asked softly, hating how breathless she sounded as she awaited his answer.

"She didn't harm herself, na. But she did something near as unforgivable. Ya see, she fell in love with young Ifan."

"Ifan...Owain's guard?" Madeline asked incredulously, though she could understand how easily Dance's harsh beauty beguiled. Who wouldn't have chosen him over an aging lord? Certainly, she was a victim herself. Beguiled out of her wits only to end up in his dungeon. "If Owain is your brother," she wondered aloud, "then surely you tried to reason with him?"

He blinked down at her as if just coming out of a fog. A strange look crossed his features, one of astonishment. Then his gaze dropped. He avoided her searching look. "Aneira was pledged ta Owain. True, I tried ta caution her, but a young woman smitten listens not ta an old man. She listens only ta her heart...." In his gaze returned that reflective glimmer of disturbing thoughts.

Riveted in place, Madeline was leaning forward, her heart pounding. "What happened to her?"

For long intense moments he didn't look as if he would

answer. Then he took a quivering breath. "Aneira's sadness could'na be hidden and we all started ta fear for her safety. Ya see, Owain took an uncommon interest in watching Ifan and Aneira together. Mind ya, Ifan took great care ta keep his distance. Until one night he came upon the fair Aneira weeping in the garden. Desperate she was, Lady Aneira clung ta him longer than another man's bride should have. Owain saw this and flew into one of his rages." He paused to recollect what followed next. "Ifan tried ta do the honorable thing and take the blame. And I tried ta be her friend until she could be brought ta understand her love could'na be returned. But she was the very vision of innocence. And every bit the noble daughter of a man of consequence. So it happened, Aneira was too naïve ta understand no good would come in telling his lordship her regrets. Poor Ifan, she never told him what she intended. Against my counsel, she went ta beg her betrothed for her freedom from the pledge. She bravely faced Owain's fury, explaining she was already in love with another."

Madeline could almost feel poor Aneira's heartbreak. "And he didn't grant her freedom?"

"Na, he did not."

She could imagine what happened next. "That's when she sought out Ifan for comfort?" she prompted, trying to sort out in her mind what must have followed that awful row and the depth of despair the young woman had to have felt. "And her sadness was beyond Ifan's bearing?" She could see it all so clearly. A proud young man in love and nothing he could do about his ill-fated feelings. But he would have sought to comfort his beloved, and likely frustrated himself, he might have unintentionally compromised her. His guilt at that point would have been great, his honorable intentions futile, yet he would offer no less of a valiant stand than that of his beloved Aneira. He would have devoted himself to shielding her from censure and danger.

Not unlike how he shielded Madeline herself in the courtyard, she thought to herself. Against the black wolf. And again that same afternoon, against the wrath of his estranged master.

"Aneira loved Ifan beyond this life," Hywel went on in grave tones. "She was blessed sweetest itself, revered by all who gazed upon her. That next morn they were bodily evicted from the castle. For a short time Lady Aneira found sanctuary with the squire and his wife, Ifan with the cotter. They both worked side by side that spring sheering the sheep. She really tried ta hide the child swelling her belly, but 'twas easy enough ta see and Ifan the proud father...well word got 'round. Aneira hung by Ifan like a doting lamb, seeking his counsel in everything. At first, they hid their impassioned tryst, snatching what moments alone they could. Of course he dearly tried ta restrain a young man's passion, but 'twas destined their love was ta defy caution." A wistful smile fleeted across his face. "Ta see them together was ta know they were forged of one soul." Sadness pulled his mouth down. "But Owain was a selfish lord and the unexpected loss of his first wife had already made him a bitter man. That bitterness became a sickness in his mind, mi *fach*."

When she shouldn't, she found she liked Hywel's endearment. "He never forgave them, did he?"

He shook his head. "Owain raved he would put them both ta death. Then shortly after that he rode outta' here shouting his curse upon the castle and leaving his people abandoned with no lord ta rule. That night the keep mysteriously went up in flames. We all knew `twas Owain done it."

"But you were here. In his absence, the people would have looked to you," she offered helpfully. "Couldn't you have set things right?"

"`Tis kind of ya ta say so, but ya must see I'm no ruler."

No, she could not argue the truth of what she had been sensing after seeing him and Dance together in the dining hall. Hywel had not struck her as a ruler of great kingdoms. He was instead, a most humble and kind healer. "I suppose Owain came back, didn't he?"

"*Ydw*, he did...the very week Ifan's wee son was born." His chin slumped to his chest, his eyes flooding with emotion, his mouth slanting a feeble line.

"It must have been awful," she murmured softly, afraid to hear more yet unable to curtail her curiosity.

He cuffed the wetness from his cheek. "By then Owain heard Aneira had wed Ifan. I think it was then he must'a made a pact with the devil. He sought revenge upon his faithless bride and her beloved. `Tis unspeakable what he did...inhuman."

"Tell me," she beseeched, reaching out in sympathy to share his burden, the weight of what he left unsaid bearing down on her heart. She saw no wife. Heard no child's peeling laughter.

Her cold fingers reached for Hywel's. Her touch brought a brief flicker of notice before grief bowed his narrow shoulders.

A moment passed where he seemed lost in grim reflection. Then just as slowly he seemed to realize by her gesture he'd said more than he intended. He slowly started to rise to his feet.

Madeline urgently caught hold of his tunic. "Help me

to leave here," she begged softly, holding tight to the fine embroidered hem.

He shook his head as he set the candle branch down and backed away from her toward the door.

"You could at least tell me why I'm prisoner here. What the curse has to do with me?"

He seemed to hesitate at the stark appeal in her eyes. Then his mouth tightened in negation.

Madeline's fragile composure shattered as tears slid down her ashen face.

Her unspoken plea held him immobile for a heartbeat longer, his red-rimmed eyes filled with overwhelming regret. "Owain will hurt ya bad. 'Tis his curse upon Ifan—"

Insistent scratching at the door halted Hywel's explanation.

Madeline gasped in alarm.

The pawing increased with fervor as if beset by panic. 'Twas Sheva—faithful insurance against her notions of escape.

Harried, Hywel pulled free of Madeline's clenched fist.

A moment's light slanted across the threshold as he looked over his shoulder before quickly slipping out.

Before Madeline could push to her knees after him, he was gone. She stumbled to the door. Shivering, she rested her head against the uneven roughness of solid oak, the grating of a heavy iron latch in her ear. The final parting sound until her next meal.

Deep in thought, uncertain he would be able to withstand another of her appeals, Hywel exited the dungeon with a lighter platter. He fumbled with the key, his hand unsteady as he turned the key in the lock. With her safe inside, he turned slowly with his burden....

Startled, Hywel jumped upon finding the master sitting on the bottom step of the stairway.

"Good ta see ya join the living, mi lord," Hywel quickly murmured in a voice that wouldn't carry, his gaze averted, his guilt masked.

Dance rose to his feet. "A temporary relapse." His gaze locked on Hywel. "How is she?"

Finally looking up from the platter, Hywel shook his head at Dance's whispered query.

Quietly Dance gestured for Hywel to come closer, his assessing scrutiny fixed on the tray.

Hywel didn't say anything, but saw what his master did. After she had refused food for the better part of two days, her appetite seemed miraculously restored.

He approached Dance. "She wants ta go home, master," Hywel murmured nervously, a catch in his voice as he glanced away. "She hasn't slept on her bed." He raised stricken eyes to his master's solemn face. "I don't know what ta do for her...."

Dance quietly took the platter from Hywel to set it on the step. "I imagine you told her something to get her to eat again. Perhaps you would like to tell me what it was?"

A glimmer of astonishment crossed the old man's face. "Ya know?"—he squinted up at Dance to discern the truth—"Yer sight—ya been having yer visions?"

Dance quietly clasped Hywel's shoulder in acknowledgement. "A few." And he waited for the explanation.

But Hywel's elation reflected like a ray of sun breaking through the clouds, his long suffering lapse in faith suddenly restored. A smile broke his grizzled face. "Then ya may get yer other gift back as well."

"Don't count on it."

"But `tis wondrous news, mi lord. I'll not let ya deny it."

Uncomfortable with the topic, Dance changed courses. "You've been in there a long time."

Hywel shrugged and countered, "Ya been sitting out here long, have ya?"

"Long enough to arrive at all manner of deductions." Dance's brow lifted. "Is this evasion I detect?"

Standing up straighter, Hywel didn't deny it. "I noticed ya rode out the other night," he ventured, diversion his best hope to evade sensitive issues. "Ya took that black devil for a good long ride, too, I reckon."

A faint smile. "Something like that."

He watched the old man sigh in relief and knew Hywel had guessed where he'd been.

"Is there anything else you wish to speak to me about?" Dance asked gravely, a marked note of authority in his tone this time. One portending a shortness of patience.

Blanching, the old man looked down at his hands sheepishly.

"Is my wife's memory not sacred in my home?" Softly uttered words full of pain.

Hywel's shoulders rose in helpless surrender. "I—I thought, the lady—she deserved ta be warned," he finished in defense of his momentary weakness.

A black brow lifted. "And you could think of no other way?"

"I didn't tell her all, master," Hywel quickly assured him. "She knows naught of your importance."

"Ah, so you told her my wife fell in love with a meager guard, and that makes it all right?"

"Na, mi lord, it doesn't," Hywel conceded. "Begging yer forgiveness, I would never cast disfavor upon ya. The girl knows none of the details—na the private ones."

"I'm sure you meant well." Dance's tone softened. "I imagine she is genuinely distressed. Probably crying."

Nodding, Hywel truly looked ready to cry himself.

"What's done cannot be undone," Dance reasoned. "And I know I can count on you to speak no more of the past."

Hywel gladly nodded his acceptance of such.

"All right, off with you then. Take her tray up and fetch the tub down. It's time our sad *engyl* was provided a warm bath."

"Maddie *fach*," Hywel called softly. He was edging closer to the silent bulge under wool blankets in a way so as to not raise his voice and startle her. "Come, *fach*, I've brung ya a bath. Ifan would have ya cleaned up for a stroll about."

From behind the altar Madeline slowly rose on trembling legs, her pitiful weapon raised to strike...when Hywel's words settled upon her sluggish mind.

"Cleaned up for who?" she accused hoarsely, her manners clearly destroyed along with her refined upbringing.

Hywel swung around with lantern swaying above his head. "Mi girl, ye gave me a fright—" Then his face drained of blood, a look of wary regard quickly shuttered at his shock. For the very devil herself was set to do him mortal injury. In her tiny fist the fork gleamed menacingly in the arm raised above her head. Skin pale, fear blazing in her eyes, her chestnut hair tangled and teeth bared like a she-wolf, she was looking at him in an unholy enough way to send him fleeing for the door. He just managed to curb the impulse. "Easy, Maddie girl, no one wants ta harm ya." He should'na frightened her with the truth, he saw that now.

"I'm leaving and you can't stop me!" Desperation trembled in her voice.

"Na, Maddie girl, I can't stop ya if ya want ta make a run for it. But I was thinking ya might like a bath first."

She gave him a mutinous glower for a long moment, then cursed.

Slowly the fork was lowered as if the effort had drained her last ounce of strength.

"I will not be left alone with him," she said shakily, suspicion in her voice, the lantern light casting pronounced shadows over delicate features, intensifying her frail beauty.

Hywel forced himself not to make notice of more prominent collarbones. "If ya wish it, I'll be close by. But you'll na be in danger—"

"Where is he?" she demanded unblinking. "I would talk to him right now."

"Would ya wish him ta see ya as ya are?"

"Yes...." But, her fierce front wavered, her appearance she knew had to be appalling.

Hywel relaxed his grip on the pewter soup bowl. "Why don't we talk over it while ya finish yer bath and eat yer mutton stew."

Her gaze dropped to the peace offering he held out and she was suddenly quite weary of it all.

When she didn't move to take it, Hywel carefully reached to set the bowl at the edge of the altar and back away. "I will return with yer bath water, mi girl," he said, glad she meant him no real harm. "If ya don't wish ta bathe

I will'na make ya, but a bath might make a girl feel better prepared for her talk...if ya get my meaning."

When Hywel returned with a crust of bread in one hand, bathing tub scraping along the floor in the other, it was to find Madeline awaiting his return with barely concealed eagerness. Already he could see her spirits were much improved, her demur blush suitably contrite for having near frightened him into a grave bare moments ago. She sat on the mattress, legs folded under her, the bowl empty beside her.

His eyes twinkled with pleasure. "I'm glad ya like mutton." Her gaze was locked on the bread. Heartened by her return of color, he gladly thrust it toward her outstretched hand.

Just remembering it, from out of his pocket Hywel produced the master's own brush as he deposited the cumbersome tub on the floor. On the bed, he laid the brush.

While Hywel was otherwise distracted, once more it was the torch light reflected from the open portal behind him that captured Madeline's attention. Eyeing her one chance with fading hope, Madeline shifted on the bed. She had one foot on the floor before Hywel said, "A good girl that Sheva. Did you know she sleeps by yer door?"

Again, Madeline's wayward notion of flight recalled to her how fruitless her chances. The temptation persisted though, and she would not give up her plans entirely.

Sullen, Madeline plopped back upon the pillow. "He can't keep me prisoner forever," she muttered darkly under her breath.

Hywel pretended not to hear her keen disappointment. "Where is he, anyway?"

He counted off the days of the week. "It would be the

Lord's Day. The day of rest. A good day to gather eggs and boil hot water for the lady's bath."

He ambled from the dungeon to retrieve a bucket of hot water from the corridor.

Her ire barely contained, she raised her voice to be heard. "He's here in the castle then?"

Sheva appeared beyond the threshold then disappeared again from sight. Hywel lumbered in with a bucket in hand, which he dumped into the tub with a great splash.

"*Ydw*, he's around—"

Water sloshing onto the ground in the stairwell beyond halted Hywel's words. He glanced up from pouring to see if the girl had also heard. After a fleeting look toward the door, she settled back with a grimace. "He's a coward, your guard," she grumbled.

Hywel smiled to himself. "Afraid of ya, Maddie *fach*? Are you certain `tis not shy he is around ya?"

Madeline snorted. "Not likely, that." Suddenly she looked pensive. "How long has he been alone?"

Hywel masked a secret grin. "I reckon `tis been long enough ta make a man uncomfortable in the presence of a lady."

"And how many years would that be?"

A yelp came from the corridor of steaming buckets before he could answer.

Madeline's gaze flew to Hywel's.

Ignoring her look, thinking her sudden interest of the one listening short feet away amusing, Hywel assured her, "That'll be Sheva. Letting me know she's impatient for her meal. I'll finish filling yer tub directly."

Out in the corridor, Hywel passed a silently scowling master on his fourth trip with hot water buckets, his amusement just barely subdued as he tread in and out of the dungeon. After the last and final trip, the door was again locked upon the lady. To leave her to her bath in privacy.

Dance helped Hywel carry the buckets up the stairs to the kitchen so they could accomplish the task in one trip. "Your grasp of English never ceases to surprise me," Dance remarked shrewdly.

"*Ydw*, well the Lady Madeline's *Cymraeg* will be coming along as well."

A brow lifted. "So you're teaching her Welsh? I see you've taken her care to heart."

Hywel shrugged. "'Tis lonely down there for her, master."

Wishing there was some other way he could keep her safe, Dance deposited his buckets near the blazing hearth. He knew how lonely solitude felt. "Just be careful, ole man, that she doesn't blindside you."

"*Ydw*, I know." Hywel dropped his buckets next to the others. "She near scared mi' bald bearing down on me with her fork. Now a she-dragon would'a pounced and run. Not yer *engyl*, she not really want ta hurt anyone. Maddie just wanna go home."

Dance's brow rose again upon hearing her name used in a familiar way. He'd need to watch that she didn't talk Hywel into something foolish. "I'll do my best to keep her alive." His tone turned grave. "And in case I haven't mentioned it, you've done well by her."

He watched Hywel's face light up. The unexpected praise taking him by surprise, his burden of late daunting. If he was feeling any of what Dance felt, his conscience was a constant nag questioning his actions.

"Come, I've got something for her."

Padding behind, his interest captured, Hywel followed him down the corridor past the kitchen and into the bailey. Dance stopped of a sudden on the front step of the summerhouse and felt Hywel stumble into him.

A momentary hesitation from Dance and then he turned the latch and entered, leaving the door open behind him. The old man hung back, waiting at the threshold gawking. Dance hadn't before allowed the summerhouse to be disturbed.

The shrine was aglow with candles. The walls a tangle of rose vines, the perfume sweetly cloying. From amber colored windows, soft light filtered in. The chamber looked as preserved as Dance's memory. His gaze drawn to the portrait of sweetness and purity—and the way the oil colors captured the fair Aneira that long ago morning—bringing it all back to him. An *engyl ael* they called her, fair of skin, hair the color of moonlit mists, eyes the soft color of heather. He'd been in attendance that day, standing out of the way and at the ready with nursemaid in case she grew too tired to continue her pose. Dance recalled the morning well, there in the garden with her, his adoration tireless, at her side in an instant to call a halt when his son grew fussy. To look upon wife and his son again was like stepping back in time. To have her die like she did not a fortnight after this very painting was finished `twas the death of his dreams.

Why he'd decided what he had, he had no idea. He didn't want to think about it. His pain contained, his senses attuned to lingering memories, he walked past his family. From the gilt-carved coffer, a newer wardrobe installed after the fire, Dance slowly withdrew a cloth-wrapped parcel. He bid the old man come forth as he unwrapped it. Hywel remained hesitant, feeling uneasy Dance knew when he thought his presence an obvious intrusion. Because Dance asked him to come forth, the old man had no choice but to join him.

Dance passed him the shapeless bundle. Hywel looked down at it as it unfolded in his hands. Buttercup gold and fine as they came, the revered gown was one of Dance's treasured possessions belonging to his wife.

The old man looked up in question.

"She needs it more than I do," Dance explained, wanting her to have something better to wear when he badly needed to give her assurances of comfort and warmth and safety.

The old man looked baffled by his unexpected generosity, tentative in thought, tracing a crooked finger lightly over the velvet softness. "It has been a long time, mi lord," Hywel remarked in a curious tone of awe. "A long time, indeed."

They departed the summer parlor together. After a brief pause to make certain the door to her shrine was secured, they were ready to proceed back to the keep.

Dance's eyes were adjusting to the bright afternoon light flooding the bailey when he halted in his tracks. His hand shot out to the side to stop Hywel.

"God—no!"

It was then Hywel looked up and saw...what made his stomach heave.

A strangled growl of pain erupted from Dance as he bolted across the courtyard.

Crimson puddles soaked the ground beneath the great black sacrifice left for Dance to find strapped to the portcullis.

It was Druidh.

Dance slid to a stop—his hands reaching out. Blood

pounding in his ears, his arms careful in lifting the staked body for fear of inflicting greater pain, Dance wordlessly pressed his face to Druidh's silky black fur. He willed it not so.

Panting, Hywel rushed up behind him.

Hands trembling, stricken speechless by the fiendish manner of revenge, the old man mindlessly worked the knots loose. After some minutes, the leather binding soaked with Druidh's life fell free.

For long endless moments Dance just stood there holding Druidh, his chest heaving in grief....

Druidh didn't move, nor would he ever again.

Dance's weight sagged against the grate. Hot tears burned his eyes, fell heedless. His heart convulsing, he hoarsely whispered, "Leave us."

Hywel stood helpless a hesitant interval, then silently retreated as asked of him.

SUFFERING, AS A SACRED TRUTH : –
A symbol of the bondage of the Spirit in matter, implying
limitation and suppression of spiritual energy or Divine life.

11.

While Dance finished saying a prayer over Druidh's shallow grave, Hywel hurried to clean up the last of the blood from the gate. It made him late getting to his chores. Late getting to the kitchen to rustle up dinner—where the everyday tasks could be plunged into with a fervor. His antidote to grief was hard work. Yet try as he did to put it from his mind, Druidh's death had thrown a gloom over the castle.

Madeline was mighty hungry by the time her dinner finally arrived.

She sat on the bed, where she'd quickly dressed before she could catch cold, the blankets bundled around her. As soon as she saw Hywel's face, drawn and pale, she knew something was wrong. "What is it?"

"The curse tis upon us, Maddie *fach*...." Hywel hung his head, his mind in a quandary about her safety. "You'll not be going for yer stroll. `Tis not safe."

Perplexed, she motioned him to deposit the tray next to her on the bed. "What happened to change everything—I thought he was letting me out of here?" she asked, reeling in disappointment.

He sighed heavily as he set the tray down. "While we be busy, the devil got ta Druidh."

The import of his words wiped the last traces of hope from her grasp. "Is he dead?" But she already knew the answer to her question for it was written on Hywel's ashen features. She felt suddenly ill. A new wave of uncertainty clenched her insides. "I'm not going to get out of here alive, am I?"

Hywel looked pained as he held out the gown for her. "He wished ya ta have this."

Her question ignored, she stared blankly at the buttercup color, her need of a beautiful gown subsequent to survival, her only wish to be set free. Her voice grew frantic with alarm. "Hywel, please." She grabbed his arm to stay him. "If what you say is true, I'm going to be next unless you help me convince Dance to let me go. He'll listen to you." Her nails dug into his arm as she beseeched him. "You're my only hope...."

Neither one noticed right away a shadow had filled the doorway.

Distracted, Madeline looked up at the same instant Hywel grew silent at her side. The gown was silently dropped in her lap. Before she ever saw him, she knew who stood there.

It was Dance.

At the sight of him, her insides somersaulted.

He filled the breadth of the portal, his harsh beauty staggering her as her breath left her.

She couldn't tell what he was thinking, but he gazed upon her in a strangely touching way, as if storing the memory against time. A look telling her he was gravely worried.

Beset by a sense of uncertainty and fear, she was nonetheless tingling all over, her heart pounding hard in her chest. He was here, his gaze caressing her like a fine sable fur, his powerful allure like soft blue mists swirling around her—a serpent of awareness moving through her. Drawing her to him as if she were connected to him by her soul. She saw his handsome face laced with traces of wetness. And quite unexpectedly, her own sorrow lay her open to him, allowing her a kinship with the man who's grieving would appear to never cease. Whatever his actions, he'd acted to protect her. And her heart bled for him. For he'd lost all. His wife, his newborn son—who Hywel told her without words, were loved more than life itself. And now Druidh, his companion.

Madeline saw it all in those haunted topaz eyes.

She saw Dance as he would have been six years ago, how he would have unfailingly sacrificed himself to save his family. To live without them, tormented by the memory of what Hywel portrayed for her as inhumane, would be worse than death to him. And she, at last, understood him.

"I want to go home...." she said softly, her gaze drinking him in and finding favor when she would rather revile him the rest of her days. Days which were now numbered by some curse.

Dance stood unmoving in the doorway. "I can't risk it."

"*Ydw*, you can," she insisted, her voice soft with entreaty, her fingers absently clenching the gown to her breast. "I release you of any responsibility. Hywel, tell him. Tell him he can't keep me."

Hywel's gaze met Dance's. A look passed between them and Hywel obediently moved to leave.

"Hywel." Madeline caught his arm to detain him. "Tell him," she pleaded, her brows drawn in anxious appeal.

Clearly troubled, strangely passive, he averted his gaze. He pulled from her hold.

Dismayed, Madeline sat transfixed. "Hywel?"

"Leave him go, Madeline." Dance shifted in the doorway to let Hywel pass.

Rising to her feet, the gown sliding forgotten to the floor, she faced him with mounting frustration. "You can't dismiss him like that."

"That's where you're wrong."

"Oh, am I? How so?"

"Wolfglyn is mine, Madeline. This dungeon. The castle. The valley as far as you can see. They all belong to the D'epanier family. As does Hywel's loyalty."

Staggered by his announcement, she blinked at him as if he had sprouted an eye in the middle of his forehead. In those tremulous moments before she accepted his claim, she believed him seriously deranged. Then the events of her stay at Wolfglyn converged upon her with the swiftness of a cleaver baring her soul. Leaving her feeling exposed, and worse, feeling a fool.

"You liar," she railed, flying at him, pounding her bandaged fists on his chest, striking him blow upon blow.

Dance held her by her upper arms because he knew not what else to do. Great sobs shook her shoulders. His arms were enfolding her close to his heart while he sought for something to say to mitigate her pain. His lips murmured consoling words near her ear, her hair as soft on his cheek as spun mists, her scent profoundly feminine, her slender body molded along the length of his own. He held onto her in stark appeal against all the months of loneliness...and realized rather inexplicably how bad he wanted to go on holding her. Take what was given him, in whatever capacity she was willing to give, for as long or fleeting the moment. He was that desperate to feel the warmth of her body against his.

His hunger unnerved him.

But neither did he let her go. He should. But he kept holding her, because as long as she was in his arms, he could assure himself she was safe and alive and for however brief—his to hold onto....

But she had been humiliated for the last time and she lashed out with words, her pain inconsolable. "You're demented and cruel and—" Of a sudden, she stopped struggling to glare at him under tear-spiked lashes, her expression heart-breaking. "Youuu—you were laughing at me the whole time...you knew all along...and"—she stammered to a halt—"Dear God, Hywel too, he lied about my father...and I believed him. Like an utter fool I trusted him."

He cupped her face between his large palms, his thumb gentle in brushing each tear away. "Na, *engyl*, he didn't tell you wrong. Not about your father. And if anyone is a fool, I am. Because I let you stay when I knew to do so would seal your fate."

She sniffled raggedly. "Then my father is out of danger?" she asked urgently. "He lives?"

"*Ydw*, he recovers."

"Thank God," she breathed, tears of relief brimming her eyes. Then her relief was overshadowed by a new danger. "Hywel said you were cursed. That man in the courtyard"—she gazed at him searchingly—"he's not your estranged master, is he?"

Dance tensed, his body going rigid.

"I'm not going home, am I?" Her voice quivered, she was suddenly trembling. "I'm never going to see my father again, and you're going to keep me locked away where they will never find me." She held his gaze with anguished eyes. "And that hideous man that arrived this morning is going to take his revenge on you by doing unspeakable things to me, too. I know because Hywel told me. I'm going to die."

"Shhh, *engyl,* he can't get to you, there's a lock on this door now. Hywel should not have scared you—"

"Please, stop it. There's no use denying it, I know about Owain. Hywel says you will die trying to protect me." Scared for a myriad of reasons, she started crying harder. "If we're going to die, I would like to hear the truth this time. You owe me that."

He did. He knew it and still he held back. How many times had he wished he could tell her? If he could bring himself to speak of it, what then? What difference could it make knowing the truth? Would it appease her if he broke down in front of her?

And yet, if he were in her place, he would want to know too.

His gaze staring fixed on the far wall, his insides roiling from the memory, he rested his chin upon the silken softness of her head and grappled for strength to venture into the black depths of his past. She stood quiet, prepared it would seem, to give him all the time he needed to put into words what he had not spoken of in the last six years. "He's my father," he said at last, his voice distant, the implication chilling.

He felt Madeline go stiff with shock and knew not if she could stomach the rest. But he sensed she was not going to stop him either. "I don't know if I can tell you all."

She sniffled against his chest. "I know how hard this has to be for you...."

He felt himself shuddering uncontrollably, his mouth going dry, the black cloud of the past descending upon him with the weight of a stone wall crushing all in its fall. "I was dragged unconscious up the tower stairwell." Owain's hired thugs had taken great pleasure in rendering him senseless, the steel shanks around his throat cutting into his windpipe and making him strangle for breath. They'd beaten him to the point he welcomed death. Blood ran in his eyes from a gash inflicted with a blunt object Dance couldn't deflect. "When I came to, sometime later, it was to find my wife on her knees weeping. I heard her begging for mercy, but I did not know why right then." Dance closed his eyes, his throat tight, convulsing with remembered fear that shook his soul. "Two thugs stood over her, holding her shoulders down so she couldn't rise...and then in my dazed state, I looked to the tower window where Owain stood, the light blinding me...."

Lost to the debilitating memory, Dance's raspy words quieted. He tried to speak, but couldn't formulate sound. His chest heaved with each crushing breath, a single tear glistening a trail down his cheek.

Madeline stirred in his embrace to slip her arms around his waist, her unexpected gesture no doubt prompted by some misplaced notion of compassion.

"Owain held my son"—his throat convulsed—"suspended from the window. I tried to rise but couldn't move. I heard my son crying...his blood curdling scream...." Then the sound of Dance's own blood-thirsty howl of misery and disbelief and abject fear carried on the morning air...in the background Aneira's frantic pleas. "The last thing I heard before I blacked out was my son wailing at the top of his lungs...."

Against his chest he felt Madeline sobbing in silence. Her grief congealed with the misery clenching his chest. Sharing his pain with her hadn't made it easier.

She held him tight. "I'm so sorry—it had to be unbearable," she murmured wretchedly. "Myself, I would have wanted to die." She stilled as if it just came to her. "You did want to die, didn't you?"

He didn't answer for a long moment. When he did the words were harsh with anger. "I prayed for it."

Thank heavens his prayers went unanswered, she thought wildly. Her heart torn and bleeding for him, she was afraid to ask what happened to his wife but couldn't seem to stop herself either. "And your wife?" she asked carefully. "Something happened to her, too?"

He had braced for her question and still felt his legs want to buckle. Aneira. His sole reason for living. Gone from this world forever. "She was spared a tumble from the tower," he murmured to himself, his gaze on the dungeon wall suddenly filled with agonizing visions. His last minutes with Aneira before, she too, was vilely slain before his very eyes. "It happened here, in this very dungeon," he intoned on a sharp breath, his hands clenching in the softness of Madeline's hair where he held her head cradled to his chest. "On the altar behind you. The bastards, there were three of them"—he sucked in a shallow breath, his heart pounding fiercely. As if reliving the gut-wrenching sight, the bile rose to choke him as they took turns toying with his sanity.

He still woke in a sweat to Aneira's tortured cries. Her valiant fight. Her unwavering gaze locked with his, both consoling and suffering in silent bearing what she wouldn't give freely. Dance had fought in vain to break free, his bare torso slickened with sweat, his breathing labored. But the chains held solid. They cut his wrists—blood splattered his legs, his boots, the floor. He'd fought his bindings like a crazed beast as he lunged for the bastards again and again, his blood boiling, the men's laughter sickening him. All the while being forced to watch his beloved mate repeatedly raped. Two vile animals holding her down while a third one plundered her with brute force. Until she had gritted her teeth against crying out. Until they had broken her, stripped her of spirit. Until she'd not been able to withstand the horror and slipped unconscious.

For what seemed hours, Dance had been up on that altar in her place, each violation to her felt inflicted upon his own body. Ripping him open, plundering fragile defenses. When they hadn't stopped, Dance had begged them with raspy voice to use him instead...fear seizing his heart at the sight of Aneira's blood...so much of it everywhere....

Still each bastard had taken his time using her to inflict as much pain as possible, their purpose—to break Dance inch by merciless inch....

Aneira had slighted her betrothed and for it she'd been vilely destroyed.

So Dance would have the memory to carry with him to the grave.

Only his vow to Aneira had kept him from driving a dagger into his own heart.

The scene in the courtyard. Druidh had been slain to prove a point.

And Madeline, God help him, was Owain's next target.

He could spare her feelings or see that she understood the seriousness in taking risks. He needed her to comprehend or he wouldn't stand a chance of saving her.

Her tears wet his shirt. "They violated my wife," he told her hoarsely, the pain of it still capable of piercing his heart. "She was bleeding to death before my eyes. I tried everything to save her, I used my powers until they left me"—he took a ragged breath—"she died in my arms." Tears streaming down his face, his distant gaze remained unfocused on the altar.

"Oh Dance, I'm so sorry," she murmured wretchedly, the horror prevalent in her tone.

Her pity, though unwanted, consoled him and he tenderly kissed her hair.

"Now he's back for me," Madeline muttered against his shirt. "God in heaven, haven't you suffered dearly enough already...surely he sees that?"

"You don't know him, Madeline." He stroked her hair. "The old barbarian ways of decades ago. The bloodshed. The betrayal. I'm sure you've heard the stories of betrayal by one's own kin, entire families destroyed. As long as I live, he will never let me forget."

She shook her head. "But Aneira did not love him, she wouldn't have made him a biddable wife. Not when she loved you. Whatever he may think, you committed no sin in falling in love. You did nothing for which you should be so fiendishly punished."

His arms momentarily tightened, his eyes closed tightly as hot tears trailed down his face. His throat convulsed against the words he would have spoken in gratitude. The relief in finding she didn't condemn him.

"Now I'm to die, too," she whispered forlornly, her fingers fisted in his shirt, "because it suits his purpose."

His lips grazed her hair, her trembling body snug within his arms, he had regretfully opened up to her. There was no going back. If he was going to succeed in saving her life, there could be only honesty from here on out. He took a steadying breath. "The curse is upon my own head—my cross to bear as long as I live. You had no way of knowing one touch from me would mark you for death."

"What do you mean one touch? There's no dishonor in touching—"

"For me there is. And I've been a long time without a woman, Madeline. He planned this with that in mind. He's not going to accept that I haven't bedded you. Believe me, I tried telling him. And I'm sure you saw his reaction, even if you didn't understand what was being said. He's beyond talk. Beyond rational thought. He lives for revenge."

"But he's had his revenge. A thousand times over."

His shoulders drooped with weariness. "In the mind of a madman, it will never be over."

"I had no idea. That's why you didn't want me coming here," she said in quiet realization. "And, I didn't listen. I was walking into a trap devised to punish you. God, how horribly unfair." With sudden insight, she said, "It is as much my fault as anyone's. Surely he knows that, since he devised a confrontation with my family so that I would seek you out. How can he place all the blame on you? Did I not walk into his trap on my own?"

A faint smile. "But you knew naught of the curse, you were merely intent on engaging the aid of a healer for your father. You're blameless." He pressed his lips to her hair. "And I should have suspected, sooner or later, it was destined that I be tested."

"Maybe I could go to Owain—"

"No!" he growled softly, "you stay away from him. You would be used in as vile a way as my wife. I can't let that happen again. I won't let that happen again."

More softly he continued, "What I need from you isn't bravery, *engyl*. If I'm going to keep you safe, I need your full cooperation. You'll be putting your life in my keeping—"

"And you will be putting yours at peril," she countered, remembering what Hywel had told her. Conceivably, he might even rush to end his own life, rather than go on living alone. Knowing what she did now, he would view her death as another failure, albeit unavoidable, but all the more unbearable perhaps. Reason enough to a man who has suffered greatly, to end his own life. What more noble an end?

With Madeline out of the way, who would stop him?

She must speak to Hywel. If things should go badly for her, Hywel must continue to stand in her stead against Dance's self-destruction. "All right, you have my full cooperation."

He sighed heavily. "Thank you, *engyl*."

A sadness filled Hywel's eyes at her request. "Mi girl, do ya know what ya ask?"

Frantic to make him understand, she was taken aback. "Would you see him take his own life? Surely, not?"

He busied himself unwrapping her hands, then inspected them to see how they healed. He didn't immediately answer her question. "'Tis all healed, ya are, *mi fach*. 'Tis his gift," he remarked kindly, his gaze prideful and reverent.

Madeline flexed her fingers, amazed herself how uncommonly quick Dance's magic salve had worked. "Give him my thanks," she said softly. With a sigh, she appealed again, "He has a gift that shouldn't be wasted. Look at me." She held her palms in his face. "Dance is special, Hywel. He's not like you and me." Her hands dropped to her sides. "He was born to do special things. He's noble and honorable and he has a power within him to save a great many people. Be a great lord. Rule these lands with kindness, where his father has failed. I know you see it, too. That's why you've stood by him through all his suffering, when he wanted to give up," she said, forlornly. "I don't know if I could bear it, if he didn't have you." Her chin trembled, her eyes swimming. "If something happens to me...I need you to help keep him from harm. Please...."

Not looking up, he stuffed the soiled bandages into his pocket. "'Tis the same thing she asked of him." He lifted solemn eyes to her. "Aneira did. She made him pledge. There on the altar, with her last breath. She begged him ta promise he would live for her and their son. And survive for her, he has. And he has struggled with that vow every day without fail for six long years." His hand came up to rest on her shoulder, the gesture consoling. "Take pity on him, mi *fach*, don't ask him ta hold onto life when he would suffer the rest of his days. You know what it's like here. His vow to Aneira, well intended it was, has kept him prisoner here. In a castle barren of warmth. Barren of solace. Barren of human contact with the fair sex. Would ya watch him destroyed in heart and mind? Would ya listen ta him as I have, pacing the halls, crying her name in his sleep?"

Wincing, Madeline's face paled, her lips trembling.

"I know `tis the hardest thing ta do," he went on. "Because I have seen him thus. And it has been no easy sight. If he loses ya, mi *fach*, he will not return the victor of this battle with evil. He knows it. And now ya must love him enough, love him as do I, and allow him his peace. `Tis merciful, Maddie girl."

Merciful? Was that what he believed? Out of her mind in fear for Dance, she realized despondently, she wasn't going to get any help from Hywel. "I can't." Tears of helplessness burned her eyes. "I just can't."

Why did Hywel's words disturb her so? Was it the thought of Dance facing his father making her sick with dread? Or was it some more terrifying thought—such as never seeing him again? Never feeling his arms about her, nor snuggling into his warmth, nor feeling protected and strangely comforted...never to smell again the clover essence he carried on him. All those things that made him human and compassionate and terribly alluring.

What was it, gripping her with desperation? Making

her die inside at the thought of him lying still as death? Was she being selfish, thinking only of herself?

Perhaps she was, but she couldn't help it. Perhaps she'd started to understand the man shrouded in mystery and his uncommon loyalty to a dead wife and child. Perhaps she'd started to care about the sad and lonely recluse, whose power to heal had somehow deserted him when he most needed it. A man spoken of in reverent tones by the very foe who led her into the forest on his master's diabolical mission of vengeance.

What woman wouldn't be in awe of Dance's unfailing devotion to a memory? And want that kind of love for herself?

A shocking thought flittered into Madeline's head. Was she hoping for the same conviction from Dance as the one he carried with him in memory?

A resounding warmth spread through her limbs at the thought. Yes. She did.

Foolish as the thought might be, she wanted to be loved that desperately. Ill-timed as it was, she wanted it all.

She wanted to experience the tender and fierce intimacy between a man and woman.

How his hands would feel on her bare skin. Her thoughts returned to that morning, waking up to find him asleep next to her, the hard contours of his warm body, the texture of his skin, the fine hair covering his body. Waking to the subsequent heat in his eyes scorching her with the hunger he'd tried to bank, but only barely. She recalled his glorious lance, swollen and red and grown to full need, and didn't doubt he must have been wanting her too. After six years, he must have been craving it quite badly.

The wonder of his craving curled her toes. She understood now where his resistance came from, how it was out of obligation to his wife's memory. It must have been a painful discovery for him. To find himself desiring another woman.

The Lord of Mists, great healer, sinfully handsome—he desired her. And yes, though she hadn't known at the time, she would have let him bury his needy lance in her body.

It was shocking. It was more. It was incredible and fascinating and tempting and had secretly been on her mind, though she had unwittingly suppressed the same heedless desires.

Now, however, when everything was about to be put in peril, she knew without a doubt what she wanted.

Certainly, if in all probability she was going to die for supposedly committing the deed, it stood to reason that she be allowed one small concession in the eyes of the Almighty. Even knowing Dance might be somewhat resistant, she could accept that. Madeline blushed furiously, her insides melting in preparation. Her heart setting itself on a heady course.

As Madeline prepared herself for Dance, her hands trembling as she toweled herself dry, she wished quite earnestly he not reject her. They were, after all, allies. And both of them about to be tested to the extremes of faith. The coming hours would be emotionally draining for Dance, as it was his father seeking to destroy him.

She'd heard the sorrow under his anger and frustration. She thought about how it would crush her were her father to maliciously seek to harm her. To suffer what Dance had suffered for loving Aneira. It broke her heart to think of it. His misery held silent. His nights filled with visions of horror and heartache. Crying out in his sleep for Aneira. Questioning his existence when he rather relished ending it. Bless Aneira, if for no other reason then that she had found a way to keep him alive. No matter the hardship Hywel was faced with, Dance needed a reason to go on. To survive in spite of his father.

Dance needed a champion on his side now more than ever. Hywel loved his master, but was exhausted to the bone by his constant vigil at Dance's side. They were both of a mind to let go.

Well, pox on that. She wasn't letting Dance give up.

Especially not now, when she would have him join his magnificent body with hers.

Was it love, she wondered, making her tremble? Could she have finally found the man of her dreams in a fairytale land haunted by evil trolls? Was it something deeper she felt or mere desperation? In all likelihood, it was a little of both. It was her desperate longing to be loved the way Dance was capable of loving.

Indeed, she had no illusions about how it would be with him.

There was apprehension aplenty. Knowing what she knew now, she doubted he would readily take what she offered.

To think—all the days she'd spent here. Under his very nose. Gracious, the sleepless nights she must have cost him. It was too late to regret that she hadn't done anything about encouraging him sooner. But not too late, she mused, to bring a smile to his lips.

BANQUET OR FEAST:
A symbol of the assimilation of Wisdom and Love by
the soul, and of the enjoyment of what it has earned
through its efforts.

12.

It wasn't exactly the smile she'd been hoping for from him, when he returned to the dungeon with their dinner in hand.

Madeline was perched on the bed, her bare shoulders loosely draped by the bedcovers.

She saw him hesitate, heard him suck in his breath the moment he spotted her from the threshold.

"I've been waiting for you." She patted the bed. "You can bring that over here. We'll eat on the bed, if that is all right with you."

He looked unflinching at her, his gaze focused on her mouth she noted to keep it from wandering into dangerous territory. "Lord, what are you up to now?"

He would have to sound disgruntled. "I'm making a dying wish. A request if you will. I saw how you hungered for me in your bed. How painfully hard you were. My brother said a man, when he's hard like you were, he's wanting to put his lance inside me. And I don't want to die before I get to feel your lance in me —"

"Jesus," Dance said softly, his heart pounding like waves against common sense — a beautiful nymph a few short feet away. Her shoulders were bare, creamy skin exposed and causing him grave discomfort. She was naked, he realized with mounting disquiet, and all the memories of her with a fever came rushing back to join those he had of Madeline, the one time he had her in his bed. "I'm supposed to compromise you, is that what you want?" In the dungeon holding nothing but pain for him. "Here, in a dungeon," he gritted out.

She gnawed her bottom lip. "We will be safe here"—he scowled at that—"and it is but a single request from a woman facing death. I will not require that you enjoy it."

"Christ's blood! What if you live to see your family again, Madeline? Have you thought about that?"

The start of tears glistened in her eyes. "Then you are going to deny me?"

She was wrecking havoc on his senses. "I'm resisting, not denying. I imagine you know the difference."

She smiled wobbly at that. "So you *do* desire me? Answer me truthfully."

He didn't answer for a heartbeat. "A man in my condition would desire you whether he wanted to or not," he said. "I can't believe you would have me callously use you. Take what isn't mine, what should only be given to your bridegroom."

"I've no use for saving myself for a husband I may never live to see. Isn't it enough that I want you? Must I also beg?"

"Damn it, Madeline, I would prefer you revile me."

How canny he would say that, when just an hour ago she'd been thinking that same thing. "Yes, I know. And I did hate you. For a short while. Before I understood—"

"Before you learned of my disgrace." His tone filled with self-condemnation. "Before you pitied me."

Her temper flared. "I don't pity you. Nor do I hate you as you hoped. I can't—leastwise not anymore."

He stood above her, his topaz eye blazing back. "Instead you wish to be ravished? While I have you locked up under my care? Don't you find that the least repulsive?"

Outlined by the light from the lit corridor beyond, so sinfully beautiful he took her breath away, he made a fiercely intimidating protector. Wild mane tousled, his heated gaze devouring her, his shirt open at the throat and his casual grace confounding, she couldn't imagine him anywhere else but here at Wolfglyn. She wanted him without reservation, without a bone of common sense in her body and she planted her hands on her hips. "I just knew you were going to make this difficult. But then I also know you have denied yourself a very long time." She looked down to the magnificent bulge in his breeches and felt overcome by weakness. "That's wanting me...and I'm wanting it." Her gaze came up, her eyes dreamy. "I want to know how wonderful it feels taking you into my body and crying out with passion. And if something should happen, I want to take a fond memory with me...."

"To your grave?" he grumbled darkly.

"Yes." Her voice soft, she willed him to understand with all her heart.

Just as softly he asked, "And if things should turn out different and you should leave here unmolested? We *could* survive. Have you thought about how you will feel when you look back on your stay here?"

God love him, he was being awfully charitable when she was intent on seduction and more sure than she'd ever been about anything before that he was what she'd always wanted, that this moment had been destined. "I would be grateful to you beyond life itself." A blush stole over her. "I would whisper a prayer that I was lucky to have stumbled into your path in the forest. Furthermore, I give you my promise, that no matter how it all turns out, I will tell no one I coerced you into this."

He gave her a grim look. "And I don't want you regretting it, *engyl*. Trust me on this, you will want to wed some day. When you do, your betrothed is not likely to take kindly to finding your maidenhead breached. I know from experience—most men will see you as ruined. You would be hurt. Whatever your defense, in this, it won't be enough to overcome his damaged pride."

"Then if that's what you truly believe, what you're saying is you would cast your wife aside after what those beasts did to her? Out of male pride?"

His gaze narrowed darkly, his look tortured and suspiciously bright. "I would love her no differently."

"There you see," she appealed softly, wishing she could turn back time, erase his sorrow, be his wife, be loved. "I could find *someone* to love me the same way. Whatever happens, I'm not going to waste what time I have worrying. Not when we both want the same thing." Her gaze drifted back to his groin, the evidence of his rampant need. "From what I briefly remember the other morning, your lance is magnificent." Her eyes caressed him with longing. "Just thinking about it turns my insides buttery." The bulge in his breeches beat like a heart, and she knew how ready he had to be. "What more need I do? Just tell me...."

Saying no more, smiling tenderly as she held his gaze, she rose to her feet and let the cover slip slowly away. The chill air made her nipples pebble.

He was deliberately pinning her with his gaze, fighting the temptation in her invitation.

When she thought he would turn and stomp out, his gaze drifted.

Against his will, Dance's gaze slid to her perfectly formed breasts, the woolen blanket further falling away to reveal dusky nipples beautifully aroused, and finally the slender curves of womanhood all flushed and eagerly awaiting more than his scrutiny.

She reached for the tray he held and slipped it from his grasp.

Turning her back on the hunger he couldn't hide in those haunted topaz eyes, Madeline set it on the altar. Then she turned back to him, her face flushed.

"I know you've seen me naked like this. I know it's been a long time for you," she added softly. "I know this can't be easy for you. I'm prepared for you to be in a hurry and I understand. It's all right, though, if you don't callously take me." She smiled encouragingly, "I would like it to be gentle, if you can. Do whatever it is you do that makes one mindless with passion." She saw him struggling, battling his hunger, his eyes blazing. "You can hate me if you want...later."

She watched spellbound, breathless, waiting.

She didn't have to wait long.

Uttering a strangled groan, Dance slowly dropped to his knees before her, his ravaged expression shadowed, his head bowed, one hand going out to brace himself against the altar as if fighting to drag air into his lungs. Her hand reached out, her fingers tenderly sifting though his raven mane as soft as mink. A tender bleeding in her heart stifled her air. And she knew in that second in eternity what rioted her emotions.

It was love.

From the moment he'd held her in her fever, he had stolen into her subconscious to capture her heart. It was all coming back to her. The memory of that comforting blue aura in her feverish dreams was him wrapping a warm spell about her senses. So convinced he was he had lost his power. Why he hadn't lost his gift at all. It was just there underneath the pain, laying dormant, and it had been there to keep her warm and safe.

He said nothing for long minutes and Madeline didn't dare move. Because whatever his decision, his struggle, she would let him go if he couldn't do this. Heaven help her, though, if he denied her it would break her heart. There was no help for it. And because she loved this beautiful, tortured man, she would find a way to hold onto him with whatever memories she could keep.

Blessedly—when she didn't think he was going to—he made the first move.

His touch subtle and gentle, he rested his forehead against her thigh. The texture of his hair was soft on her skin. His breath warm and sending tingles shafting through her to pool in her belly. A heavy sigh released from her lungs sang from her soul. In those first unsure moments, she feared making a sound, making any sudden movement, making a mistake that would drive him away. She could only stand there in her nudity, her heart slamming joyously against her ribs. Her skin tingled, soft hairs on her legs and arms standing erect.

Very quiet, she heard him whisper, "God help me...I'm going to have you."

Silent in response, she dared cup his head between her hands, her instincts guiding her, her breath held in wait for she was frightened. Of scaring him. And it struck her, that amidst all the upheaval of an uncertain future, she'd somehow found her way to him. Being here was somehow her destiny. It was sobering and frightening to think she might have missed him in the forest and been searching forevermore.

Here they were, two perfectly wretched souls.

He was taking care with her and she was thankful, since she couldn't abide lovemaking carried out without thought for her feelings. Nor could she imagine the mating ritual embarked upon more carefully. His hand roamed up her leg, skimming over the taut globe of her buttocks. There he kneaded her pliant flesh with warm fingers. `Twas humbling his care of her, his utmost regard for her, and she could see how easily he must have captivated every maiden's heart with such reverent intimacy. Twas no wonder he was loved the breadth of his world.

His nose nuzzling the apex of her desire riveted her senses, brought a stifled moan to her throat. Her attention was now fully engaged, liquid desire melting through her. Her legs grew weak, her head faint, and it took every ounce of strength she possessed to keep from slipping to the floor. When his nuzzling grew gently bolder, she clutched his head for support against the spasms of sensation he stroked to a wild pitch.

At the height of his exploration, he penetrated her nether lips.

A strangled cry broke from her throat, a softly agonized whimper giving her away. "Help me," she murmured in her throat, her mind delirious, "I feel weak...."

And she mortified herself by swaying off balance.

She didn't get far for he swiftly caught her up.

Dance scooped her into his arms and held her to his heart, blood pounding while he took a moment to regain himself. "I can't take you out of here," he apologized, wishing like hell there was any place else in the world to take her for what he was about to do.

"I know," she breathed contentedly. "We shall use my bed." She gestured lazily toward the tangle of blankets. "If it's all right with you."

He hesitated a moment, apparently still indecisive. But since the alternative was a cold stone floor, he slowly deposited her on the bed. It groaned under his weight as he knelt on the edge. With one hand, he swiftly removed his belt to prevent it from jabbing her, then he followed her down.

She felt him trembling, holding his weight off her, his mouth descending to strip Madeline of her last breath. His tongue tasted her. He hungered for her, and she reveled in his tender exploration, his mouth sucking at her bottom lip—whispering kisses grazing her eyes before moving to the soft shell of her ear. A strangled moan of pleasure sang from her throat. His hot breath in her ear made her wild and impatient, goosebumps springing up all over her flesh. His lance felt hot through his breeches, the texture of fabric soft in contrast to the pulsing heat of his thickness nudging her aroused portal of desire. His breathing was agitated and she took pleasure in being the cause. She liked his weight pressing her into the mattress, the feel of solid muscle beneath her fingers. The way each muscle rippled with the shift of his attention. And she never wanted him to stop, she never wanted this closeness to end.

His mouth sought the tender flesh in the hollow of her throat, brandishing her senses with new sensations. Brushing tantalizing kisses there until she was mindless and needy and clutching him tightly while a fierce aching streaked through her vitals. It was beyond bearing and it was poignant and sweet and painful and she needed surcease desperately.

When his tongue found her nipple, she was trembling on the brink. Then he sucked her breast deep into his mouth. Madeline cried out, intense pleasure streaking through her nerves. It was there she shattered, her hips rising into him of their own accord, seeking what pleasure he promised as the sweet pain of longing engulfed her.

Again...and again...and again, he laved and suckled until she was panting and whimpering his name. He mimicked her grinding, his legs quivering with each powerful thrust. His breeches were damp with her love fluids, the thin barrier of cloth stretched taut—his pulsing cock straining for penetration, craving more friction.

Through the delirium of it all, on the fringes of perception, she heard his response, his labored breathing, the pained growls as he repeatedly mashed his constrained lance against her aching. She felt wet, tormented and feverish and his suffocating gasps of apology made her heart ache.

"Shhh," she panted near his ear. "No apologies. Not for this."

Responding to her plea, he ate a soft trail from one lavished wet nipple to suck and tantalize the other. She whimpered on a suffocated intake of air, the intensity of her feelings hurling her near tears, her hands frantic to divest him of clothes....

So his thickness would be blessedly free and she could take him into her body where she was dying to take his lance deep. Where instincts told her he would quench what ailed her.

The bed groaned as he rose to hurriedly help her remove his breeches, then his beautiful lance was blissfully free and hot and pulsing fiercely against her thigh.

She heard him moan, "I'm sorry, *engyl*," and he was drawing back to fit himself, the tip of his pulsing cock wedging itself in her yearning cleft. Seeking to assuage her aching, she felt him ready himself. He was shaking. And in the intensity of the breath-held moment suspended for the heartbeat, she sensed he was fighting for control. She feared then he might change his mind. It was an awful fear galvanizing her, her hands gently gripping his buttocks, her consent unmistakable. The next moment before he thrust himself into her, she braced for the pain Philip told her would rend her asunder.

And true it was...the tearing pain pushing into her. Oh, God, it hurt...his thickness filling her full. Tears sprang to her eyes as she held still, her body taking him deep....

Dance felt his heart hammering in his gut, stampeding in his groin, his cock relishing every welcoming spasm; the sweet tightness of her sheath swallowing him in waves of rapture...his world on the brink of exploding into a thousand bright stars behind closed eyes. This was heaven the way he remembered it. Only sweeter than he could recall it ever being. The tension draining from him like sands of time. He could die inside her and relish death, relish the gift she presented, his desperation far surpassing hers, his experience keen and monumentally unique. The mating dance, having been withheld for so long, came in a wave of sweet pain releasing him of his long suffered celibacy. It was celibacy, he recognized now, that had held him in bondage for so long he'd almost forgotten. That it could be like this.

That it could be better than food, or sleep, or air.

Every nerve twitching and spiraling and orgasm pounding through his blood until he couldn't breathe.

It was all he could do to keep his weight from crushing the delicate *engyl* of mercy looking shyly up at him. In her eyes glistened unshed tears. Partly for profound joy, partly in pain. Her pain pierced his soul.

With an overwhelming sense of gratitude spilling over,

he felt an indisputable wetness cloud his own vision. "Soon, it will hurt no more," he whispered consolingly above her.

His own pain pulsed through his body. The thick lump in his throat convulsed.

What he felt escaped human capacity for expression.

His body joined to hers was fundamentally the only saneness in life. It was as natural as breathing. And he'd missed it so damned much, he wondered how he had held onto any semblance of sanity at all. Right now he couldn't dredge up even an ounce of guilt for the senseless deflowering of an *engyl*. Dear Christ—he was pouring into her with unchecked recklessness that left him momentarily paralyzed. It was callous and unthinkable should he get her with child. Yet he had not the physical strength to withdraw.

His body shook with a climax so strong it hurt. Her keening cry washed over him as he fell over the edge with her clasped close to his heart.

The only sound in the aftermath was lungs gasping for air. In the back of his mind, he knew the only outcome of such abandon was to give her the benefit of an honorable proposal. Dance looked down at Madeline and found the possibilities strangely appealing. He would no longer be alone, his bed at night empty and cold.

Yet doubt crept upon him. To forsake the memory of one woman for the more convenient one in the flesh would be callously self-serving. His past presented more than one burden. He wouldn't ask Madeline to bear more when she already had enough to shoulder.

In truth, they needed no further complications on top of what awaited.

He'd fulfilled her wish. It was unfortunate the experience was undeniably remarkable—unfortunately more memorable than he would later care to reflect on.

God help him, he already wanted to plunder her again and again, until he grew numb...until he lost himself in her.

Yet if he did what he entertained, where did that leave them?

"I can bear anything, but not regret," she breathed, her gaze cloudy with emotion, adoring and unabashed.

Judging by her incorrigible smile, he was going to regret more than he ever dreamed possible. "The only regret I bear, is the thought of now returning to my bed alone."

His sadness would have to console her, she decided bravely. Affecting a lightness of heart, she gave him an undiminished, if tremulous, smile. "You don't have to leave just yet, do you? I mean"—she blushed profusely—"we could stay abed, could we not, a little while longer? That is, if you don't mind." Frowning, she traced a finger over the marks left on his shoulders by her nails. "I hurt you, again, I fear."

He lowered his head to gently kiss the bridge of her nose. "I never felt it, *engyl*."

"It was because you were lost to lust—the same way I was, weren't you?" She smiled sublimely. "Oh, Dance, making love is wonderful—no, it's better than wonderful. This part, the feel of you inside me, the wonder I feel—there are no words to express it."

Inexplicably, he felt the same. "It can be better for you, *engyl*. I don't want you to misunderstand and think this is the extent of pleasure. I rushed things."

"I'm not so sure it was *you* rushing things. But then you *were* trying so very gallantly to control it." She sighed contentedly. "I'm rather flattered, since it has been so very long for you." To his look of chagrin, she kissed the cleft in his chin, felt the masculine stubble abrade her lips. "Don't worry, I promised never to tell anyone our secret, and I won't. You're completely blameless."

He heard the sincerity in her promise and wondered how she would feel about her promise if her belly were swelling with his child. She had a tremendous capacity for forgiving—for making the best of her situation. When any other woman would be clinging and weeping in fear, Madeline embraced opposition with daunting courage. He couldn't help thinking she would have chosen to endure Owain if faced with the same choice as had Aneira.

True, Aneira hadn't been dealt fairly, she hadn't received the support she sought from her father. According to old rule women were thought of as the spoils of war.

Dance's own mother had been such a pawn, a princess uprooted from her Russki homeland, captured in a boarder raid and sold into slavery. Did she have a choice, Princess Tolstaya would have forsaken all in the name of love.

With the same hot-blooded streak in his veins, Dance had fallen in love with Aneira and got her with child. Never did he regret loving her, until it cost her her life. In contrast, Madeline wanted no protection from him. All Madeline asked for in return was to experience passion. Her one dying wish.

He had taken her in the name of granting her dying wish. He had benefited from her dying wish. She had known he would, and still she encouraged him.

Hell—how could he have been so thoughtless as to risk siring a child on her?

"I should have been in control more, Madeline. I should not have spilled my seed in you." He would have her know his travesty. "I've likely got you with child."

Though only slight, he felt her go still beneath him.

"Is it possible you think"—a smile leapt to her eyes, disarming him—"my first time?"

It wasn't only possible, it was probable. "In my experience, it is more likely than not."

The damning news should have brought her regret. "Then I could be carrying your child right now," she remarked softly while smiling up at him.

She didn't appear the least perturbed, which disconcerted him. "I should prepare a solution for you. One to wash my seed from your body."

"I rather expect it is already too late. Don't you?"

From the mouth of innocence. "You have my sincere apology, *engyl*."

Giving him a stern look, she nipped his chin playfully. "That will be your last apology to me." Then more solemn, she went on, "Besides, I think you are forgetting, I may not need worry about motherhood if Owain has his way."

He glowered at that.

Braced on his elbows, joined still to her body, Dance cupped her head in his hands. While his gesture was reverent with genuine affection, a seething hatred boiled just below the surface. There in silent contemplation, he vowed he would find some way to end her life before he would let Owain violate her. "I don't intend to let him near you."

The resolve in his tone made her suddenly fearful he might do something recklessly heroic. "Please, could we not pass the rest of the evening in a more pleasant way?" Her legs entangled with his, she smoothed her hand down his back, over heated muscle and the fine dusting of hair covering his skin, her tentative smile speaking to him in a language that needed no translation.

Dance could have resisted the temptation to kiss her if

he tried harder. But she was moving beneath him in a way that scattered one's senses. Lust ruled over rationale, and though he had intended to get up and leave immediately, the way her slick sheath was clenching his cock proved a powerful inducement. His mouth covered hers with masterful swiftness, his hunger simmering, her bottom lip gently captured between his teeth, possession once again igniting his blood.

"You're wonderfully swollen, which means you are wanting me still," she taunted against his mouth, her hips grinding against his shaft.

"So there's more you want than *one* dying wish?" his voice rasped with desire, common sense obliterated by a recent taste of plunder. Sharp-seated desire pumped through his veins, his need unquenchable after the long-suffered loneliness, and he might have resisted if his cock wasn't stiff and embedded to the depths of her womb...and the remembered promise of mind-numbing release another few thrusts away.

Desperation goading him, he felt moisture burn his eyes. His state was appalling and nothing he seemed able to do about it, except give into Madeline's wishes for more.

He told himself she didn't know any better.

His teeth scored the tender flesh of her ear lobe, her lush body pressed snugly against him. His hands locked on the globes of her delectable buttocks, his shaft unrepentant...he thrust to the depths of her heart...again... and again...slowly in...and slowly out...each thrust lifting her off the mattress, each whimper of pleasure in his ear spurring him on in an agonizing frenzy of mating. She mercilessly impelled him and he took her like a wild animal in rut. His blood burning, his whispered words solacing and praising and encouraging her to higher planes of surcease and surrender. He teased and played and loved her body with tender attention, his lust engulfing her, carrying her toward the shimmering peak.

He sustained her orgasmic peak for unending long minutes, until her fitful cries of pleasure rent the air and still he gave no quarter, his cock slick and hot and painful and hard, he riveted her world with shattering sweet sensation.

Dazed by passion, her senses alive and screaming with pleasure such as she never thought possible, Madeline held on tight. His face was buried in her hair. His breath hot on her neck, she tightened her arms around him, her heart beating rapidly in rhythm to his and felt the magnitude of wonder split her open.

And she cried out in rapture, her neck arched in shattering splendor as she clawed wildly—her nails leaving a slash of red welts—against the dizzying effects of unrestrained passion.

Clover scented the air, his body slick with sweat sliding against her skin....

When a heartbeat later she plummeted head over heals, he followed her over. Release shafted like needles through his limbs. It traveled up his spine to rush to his brain. His fingers tingled wildly. His toes cramped. Every nerve screaming out in carnal exhilaration. So that he had scant seconds to act before wasting himself. He was erupting as swiftly as he withdrew.

Following on the heels of release, somewhere in the region of his soul, he felt the intense loss of her heated sheath and almost re-entered her immediately.

Instead, Dance lay atop her, his harsh breathing the only sound in the sparsely lit cell, the life of his loins spilling endless streams of semen onto the coverlet between her pale thighs as he grappled for a hold on his world.

And the tears came. Choking him. Lingering sorrow, intense relief, a culmination all coming together—emotion brimming. Some recess of his mind told him he needed to flush his semen from her womb, but that required he sit upright.

"Don't say it," she whispered between gasps of air. "Don't you dare apologize."

He didn't answer her right away for he was fighting for breath.

When at last he could manage it, he rolled to Madeline's side. He lay on his side, his back to the stone wall, one arm draped heavy across her waist, his thigh resting slack atop hers as a sinking sense of peril enveloped him. The irreversible damage he had just done her should have angered him more for it changed everything between them.

"I wasn't going...to apologize," he groaned softly near her ear, his emotions now carefully disembodied.

She smiled, her eyes heavy, surveying him through drowsy lids as she raised her lips to his to bestow him a grateful kiss.

He was spent, the tension gone from his body. The struggle over. And his lashes, she noted sadly, were glossy wet crescents against his skin. She wanted desperately to comfort him, assure him things would be all right. But it wasn't over. She didn't know how things would turn out.

All she knew was that it was criminal he'd denied himself this kind of soul-stirring splendor. But then, of course, she could pretend he'd been saving himself, albeit unknown to him, for the night she stumbled into his path.

Certainly it wasn't that long ago she'd thought him a

pagan forest creature. At the time, it had been no more than a fanciful reflection, but closer to the truth than she had suspected. This man who held love sacred, while others only dreamed of that kind of love for themselves. And just when she'd started to think love wasn't something men held in high esteem. But the Lord of Mists was master unto himself. Fearless. Honor-bound.

Now reduced to availing himself where he could. And poignantly gentle with her in his most ravaged state of need.

The wetness on her neck—his suffering—made her throat convulse with pain. She couldn't bear it—him wishing she was Aneira. Maybe, she consoled herself, he was grieving his faithful companion, Druidh.

"I'm so sorry about Druidh," she whispered into the long silence.

Beside her he remained still, said nothing.

What he felt, whatever his thoughts, she could only guess. She gathered to her breast what comfort she could in sharing his private pain, in being given the unexpected privilege now of understanding.

Did she feel any regret? Honestly as she searched her heart, the answer was an astounding—no. `Twas the curse which brought them together. And together they would somehow survive.

This beautiful man had paid far too dearly, and it was time he was released of his noble bondage—the crushing guilt.

And if, as she suspected, he left behind traces of his seed to grow in her womb—careful as he might have preferred to be, she would be carrying his child. A secret smile touched her lips. She could imagine the babe in her arms.

A beautiful pagan child with amber eyes and silky black curls.

Dance shifted his weight to accommodate her better, his mouth tender in nipping the delicate skin behind her ear. "I'm not going to let anything happen to you," he murmured so quietly she almost didn't hear him.

Coming out of her dreamy musing, Madeline felt her heart race with the dread she heard in those words. "Where do you think he is right now?" While reality came crashing down around her once more, she unconsciously pressed closer to him as if by melding herself to him, she might hide from what she had no wish to confront. Not yet, anyway, after being so recently awakened to love.

"He'll be far away from here...." Owain had had enough time to be miles away by the time Druidh was discovered. Likely the bastard was out there waiting—hoping Dance would be just furious enough to rush headlong into whatever danger awaited. Whatever trap he devised, it would be for both Dance and Madeline. For what satisfaction was there for Owain in slaying Madeline without a witness?

Dance didn't tell her he found Druidh hanging *inside* the courtyard. Which meant Owain had found a way inside. By the same route Owain probably used to breach the fortress to get to his wife and son the last time. He thought about Madeline, and decided it served no purpose to alarm her more than she was already. "I know you don't want to hear this, but the only way I know to keep you safe is to keep you locked up down here." He anticipated her next question before she even voiced it. His decision a heavy burden, his instincts screaming at him to the contrary, he nonetheless said, "But you can't stay in the dungeon indefinitely. And therein lies my problem—"

Madeline tightened her hold on him. "How long do you think we have before he finds a way to get to me?"

He wanted to refute all possibility of that but knew he couldn't. "I wish I had somewhere else I could take you," he said aloud to himself, a very real threat backing him into a corner. "I've thought about giving you the one key to the door. The dungeon is impregnable. That way he couldn't get to you. That way the key couldn't fall into the wrong hands."

The concern in his voice fed her own fear. "Let me go with you—follow you about. If I'm with you, you'll know where I am at all times. I can help you—I vow I won't get in the way—I won't slow you down—I'll do exactly as you say—"

"Madeline—"

"Please," she implored.

His expression reflected stern vulnerability as conflicting emotions danced over his features. She could see him wanting to deny her even while he regarded her with a raw tenderness that stole her heart.

There was but a moment's hesitation, then he slowly lowered his mouth to hers. His kiss spoke the words he didn't voice, his kiss imparting a silent promise...in turns consoling and desperate, the heat of his lips moist on hers, his breath warm and stirring. She wanted to rail at the heavens, the unfairness of fate. She could die right here in his arms, right now with a smile on her lips.

Madeline snuggled into his warmth and suffered in painful silence. She knew her life before Wolfglyn was lost to her, she had accepted that days ago. Each day spent now with Dance filled the void she spent missing her family. She could no more leave Dance behind than she could go back to being Miss Madeline Carlton from Boston.

To some degree, she supposed Dance had changed, as well.

It was strange how not that long ago, her pagan in armor had been all harsh edges and cold steel. But at the moment, with his shield down, she saw him much the same way he must have been before tragedy turned on him. The healer underneath the armor—a compassionate man, caring and loving and generous in his affection.

Love made her weak and fearful and suddenly every silly thing that mattered to her before seem inconsequential. The thought of somehow losing him terrified her.

His lips grazed her jaw. Against her cheek, his mouth close to her ear he softly commanded, "If I agree, I will be merciless, *engyl*. I won't compromise. It will be my way or none. If you break trust with me, I will have to punish you. There is no other way." His voice dropped to a whisper, sorrow shadowing his tone. "I can't risk losing you...."

She felt a moment's unutterable joy...before she realized he was speaking in terms of his past. Pain welled in her throat. "You won't lose me," she assured him hoarsely.

"I can't let you go running about the castle—"

Tears burned her eyes. "Then I'll need a leash—"

He smiled against her ear. "I've got just the gold chain for you. Lightweight, fitted with emeralds, it would make a nice collar—"

Bearing her pain in silence, wanting nothing more than to be loved by this beautiful man, she shivered as delicious heat tingled through her. "Perhaps you'll also be wanting a whip to keep me in line—"

A gravity returned to his tone. "I won't lose you, " he repeated.

"Nor I you," she answered shyly, holding him tight against an uncertain future. "And you will not mind, since we must be together night and day, if I sleep in your bed with you?" She forced a levity she was far from feeling. "And you'll tell me if I snore?"

She felt a margin of tension leave his body finally, her frivolity easing some of his concerns. A velvety rumble of laughter fanned her neck. "I suppose, I could find ways to keep you awake."

"Mmmm, there's that." Trying to be brave, she shoved her pain away.

"My very own love chattel."

"I may need a nap in the middle of the day," she whispered, "now that you mention it."

A soft growl in her ear. "You can count on it."

Suitably distracted and danger relegated to some obscure place in the back of her mind, she could live for the moment. "So eager, my lord enchanted, indeed, I'm very lucky to be your chattel." Her body tingled and she shivered pleasantly at the thought. "In fact, to show my appreciation, I may even polish your armor and clean your boots."

He grinned. "God help me, my very own *engyl* at a whim."

"And I can be most grateful," she cheerfully responded, squirming under him and bringing his attention jolting back to their present state of disrobe. Predictably, her squirming enflamed his blood, his desire hardening with little provocation. He sucked in his breath as her eager fingers closed around him. "I can see," he breathed tightly, "I'm going to need to reward you somehow for your good behavior...." Her hand moving down on him momentarily stifled his air, cutting off what more he might have said... his muscles quivering, his hips flexing under a euphoria that he gave in to willingly...and his last thought before lust clouded his every thought...was of *engyls.*

Thank you merciful saints for engyls.

In his present condition he didn't question his attraction, nor the bond of understanding that came from exposing one's darkest fears. All fears culminating so that nothing stood between them any longer. For a time nothing else existed. They made love long into the night, the flames of desire keeping the dungeon heated, keeping at bay the encroaching fears — their passion fierce and all consuming in the chamber that had previously held nothing but pain. They made love until dawn gave way to a new day and with it a fatalistic sense of peace. A peace as fragile as mists against that which threatened to destroy all in its path.

GARLANDS OF FLOWERS : —
Symbolic of assemblage of higher emotions and virtues,
tokens of joy and gladness in the buddhic consciousness.

13.

Early the next morning, Madeline was roused from sleep by the loss of Dance's body warmth. She squeezed her eyes tight, willing away the start of a new day. Willing time to stop. It was fruitless, she knew. She lay there, shoring up each blissful hour she'd spent with him. His magnificent body joined to hers in fiercely possessive ways. As her head cleared of fog, she vaguely felt a nagging stitch of pain between her legs. Her maidenhead, or rather the loss of it.

For a while longer she laid abed, curled into a ball against the invading chill of another day, and reflected on her wondrous dreams. She and Dance alive and well, the spring rains drizzling outside while within the warmth of the castle their children romped wildly about the chamber, fierce feats of swordplay going on, shrieks of bubbling laughter peeling around the bedchamber. Her beautiful pagan giving chase, his deep laughter warming her joyous heart. In that dream, she even allowed herself a moment's contentment.

Nothing would take him from her, she'd decided that already. Her boundless love, her deep conviction had grown with his each tender caress throughout the heat of night. So that by this morning her beautiful pagan was implanted firmly in her heart where she could nurture her love for him, if in no other way but in secret. This morning in the aftermath of blazing passion, she knew in her heart she belonged with Dance. Here at Wolfglyn. The only shadow on the dream was the ever-lurking presence of evil. Evil she would fight with her last breath, if need be, for Dance.

A shuffle of noise, a fastening of a buckle interrupted her musing. Her pagan was near. With her eyes still closed, she could feel him standing at the foot of the bed. Yes, and she could smell him. His clover. As if he'd been out rolling around in the dew-dampened fields.

Today he would be dressing to slay the evil troll alone. He didn't know it yet, but this time she would be at his side. So ordained by a mutually pleasant arrangement.

"Promise me, when the fighting starts, you will run. If something happens, I need to know you will get away from here in time. I want you to make for the village. Don't look back..." And he'd made her promise him, while she was crying out in rapture loud enough to bring the rafters down. Smiling secretly to herself, she knew she couldn't really complain. The extent of his resourcefulness had brought a flushed glow to her world, which now accounted for the contentment settled deep in that place where she held him in her heart.

Though she knew he was up and readying himself for the day, Madeline wasn't yet ready to get out of bed. She wasn't adapted to endless love play, she ached to her bones, not to mention in other places. Oh, if she could but lay abed just a while longer. She could go on dreaming of things happy and noble, like fairy tales and castles and life with a pagan healer.

Madeline's eyes flew open as soon as she felt him kissing her there.

Her half-hearted objection dissolved under his mouth.

She was melting, her flesh tender and oh, his tongue so utterly tantalizing. She felt the stubble of his unshaven jaw abrading her where he was nuzzling her. Her hands sought hold. Like a flower opening to a cozy ray of sunshine, her thighs fell apart for him, her fingers clutching his head. In her fists, his hair felt like silk, his tongue...dear heaven... that perfectly wicked tongue....

"I thought you might like a hot bath before your *brecwast?*" he murmured against her velvety pelt, her squirming reminiscent of last night. Scented with his own fluid, she tasted like a vessel of passion. A musky sweetness filled his brain, his gaze shuttered, his regard focused on her dusky nipples wanting some of the same attention.

Lord in heaven, he could bed her again in a heartbeat.

With his loins throbbing and his cock standing stiff, he very nearly crawled atop her. But her swollen cleft was yet too tender for more ravishment and he didn't want to do her permanent injury. More a priority at the moment, she needed to adjust to her new role of dutifully obeying him.

He was smiling as he disengaged her hands and got to his feet. Straightening to his full height, Dance stood looking down on her with a raw hunger that couldn't be masked.

"We don't have to go out...." she replied around a stifled yawn, her hand lifted, reaching for him.

He clasped her fingers and when she tried to pull him into bed again, he instead turned her palm to his lips. His tongue flicked her, tasted her saltiness. He smelled himself on her skin, his body reacting with raw hunger.

In the next unexpected move, he deftly dragged her from the bed to her feet. Taken by surprise, Madeline laughed up at him with unabashed delight, her body melting into him. Well warmed by his nearness, she hardly noticed the chill as she wiggled enticingly against the enormous length of him.

Her little cry of protest fell on deaf ears as he hauled her into his arms and without any warning carried her out into the corridor naked as a newborn babe.

"Are you mad?" She scrambled to cover herself, her arms covering her breasts as she shot him a rueful smile. "What about Hywel—"

"Off collecting eggs and feeding the flock. Relax, *engyl*, we've got the whole castle to ourselves for a time. Now which would you prefer first? A bath or *brecwast?*"

"Bath," she answered in his own tongue. Having already guessed which she'd prefer, he was marching up the climbing staircase with her.

Dreadfully self-conscious, she hugged herself, her nakedness suddenly making her shy. They emerged from the shadowed passage into the foyer off the dining hall. A blush stole over her as she looked quickly about for Hywel.

Within minutes Dance had traversed another stairway to the upper chambers where twin towers bracketed a familiar corridor. At the corridor's end awaited the master bedchamber. The bedchamber where she'd first awakened next to him, and where she had her first look at a man's magnificent lance. It was hard to believe that was a mere four days ago.

How could she have guessed she'd now be consorting with him?

The two of them shackled to one another out of necessity—Madeline dependent on him for protection and shelter and food.

She saw the bathtub right away. Steam danced upon the water's surface. Her gaze swung around the room in quick survey. On the bed, next to the fine silk chemise, she spied a gown. Ice blue velvet and simple in design. The bodice was cut low, the fit designed to cling to her body. Well-preserved, the skirt of the gown flared out in a sort of demi train that proclaimed it very old. A fine jeweled belt, one she believed she once heard called a girdle, lay atop the chemise. Its precious stones twinkled in the sunlight streaming across the bed. All bathed and dressed, she might easily resemble a maiden from medieval times. Dressed to slay the evil troll hidden somewhere beyond the castle in the silvery mists. All she could pray was she'd be up to the task of facing the enemy when the time came.

By the time Madeline finished her bath, she was wrinkled all over like a shriveled plum and ready for that *brecwast* Dance mentioned. She was just wondering about him, her eyes half-closed in drowsy repose and her hair swirling about her shoulders in the water when she heard him returning, his footsteps quiet in the hall outside the master bedchamber.

She was waiting for him with a content smile. He returned her smile with a patient one as he nudged the door shut behind him, balancing a silver tray in one hand. Madeline was seated in the tub and couldn't see what feast he held aloft. "Mmmm. *Brecwast* sounds divine," she remarked eagerly, her stomach rumbling after what felt like days of fasting.

The disappointment on her face when he set the tray of assorted glass vials on the nearby footstool, was almost comical. "Where's *brecwast*?" She was rising to her knees in the tub, prepared if she had to, to march down to the kitchen and rustle up her own meal.

He held up a hand to halt her. "Stay put." Then he was filling a flask with something that could only be described as offensive-looking. It smelled worse than ever. Madeline quickly pinched her nose.

Wary, taking in his speculative look, she shook her head. "Don't you dare come near me with that." He looked engrossed in what he was doing. "What is it, anyway?"

"Sterilizing salt." Dance was busy counting drops of another mixture he dribbled into a long-necked flask. "You need but to lay back in the water. This won't take but a minute."

"Sterilizing salt—for what?" Eyeing him carefully, she just subdued the urge to bolt for the door. She didn't lay down in the tepid bath water. "Whatever you have in mind, you can forget it. I'm not ill or injured—I won't drink it—"

He turned his head to take in her mutinous stance. "Trust me, *engyl*, you won't be drinking this. It goes between your legs."

Madeline let go a bark of laughter at the ridiculous suggestion. Until she realized he was serious. Laughter died on her lips as the full import of his intent washed over her like a bucket of cold water. "Dear God, you can't mean to use that to—"

Oh, but he did, she saw it now, and the unexpected sense of loss tearing at her heart matched the haunted reflection in his topaz eyes. The painful truth lanced her wide open.

How could he do this? He was a giver of life, a healer who would detest the very thought. What he was asking her to do went against his every principal. Her more rational mind, of course, understood he would not want to leave his seed in her where it could give life. After his last painful experience, he was leaving nothing to chance. She knew he was right, still it hurt her deeply to have to accept he didn't love her with the same heedless passion he had loved Aneira.

He was offering her the flask, his gaze compelling her to be sensible.

Don't ask this of me, she wanted to rail. *You can't want this.*

Even knowing her love wasn't returned she wanted to plead he give her a fighting chance.

Her heart aching, she didn't want to wash his baby from her womb.

The sad thing was, she knew he was being practical. So how could she not do the honorable thing by him after he'd been so gracious to accommodate her dying wish?

"You're right. Forgive me. Of course, I'll do as you think best." She wasn't going to cry, she bloody well wouldn't. "Here, I'll do it," she mumbled hoarsely.

Her insides wrenching, she took from his hold the odd-looking pewter piston with an elongated bone nozzle. It was fashioned like one of those offending reservoirs. She remembered Philip the one time he'd been ill and doubled over in pain. Nanny had used on him just such an instrument, while Madeline listened outside his door—thinking him dying, her heart breaking, his hollering and cursing unbearable.

Feeling her legs tremble, Madeline turned her back to Dance and sank to her knees in the water. Tears flooded her eyes. "What do I do?" she asked over her shoulder in a small voice.

Dance closed his eyes, his resolve close to wavering. When he stood there teetering on the precipice of doing the unthinkable, he dragged air into his lungs and at the last moment, drew himself up. God, if she wasn't the sweetest possible form of revenge.

He had to remember that. How could he bear holding another babe in his arms again?

Dance opened his eyes, his gaze following the proud line of her spine...and could almost feel the silken texture of her heated skin under his fingers. He could recall it all—the heavy fullness of her breast in his palm, the way her each slender curve felt under his hand—and the wild abandon of her passion flourishing under his touch. In his ear, he could hear the catch in her breath when he sank himself to her heart. Her impatient whimpers when she peaked. Her nails scoring his back as he pressed that finite inch more. The delicious pain and pleasure melded in sensation. And to peer into her eyes as gray as mists—God in heaven—to behold the sated smile on her lips, and taste her tears of release when he was holding himself deep against her womb.

As unforgivable his part in this, as much as it made him sick to go through with it, he wouldn't change his course. He would not allow her dying wish to end up a young woman's shame to be dragged through the streets. "Gently, *engyl.* Hold your finger over the top and shake. Then you put it—"

"I know"—she interjected tremulously—"between my legs."

He waited for her to continue, but she just sat there unmoving.

Giving her privacy, abhorred to watch, Dance moved away, his steps carrying him the safe distance to the window. What was wrong with her? God knew, she wouldn't want to be breeding when she returned to her family.

Warmed by a roaring fire in the hearth, he quietly gazed upon the landscape below in the drizzling mists. He could smell the way the rains scented the air on an early winter's day. Feel the chill draft sifting in through the tiny fissures in the walls, reminding him of tiny fissures of mortality notched upon his soul. He stood with his back to her lest his resolve weaken. "It would not go easy for you, Maddie, if your family discovered you were increasing when you returned home. You don't want a child, not this way...."

Pride stiffened Madeline's spine even as her throat lumped with pain. For pity sake, he'd only spilled himself inside her the first time. Even Aneira could not have gotten with child her first time. "I'll take care of it. You can go. See to *brecwast*—see if Hywel needs help."

Brecwast turned out to be a quiet affair with Sheva waiting patiently under the table for scraps. Hywel did most the talking, which was fine with Madeline, since it left her with nothing more than an occasional comment to add. As it was, she felt ill to her soul. Her throat convulsed every time she thought about the unnatural deed she'd done.

It was beyond foolish to expect his love in return. She could never replace his wife. She saw that now, painful as the revelation.

Dance sat across the narrow table from her, his expression unreadable, and yet imparting more than he suspected. The pain of his past weighed down upon them both like a suffocating cloak. Was this it, then? Was this how lovers behaved after a dazzling night of pleasure? How could one go on like this? she wondered. The strained smiles, the pretended indifference, the pounding in her vitals at the mere thought of his thick lance filling her body. Simply being near him making her want to scream with frustration.

If she were miserable, he looked equally preoccupied with his own demons, his brows drawn into a scowl. The fierceness she'd come to recognize behind which he hid a deep sorrow. Certain she was, he still wanted her—she'd seen his glorious arousal straining his breeches in that fleeting glance she stole when she stepped from her bath. His fists clenched at his sides, his amber gaze alight with hunger while she had brazenly exposed herself at every opportunity.

It was torture of the worst kind, this pang of hunger clawing at her vitals. Newly awakened passion was an unruly child of havoc. It held a power to make one squirm.

Certainly, as new to her as was being his lover, she could see now how a month or two of this unbridled yearning would have caused young lovers grave suffering.

Merciful God—was Dance going to make her last wish unbearable? The question churned around in her mind with regularity through breakfast. Her one consolation that he might have recklessly fallen in love with her, were he not burdened with the past, had to sustain her.

He had changed since her bath. For *brecwast*, he wore a black velvet tunic and black leather breeches that hugged his muscled legs, his long raven mane wet, freshly washed. He wore no adornment, no ring, no evidence of his noble birth other than an inherit grace. Looking upon him recalled to her every inch of masculine muscle, the fine dusting of hair covering his chest, the crisp way it tickled her when he was joined to her body.

Dance held his own counsel throughout the meal.

She watched him in silence while she picked at her plate and wondered if ever he would want another heir. Occasionally he would slip a chunk of veal to Sheva under the table. Sheva was wagging her tail; the soft fur brushing Madeline's thigh. Before long, Madeline followed Dance's lead. Minute by minute her confidence grew and it gave her immense satisfaction to partake in so brave an act. It had to be a sign she was growing more at ease in Sheva's presence. She suspected Dance knew he was helping forge a trust between them. If nothing else, it helped keep her mind occupied for a while and off her worries.

Hywel, bless his heart, kept the conversation from dying, sometimes talking to Sheva, sometimes answering for her. It kept the meal from becoming a total disaster. For her part, Madeline was the picture of calm. It wasn't easy being subjected to Dance's watchful eye.

The absolute worst part was pretending not to notice each time he halted in his meal to listen for the faintest sound.

The clock chiming in the hall made him flinch. Howling outside actually made him pause in chewing until the noise diminished. Whether a rustle of wind or a groan in the rafters, Dance was glancing up from his plate every ten minutes to slide a look at the shadowy foyer. It wasn't long before he had her ready to jump out of her skin.

Madeline set her napkin aside with a forced calm and addressed him. "I don't know about you, but I would very much like to visit the stable to look in on Ole Bones."

In chorus, Hywel and Dance both said, "That's outside."

Sighing, throwing up her hands, she peered from Hywel to Dance. "All right. What would *you* two like to do?"

Into the awkwardness, Hywel cleared his throat. "Ifan here plays the flute."

Madeline looked at Hywel, stupefied. She swiveled her attention back to her silent *brecwast* companion. "You play the flute?" she asked incredulously, then realizing how rude her surprise, she quickly recovered, "I would love to hear you play something."

It was the first time Dance gave her his full regard. "Perhaps when I get back."

Madeline quelled. "Are you going somewhere?"

"I must hunt *prynhawn ma*, this afternoon, before it grows dark." To her sudden anxious look, he said softly, "I will need you to lock yourself in the dungeon while I'm gone—" She was shaking her head, her protest ready, but she didn't get to voice it fast enough "—Madeline, you promised me." His voice dropped to a soft rumble. "Please. I would have you safe, *engyl*."

When he used that seductive murmur on her, it transported her back to bed and the velvety tone he used when coaxing her to a fevered-pitch. "Can't I go with you?" She gave him a breathless sigh of despair. "I can hunt, I can help you. I swear I'll be good." Unconscious of her action, she leaned forward in entreaty. "Please, say yes."

His gaze was drawn to the soft swell of her pale bosom straining the low neckline. She could have been his wife sitting there in that gown, her slender curves molded by loving hands under the palest of blue velvet, her skin flushed and her eyes begging him to satisfy what ailed her. He wanted to dismiss Hywel. He wanted to lay her upon the table and run his fingers through those silken tresses the rich color of autumn...while lower he would stroke her soft mound of damp curls until she was panting and writhing. She would smell like soap, her skin fragrant and clean, her woman's heat lushly swollen. He could think of a number of secluded niches in the forest upon a bed of damp leaves perfect for pleasuring her.

He cleared his suddenly dry throat. "Must you tempt me?"

"What?" she asked innocently, a sparkle in her eye telling him she guessed the path of his thoughts, her breasts overflowing the low neckline.

The two of them hardly noticed when Hywel rose to his feet to mumble something having to do with rounding up Sheva's mother and sisters. The chore needed his attention right away.

Dance waited until he had her alone. Curbing lustful cravings, removing something from his pocket, he slid it to the middle of the table, his gaze holding hers.

Intrigued by what he held in his fist, Madeline lowered her gaze. He opened his palm to reveal a heavy brass key affixed to a gold chain. The key, she suspected, to the dungeon.

She looked up at him in question.

"We can eat no more veal," he explained. "If we do, I won't have one sheep left come spring. Hywel would never find the traps, even if he knew where to look. This is something I have to do myself." He held his palm open to her. "Take the *allwedd, engyl*. Lock yourself in."

Her hand reached out to cover his outstretched palm, her pulse pounding. Panic dilated her pupils, darkening the gray irises black. "You could take me with you."

He felt a moment's hesitation, her plea almost tempting. "You have no idea how hard this is for me. Leaving you behind...." And what her thoughts imparted, flashed before his eyes—fear—death—grief—as if her each thought sped through him.

The shock of it, the strength of the vision was almost painful. The seer in him felt each fleeting emotion. It was as if a river opened up inside him, his long suppressed gift pouring through. It came unexpected. The sight almost as strong as it was before the deaths. And intuitively, he knew it was back, like a long lost friend returned to him. Only he wasn't sure if he could trust it, yet.

A faint grin curled his lips, the wonder of what just happened slow to rouse in him unbidden joy. "You're safe here, *engyl*," he assured her. "While in the forest you would be an easy target. Sorry, you must stay behind...."

"But—"

He arched a black brow that halted her appeal. "Surely you haven't forgotten, already, the rules of this arrangement?"

Biting her lip, lowering her gaze, she shook her head. "I haven't forgotten," she whispered contritely.

Dance got to his feet and stood over her.

She raised her head, gave him an equally daunting look. "You must be careful for me, then. Won't you?"

A twitch of his lips and he was grinning. What a fierce little *engyl* he had on his hands. What in the name of heaven, he wondered, was he to do with himself once he returned her to her family? Unfortunately, the answer wasn't as neatly forthcoming as it might have been mere days ago. "I'll do my best..." And his hand came up to cup her nape, gently draw her to her feet. He slid the fine gold chain bearing the key over her head to settle between her breasts. "I trust you will be waiting for me in the dungeon when I get back...."

"I wish you didn't have to go—"

Slowly his lips came down on hers—effectively silencing her. He claimed her mouth in ravaged possession, and she kissed him back as would a frantic child seeking comfort, his body crushed tight to hers, his hold on her most desperate. It was a poignant kiss of realism. He hadn't intended to scare her, but he knew she was feeling it too. The helpless sense of impending peril.

The heated tension existing between them intensified the desperation.

It curled languidly through Madeline's blood, and her fingers clutched his arms in urgent appeal. "And I trust you will come back to me in one piece...." she whispered against his mouth.

Cunning in her timing, Sheva nudged Madeline's thigh with her muzzle. The gesture affectionate in nature, indicative of friendship. Madaline gave silent thanks, Sheva's presence oddly comforting. Sheva would protect him. Sheva would not let anyone harm him.

Dance ended the kiss first, and Madeline stifled a small cry of objection.

Her sadness unsettling him, he gave her a brief kiss to the end of her nose. Then he reluctantly turned her in the direction heading back to the dungeon deep in the belly of the castle. "Don't fret, *cariad*," he murmured in her hair, "I'll come back in one piece."

Through the fog of her fear, she heard him call her 'love' in his own language. It was just a figure of speech, like when he called her 'angel', and though she knew better than to read anything into it, it still gave her unimaginable pleasure. She wanted to voice her love and see his reaction, but she wasn't that brave. So instead she slid him a parting glance, ripe with feeling.

Dance smiled reassuringly as he gave a playful swat to her backside to send her on her way. "Remember, don't unlock the door for anyone."

Madeline could barely see where she was going, but she held her head high, her tears undetected as she made herself walk calmly from the dining hall. To her left, as she passed the foyer, she glimpsed Hywel trailed by three unfamiliar fur forms. Her feet hurried as she made for the dark portal to the dungeon. She heard him call out to her that he would be down later to keep her company. She nodded acknowledgement, then disappeared around a corner.

Only when she reached the dungeon did she let herself weep. She gave vent to the emotions strangling her. The key locking her in was tossed upon the altar as she flung herself onto the bed. Where she sobbed into her pillow. In the chill cellar, she hugged the blanket around herself, and tortured herself wishing with all her heart Dance could love her even half as much as he loved Aneira. Feeling abandoned, she could stand being alone in the dungeon no more, the smell of him lingering on the bedding. Reminding her how beautiful the last two days had been.

She'd wait half an hour.

It would be her first time out in days.

She was near crazy being confined.

She would stay out of sight, she told herself, while watching from the battlement for Dance to return. As long as she remained within the castle walls she was safe. Besides, she knew he wouldn't have gone hunting if he thought there was immediate danger.

Half an hour, she repeated to herself. *That's all I want.*

She'd only be out long enough to stretch her legs, get some air.

Dance need never know.

A gust of chill wind whipped her hair in her face as she flattened her back to the stone wall in the late afternoon shadows slanting across the courtyard. Her hand went to the key resting against her chest, her heart pounding excitedly. Listening a minute, she peered about the inner yard. One corner of the yard snagged her attention. Newly churned earth topped the small mound where Druidh now rested beneath a stick cross. A brittle shiver raced down her spine as she looked about the courtyard to assure herself she was alone. The bailey looked quiet and deserted.

The feel of sunlight, though diminishing, offered her scant warmth, but she reveled in it just the same. Madeline turned her face to the sky with closed eyes and breathed deep the scent of fresh air. Earth. Wet stone. And freedom in which to bask. She hadn't thought one could smell freedom, but she did. Nothing could make her regret this one indiscretion. The cloak she borrowed from the foyer, one of Dance's, hung off her shoulders to drag the ground. It provided adequate protection from the chill temperatures.

She opened her eyes. Beyond the machicolated parapet she saw in the distant sky angry storm clouds gathering. Winter was approaching. She sighed. Soon the Atlantic crossing would grow fierce. Her brothers would be preparing *The Boston Lady* for the return trip home. By now, they would have unloaded the hold and made a substantial profit on the steam winding engines. Did they still wait for her return? And her father. Was he yet strong enough for the voyage home? Philip—did he survive the beating Leroy gave him when he found her gone?

Did they search for her? Miss her?

A twinge of sadness darkened her thoughts of them. She'd thought several times about somehow getting a missive to them. Then she just as cowardly talked herself out of it.

What would she tell them, anyway—that she'd fallen in love with a Welshman, that she'd become his leman and she wanted to stay with him? She knew her brothers. They'd bodily drag her back to Llandeglay and set a hasty course for home—and she'd never see Dance again. She could rail to the heavens all she wanted and not be given a chance to explain. Once back in Boston, she'd be heavily escorted until she was married off to the first eligible suitor—and his silence handsomely rewarded in gold coin. She would bear his touch while missing her wild Welsh healer. Her husband would get his children on her, and remind her every day, that he was obliged to keep her shame quiet as long as she stayed faithful to him the rest of her miserable life.

Her independence would be stripped from her as soon as she returned to Boston.

And what of Dance? Would he even care or try to intervene—or just let her brothers bully her into leaving?

God in heaven, she needed to warn Dance. If they survived, she must not forget to warn him about Leroy's temper. No matter how outnumbered she might be, whatever she did, she simply would not allow them to string him up.

A sudden cold gust whirled dried leaves against her face. A tiny branch stung her cheek, her attention returning to the growing ferocity of the storm. She wasn't yet ready to face the dungeon. She sent up a silent prayer for Druidh and hoped he hadn't suffered unmercifully. Across the open courtyard, Madeline spotted shelter. Quickly, she drew the cloak's hood over her head to shield against the elements and made a run for it. Thunder rumbled over her head.

The door was stuck but finally gave way with the last shove. Inside at last, her lungs gasping, she hurried to shut out the howling wind. The force of the storm had grown. For a moment, she worried she would have strength enough to get it closed. Struggling, after putting all her weight into it, she finally succeeded.

Madeline was shivering, her fingers icy cold. She took

a relieved breath and hugged herself as she turned to face the room.

Her heart stopped mid-beat, her eyes going round in astonishment. Her first thought, she was in a place of worship. Or rather she saw now, a shrine. A shrine of vast importance, she realized as her shock subsided. She stood rooted not daring to move, her gaze fixed on the portrait of a woman and child. She knew instinctively it was his wife.

In the woman's arms was a child. It was Madeline's child, the one she saw herself imagining earlier. A pagan child with amber eyes, his hair as black as coal—it was Dance looking back at her from the infant's eyes.

Heart pounding, Madeline lifted her gaze to the woman's face.

Envy, pain, jealously, all the emotions swamped her. Aneira was exquisite.

Like fine china, delicate and fragile, she was everything Madeline expected and more. She was the woman to whom Dance gave his heart. Her beauty flawless, her flowing long hair pale as a winter mist. Her remarkable eyes the color of heather. Everything about her radiated serene contentment. Her shy smile intimate. By her expression, she had to be posing for Dance. Love expressed in every gesture. The garden behind her in the portrait was vivid with spring flowers. She would have died shortly after the painting was done.

A foreboding shiver raced down Madeline's spine at the thought.

This woman brought the death of so many dreams. And Madeline's fragile happiness was fast crumbling.

Dance had deeply loved this beautiful woman, he still loved her. Dance's son would have been six years old if he'd been spared.

Owain, demented and numbed by bitterness, he had to have wanted very badly to possess this beautiful woman. From what she'd seen and heard already, she didn't doubt Owain had tried to bend her to his will. What Owain had felt wasn't love, not when it destroyed. Aneira must have sensed that in her betrothed. Dance on the other hand already knew how his father was, which explained his reluctance to interfere where it would be foolish to do so.

Madeline stood there trying to imagine Aneira here at Wolfglyn. The castle as it was back then, a thriving stronghold. Dance in love. His gift for healing. How he might set a broken bone, stitch up a wound, bring an infant into the world. His calling alone would have gained him everyone's respect. He would have lived the life of a noble lord. Worn the finest of linen next to his skin. His family's possessions many. Their wealth enormous. His table would have groaned under the weight of gold plates and candelabra. Precious stones set in the hilt of his sword, worn on his finger, adorning the clasp of his cloak.

All of the wealth and wild Welsh beauty of a rugged land inherited by God's favored wild one. So named Ifan, Lord of Mists. Guardian of the forest and keeper of wolves.

To Madeline — he was simply the man she loved.

If she hadn't felt the full impact of unrequited love before, it was staring her now in the face.

Aneira's shrine was Dance's tribute to love. Madeline could see his affection in every detail. The placement of several beeswax tapers in long-legged stands — now left smoldering after being blow out — they surrounded the painting as if there to keep his family's memory alive. At the base of the candles were scattered wild flowers. Likely put there by Dance himself. There was a kneeling bench flanked by more candles and clumps of wilted heather, where Dance would spend his time in prayer. A thick carpet of brocade blue to warm the stone floor beneath his feet. The space adjoining Aneira's portrait held her personal items. A finely-carved chest. Crested silver hairbrush, mirror and a strand of pearls atop a mahogany dresser. In its own special place next to the pearls was a plated length of her pale hair, bound by blue ribbons at each end. It was one of those Welsh traditions, Madeline read about, to braid the hair of the deceased for keeping.

A small jeweled chest sat atop the bed in the middle of the white lace coverlet. Inside the chest would be his wife's jewelry—each piece he'd given her. Their wedding rings.

Something, Madeline thought sadly, she would never have.

The weight of despair filled her with such melancholy she couldn't breathe.

Never would there be a shrine like this for her.

Her tears spilled over, trailed down her cheeks.

She had no one to love her like this.

Dear God, she would die unloved.

The strain of the past weeks bore down on her, draining the last of her feeble courage, the floor under her feet wavering....

Grieving for herself, she turned and stumbled for the door and somehow wrenched it open. A cold blast of rain pelted her face. A bracing gasp and she darted out into the pouring rain, her feet carrying her without conscious thought...her hem slapping puddles. She was out of breath when she reached the foyer, her insides heaving as she ran headlong down the stairwell—half stumbling down the steps carrying her to the dungeon and safety.

She just made it inside...her bed within sight.

And she was sinking to the floor before she could reach it....

SLAUGHTER OF ENEMIES : —
A symbol of the subdual and dissipation of the passions,
desires, and illusions of the lower nature, which are the
foes of the Higher Self.

14.

The crashing of wood, the banging of a door resounded through the stone walls.

Dance stood on the thresh-hold, his hair slicked to his face, water dripping from the hem of his cloak to pool at his feet. His lungs gasping, his heart thumping hard—he'd just left the sanctuary after finding the door wide open to the rain pouring in. He'd spent some minutes searching for Madeline, praying fiercely...his search seeming endless... time suspended in a void of fear and confusion and panic. He'd come back to find every last sheep slaughtered, chicken carcasses dotting the courtyard, blood running like crimson rivers over the ground. Fear driving him wild as he ran for the castle.

And what did he find—the damned door unlocked!

He shed his cloak in one swift move. He should beat her for disobeying him in this!

And yet, as he rushed to kneel on the floor beside her crumpled body he felt such relief in finding her, his anger evaporated.

Hywel had followed him, his legs more feeble and therefore taking him longer to manage the stairs. He stood out of breath and bent over just inside the door.

Dance glanced up wordlessly to see his relief mirrored and Hywel going down on his knees to huddle at her feet. "Is she...?" He couldn't voice the words.

"Alive, *Ydw*. And I don't see blood," Dance answered and turned back to Madeline as Hywel praised the saints. "Bring Sheva in, put the others with her. Secure the doors. Can you do that?"

"*Ydw*, I go now." Hywel pushed to his feet, and stepping over the discarded wet cloak, hurried out.

Quickly removing his gloves, Dance gently lifted Madeline's head, and being careful of injury, cradled her limp body in his arms. A quick assessment assured him she was breathing and very much alive. Hot tears burned his eyes. Relief staggered him.

He'd found her!

Unconscious what he was doing, his only thought for her, he knelt there rocking her. Trying to regain himself, his lips tenderly grazed her temple. Inside his chest, his heart hammered loudly with each passing minute.

"Madeline," he urged softly in anguish, his shock residing and yet unsure why she was unconscious. "God, I could strangle you myself," he murmured, his tone not the least threatening. He gently kissed the warm shell of her ear. "Wake up, *engyl*."

Her lids fluttered, but still she lay limp.

Thunder rumbled through the walls, shaking the earth and portending a bad storm that would last through the night.

A little more urgently, he shook her. "Wake up, *cariad*." He hugged her tight. "I will have you awake, so I can beat you for scaring me."

"Dance?" A faint cry from her.

He was looking down into her face with anguished joy when her eyes opened. A little sigh from her and her arms came up to clasp around his neck. "You're home. Oh, Dance, you're home."

"Aye, I am. And you're in grave trouble."

She squinted up at him in dazed confusion, then her unfocused gaze cast about the room. She seemed to remember then, her fingers clutching for the key at her neck. "Oh, dear, didn't I lock it?" Her gaze came back to him as she became aware he was on his knees and holding her in his arms.

"Na, you did not!"

By his tone, she knew instantly she was indeed in trouble for she must have alarmed him when he came back to find her unconscious on the floor. "I'm so sorry. Oh, Dance, I didn't mean—"

"Save your apologies, *cariad,* for after I beat you." He said it with a strained grin.

Warming under his tender regard, she impulsively kissed him. "Beat me, I don't care. For you have returned."

He wanted to punish her in the worst way for scaring him the way she had, but he decided he would think on a punishment deserving of her crime after he got her safely tucked in bed. "*Ydw,* I have returned and our meal is being cleaned by Hywel..." There would be no more mutton or eggs for a long while, but they had rabbit. "Who, by the way, is in trouble for being remiss in his duty." In truth, he was angrier at himself, because he hadn't told Madeline all he knew. But then he shouldn't have to, he recanted, if she listened better to orders. "Why didn't you lock the door?"

"Please," she asked softly, his body solid and warm around her, "please, don't punish Hywel. I am at fault. Visit his punishment on me instead."

He didn't know how to tell her what he came home to find, so he didn't try. Nor could he so quickly let her off.

Nor could he let Hywel take total blame, he knew, when Madeline was wearing the *allwedd* around her neck. He moved aside the candle branch left behind by Hywel to lift her onto the bed. He sat beside her.

"Lift up." An arm supporting her, he helped her sit up and with very little struggle drew the borrowed wet cloak from her shoulders. Her gown was as deftly removed and joined his cloak on the floor. One of his nightshirts lay atop her pillow—left there for her by Hywel. "I'm not going to ask you where you've been." He did his best to see she was comfortable for her coming punishment. Outside the rain was fierce, the Welsh sky angry and relentless. It had slowed him down. Sheva had lost Owain's scent in the River Edwy. Dance had no idea how Owain had doubled back and made it to Wolfglyn ahead of him, but it was obvious he had.

It scared him stiff knowing he could have lost her in the few hours he'd been away. She had to be taught a lesson. He wasn't going to let her forget her breech of trust. "I've decided two days will be your punishment for breaking trust with me. I thought about a leash, but this will be better." He held up two lengths of silk ribbon he'd impulsively selected from Aneira's chest for Madeline's hair, which he'd intended giving her on his return. "You'll spend it tied to this bed, where you can't go wandering off—"

"You can't be serious," she chided.

"Give me your wrists, *cariad*." He held his hand out, fully expecting compliance.

"This is awful," she lamented anxiously, wondering if he'd have grieved the least little bit over her. Wondering if he might have returned her love, had he not first loved Aneira. "I've never been tied up. Can't you think of something else?"

He shook his head, his expression unbending.

"Oh, very well." She held her hands up, her gray eyes simmering. He'd never have tied up his precious Aneira.

Dance neatly and expediently fashioned a bow at each wrist. He checked that they weren't too tight before tying them to opposite sides of the bed. He sat gazing down at her, her body warm against his thigh.

Out of immediate danger, his *engyl* lay prone on the narrow mattress in one of his nightshirts looking every bit the recalcitrant damsel in distress. She looked incredibly young, the white of his nightshirt contrasting her fiery beauty. He wanted her more with every breath he drew—it wasn't a question of wanting her. His groin ached just contemplating ways to ease her distress. He wanted to ruck up the nightshirt right now, slide between her shapely thighs and bore himself into her sweet body...and he would in an instant if he didn't have a very important lesson to teach her first. In the meantime, she'd not suffer from chill or be uncomfortable, he'd send Hywel down with another blanket. The candles lighting the cell would afford warmth.

Watching him under her lashes, Madeline struggled to sit up on her elbows. She found her bonds had very little slack. He removed the key from her person and slid it into his pocket. Blinking in consternation, she hated yielding, even if she deserved his lesson. He had the audacity to smile. "Where are you going?" she asked sharply as he pushed from the bed to make his way toward the door. "Dance? How am I to eat and relieve myself and—"

"With my help," he told her, giving her a wicked flash of teeth from the thresh-hold. She was bound to find out sooner or later what happened today. But if he kept her distracted, he might forestall the explanations a little longer. "Peaceful dreams, *cariad*, I'll see you at dinner."

He exited the dungeon and shut the door. The sound of the key grated in the lock.

Wordlessly, Dance worked beside Hywel in the rain to sweep the blood from the courtyard. It gathered in a pool at the drawbridge and ran down the sloped embankment to the moat. They piled the scattered carcasses for latter burning. Dance had no choice now but to hunt each day for their meal. That was, Dance was sure, what Owain planned. To get him away from the castle. Which would leave Hywel and Madeline alone and unprotected.

"We'll leave the girls to roam freely about the courtyard. They will sound an alert if he should come back."

Hywel looked about at the mess, the death, the more recent grave with its hand-made cross, the door to the shrine hanging open. He bowed his head, his shoulders slouching. "Forgive me, mi lord."

"Dwell on it no more, old man." Dance had noted the direction in which Hywel had been staring, but he said nothing.

In truth, no one had ever trespassed his sanctuary. Not until Madeline. He knew that he should be furious. He would have been, no question about it, if it were anyone else. How did he explain it, then? Except that he was starting to care for her.

When he'd returned, saw the courtyard littered with bloody corpses and the door hanging wide to the summerhouse—Christ, he never wanted to feel that way again. His heart was still pounding in his ears.

Would that he could allow himself to take a mistress,

he would be tempted to keep her. And that thought was useless. Would that he could have sent her away after her illness, he might have saved her. As it was, things were fast deteriorating. When he'd never thought it possible, Madeline was swiftly displacing Aneira in his thoughts. Somehow she wielded a power to help him forget. It would be only a matter of time before he gave in to destructive desires.

It's what Owain was counting on.

What better means of revenge was there?

Before that happened, Dance would sell his soul. He still had choices, even if they were limited. His conscience demanded he send Hywel with a message for her family. Telling them the gravity of the situation. He should do it before anything else happened.

He could do that...and sure as he was breathing, he would never see her alive again.

It was certain, Owain didn't care who he had to take down to have his revenge. There was ample opportunity on the path between here and Llandeglay for an ambush. Madeline could get wounded in the cross-fire.

The vision of Druidh staked to the portcullis flashed before his eyes, blood draining from his mangled body.

Dance felt a sweeping, uncontrollable rage.

All he could think of when he couldn't find her today, was that brutal and unprovoked attack...and finding Madeline the same way.

The day of reckoning was upon him. He was powerless to prevent it. He was forced to accept the truth, that his Welsh blood was rooted in origins of bloodlust.

His fate ordained by his ancestors. Where power clashed and greed ruled. The Welsh had survived by their cunning, their brute strength, their fortitude.

Owain gave him no quarter for retreat.

So be it. His decision was made. He wasn't going to wait around for Owain to strike. As soon as he could get away, he would pick up the search at the river and with Sheva and a bit of luck, he would find the tracks leading to his foe.

He had just one thing left to do before he could leave Madeline alone again. He had to somehow instill in her the importance of following orders.

Madeline squirmed on the mattress, her skin tingling and her nipples pebbling and her heart breaking, for Dance wasn't going to quench her yearning. 'Twas her lesson. The aching, her unfulfilled passion. But that was the point. He knew she had to need release as badly as he did.

He was kneeling on the floor beside her, the weight of his head resting heavily on her stomach. Madeline strained against her bindings to try and curtail him. The bindings made her efforts futile. Tears of remorse burned the backs of her eyes for bringing him to this point. Dance's thick mane fell over his face, shielding his ravaged expression from her. Madeline would have given her soul to take back her deed.

Her foolishness caused this. She understood that now.

That the punishment he had in store would be his own. And that she must witness it, hurt her beyond bearing.

His breath burned her skin where his mouth suckled her navel. "Dance, I'm so sorry."

His fine linen shirt was stretched taut over the breadth of his broad shoulders, it was damp and plastered to his skin. "I won't disobey you again." Her voice trembled. "Please let me do that. Please let me help you."

He wasn't capable of more than shaking his head, for

the strain he endured in silence pushed him to the limit. He'd already told her he wanted her. He'd whispered hoarsely, he desired her more than he should. He'd related to her exactly how he was going to touch her. And he told her how he was going to touch himself. And do it while thinking of her.

He'd told her how wet and hot and tight she felt...while it was his hand he used to torture himself.

He told her how it felt to lie in his bed alone and crave a woman's touch until he could feel no more. How empty his life, the darkness never leaving him and wishing his life over, so he wouldn't miss her anymore. That he would gladly forfeit his life before he would lose her too. She would know during the next two days how he had felt every day for the last six years.

And how she would feel in his place—the endless despair that never ceased. And she would understand why he couldn't lose her and why she must never take risks such as the one she'd taken today.

Madeline didn't need convincing, her heart was already torn asunder by just a brief few minutes of it.

He was tiring. Or the hand that worked so furiously toward release seemed to tire...for it stilled. Into the numbing silence that followed, his breathing sounded harsh and broken.

Madeline couldn't see, for the lower half of his body was shielded by the bed and below her line of vision. But she sensed he'd reached his release.

Between her thighs she was weeping for him, her own craving unfulfilled, her dire need evident.

He was strangely silent, unmoving.

"I hurt," she whispered in comprehension, tears scalding her eyes as she beheld his bowed head. It hurt to the depths of her soul, and she couldn't contain her pain.

A heart-wrenching sob bubbled up from her throat.

Madeline didn't know when her bindings had been freed, she didn't know how she suddenly found herself cradled against his chest, his warmth enveloping her, his apology warming her ear. She was lying against his heart, listening to the steady rhythm beating in her ear. She was beyond comfort, beside herself in remorse and anguish and the sorrow she felt overwhelming. Over and over she sobbed she was sorry, and his each tender apology in response echoed in her head.

Tell him, tell him you love him, her heart cried.

"Dance...."

He cupped her face with one hand, lifted her chin to peer down at her with stark regard. Before she could say more, his mouth came down on hers, his kiss gentle and repentant and asking forgiveness.

A strangled cry sounded in her throat, poignant with longing.

His lips released hers—yet whispered a hairsbreadth away, "Shhh, *engyl*." He pulled her head to his chest. "Easy, *engyl*. Rest now."

Her arms went around him to steady herself. "I'm so sorry,"—she hiccuped—"I scared you."

"I know, *cariad*, I know."

"I won't do it again—"

"Shhh," he soothed, stroking her back, easing the tension from her muscles. Pooled on the floor between his knees lay his seed. Evidence he'd suffered shame alongside her. Remorse vying with fear for domination in a situation where there were no winners.

Weakly, she held onto him, her body trembling. "I've learned my lesson," she whimpered.

"Shhh, *cariad*." His lips grazing her temple, he eased her

slight weight gently over to make room on the mattress, and joined her, spooning her against his body warmth. Her delectable bottom crowded his arousal.

He nibbled her nape, the fine burnished hairs soft on his cheek.

Soon Madeline lay snuggled against him, her throat purring.

"You can't go to sleep like this," he told her tenderly, his thigh wedged between hers, his lance still painfully engorged again and seeking surcease.

She stretched out along his length, bringing to sharp focus every nerve.

"You need to be loved, *engyl*." And so saying he penetrated the damp petals of her desire...and she arched against him...driving him deeper...her fitful whimpers now those of pleasure.

Dance cupped her breasts and flexed his hips, his cock plunging against her womb. The surfeit of heat engulfing him as sweet as honeyed-hands.

It was there he held himself against the first tiny flutter of rapture jolting down his spine, her orgasm throbbing through him, her greedy sheath pulsing hot and slick.

Cradled in his arms, Dance made love to her long into the wee hours of morning. They ate a cold bowl of rabbit stew in bed for a brief respite when they needed strength and he then took her soaring over the cliffs of blissful rapture. Dance finally exhausted himself in her sometime close to dawn. Madeline kissed him sweetly, and well loved and sated, fell asleep with a smile on her lips.

They neither one thought once about the peril fast approaching.

It was some hours later before Dance stirred awake. Making no sound, he rolled from bed. He used his discarded shirt to wipe the drying semen from the stone. He knew he should find Hywel. There was his bow and quiver hanging in the foyer; preparations for today's hunt to be made. But he sat there a moment gazing upon the woman who had managed to bring him moments of unquestionable joy.

She wasn't betrothed to another. Madeline wasn't here to marry another, she had come to him on her own. Looking for a healer.

Would that he could forget that he'd put her in grave danger. That she might stay at Wolfglyn and warm his bed and heart.

But then he knew better than to let himself believe there was hope.

Would that he could return her love, he might find peace.

Shaking his head, knowing he couldn't afford to let a glimpse of heaven sway him, he sighed and turned to exit the dungeon of his sleepy *engyl*.

The feel of something slipping over her head roused Madeline from her dreamy slumber.

She'd already decided if she couldn't displace Aneira in his heart, she would focus on what she did have. She had moments like last night. Moments when he called her his 'love' in a way that almost made her believe he cherished her. Moments of impassioned madness when nothing else existed.

"Good morning, my enchanted pagan," she whispered sleepily from under the blankets twisted about her, her smile replete with warmth enough to chase the chill away.

His lips brushing hers aroused foggy memories in her of kisses to steal her heart. She loved the way his breath smelled of mint, his clover scent familiar to her senses.

Pretending to ignore him, her eyes closed, she burrowed deeper under her covers. She didn't feel like waking. She felt too content. Too well loved to care if she ever tumbled out of bed again. If he kept up the assault of her senses, she would soon be clinging to him again in fitful need of his glorious lance. His tongue tracing her jaw was hot and wet. Mercy, how she loved her pagan healer.

Warmed metal slid between her breasts—her key. He must have first held it in his palm, for it lay warm against her skin. His thoughtfulness was just one more small way in which he pleased her greatly. She suspected he had been exceptionally good at pleasing, good at making a woman deliriously wanton. And in that moment of reflection, she was painfully envious of all the others before her whom he had extolled his unearthly pleasure.

"I'll be back soon," he whispered softly in the curve of her neck, his open mouth kisses sliding over her collarbone. "Wake up, *cariad*, and lock the door behind me."

Her arms came up to fold around him as she came awake to find his penetrating gaze hovering inches away, heat of desire smoldering in stark topaz eyes.

"Must you leave?" she asked drowsily, the coverlet slipping to expose her breasts, cold air puckering her nipples. His gaze held hers with some raw emotion that gave her silly heart flight. Then reality cautioned that, no matter how blissful these last few days, his heart still belonged to Aneira. That any other woman was a miserable substitute for the one he lost. It was awful wishing for silver linings that weren't to be hers.

"I must hunt for our meal today," he said simply.

"And you're going out alone, again," she groaned softly, her arms automatically tightening about his neck and locking in an anxious embrace. "Don't go. Stay with me.

Come back to bed." She gave him a sultry smile. "And I'll let you punish me with your wicked lance."

He laughed softly, a rumble of velvet sound coming out half-groan, half-surrender. "If I stayed in bed, we would starve, and you would have no strength to meet my lustful demands. I think I should rather have you fed." He gave her a wolfish grin. "When I return, I shall see to it my lady is plundered until she whimpers for mercy."

She loved the sound of that. She loved his plundering. "We shall see who begs for mercy first, my pagan prince."

Laughing, Dance moved in haste to disentangle her arms before he could change his mind. In and out, he carried buckets of hot water from the passageway into the dungeon for her morning bath. He placed a dry towel on the altar for her. While she bathed, her *brecwast* would be heated in the great black kettle. He hoped she liked Hywel's rabbit stew, because they were having rabbit again.

Madeline was squatting over the chamber pot, relieving herself when he bent down to give her a quick departing kiss. "Come back safely to me," she murmured against his mouth.

Dance smiled and tousled her hair. "I will be counting the hours."

Incorrigible man, they both knew he would be preoccupied with ferreting out their dinner, but she liked the dream they shared. It was their little game—created in the illusion of happiness. And if he told her he would count the hours, then she would be content to let him tell his small falsehood. As long as he came back in one piece, she could be graciously tolerant of anything.

Madeline locked herself in the dungeon, then stepped

into her bath. Warm water splashed the floor as she ducked under to soap her hair with vigor. She smiled to herself at the memory, the water's heat soothing the swollen petals of her sex. Dance had a variety of endearments he used for that part of her body. Through the night his lance craved her "honeyed slipper" as she in turn craved him.

`Twas wonderful the craving. Almost as wonderful as his cure.

Still as much as she wished it could, the day couldn't be spent in bed. She had to go on with life. She had to prepare herself somehow. For whatever might come. The key dangling around her neck sloshed in the water between her breasts. A reminder that she put Dance in grave danger of becoming entrapped by her own foolishness. She'd already caused him undue distress, she told herself. `Twould be better for him should she not have come here. She would not be in this mess, she railed silently, if she'd not been so intent on being granted the same respect as were her siblings. Were she a man, she'd be out there right now, with Dance, hunting their meal—not confined to a dungeon for her own protection.

The truth of it, she'd learned more than one lesson these past weeks. Still, she'd never understand how the dominant sex got it in their heads that they could dictate the rules without the least resistance. And yet, she saw how Dance ruled differently than did her brothers. He didn't dictate, he wielded a subtler power. By allowing her a place at his side. Unlike Owain, Dance wasn't threatened by opposition, he didn't need to bend anyone to his will. For Dance stole into one's heart instead. It was how she imagined the great chieftains of old ruled. How they wielded their power by first gaining one's loyalty. Dance was born to be a great chieftain. That apparently was his downfall, for it made him a rival with his sire.

And yet she couldn't believe Owain never tired in his vigil. Why chose Aneira for his bride? When she was years younger than he, and incapable of loving him?

Dear God—the path of her thoughts! The implications that arose from nowhere were staring Madeline in the face!

Owain wouldn't just settle for banishing his rival, he would want him destroyed.

It was fiendish and cruel and heart-breaking and it was the way of his kind, Dance told her. The stories came back to her of betrayal and bloodshed. The constant battling between clans for absolute power. As long as Dance lived, he would be a threat to Owain.

What better way to bring about his son's end than to create an irreconcilable riff between them? What better way, than use a woman to cause a confrontation?

The chosen woman would have to be young and beautiful enough to snare Dance's attention and....

Madeline sat deathly still, her heart pounding with dreadful insight.

Dear God—it had never been about Aneira. Not really.

Nor was it about Madeline this time. Why hadn't she seen that until now?

It had never been about a woman!

This whole time it was about Owain's son. About Dance's eventual demise.

Dance, whom the people of Mynydd Castle had trusted and given their loyalty.

And Dance knew—dear God—he knew his father harbored jealously.

That was it! That explained why Dance had resisted

when Owain insisted he instruct Aneira on her duties at Wolfglyn. When anyone could have done that, Owain had given the task to his son. Owain had been devising his trap to provoke his son into a battle, and Dance held his hurt and shame for his father silent. Dance had resisted Aneira, resisted his attraction to her...

Because he knew his fate ordained, he knew it was a trap.

Poor Aneira, she had had no defense against Owain. If she had not unwittingly brought Dance to heel, she would have been slain in her sleep or poisoned or worse. For if she failed, she would have no longer been useful to Owain. She would have been subjected to worse than torture and she would never have understood why.

Who knew how long Dance lived with the silent knowledge his sire desired him dead? That's why Dance had accepted the refuge of solitude—why he chose to live a recluse. He lived with his pain and the shame of dishonor, the shame of his father's deceit. He'd not fight his own flesh and blood and become the same thing he despised, so he'd surrendered.

Sadly, it was the one power a son had over a bloodthirsty sire.

As long as Dance suffered, Owain would allow him to live here. But at what unspeakable sacrifice?

It cost Dance his gift for healing and ultimately his wife and son. He'd quietly thrown down his sword in defeat. His honor had trapped him in the middle. Aneira on one side, his father on the other. And she'd made him vow on his honor that he'd not take his own life.

But Owain could and Owain held a timeless grudge.

Dear God—Madeline saw it all so clearly now.

Owain would stop at nothing. Madeline was just another

casualty of rivalry. She was going to be used to strip Dance of the last of his honor and in the end his life.

Hywel knew it too. It was in the way he looked at her with silent pity.

Because Dance would not survive another slaying.

Oh God, Dance—he was going to fight this time! He was going to fight his father!

And Owain would succeed this time.

Because Dance would turn his dagger on himself in the end....

DEPRAVITY, UNIVERSAL :—
Symbolic of the vehemence of the unruled lower
desires in the soul, which require to be disciplined.

15.

Suddenly cold to her core in fear, Madeline rushed to dress so she could find Hywel. Together, they had to come up with a plan to save Dance from himself.

She was reaching for the blanket to pull it around her shoulders for added warmth, when a banging on the dungeon door made her jump.

Her borrowed gown sticking to her chill, damp skin, she shivered. "Hywel?"

A moment's hesitation and she heard him call back. "*Ydw,* mi *fach.*"

Something in the pitch of his voice halted her mid-stride. "Hywel, is that you?" Stepping around the tub as she wrapped a blanket about her, she leaned her ear to the door.

No sound.

Her heart started racing. "Hywel, what's wrong?"

He answered her in English. "Maddie, don't open the door—"

Faint, coming from the other side of the door, she heard a strangled groan from him.

Panic pushed up Madeline's throat, suffocating her. "Hywel?" she cried, willing him to answer.

"Unlock the door, Miss Carlton," came an unfamiliar voice. "Or he dies—"

"Na—don't listen to `im—"

Just as relief washed over her, she heard the thud. Heard something that sounded like a body slumping to the floor, and her heart dropped into her stomach.

"Whoever you are, please," she pleaded desperately, "leave Hywel alone. Don't harm him!"

"Open up or he dies with my blade in his gullet."

Cringing, recognizing now the voice as Owain's, Madeline shivered as blood congealed in her veins. How had he gotten in? Her stiff fingers clutched the warm brass key between her breasts. Dance had told her not to open the door. "I can't open the door," she anxiously stalled, "I don't have the key."

"Ah, *mi fach*, don't play me for a fool. I know Ifan gave it to you. That you wear it between yer perty breasts."

How did he know that? How?

She closed her eyes and frantically prayed—dear God help her—she would be used to bait the man she loved. But if she didn't do as Owain ordered, Hywel would surely die.

Everything Dance had told her about Owain assailed her. Madeline didn't want to die, she didn't want to do this! Neither did she want to choose between her friend and the man she loved.

Bile climbed up her throat to choke her. "He won't come after me. You are wasting your time."

"You're sure of that, are ya now? After I heard him rutting with ya, *mi fach*? Ya forget, I know my son, his weaknesses, and we both know he will feel responsible for ya. Think ya not, he would want ya back?"

It made her skin crawl to hear Owain had been close enough to hear them making love. Owain had obviously gained access to the dungeon—by some passage unknown to Dance. "Don't do this to Hywel," she cried through the door. "I beg you."

"*Ydw*, you will beg me, *fach*. You will beg Owain for mercy and I will decide whether to let Ifan live."

"You lie," she challenged fearfully, "you're going to hurt him, I know."

He tsked. "I'm going to *hurt* yer friend here, lass. Come now, I will not ask ya again to unlock the door."

Anxious he would kill Hywel, Madeline quickly fumbled for the key. "Wait!" she pleaded, her hands shaking so badly she almost dropped it. Again she fumbled with the key in the lock, her heart pounding hard in her chest.

Abhorred to do it, she pushed the great oak door open. Bravely, she faced her assailant as the door swung into the stone wall with a shudder.

Huge and menacing, Owain stood over Hywel.

Dance's father seemed taller when facing him alone, his shoulders broad as an ox. A frightening sight, he was covered head to toe in animal skins, a shaggy beard obscuring most of his features, his smile feral. Triumph gleamed in his black eyes. Madeline quelled, her gaze shifting to the dagger glinting in the candlelight.

Her face must have given her away. His smug laughter brought her gaze up.

His smile said he had her right where he wanted her. Fear sliced through her as those leering black eyes skimmed down her body—their descent making her gown feel transparent.

To show fear of any sort would be a mistake.

At the moment it wasn't herself in immediate danger. It was Hywel. Her friend dangled unconscious in the barbarian's grip, his head cocked at an awkward angle, a trickle of blood oozing over the lethal blade pressed to his throat.

Galvanized by panic, Madeline shot out a hand to stay Owain. "Please," she pleaded, raising haunted eyes to black ones. And she just curtailed the need to shrink from the cold ruthlessness in his sneer. Knowing he could just as swiftly gut her, Madeline suspected she would be spared for something more diabolical than mere death. "If you let Hywel live, I will go with you peacefully." Afraid Dance might appear anytime, afraid she would be used to trap and hurt him, Madeline would do anything she must to forestall more bloodshed. "But know this...I will not let you harm your son."

He chuckled at that, his chill gaze snaking over her from head to foot. "By God, yer a fiery beauty. Poor Ifan, he didn't stand a chance. But then I knew ye was more his match than that faithless bitch come here last time. Ahhh, don't look so sad, girl, he's not gonna want anything to happen to ya. Rest assured he'll come lookin for ya."

Owain laughed as color leached from Madeline's face.

Giving her a lecherous grin, he dropped Hywel like a burlap bag to the cold stone and kicked him aside.

Wincing, Madeline was dropping to her knees to help Hywel when a beefy paw closed around her arm. She was jerked up. His brutal grip on her bruising, pain shot through her limb, and then she was being propelled forward. Madeline shot a quick glance over her shoulder at the motionless form of her friend, and prayed Dance would find him before he bled to death.

Leaving Hywel where he laid, Owain yanked her along. Several times, Madeline lost her footing in the dark and stumbled.

They made a couple turns to her left; going deeper into

the belly of the castle. Taking the winding dark corridor that led seemingly nowhere. Then Madeline was shoved through a hidden portal into broad daylight. Suddenly, they were outside the castle. Her arm came up to shield her eyes and barely had she time to catch her breath before she was being roughly dragged along. For a man twice her size, she found Owain moved with surprising speed. They were practically running, their steps carrying them swiftly through the hip-deep grass. It had rained. The grass was wet and soon her soggy skirt was slapping against her legs. Her feet were bare and cold, her shoes left behind in the dungeon. Bits of branches pricked her tender soles. That kind of pain she could endure.

It was the crushing pain of what would happen to Dance that she couldn't bear.

She was being dragged along, her lungs screaming for air. Just before they broke for the cover of the forest, Madeline took a long glance over her shoulder. Her last glimpse of Wolfglyn. A misty white phantom of limestone, black standards slapping in the breeze. Choking on regret, she said her silent farewell.

Her love, she sent soaring over the valley to Dance was her one solace she could leave behind.

She knew not what Owain planned to do with her, but she knew she could not bear seeing Dance chained. Fighting like a wild animal against his bindings, and witnessing what no man should have to witness once, let alone a second time. She would not be the cause of more suffering for him. She would not let it go as far as Aneira had. That she vowed.

Somehow she would find a way to escape Owain before Dance found them.

There was a horse tied and waiting for them in the thick of trees. Without breaking stride, Owain roughly hauled

Madeline up onto his shaggy, short-legged steed. Then he swiftly climbed up behind her. He kicked the beast into a trot and soon they were swallowed up by the dense forest, their path taking them into shadow-dappled cover. The cold chill of evening swept over the forest. Mists tangled about the ground like tendrils of smoke. Her captor wore a fur-lined coat to keep him warm. Madeline had no such protection. Her gown lay plastered to her like a second skin.

She could feel her captor's leering eyes on her back and imagined what he was thinking. She thought of Aneira and how Dance had watched her being brutally raped. Soon as the immediate danger of discovery passed, she didn't doubt he'd be all over her. In this she had no illusions.

Owain was coarse and dirty and wearing animal pelts on his body. Being forced to ride with him made her skin crawl. It was hard to imagine him a once powerful lord betrothed to a refined and beautiful princess. It was even harder to believe—though the resemblance was there—he was blood kin to the man she loved.

Madeline kept her spine rigid and listened to the forest sounds around her. Was Dance already in pursuit? The tree-lined path veered seemingly in circles. Dance would have to travel in the dark. Did Sheva remember Madeline's scent? Was she out there right now leading Dance into danger?

She hoped not, with all her heart.

It had grown dark sometime ago now, the moon the only light guiding them to their destination by some indiscernible path leading deeper into the tangle of dense bracken. Under them, the horse's great hooves crunched the ground. Puffs of moisture snorted from his nostrils like steam. The animal had to be as tired as she was herself, but he never slowed.

Madeline was slumping forward with exhaustion when up ahead of her, an orange glow of light caught her eye. A camp?

She sat up straighter. Had he finally reached his destination?

With their arrival, her fear of the unknown resurfaced. Would he attack her right away?

Without warning and before the horse came to a complete stop, Owain shoved her from the saddle. Madeline felt herself tumbling. Hard ground slammed into her. Her lungs gasped for the air knocked out of her. Pain shot through the arm pinned under her. She lay still for fear it would hurt worse if she moved. Heat from the campfire blazed in her face.

She hurt bad, her arm maybe sprained, her muscles screaming as if she'd been beaten all over. She didn't know in which direction even to run. By her estimation, it had to be close to midnight. Enough time had passed that Dance would have found Hywel; with any luck he would still be nursing Hywel's wound.

Poor dear Hywel, he'd tried to warn her. But his cunning nowhere near matched Owain's. What would Dance think when he found the dungeon unlocked a second time? Would he think this her fault, she wondered forlornly?

A thought that didn't bear close scrutiny.

A flitter of shadow from the corner of her eye caught Madeline's attention. She had to twist around to see better. A silent form wavered in and out of her vision. A woman?

Yes, it was another woman. She was opposite the campfire from Madeline.

Madeline's gaze swept down, rested on the chunk of

rope binding the woman's wrists. Her gaze swung back up with sympathy, but the eyes peering dully into space saw nothing.

What was wrong with her?

Upon closer scrutiny, Madeline saw tattered shreds of dirty linen hung about the woman's neck, off one shoulder. An ugly purple bruise blackened her arm, her jaw. Dried blood matted her copper tresses. She sat cross-legged in an immodest slump. The blanket she'd been given was blood-crusted and riding up her thighs.

With disturbing clarity it dawned on Madeline what she was looking at...and her insides recoiled.

Outrage burned inside her, distracting her from her own injury.

Before Madeline could call out to the woman, a crunch of footsteps sounded. She had little time to worry it was Dance as two definite human shapes stepped from the cover of darkness.

Madeline gasped in alarm, her heart kicking.

"Come closer boys, take a look at her." The two men came into the light of the fire.

Blinking in shock, Madeline recognized Llwyd, the despicable coward!

His hand roaming possessively over the woman's bare shoulder, he gave Madeline a lewd wink.

Owain snickered. "I think ya two have met."

Overcome by panic, Madeline made to rise. A cry of pain burst from her throat.

"Bind her hands," Owain ordered the foul-looking giant with gaping holes for teeth.

He lumbered around the fire toward her. Alarmed by this new development and suddenly finding herself outnumbered, Madeline grit her teeth and tried to roll out of his reach. He was upon her, knee digging into her back, pressing the air from her lungs. Sharps twigs and earth dug into her cheek, the ground under her cold and unyielding. Madeline yelped as her hands were roughly bound. Tears of pain sprang to her eyes. Gritting her teeth, she blinked them away. Her bonds, she discovered some seconds later, were tied unnecessarily tight. But she'd not give the bastards the satisfaction of complaining about it. Instead Madeline focused all her hatred on the rotten bastard who had deserted her that first night in the forest.

He grinned at her from across the short distance. A look that said he'd make her pay for withholding the code-word devised by her brother.

She glared back, giving him an equally threatening glare. One promising him she would skin him alive if she ever got a chance.

At least they hadn't ordered her gagged like the helpless victim of their lust.

Would Madeline's turn be tonight? Was rape the only thing they had planned for her? Would she be raped like they had Aneira? Raped as they had the mute woman with sightless eyes?

She would not, she vowed, let herself give into despair. She would not let them see how terrified she was. She had to be brave. For herself. For Dance and what he'd been through already.

Madeline spent her first sleepless hour on the hard, cold ground where she curled close to the dying embers praying Dance would stay away. She forbid herself to show weakness. Forbid herself to fall asleep. Her muscles screamed from being cramped in the same position. She lay there numb and cold, her fate awaiting like a brutal hand clamping over her mouth, suffocating her.

By morning, the despair she tried to hold at bay overtook

her like the fog circling the sleepy camp...it robbed her of the last remnants of pride. She wept silently into the earth where her pain would be muffled.

She heard them waking up. The giant who bound her hands grunted as he hefted his bulk to his feet to poke a stick at the dying fire. Llwyd, who woke next was staggering over to a tree to relieve himself. Finding apparent delight in her moment of weakness, he laughed down at her. "I'll be happy to help ya out, *fach*, just as soon as Owain gives the word."

Face flaming, Madeline swallowed her tears to glare back unflinching at the lewd suggestion in his gaze. She forced her gaze not to waver as the weasel unsheathed his pitiful lance. His intent to leave her with a vivid impression of what she would soon encounter.

Watching, the slack-jawed giant guffawed. Not to be outdone, he reached out and gave the sleeping woman a smack on the leg to rouse her. When she didn't rouse, he shoved his hand up her skirt, between her legs. Madeline squirmed against her bonds in protest, her gut roiling.

She wanted to cover her ears, block out the pitiful, incoherent words uttered by the woman. Madeline silently screamed for her, her ears filling with sickening sounds, her mind rejecting the violation to her own senses.

Dance had had to watch his wife raped. Hear her cries. It lay open Madeline's heart to the pain of ruthlessness. Her own vulnerability keen.

Her own humiliation was coming.

And Dance had tried to spare her this.

He'd done all in his power to send her away.

Madeline's stomach heaved as she watched Llwyd crawl under the animal skins to join the giant in his ugly act.

So intent she was on the squirming heap of animal skins, her anger fulminating, she hadn't heard Owain approach.

He was suddenly looming over the squirming mass, his feet planted, hands on hips, a smile slow to crack his face. Neither Llwyd or the giant knew yet he was there, so busy were they. She felt a fleeting sense of retribution. Owain would have something to say about this.

It was not what she expected.

Before she realized what he was doing, Owain bent and pulled the cover from the contorting shapes hidden beneath. Shocked to her core, the sight rendering her ill, Madeline turned her head away from the vision.

Instead of outrage and shouting, she heard Owain chuckling. "Ahh, *mi fach*. What be the matter, girl? Never seen this before? Men taking their pleasure in the same woman?" He tsked and laughed some more.

Fighting waves of hysteria, Madeline curled into a ball. She tried to shut her ears to the grunting. Shut her mind to the vision, her eyes tightly closed as if she could escape it.

When she next opened her eyes, it was to find all three men looking at her.

They sat across the fire from her as if waiting expectedly for something to start. Madeline had tried to reconcile herself to dying—but her time came far sooner than expected.

Owain approached her on the bed of earth where she'd been lying since he dumped her off his horse. She'd not relieved herself that morning. And she was needing to very badly.

In her face he dangled a limp rabbit. "Dinner for our guest." He laughed down at her.

The rabbit was skewered and hung over the roaring flames. The sun was sinking. Half and hour later, Owain crouched down next to her with a hunk of roasted meat, still sizzling and hot off the skewer. He dangled it in front of her face, knowing she wouldn't be able to hold it herself.

"I'm going to let ya run for it, mi *fach*," Owain chortled above her.

He smelled revolting, his statement terrifying her.

"But first ya will eat, so ya have strength ta run. Llwyd and Boar, over there, they like a fighter. Ye'll give em a good fight cause ya got yer wits. Not like the mute lass there. Her kind not much sport, if ya get mi meaning."

A motionless heap lay prone under the animal skins on the ground beyond.

He was going to play with Madeline now. Torment her like his cohorts tormented the snoring woman. Sickened by the thought, abhorred to eat from his hand, she none-the-less forced herself to take a bite of his offering because she wouldn't cower.

As she savored what was probably her last meal, the taste of charred meat, she noted Llwyd and the giant named Boar had risen to their feet. They were making ready for her. Like predators waiting for their prey to flee.

The moment she had both waited for and shrank from was upon her.

They'd be on her in no time...unless she could outrun them or outsmart them.

One thing she did know, they would not simply rape her and be done with it.

She was Dance's woman. Dance's women were to be tortured.

They'd do it while keeping her alive.

Madeline felt her bonds being cut. Fear such as she'd never felt closed her throat tight. She swallowed hard and felt Owain behind her, his close proximity suddenly terrifying her in wholly new ways. The giant looking at her from across the campfire licked his lips as if savoring her in his mind. He was big, his lance monstrous and visibly protruding against the fit of his filth-stained breeches. She'd no doubt he'd hurt her badly. Llwyd, the slimy bastard—Llwyd had repeatedly joined himself to the mute woman under the cloak of covers as if she were there for his sole pleasure. They'd make her revile what had been beautiful between her and Dance.

"You can wash yerself, mi *fach*, but ya will never get my smell off ya. Ya will remember me every time he touches ya." Madeline knew it to be true, the smell she would never in the rest of her days forget.

The giant was grumbling, he didn't want to wait any longer, he was already salivating. Owain's revenge though, she knew, required methodical torture.

Sick to her soul, Madeline forced herself to drink from the cup her captor held for her. Water trickled over her lips, down her neck. When her chance of escape came, she had to be strong enough to flee to safety this time. She would not be hunted down to be brought back here for repeated raping.

While she contemplated the extent of her injury, whether it would slow her down, the insidious memory of Dance's anguished words came back to her..."*the bastards, three of them, they violated my wife...she was bleeding to death... she died in my arms.*"

"Come, darlin', it's time for a walk." Owain lifted Madeline by her uninjured arm to her feet. Pain jolted through her. Her heart hammered with fear while her legs cramped under her. She was loath to accept his support until the painful tingling subsided, but she had little choice.

"I need to relieve myself," she told Owain, repressing a gnawing panic.

He snickered. "Get ye ta the river."

Shoving her forward, Madeline was escorted along a mossy trail. Until they came to where an icy cold stream cut across the path. Llwyd and the giant brought up the rear. To Madeline, the river's dark depths looked bottomless. She couldn't help shivering.

"You can relieve yerself here, mi *fach*." He shoved her closer to the grassy bank.

Numb already from the chill night air, Madeline looked behind Owain to her audience. "I suppose I have to do this with you all watching."

"Na—we will turn our heads so ya can make off." He chuckled menacingly.

Cold and frightened, she lifted her chin and her skirt and squatted. She did so without pause, without modesty, without thought for appearances.

Obscured by the cloak of darkness, the moonlight dim tonight, she used the pretence of relieving herself to gather her scattered thoughts. Behind her she knew they waited, her chance of escape cut off that way. The icy river facing her was wide open, no one to block her escape. The current was swift, the river wider at this point than where she'd crossed it all those nights ago with Dance riding behind her on ole Bones.

The cold shock would certainly take her breath away, she'd not be able to stand it for long. She had maybe a handful of minutes before she'd be rendered numb, incapable of moving her limbs. The spiking cold would be near unbearable. Not as unbearable though as knowing she was instrumental in luring Dance to his death.

If her captor's followed her in, their clothing would drag them to the bottom.

Death by drowning, she decided, was kinder than rape.

Without another thought, Madeline dove for the black viperous depths.

Spikes of pain sliced through her as she sank, the cold seizing her muscles. Roaring water closed over her head. Around her ears the current swirled, her arms flailing a wrathful and watery grave. She tried to breathe, but her mouth filled with water. She was being drug along by the current, her lungs screaming for air, but she dared not surface.

Seconds seemed like hours. When she felt herself fading, her fingers curled and frozen, she clawed for the surface...and felt a brutal hand latch onto her throat.

Debris in the river crashed into her, making her cry out. Drowning, suffocating, gasping for air, she fought the hand off. She was losing consciousness, the water rushing around her head...then she was free of the hand...drifting... no more pain.

NIGHT AS NULLITY :—
Symbol of the forgetting of all past experience on entering
a higher level of consciousness. Implies the expunging of
sorrow and pleasure, the wiping out of pain in passing out
from the "night" of the soul—the delusion of the lower
planes—to the "day" of the higher planes.

16.

A howl of anguish rent the night air, echoing through the mountains, stilling all other sound in its wake, the wretchedness of grief assailing the ears of forest creatures in the night. Wings scuttled in the tree tops, birds startled, taking flight. Moonlight lent shadowy shapes to barren branches, the ground undulating foggy wisps. A stark quiet fell upon the shoulders of the man doubled over on the ground. His dark head bent, his body trembling.

God noooo!...Dance howled in pain.

He absently peeled off his gloves. The gown, his gift to her, had been shredded by whatever fed on her—buttercup velvet mired with scarlet drops.

Sheva stayed her distance, head hanging, helpless to know how to comfort him.

On his knees, Dance reached out to the mutilated body illuminated in moonlight—his fingers curling into a fist.

He'd followed blind instincts to find her...he'd felt something unmistakably dark shift through him, a sense of overwhelming urgency shaking him to the core...something he felt was terribly wrong as soon as he'd entered the forest.

The moment he'd felt it he'd broken into a run....

Na, engyl! The hand he held suspended above her shook. *God no!*

It hurt to breathe...hurt to kneel over her and do nothing. It hurt inside him with a wretchedness cutting his heart from his chest....

Yet he couldn't bring himself to touch her, because as long as he left her lying where she was, she might yet open her eyes. She might yet live. The blood wasn't real. She'd not be here and she'd not be dismembered beyond recognition. She'd not have cried out to him for help.

She'd not be wearing the key he'd given her around her broken neck....

And he could go on living...and breathing...and remembering her the way she was just this morning. The tenderness in her smile, the gentleness in her touch and the purity of her heart. He could go on holding her...kissing her lips...her hair...loving her body...bringing her joy. She would awaken to wrap her arms around him and hold him tight against a lifetime of loneliness.

His gut knotted in despair, Dance reached out unconsciously to find Sheva, his fingers in her fur curling into a fist. She yelped and he instantly loosened his hold.

His blurry gaze swam with pain.

He hadn't noticed right away that Sheva was licking blood from Madeline's snarled hair.

"Get away," he scolded fiercely, shoving her off.

Sheva slinked away, cowering on her belly before circling again to crawl back to him.

Doubled over, Dance dragged a sleeve over his eyes.

Sheva inched her way closer to him. Her wet nose rested on his thigh, her sympathy given the only way it could be.

This time Dance didn't shove her away. He reached out for her—and pulled her into his arms.

In her fur, he buried his face and wept....

Back at Wolfglyn, after Hywel was suitably recovered from his close brush with death, his wound bandaged, he burned the carcasses. A great billow of smoke rose from the courtyard, blacking the sky. That done, Hywel took himself off to the keep to wash up. Because the master had said Lady Maddie would want her a bath when he returned with her, he had her a bath ready. She'd saved him, Maddie *fach* had. And he'd hoped to thank her.

Hywel's gaze blurred, his throat tight with emotion as he watched Dance approaching the drawbridge as dawn peeked over the treetops. The sight of blood stopped his heart. Hywel found himself gripping the wall for support, deep sorrow rendering him incapable of speech. He'd been waiting for Dance to return since last night. He'd been praying for miracles and an end to the suffering.

It wasn't to be granted.

Dance looked ready to drop. He had carried his precious *engyl* all the way back to Wolfglyn from wherever it was he'd found her. Her body was wrapped in the master's cloak. Dance's fleeting gaze met Hywel's. The rawness in it saying what couldn't be voiced aloud.

The silently grieving man who passed Hywel in the courtyard, looked ravaged by death, pain and desolation. He looked neither right, nor left, nor did he pause but to kick the door wide as he disappeared inside with his *engyl*. Hywel just caught up to him as he made for the stairs to the watchtower.

"Ye canna be taking her up there ta leave her."

Dance said nothing as he elbowed Hywel aside and

traversed the stairs. "Think ye what is best for her," Hywel called after him. "Take her home ta her family, mi lord."

Dance never slowed his pace. His face was set in stone, his topaz eyes sightless in misery. Hywel knew the signs well. The inconsolable grief that rendered a man temporarily mad. And every time before that when Dance had eventually recovered. Why did it scare Hywel then, this time?

Why did Dance shut himself in the tower with her? Where she would begin to rot?

It was dinnertime before Hywel gathered courage enough say what must be said. Before he felt strong enough to traverse the tower stairwell and the endless corridor of steps reaching skyward. This time Hywel had had the foresight to hide the key to the tower room. So that he might rescue Dance before the master grew too weak to lift his body off the floor. Hywel had porridge for Dance. He would somehow make sure Dance didn't starve himself. None of his nonsense was he listening to this time.

Hywel heard the mournful tunes of the flute playing as he climbed to the tower room.

The door was ajar. Sheva greeted Hywel with a wet nose, her tail wagging as if to say, "it is about time someone came to relieve me." Hywel soundlessly stepped inside the round room. He saw Dance at the window staring out, the flute now quiet in his lap, the body of his maimed *engyl* cradled in his arms. He saw Madeline's arm dangling from the cloak in the full light and reeled on his feet. Black and blue bruises traced what he could see of her arm above a fleshy tear. Something had gotten to her. The master's poor *engyl* was stiff, lifeless. She'd fought for her life, Maddie fach had, she'd not given up easily. It made him pray she had died quickly.

She was beyond anyone's help. Yet his master was not

going to part with her either. He would mourn her as he had mourned his beloved Aneira. Thankfully Dance had covered the worst of the carnage with his cloak.

Hywel bent to pick up the *allwedd* dropped to the stone floor. He looked at it in his hand—the key to the dungeon. Emotion choked him. The bowl of porridge burned his fingers until he remembered he held it. Slowly, he approached the overturned table at Dance's elbow. Hywel righted the table and set the porridge on the scarred surface, pushing it closer to Dance.

"I'll expect ya to eat every bit of yer porridge, ya hear me?" he insisted sternly, "or I'll be forced ta feed ya miself."

Dance said nothing.

Hywel hung back. "Tis me yer *engyl* was protecting," he admitted tearfully, his hand going to the bandage at his throat. Aneira had saved his life. "She did'na want ta open the door." He took a deep breath and would have gladly taken her place for he knew living was crueler. "She loved ya. Ye know that, don't ya? Yer *engyl* she wanted to stay with ya."

After a long hesitation, Dance turned his harrowed gaze from the window to stare at Hywel. "She wanted to hear my flute," he murmured softly. His gaze, stark with sorrow, returned then to the sky beyond the window. "I told her I would play for her...." His husky voice trailing off with raw emotion.

"*Ydw*, ye did, master, and yer *engyl* rests quiet, no one can hurt her now...."

"I'll take her home," Dance acceded quietly in answer to Hywel's unspoken question.

"*Ydw*, ya will get her back ta Llandeglay. That be good. Then ya will want to find the herder in the village and bring woollies back with ya. I'll load the cart with supplies and together we'll come back home and we'll weed yer garden so yer healing plants grow strong. Ye'll make yer medicine and come spring we'll trade many bottles at the *Eisteddfod*." And life will go on...he could have said. "Come mornin' I'll hitch the cart up to her beast."

Dance sat quiet, a stone effigy of a battle-scarred noble lord. His stark gaze held raw pain, tears glinting in his eyes. Hywel said nothing more.

Dance spent the first day in a cold tower chamber, the wind and rain lashing against the shuttered window. He'd refused each crust of bread set before him. He played his flute endlessly, the melancholy melody heartrending, driving deeper the finality of his last days with her enshrouded body held in his embrace. The second night, in a despondent rage he destroyed his alchemy chamber, sweeping the vials of herbs from the tables, tipping over a vat of lukewarm water in the rushes by the dying embers in the great hollowed hearth in the wall. He shattered glass, and then weak from his rampage, he dropped to the cold stone floor on his hands and knees and cried in silent agony, head hanging, trembling, chest heaving in misery. He cried her name in his mind over and over while trying to let go of her in his heart. When he couldn't stand being alone in the alchemy chamber, he numbly dragged himself back up the tower steps to hold her again.

Hywel sat with him that night as it stormed the worst, the wolves howling from the chamber at the other end of the castle far away from the tower room. Diligent in watching over his master, he planted himself just inside the door on the floor next to Sheva. His back propped against the wall, he watched over Dance and repeated his plea that she be taken home to her family waiting in Llandeglay.

Lost in grief, Dance played his flute, his lungs rasping,

weak, but he played for her until he slipped unconscious—exhaustion finally claiming him.

He held her in his sleep, his body shielding hers as if she were still in need of protection. That's where he remained with her until Dance roused himself from the mercilessly cold stones to sit by her side in the dark and try to formulate coherent thought. He stopped playing his flute. It sat untouched next to her. He sensed Hywel was awake, listening.

Dance's voice sounded disembodied, barely a whisper, "I'll take her to the village in the morning."

It was still as death in the pre-dawn hours the next morning, a faint stirring of light just shimmering on the western horizon. Everything was damp, sprinkled with rain. The air heavy, freshly washed. Patches of fog swirling the ground like silver mists. The courtyard was in semi darkness. Only an occasional shuffle of a hoof striking stone as her horse was being harnessed to the cart, clouded moisture snorting from his nose in the brisk morning temperatures. Even Lucifer was quiet in his stall. Not a sound could be heard from the stable. No bleating from sheep, no squawking from chickens. Just a bone deep quiet. The silent whisper of death. Like the days of old after a bloody carnage, the hollow stillness in the aftermath of war when one gazed out upon the tangled corpses of a battlefield and felt the wretchedness of victory in the foe's sightless eyes.

Hywel waited with ole Bones in the courtyard after letting the master know everything was ready for their departure.

When sometime later, after the midmorning sun was streaking over the verdant valley, Dance still hadn't joined

Hywel, he started back for the keep—trudging up the front stairs to the heavy oaken doors, his steps weighted down.

He approached midway when the doors banged open before him.

Hywel looked up—whatever greeting he was about to voice dying on his lips.

Dance held her cradled in his arms, her head tucked under his chin the same way he'd held her all through the night. He hadn't changed clothes, her blood still smeared his breeches. She was enshrouded in a plaid woolen blanket taken from his bed. The grave lines of grief hardened the angles of his face, his ravaged expression suppressing pain barely controlled. His lips set in a tight line, teeth clenched.

Wordlessly, Dance descended the steps and made his way to the rear of the cart.

The old man rushed to his side.

With little more than a passing look, Dance laid her gently on the straw. Which had been piled to cushion the ride for her, even though she couldn't appreciate it.

Dance climbed in with her, drew her into his arms again and held her tight, his gut clenching. His hands shook as he cupped her head to his heart. Weary, emotions shredded, he looked down upon the covered head of the woman who had come here for a healer. She'd come to him innocent, a vibrant streak of light in his dark world. She'd been his one brief comfort. She'd given him her child's heart to awaken. He'd joined his body to hers. She'd bled for him—her gift of womanhood—he'd touched her where no man had been before him. She'd bedeviled him, tormented him, and given of herself in tender ways.

Holding her, not wanting to think about when he would have to part with her, Dance rested his back against the cart's side. Head back, his gaze lifted to the black standards high above the stone walls — the splash of a crimson where a dragon fiercely defended his territory—and knew he might soon join her.

Madeline who filled his last days with warmth was cold and stiff in his arms. Her beauty, her laughter, her valiant last wish still echoing through his soul, her hours of pleasure as fleeting as her days spent in his arms. She'd offered him unconditional happiness, a precious glimpse of hope. And he'd given her nothing but empty promises to keep her safe. He'd been blinded by a past he couldn't change. Missing what he couldn't bring back, and he'd foolishly forsaken what he could have had right under his very nose.

He should have told her while he could that she'd become his ray of sunshine. He should have cared for her better. Kept her alive. Gone down on his knees and thanked her for every day she spent teaching him how to live again.

God—he should never have left her alone—not for one hour, one minute, one second.

Closing his eyes, he pressed his lips to her covered head. Felt his heart well with pain. Inconsolable loneliness. Piercing grief.

Today he would accept his fate as he should have done so years ago.

He would hunt the bastard down and finish it.

Choke the life from him with his bare hands and watch him fight for his last breath.

Put to death his own sire.

Tears scalding his eyes, Dance embraced his chosen path, blood-chilling resolution thriving in his heart. He looked to the black emblem of his crest stir in the breeze.

The remnants representing every sorrow he held for this place. His home. His comfort and his torment.

Dance returned his thoughts to the present, settled himself for the long journey to Llandeglay. He felt a moment's disquiet about leaving his faithful friend with the castle to look after by himself, then he shook off the thought. The cottage in Llandeglay was Hywel's now—he would be allowed at long last to live a normal existence. Free of the shadow that haunted Dance.

Dance thought of Madeline's family—her brothers. A wry grimace settled upon his mouth. He remembered clearly what she had told him. Her brothers would want his blood, they'd settle for nothing short of tearing him limb for limb.

He'd have to somehow extricate himself from the lynch party that would surely be waiting him when he got to Llandeglay with her.

It should have worried him.

As it was he couldn't feel a thing but numbing emptiness.

His heart pounding, he looked down at Hywel who was waiting for his signal.

"Let us go from here," he replied, and took a steadying breath. As the cart pulled away from the courtyard some minutes later, Dance's thoughts turned once again to the cold body in his arms.

His head rolled back to rest, his eyes unfocused and heavy as they made their way over the drawbridge, the clank of hooves resounding in his brain, the churn of wheels under him, the jostle and creak of the rickety wooden cart. A dampness in the air beaded on his skin, the squall of a pine marten high in the sky lulled his groggy senses. Pitiful warmth from a faint sun seeped into him, drugging him.

In his mind's eye he followed the muddy ruts in the rain bogged road, the lush green landscape rolling by. So dazed and lethargic was he, he didn't at first notice when the cart stopped jostling.

They had stopped.

He sensed Hywel's wordless alarm, and it roused him to turn his head, peer up.

The old man seemed incapable of speech, his face chalky white, eyes wide in shock.

God—what now?

His gaze turned in the direction the old man was staring.

It was then he saw it...saw her...saw the ghost of familiar beauty emerging from the forest as if borne from fertile earth. He blinked—rubbed his eyes with one hand.

The apparition kept coming, floating toward them... not floating...walking, his mind registered incredibly. In stunned disbelief, he sat riveted in place, his heart hammering against his ribs, his mind playing him a wicked trick, it couldn't be—

Madeline?

Alive?

The white shift she wore stood out against the darker verdant copse of woods.

Anguish rose up from his soul to choke him, her ghostly beauty haunting him, coming to see him off, pay some tribute to her lifeless cold corpse. Not taking his eyes off her across the valley, shifting his burden gently to lay her down, he stepped down, left the cart behind. He stood there at the edge of the road. The grassy pasture stretched out before him to the blessed vision he couldn't take his eyes from.

She waved then...and he felt shock waves crawl down his spine.

If Madeline was here...who was it in the cart?

He started forward on unsteady legs, his steps carrying him through the grass, faster his pace, his hurry to reach her before she disappeared from sight, his need for her so great he reached for her with his soul.

"Madeline," he appealed loud enough it would carry, a question in his tone, disbelief making him feel foolish and yet he couldn't stop himself.

Carried on the air over the fragrant wet field, a sweet reply reached his ears. "Dance."

He knew he wasn't dreaming, he was awake and the ground solid beneath his feet. She was in the cart he left behind with Hywel, but he wanted to believe....

She held up a hand to halt him when he was still a great distance away. Her features were clearer, the ghostly dreamlike quality dropping away to leave him reeling. He started walking faster.

"Stop," her voice firmly called to him.

It was indeed Madeline's voice he heard. Baffled, not understanding, he faltered in his steps, came up short... afraid to move and so afraid if he didn't she would vanish.

Her heart reached him in her dove gray eyes, a glimmer of fatalistic sadness...giving his heart a sudden pause. "What's wrong?" he heard himself ask, but didn't move.

She just shook her head, tears glistening, her gaze filled with an emotion he would never forget...telling him she knew she was going to die.

Tragic, fragile...he sensed her inside him, felt her heart beating for him...touching him across the distant expanse of green. He smelled her when he knew he couldn't be close enough. Senses highly attuned to her, he felt her soul reach for his, their bond timeless and everlasting and infinite....

"I came to say bye," he heard her whisper...his ears picking up the subtle pain and joy.

Jesus God—what's wrong? his mind screamed. He started forward. That's when he saw out of the corner of his eye a shadow emerge from the heavy cover of the forest.

Still reeling from one shock, another one hit him in the gut.

Owain!

Black eyes malevolent, Owain held his bow drawn—

Feet skidding to a stop, Dance knew in an instant what was going to happen. Madeline stood between them. His eyesight keen, Dance saw a glint of light reflecting from an arrow aimed at her back.

Panic swelling inside him, his gaze swung back to her, all of it registering on his bemused senses that Owain held her in his sight. "Madeline, run!" he shouted, his voice carrying a heart-gripping warning.

She helplessly shook her head.

Fear held Dance immobile.

"Say good-bye to your lady," Owain called out from his vantage, his voice ringing clear in the stillness of the morning hours.

"Don't!" Dance managed to yell, "don't do it!" The air in his lungs stilled; his father's instability unnerving.

A sinister sneer. "Down on your knees, boy."

Stricken, Dance turned his gaze back to Madeline...this time his scrutiny taking in so much more...noticing her soiled chemise...how it fell from one shoulder...spotted with crimson stains...blood.

"Beg for her life!" Owain shouted vehemently.

All of the past memories rushing back, Dance kept his

focus on Madeline. The pain in his eyes, the silent suffering in the look he shared with her conveyed what he couldn't with words.

Then one leg buckling, he dropped to his knees in the damp grass. His knees sank into the cold wet earth. A chill pervaded his body, shook him, he couldn't stop the tremors....

He bowed his dark head and begged, "Please," he cried harshly, "spare her." His body shook uncontrollably. Fists clenched at his sides, more softly he prayed, "Owain, I beg you, don't take her!"

Demented laughter.

"Say good-bye," Owain gloated from a distance as he nocked his arrow and let it fly.

In a blur of motion, Dance sprang to his feet...a roar rasping his throat....

The howl echoed over the *glyn* as Madeline shrieked and fell forward.

Dance's heart took the impact, his lungs seizing and his legs too slow to reach her before she landed. She crumpled to the ground, the arrow quivering, finding its deadly mark. Heart pumping, Dance ran full out, legs thrashing through the deep grass to reach her. He slid to the ground the last few feet and reached to cup her head, drag her close as she lay still, her breath panting, growing fainter, pain contorting her face. Her whimpering sobs cutting through him.

A cursory glance at the wound brought tears to his eyes. Blood oozed from the arrow imbedded in her back through her shoulder. The shaft was deep. He tired not to hurt her as he gently turned her a fraction to see the head sticking out the other side a hand's span above her heart. Elation rose in his throat before he saw the greenish tinge surrounding the wound, smelled the putrid odor. His hands stilled.

Fucking bastard poisoned the arrow!

He bent his head, mouth near her ear. "I'm here, *engyl*," he softly soothed, glancing up swiftly at the cart a hundred yards away. "I'm not going to let you die, you hear me," the last a strangled promise, determination in his words when every minute he delayed left her slipping from this world.

The mix of dwale and hemlock, if blessedly slower acting, was fatal. He had to hurry. Get her back to Wolfglyn.

"I'm going to lift you...." he told her as he shifted her carefully as possible into his arms.

She made no whimpering sound—she was fading, already the poison feeding into her blood.

Vague awareness reached him—a distant sound—a blood-curdling scream of death.

His head shot up, his gaze scanning—riveting on his father who staggered, Sheva latched onto his throat, hanging there snarling, dragging Owain down to the ground. Dance felt unexplained emotion overtake him...something fragile snap inside him, twisting inside his chest. A young boy's love for his father stealing into his thoughts...the sad events that separated them in later years...the father who had turned raving mad.

As Dance had himself turned mad in grief. Done things he wouldn't have ever thought he'd do.

He watched with sinking absolution as Sheva enacted her chilling justice, her loyalty to him far surpassing human understanding, all-encompassing and primitive and unfailing.

In a matter of seconds Owain stopped struggling, no more did he flail his arms.

His brutal reign over.

Still Sheva held onto her foe, her fangs buried in his throat.

"*Bledig*—" Dance called her off with a raw voice, his soul momentarily divided, his deepest pain exposed in that moment of loss.

He'd buried his mother. His wife and son. Druidh.

He'd lost all....

Lost a father he'd long ago banished in his heart.

Unable to do anything for Owain, turning from the sight, he looked down upon his last reason for living. The *engyl* who'd possessed him.

His precious *engyl* slipping away....

Stirred to action, he cradled her to his chest, straightened to his feet and hurried through the grass straight for the castle. On the road, Hywel turned the cart around.

Dance kept a grueling pace until he reached the drawbridge, then he called upon his last resources of strength and dashed with her through the courtyard, up the steps and kicking the doors wide hauled her into the keep. He got her inside and up the stairs, his lungs rasping, heart pounding. Down the corridor and elbowing his way into his bedchamber to gently lay her on his bed.

He rolled her softly to her side—gripped the arrow— and glad she was unconscious, snapped the end off. Then slowly pulled it from her shoulder. He tossed the bloodied shaft to the floor.

It was a small relief, but relief it was that the piercing hole was high, missing bone, her lungs. Blessedly somehow missing her heart.

Owain had taught Dance everything he knew about hunting, there was no better shot with a bow. He could have hit her heart....

Dance thought on it no more as he hurried from the

room to search for what he needed from the unbroken bottles strewn about his alchemy chamber. Glass crunched under his boots as he carefully knelt in the chamber, sorted through the shattered mess. The chamber reeked of scents all blended. He hadn't destroyed everything; a small blessing. The bottle he needed though lay tipped over. He saw in a heartbeat of dismay, the cork was partially displaced, the precious antidote all but leaked onto the floor. There was hardly enough to save.

It had to be enough!

He didn't have time to waste distilling more, Madeline would die within a matter of hours without it.

Dance met Hywel at the foot of the stairs where he paused only long enough to say, "Bring mustard water, blankets and hurry. To my bedchamber—" Then he rushed past the old man, taking the stairs three at a time.

Hywel entered quietly some minutes later, his brows drawn with worry. Dance looked up and motioned him over to the bed. He sat on the edge, holding Madeline against his chest, one arm supporting her shoulders, her head back as he dribbled the last drop of strychnine between her lips. Her head hanging back over his arm, he tossed the bottle aside and tenderly traced a finger down the pale column of her throat...encouraging her to swallow, praying she didn't choke and expel the precious elixir he so badly needed to get down her. "That's it, *engyl*," he whispered against her cheek as involuntary reflexes worked to swallow. "I'm here. I'm with you. Hold on for me," he rasped thickly, softly compelling with his heart things he didn't want to reveal to Hywel. The way he sat on the bed, his shoulder partially shielded both Madeline's body and his face.

"Start a fire," he said to the one awaiting his next command. "I want her kept warm. I also need a bath prepared." It would take both of them keeping the fire going through the next three days. He needed egg whites, but since there were no chickens, the mustard water would have to do. That he'd give to her next, if she kept the drops down.

Hywel set the blankets next to Dance on the bed before he shuffled off to toss wood into the cavernous hearth across the room. Behind him, a few minutes later, Dance heard the fire roar to life. He needed the bed closer to the heat, but couldn't risk a sparking ember sending the bedding up in flames. He needed his damn powers back, he railed silently to the God who had forsaken him. He reached out for the blankets. Dragged them over to bundle around her. He quickly had her cocooned in wool. His gaze riveted on the weak pulse in her throat. Her skin was paler than he remembered it. Behind him the fire blazed, already the warmth reaching him where he sat. Paralysis would come. The poison would gravely impede her breathing. Her respiration was already dangerously shallow.

"Come on, *engyl*," he raged hoarsely, waiting for some sign the antidote was working, his need to shake her awake almost overwhelming when he knew it did no good to panic.

He had to keep his mind clear, focused, his senses receptive. He needed a moment's privacy to get her out her soiled gown, his own breeches off so he wouldn't bloody the sheets. Hywel's presence behind him offered unswerving fealty. "I need the bodies taken to the chapel. Then bring the bath. Can you manage?"

Only a slight hesitation as the impart of "bodies" was digested. "*Ydw*, I will manage."

There was no clarification needed—no question as to whom Dance referred.

"Go then. And hurry back."

"I will," the old man assured him as he turned away to carry out his task.

SAVOUR, SWEET:—
A symbol of the yearning of the lower self after
righteousness and truth, which draws down the
Divine blessing.

17.

Dance waited for the door to close then he brushed his thumb over her bottom lip in a whisper-soft caress, his head lowering, his lips claiming hers as he'd never let himself claim her. His heart wrapping around her in his kiss, his touch reverent and solacing.

His eyes glistening, he willed her to open hers, stay in this world...not leave him. "Stay with me, *engyl.* Don't let go...don't you let go," he softly invoked of her, the litany tumbling from his lips as he feathered kisses over her cheek, her closed eyes, her downy brow, the soft whorl of her ear. His heart calling her back from the darkness to which she sought escape.

His blood chilling, he'd seen the bruises, the ones lacing her throat like fingers. She'd fought him. Using her small fists. Dance remembered well her claws raking his face in her fever. Had she clawed Owain? Or had the bastard had help?

He couldn't evade the merciless visions.

This time...Madeline struggling and no one to hear her screams. Everything in him shrank from what he was certain he'd find. The unspeakable memories were upon him, the blood and the pain. His gut clenching, seeing in his vision Madeline pinned to the ground. Violently hurt, repeatedly raped.

The evidence of which would kill him, but he couldn't leave her with another man's seed in her. If she were able, if she were conscious, she'd want a bath. She'd need to be held and told she'd be all right.

Very slowly he reached for the blood-streaked sleeve of her soiled shift and slid it from her shoulder. His eyes following the path of bruises he found underneath. Controlled fury raged through him, his eyes closing as he imagined what more he would find. Quicker, he peeled away the bodice, saw the larger purple welts marring her breasts. His throat constricting, his hand shaking, he locked his gaze on her face as he pushed the gown to her hips. His hand shifted under her bottom to lift her and then the shift was stripped down her legs and tossed to the floor.

Her bath water was brought in while Dance ran his hands over her, searching for broken bones, his touch careful around the worst bruises. His hand stilled over her abdomen, slid lower, her skin taut under his fingers. He held still for a moment...closed his eyes. His fingers slower to cup her soft woman curls, then brushed over her cleft...feeling for injury. He tenderly penetrated her petals, felt wetness, and he clenched his teeth—not knowing if blood or semen, his mind assessing. No tearing could he detect, yet. Opening his eyes, he watched her face for signs of waking and then slipped deeper into her hot body. His gaze dipped low, wanting visual confirmation of what his penetration found—she wasn't torn or damaged.

Breathing easier, he nudged her thighs wider and looked where he had her open. No blood—thank God.

He could see no trace of semen, yet he couldn't be completely sure there wasn't. There was no sure way to know if she'd been violated recently, how often, or by how many by looking.

Pushing a gut emotion out of his mind, he carried her to the bath scented with lavender, and lowered her in. Water sloshed over his chest as he supported her head, adjusting her weight. He left her hair unwashed, his attention instead devoted to her body. Quick and efficient her bath was—all of five minutes. He didn't want her chilled.

That taken care of, Dance quickly got her near the fire. Gently set her on his lap, the warmth of the blazing hearth soon warming her skin as he expediently toweled her dry.

Dance gently pulled the silk coverlet back, got her comfortable in bed and shed his own clothes on the floor. Beads of sweat dotted his brow, the heat of his body sliding in the bed next to her flushed skin. Cradling her close, her softness welcoming, her spine snug to his chest he covered them both. Conscious she wasn't worse, waiting for the first signs of improvement, he feathered open mouth kisses to her nape, her hair soft on his skin, her usual scent reminding him of their first coupling. His kisses moved to the gentle slope of her shoulder, the rigid curve of her spine. Lower he flattened his palm over her abdomen and pressed her up closer to his groin. He was glad she couldn't feel his body's shameless reaction, his flaring arousal flush with her lush bottom, the way she fit him like nature intended she fit him. His thigh atop hers, locking her too him in primitive ways that had him stiff and throbbing.

He'd missed her more than breathing...more than life.

The first tremors started low in her limbs, a gentle quivering and he braced himself for the long day ahead.

Dance held her in her delirium, his hold tender through the afternoon and into the evening. His litany of endearments whispered into her ear, holding onto her tighter when she trashed about. Hywel had come back hours before with the mustard water and set it on the bedside night table. He'd said nothing about finding Dance under the coverlet obviously naked with her; he'd kept his gaze averted and Dance knew he'd accepted the natural development of intimacy between them. He allowed himself a moment to consider how right it felt having her in his bed, having her back in his arms.

Dance was still alone with her hours later when her dreaming took on the shape of hell. He listened to each of her fitful cries, deep sobs shaking her curled body, her heart-wrenching pleas tumbling out and felt in his gut each harrowing whimper. As she fought and struck out at an imaginary assailant, her fists clenching and lashing. He would have closed his ears to it if he could have, for he knew of no way to take back the vile things that had been done to her.

The strychnine wasn't enough as he'd feared. It wore off around midnight and she lapsed into a death-sleep that had him out of bed, clamoring across her to wearily reach for the vessel of mustard water. He was vaguely aware through the daze of his fear that Hywel came and went and the fire never died. The firewood was gathered, the blaze fed and then he was alone again.

He was losing her...it came to him in that moment between wakefulness and sleep, where he teetered on the edge of exhaustion so great he could scarcely keep his eyes open.

It lanced his heart the feeling sinking into his soul.

Rousing her, using his mouth to tantalize and comfort, he kissed her savagely, his chest heaving with each frightful breath, and when he couldn't get a response from her the panic he held at bay came washing over him. He pulled himself to recline against the headboard, dragging her with him, his reserves of strength nearly depleted and he begged her to hold him back. Kiss him back. Don't let go....

Into his mouth he sipped the mustard water, tasting the bitter respite. Bent his head and lips lowered to hers, hers parted under his, he let a scant bit dribble from his lips into her.

A tear slid down his cheek. "*Engyl*, my sweet *engyl*." Her throat flexed to swallow. "Come back to me." Gently he jostled her, willed his life into her.

"God, don't let me lose her," he pleaded against her lips. *God in heaven, hear me this time and let me help her. Use my body, take my soul, my last breath....*

That's when a tiny tingle of awareness flared somewhere deep inside him, shifted like heated vibrations of light through his heart...spreading...feathering outward to swirl through his senses. Move up his spine like dancing spindles of blue heat. His scalp tingled and he felt enveloped in a familiar all-consuming infusion of prickly energy.

Tears streamed down his face....

He didn't dare to move a muscle, he kept utterly still, his most reverent prayer somehow happening. Alive inside him. His unspeakable relief and humble gratitude so intense....

Then he tensed as his body screamed with power. Painful—sweet—strong all at once. Flowing to his extremities, he felt his long dormant gift traveling through him, around him, embracing him with heavenly intensity.

A roar of elation burst from Dance's throat as his arms tightened around her.

Make me your servant, your instrument, God. Take the pain away from Wolfglyn...bring us peace...heal your little engyl. Love her, God...please don't forsake her.

With his whole heart, Dance solemnly vowed. *Give her life and I will go down on my knees to you.* A weaker whisper of conviction in his reverent prayer, *I will make my peace with my father...I give you my pledge....*

From her deep dark hole of emptiness, Madeline stirred, peace enveloping her, warmth cradling her close, her heart throbbing stronger...almost painful the beauty inside her, bursting forth, molten warmth igniting her blood, calling her back from the cold darkness of her cavern of death. The beautiful heathen of her nightmares held her anchored to the pulse of life shimmering between them. He wasn't letting her drift. Oh, but so very tired she was, so heavy.

Behind her eyelids came a blinding light, sudden sunshine wrapping her, shafting through her, blue—green—white spikes of vibrant light centered inside her chest streaming heavenward.

A moment of stillness followed and she was jerked out of her death trance. A soft voice, warm on her skin, whispered into her ear. *Stay, engyl, stay. Live, engyl, live.*

Mindless in his reverent focus, Dance spoke from the heart, his words tumbling forth, *let me love you, engyl, as our God loves you...come back to me...I need you....*

In a region of his soul, Dance felt her life force awaken, join his and he fiercely hugged her to his chest, her name on his lips....

His shoulders shook, his head bent to hers, silent sobs of happiness overcoming him. Divine love lit his heart, chased away the darkness and sorrow and he realized the sweet miracle for its greatness and grace and beauty.

"Thank you, God," he whispered at her damp temple.

He pulled back to peer down at her serene face in

sleep. How very precious she was to him. "Madeline," he encouraged softly. "Can you hear me? Answer me, *engyl*."

"...Dance." The faintest of answers from her lips as they worked to speak. Her eyes fluttered open. The beauty of her heathen greeted her. Her groggy gaze flitting over his face with love. Weak yet dazed by his nearness, the shimmering power still connecting them in a haven of warmth, she tried to lift one arm to embrace him, but it fell heavy to her side. His tears ran unchecked and she so wanted to hold him back, tell him she loved him, that he had nothing to worry about, she would take care of him. Then a shadow darkened her features — the memory.

Dance saw the unspoken fear. "He's dead, he can't hurt you, *engyl*."

Nor you, her gaze spoke to him, her adoration shining.

Gladness swelling his heart to near bursting, Dance lowered his head and brushed feathery kisses over her lips. "You're my sunshine, my life and I should have told you days ago," he breathed against her mouth. She was limp in his arms; her strength would take some time yet to recover. "Rest, *engyl*, rest now. I'm right here and I'm staying with you."

He stayed with her as he gave her his word. For the next two days as she reclaimed more strength and healed and the last of the poison left her body, he cared for her around the clock. He read to her while she slept. He composed poems in his mind and recited them to her. He brushed her hair with his boar-bristle brush and fed her because she couldn't feed herself. He gave her watered wine to relieve her thirst and when he knew she was sleeping soundly, he rubbed salve on her bruises. His hands roaming tenderly over her skin, the soft texture under his fingers making him think of pearls. His each touch cherishing, bonding her life force to his with gentle strokes. And he tried not to think beyond each hour spent with her.

Still it was there, his promise, in the back of his mind. He knew he had one more thing to do before many more days passed.

And he could even be benevolent because he had her back from the dark side.

All in life was perfect. Fragile still, yet perfect.

Dance had left Madeline safely tucked in bed where she spent the last three days sleeping, regaining her health. He'd bathed, shaved and put on a clean shirt and breeches and caught himself actually whistling a gay tune as he tugged on his boot.

As he made his way to the chapel, he peered up at the shimmery night sky and felt peace permeate his soul. He felt alive as he hadn't been alive for years.

He had decided to take no chances that something would come along to change things. So he left Madeline first thing he felt it was safe to leave her unattended.

The chapel as he strode over the threshold was chilly. Kept cold to preserve the occupants. A tingling finger walked down his spine the moment he spied the two wrapped bodies lying on the stone floor where Hywel had tended them the afternoon he brought them back.

Superstitions were ingrained in the *Cymry* and some believed a corpse candle hovered about one a few nights before the eve of death. Others claimed they heard the knockers or the ghost voice. Unfortunately, no such warning did Dance get either time. Nor had he really expected to. Death wasn't so easily predicted as he well knew.

He looked down at the smaller corpse. The other one

bigger. Both of them shrouded in wool blankets fetched from the keep. The nameless woman would be buried at Wolfglyn and the authorities in Llandeglay notified. He just remembered the braid of hair on his finger and pulled it off; let it fall to the ground in the dark.

Moonlight filtered in through the one tiny window casting shadow about the lifeless forms, illuminating the mounds. No fire heated the hearth, no sound broke the stillness of darkness. Dance's heart thudding in his chest was the only sound pounding in his ears.

His promise to God, his vow he would now make good.

He'd come to put the past behind him where things of the past belonged.

He'd felt disconnected these last days, untouchable by the past. When he should have felt grief with his father lying still as death, he could feel nothing. Something had happened to his hatred. It had been replaced in his heart with humility. It was simple, once his prayer had been answered, to shed what could no longer cause him grief.

Dance made his way carefully through the dark, his steps halting at his father's side.

He looked down, saw no threat in the lifeless body. Inexplicably he crouched down, his hand going out to rest on the heart that no longer beat with loathing and madness. Dance's fingers clenched there, his head bowing as deeply hidden sorrow burst from its hiding place in his soul. Pity welled up in his heart for the man who'd been his enemy for so long.

Aneira couldn't have healed Owain, but Owain had been too far gone to see that.

When a man lost his reason to live there was little in the world worth cherishing.

Under Dance's fist his father lay cold, unmoving, his mindless devastation over.

Dance would one of these days find the memories less painful, each passing year a balm distancing him from the events until there was nothing left of the memories...not this one here in the chapel either. They would fade as the red woolen blanket would fade with age. As mortality faded with each passing year.

Here in the chapel, amidst death, a sense of peace laid its hand on Dance's shoulders. It offered comfort.

His eyes filled with shimmering tears.

Relief. Regret. Renewed hope. All washing over him.

Each tear streaking down his face, dropping onto his hand with cleansing finality.

He cried there at his father's side for several minutes — his chest heaving.

How did one both love and loathe the same person?

Shocking as his admission of two days ago, he'd never truly hated his father.

He despised his sire's existence, reviled his sickness — mostly he felt shame. Helplessly embarrassed by his father's infirmity. His capacity for cruelty.

Dance also understood why it had been hard for a father to live with a son who possessed the power Dance did. He'd often wondered why he'd been chosen over his father to bear the gift. Owain understandably attacked that which he feared. He let feelings of inadequacy obsess him.

Owain found his peace in death. He would be haunted no more by his own son.

And Dance would live the rest of his life with the memory.

"I once loved you," he whispered brokenly to the still body of his father, his fist clenching in the blanket.

Blinded by tears, he pushed to his feet and stared down at the shapeless mass for a minute more. Then he left the chapel.

He told himself as he made his way in the dark across the courtyard, he had better memories to look forward to. Reasons to rejoice. When he'd never thought it possible he would one day say that.

He had one more stop to make.

In the dark, Dance knelt at the shrine below the painting of his wife and son. The summerhouse was cold, the candles gutted. He lifted haunted eyes to the spot he knew held their faces. The smell of them poignant in his memory, he needed no light for his good-bye. In the darkness of the room devoted to them, he sent them a prayer for eternal peace. A heartfelt apology for his appallingly inadequate love.

"I've been given another chance," he murmured softly to the family he had no more, "to be whole again. I will never understand it, but I do understand I was meant to stay behind. Meant to find the girl in the forest. She's here now in the castle in my bed. Where I've had no woman besides you. You'd have to know her to understand. Believe me I tried to avoid her." He drew a deep breath. "I've changed. Things have happened. She's inside me and I've been in her where she's taken no man before me. Her blood stains my sheet. Somehow, through her, my powers are alive and well. And I've since learned things are best left to Him who grants life as he takes it away."

He sighed heavily. "I've come to say good-bye tonight. May you find eternal peace in the arms of a noble knight in your realm." His eyes filled with tears. "Give my son a kiss for me—tell him I will see him one day in the future. When we are both together again and he can understand I didn't wish to be separated from him." He swiped his face with a sleeve. "I've loved you for so long...I never wanted to let go of you. God forgive me, Aneira, I don't want you waiting for me...."

For a long time, Dance remained there beneath his family of another life. He willed them happy...and finally...as the night wore on, he left them to their destiny as he took his own to account. When he left the summerhouse he pulled the door shut without looking back. Tomorrow he would have Hywel move everything from the summerhouse to his mother's bedchamber. Lock all the memories away in the room with the part of his heart devoted to that memory.

Back inside the castle, he found Sheva waiting in the foyer, sleeping by the door where she knew she'd be first to see him return.

He crouched down beside her as she licked his hand in welcome.

They'd shared much Sheva and him.

He scratched the scruff of her ear. She panted happily. "Shall we awaken sleeping beauty?" he asked Sheva, smiling at his own foolery, his heart unburdened and free to indulge in unhampered joy.

They traversed the stairs in lighthearted play. Sheva bounding ahead of him, his hand swinging down to tag her tail and send her darting out of his reach. They played down the long corridor to the master bedchamber.

Outside the door, he looked down into Sheva's bright amber eyes and brought a finger to his lips in a gesture asking for quiet. "I'll kiss her while you lick her hand," he told her, grinning. "And we'll see if our sleeping beauty remembers us."

His hand reached the latch, but before he could open the door, it swung in and suddenly Hywel stood facing him, his eyes blinking. Dance's gaze lowered to the empty broth bowl his friend carried. The old man shot a glance over his shoulder and lowered his voice, "She woke while ye were away. Said she was hungry and she missed ya." A smile cracked his wizened face. "Told her ye was coming back soon. Just settled back ta bed, our Maddie *fach*. So don't ye be wakin' the poor mite."

Unabashed, Dance looked beyond Hywel at the bed and murmured, "I'll be down later to help with the graves."

He debated what he had yet to do about notifying Madeline's brothers of her whereabouts. If he even did, how much did he tell them? And how much would they guess had already transpired?

"I know I'll need to do something about getting word to Llandeglay about the other body I found. Someone's bound to be looking for her, whoever she is." He sighed and wouldn't let himself dwell on the missive his conscious demanded he send to Madeline's family.

Hywel nodded back over his shoulder. "Our Maddie 'tis not herself, yet." His brows waggled. "I've been thinkin' she'll want a weeks rest and quiet," he helpfully pointed out. "Them that's lookin' for her would only trouble her thoughts and stir things up."

Heartened by Hywel's understanding, Dance clasped his shoulder in silent appreciation, the weight of making a decision postponed by unspoken agreement for another week.

His face cracked with a broad smile. He had a week's reprieve. A week to indulge in fanciful abandon. She might need even two weeks before she was returned to glowing health, he decided in high spirits.

Dance sat himself in the chair next to her bedside and

watched over his *engyl*. He hadn't wanted to examine too closely his feelings, but it was already too late. The reason his memory of Aneira was fading was he'd replaced her in his life...with an *engyl*. Cupid's arrow had penetrated to the depths of his soul.

He wanted Madeline in his life...in his bed...his child planted in her womb, and he wanted her to have a choice in staying or leaving. Unfortunately, he didn't expect she'd be given much say one way or another once her bloodthirsty siblings had her back.

No surprise there. Dance had nothing to offer her except a tumble-down castle.

His heart.

His bed and the warmth of his body on cold nights.

What did he tell her? Stay with me? Forget everything that's happened? Forget that I left you unguarded? I'll never let you be hurt again?

He would simply demand her family turn her care over to him...as they staked him to a bonfire and roasted him alive.

Were Madeline his sister, he'd want his head. No way in hell were they going to give him a chance to atone for her unspeakable treatment.

Sheva planted herself at Dance's feet, her head resting on her paws.

They both waited in silence. Behind them the fire crackled and spit.

The smell of lavender was heady in the room, drugging one's senses, the ambient silence peaceful. Light rain pattered against the glass panes and Dance found himself—at the end of his strength now that he let himself relax—growing increasingly tired.

There was no danger lurking over his head. No reason

he couldn't let his guard down and catch a few minutes rest himself.

He drifted off in his chair perched near the bed.

That's how Madeline found him when her eyes fluttered open a handful of minutes later.

Her mind was clearing, her terrible headache gone this time. She was lying on her stomach, one hand dangling over the side of the bed, the other under her pillow, pristine linen soft on her cheek. She stared at the hauntingly beautiful man sleeping not three feet away and she smiled a dreamy smile rife with love. He was sleeping and couldn't see her looking at him the way she was, so she let herself linger in her perusal.

His sensual full lips were faintly curved, his features restful. With one rakish ebony lock falling across his brow, he looked the very image of a sleeping prince. From a romantic fable. White linen molded his broad shoulders, his shirt open at the neck.

He slept in casual repose; the sleeves of his shirt rolled up, baring forearms dusted with dark hair. Black leather breeches molding narrow hips, every inch of him raw masculinity. Every inch a creature of virile grace and strength. He'd fallen asleep watching over her.

She still couldn't believe it was over. A residual of fear shivered through her when she thought about her capture. She had to remind herself she was safe. Hywel had reassured her Owain was dead.

It was near sweltering in the room, and she soundlessly kicked the cover aside. The coverlet came to rest low on her hips, exposing bare skin to the waist. Limp auburn curls lay tangled about the pillow beneath her cheek. Lavender a prominent scent in the over-heated chamber. Her skin was clean, she realized. Dance must have bathed her.

Should she wake him? she wondered. Demand he crawl back into bed with her?

The poison, Hywel told her, had near killed her. When she'd gotten worse instead of better, how she'd scared them. He'd talked animatedly while he told her Dance's healing magic had returned only at the last minute when she was slipping away.

Dance had nursed her back to health.

Her pagan prince. He had his powers back.

What now, she wondered, would he do that his gift was restored him?

It shouldn't be wasted.

Certainly, he could do all the things he'd once done. Deliver babies. Put a stitch to a wound. Bathe a fevered brow. Restore, if he wished, Castle Wolfglyn to its former beauty.

Take another wife, she thought despondently, the idea painful and abhorrent.

What would become of her? How did she figure into his life now when he no longer needed to protect her from his father?

Suddenly afraid of facing an uncertain future, she held her breath and prayed things between them wouldn't change.

She didn't want to go back to Boston.

Incongruous thoughts flittered through her head, all of them posing obstacles. Her brothers. Her father. The awful moment when she'd need to face them with what they would view as unacceptable, shameful, her virtue heedlessly given to a Welshman. She would just have to explain she was the one who compromised Dance. And somehow she would make them to listen.

And Dance, if he didn't feel the same way—if he didn't

love her—he surely felt something for her. He couldn't just send her away, not now after all they'd been through. Could he?

So engrossed she was in thought, she jumped when a wet tongue licked her fingers.

Gasping, she jerked her hand up before she realized Sheva wasn't gnawing her arm off. She was just saying hello.

MIRACLES OF HEALING :—
These are symbolic of certain facts of spiritual growth which laws are as yet unrecognized by people at large. They occur as the Higher nature becomes more powerful in the soul, and they are psychic and spiritual endowments which come in due course according to the soul's preparedness for them, and which are added to the human nature as the souls evolve. They are not external phenomena exciting wonderment.

18.

As a silver head emerged above the edge of the mattress, Madeline suddenly found herself eye to eye with Sheva. It brought back memories of that first night when she'd thought Sheva was going to eat her.

No pet dragon here, just a silver she-wolf with amber eyes the same color of her master.

Tentative, experimentally, she lifted a finger where her hand rested near the bed's edge. Sheva flicked an ear upright and nudged closer to lick her finger. This time Madeline didn't gasp. The reunion was a pleasant one. Both of them previously acquainted and forging a bond in an elemental way. Sheva's tongue felt like sandpaper on her skin. Wet and rough and gentle.

Who would have thought Madeline would make a friend of Dance's shadow?

"Thank you," Madeline whispered gratefully, her fingers hesitant before venturing up to pet Sheva's furry scruff.

Tongue hanging, Sheva basked in the attention, her weight fully pressed against the soft mattress.

"Sleeping beauty awakens," a rough-soft murmur came from the chair.

Sheva, hearing her master, circled to lay her muzzle on his thigh. Idly, he reached out to stroke her ear while his heavy lidded eyes regarded Madeline with open affection.

Smiling like a guileless child, Madeline blew him a kiss from her disheveled sprawl atop his grand bed. "My healer has his powers back, I've learned." Her purr was infused with joy, her skin warming under his heated gaze.

"How are you?" he asked softly, leaning forward to tenderly lace his fingers in hers.

Instant warmth flared to life in the shared touch, in the breath-held moment of awareness shimmering between them.

Squeezing his strong fingers in hers, she heard in the question, no matter how lightly broached, an underlying concern about how she'd been treated by her captor. "I fell in the river getting away and washed downstream," she explained quietly, her thoughts shying away from further reflection. "I must have near drowned because I don't remember anything after getting away," she added emphatically in a softly murmured sigh that which was mostly true.

He briefly closed his eyes, his throat convulsing around a lump of relief...and didn't seem to breathe for a long moment. Then he opened his eyes and she found them glistening.

Fathomless topaz eyes, shuttered by dark lashes, regarded her with curious tenderness.

Their fingers were locked, his strength steadfast, his hold on her almost painful.

"I'm fine," she prevaricated softly, bringing his hand to her mouth. Her lips brushed his knuckles with a light kiss. "You said I'm your sunshine, your life." She affected a faint smile because he was being patient when he wanted to ask her more questions. "I wasn't dreaming that, was I? You missed me a little, maybe?"

He swallowed a soft growl and without a word, moved from the chair to kneel on one knee by the bed—Sheva backing out of the way. He dragged their twined fingers to his lips, bowed his head over her hand and pressed a lingering kiss to her palm.

A long poignant moment of silence eschewed while they neither spoke.

His mouth felt warm on her skin, his kiss repentant and remorseful and reverent. Tendrils of vibrant heat spiraled though her. She used her free hand to reach for the inky silkiness of his hair, her fingers spearing through his thick mane. Then her hand moved to cup his head as her heart swelled with heartrending adoration.

"I thought I'd lost you," he finally whispered against her palm, his head lowered still so his expression was hidden from her.

In those words, though, she heard an implicit note of sincerity that couldn't be mistaken. As if he'd feared he'd lost the only thing that mattered to him.

What would he say, she wondered, if she bravely told him she loved him? Would he retreat? If he did retreat, if he did get a wary look in his eyes, could she pretend a lighthearted levity when her heart was breaking?

Was he already planning on returning her to Llandeglay in a few days?

Coward at heart, she clenched her eyes closed against the threat of tears. *I won't leave you, I won't go.*

So lost she was in thought, she didn't notice he'd stopped kissing her palm until she opened her eyes to find him peering beneath his lashes at her in a way that immediately brought a flush to her cheeks. Good lord, had he guessed what she was thinking?

"When you feel stronger," he suggested, "I thought we'd have a picnic in bed."

She breathed deeply. "And you'll read me another of your poems," she queried unabashed, trying to evade the irreconcilable emotions for which there was no resolution.

He looked momentarily uncomfortable. "You remember those?"

"I was sleeping. Not dead. And they were beautiful as I recall." Her brows pinched in concentration. "Or at least they sounded lovely in my delirious dreams." She absently toyed with an ebony strand of hair. "Can I hear them again"—a pleading suffused her words—"now that I'm awake?"

He laughed softly as his finger reached for and gently tugged an auburn tendril at her cheek. "You weren't supposed to remember so well."

"But now that I do, you will read them to me again, won't you?" Her smile intimate, bright, cheery. "Every one of them."

How could he resist her simple request after so nearly losing her? "Maybe later."

Her brow arched. "When you're ready, you can surprise me."

He squeezed her hand affectionately. "I must go out for awhile."

A shadow darkened her gaze, a flicker of fear resurfacing—then gone. "Will you be gone long?"

"How about if I hunt nearby." He knew where the deer bedded down and when he wouldn't ordinarily hunt his prey while they rested, a depleted supply of fresh meat required an exception this time.

"Take me with you," she breathlessly extolled, though her lazy sprawl was more indicative of slumber.

He gave her an assessing look. "Tomorrow maybe. After you've had a solid meal and you're stronger."

"But I feel fine." Yet she was already dozing again, her close call with death too recent.

"First our picnic," he murmured as her eyes grew heavy, "then we'll see."

She was asleep before he finished speaking.

Dance watched her for a moment more, then bent and kissed her before standing up. It was warm in his bedchamber, but he covered her up, tucked the ebony satin coverlet under her chin against the chance of her catching a chill.

Out in the courtyard some minutes later, he joined Hywel for the burial. Hywel's lantern light cast long shadows from the corner of the courtyard. It had drizzled while Dance was with Madeline, the night air damp. Rain clouds drifted by a full moon, parting to a clear night sky sprinkled with stars.

Soundlessly, Dance set his lantern down next to Hywel's. The old man looked up, nodded across the gaping dark pit in the earth, and continued to dig without pause. Dance reached for the pick, hefted it over his head and let it fall. A rhythmic sound set the pace for pick and shovel, the chipping and digging of wet earth as they worked.

The girl was laid to rest first, a short prayer said over her grave as Dance tapped a cross into the soft dirt.

It took longer to dig the last grave, which was deeper. Both the freshly dug graves sat apart from the common area already holding three rain-battered mounds covered with grass.

His mother, his wife, his son. Undisturbed graves, the grass on them lush, overgrown, a wildly tangled vine lacing the ground, curling up each cross. Lungs heaving, Dance reflected on happier moments and turned back to help Hywel finish.

Twenty minutes later they stood in the dark at the edge of a circle of lantern light and Dance said what prayer he had prepared. "God rest you," he murmured over Owain's cross and drove it into the ground. Beside him, he heard Hywel say "amen" in chorus to that which Dance finished in silence.

The burial was done. The last of his past, the last of his family laid to rest.

With his longbow in hand, Dance left the keep a short time later, melting into the shadows as he followed Sheva's path over the drawbridge. In a clear black sky a full moon shimmered, illuminating the jutted road ahead of him.

He knew when Madeline woke this time she'd need more than broth.

His prey would be bedded down for the night, making his task a bit of a challenge in the dark. But then he knew where the deer traveled; he would need to go deeper into the forest. Fresh venison would be a welcome change. With the sheep and chickens slaughtered, he now would hunt for their meal. Which excuse also provided him the opportunity to do some scouting along the trails for tracks. Those belonging to a party of riders. He'd prefer no surprises from unwelcome visitors.

He didn't want Madeline to be disturbed, he didn't want her distressed over a confrontation right now when she was yet so weak. He had a week's reprieve yet.

She needed time. Time to deal with things in her own way.

Sooner or later she'd be confronting that which lay suppressed beneath a thin veneer of civility. Where she held her pain and rage buried. Waiting like a putrid wound needing lanced.

When that fragile thread of composure broke...he wanted to be with her.

If her family interfered before she could purge her soul, she might never overcome the mental scars. She'd return to Boston, go about her day to day duties with a brave smile for everyone, while inside she was broken and suffering.

If he did nothing else right, he could help heal her inside.

Before they came to take her away, he prayed he be allowed enough time to transplant some of the pain with happier memories.

Dance found their evening meal sleeping in the tangled forest cover near the stream. His arrow found its deadly mark; the young buck had scented him and was getting to his feet when Dance dropped him not twenty feet away.

He skillfully and expediently cleaned his kill; fed Sheva the entrails and heart. Then he filled the burlap bag with fresh meat while his thoughts filled with an urgency to get back before Madeline gained complete consciousness. She'd be wide awake this time and hungry.

Dance kept to the forest trails covered with a dense blanket of damp leaves, his footsteps soundless as he moved over the familiar paths, Sheva like a sleek gray shadow at his back. He avoided the roads where they might be spotted if someone were out there in the dark searching. Relieved he was, he didn't see any trace of hoof prints as he scanned the muddy road winding its way through the torn barrier to the castle. Wolfglyn sat quiet in the distance like a shadowed sentinel shimmering in the silver moonlight. All was peaceful within, the woman he adored waiting for him in his bed. He was alone no more. All was secure within those stone walls. His past deeds and sorrows forgiven and already relegated to less important realms of memory.

Madeline was his lodestone, his fierce little champion, and she'd brought him out of the darkness into light. He could feel her in his soul, in his heart. She was a part of him now.

Tomorrow he would take her with him to hunt. She would be at his side when he showed her his private retreat. He would teach her how to call to the deer, how to spot their trails. He'd hitch the litter up to ole Bones and take her for a short ride around the castle. And one day soon he'd show her around the garden where he cultivated what he needed to distill more medicine.

They'd have their first picnic tonight...in bed.

In the kitchen below the floor of the master bedchamber, Dance handed Hywel the burlap bag holding what was to be their evening meal. Then he went to the wash basin, poured water from the earthenware jug. While Hywel lifted the lid to the boiling kettle of water, Dance shed his bloodied clothes and scrubbed up. Sheva, fed and content, plopped herself down on the floor under the kitchen table.

"In the morning," he told Hywel, "I need you to move everything from the summerhouse to my mother's room. I'll have Madeline with me. You think you can manage it while I'm gone?"

Over his shoulder the old man, smiled. "Don't worry 'bout me. I'm glad ye be takin' our Maddie *fach* out for fresh air. Give her something ta do with her time. Ya see anythin' suspicious tonight?"

A faint scowl. "As far as I could tell, nothing within two miles. I'll know better tomorrow in the daylight."

"Ye keepin' her ta the forest trails, I reckon?"

"I thought I'd stay in the north *glyn*, show her the new fawns." He dressed quickly in a clean shirt and breeches he found draping the chair by the washstand. "I'll scout around while she rests."

A silence stretched between them for a moment.

"Maybe them that's lookin' for her will give up and go home," Hywel murmured thoughtfully.

An echo of the same, yet more fiercely possessive speculation sifted through Dance mind—each minute ticking by bringing him that much closer to the inevitable. He felt powerless against the odds and yet who knew better than he how fate had its own agenda.

Yet on his way up the stairs to his bedchamber, he considered drawing on his illusive gift of sight. What would the future reveal? he wondered, if he indeed called upon the visions. Did he really want to know?

He paused on the landing of the long dim corridor stretching out before him. What if it wasn't what he wanted to see?

Dance shook his head clear of that thought. Yet it still stayed with him as he opened the door to his room and stepped inside.

He saw no more than a glimpse of bare flesh as Madeline ran toward him. Tears streamed down her face. Then she was melting against him, his arms going around her to hold her close as he scanned the room for the cause of her distress. She was soft, trembling, heat from her body warming him as he quickly contemplated and discarded a number of reasons for such a greeting. He dropped his head, his lips grazing her temple, his whisper consoling, "What's wrong, *cariad?*"

"You're back," she sobbed against his chest

Her fingers were fisted in his shirt; she was clinging to him, the fear in her voice unmistakable.

And he silently castigated himself for not coming directly up to her the minute he got back. "I'm here, *engyl*." His arms tightened as he scooped her up to cradle her in his arms. "I'm back and you're safe...don't be afraid, I'm right here."

But her sobbing only grew more hysterical as he carried her to the chair near the fire and sat down with her. She immediately curled into him, her legs drawing up so she could get closer, her face hidden in his neck. He said nothing for a long number of minutes because she wasn't capable of conversing. A floodtide of misery, all that she'd bravely contained for the last week came pouring forth. Purging its way out. And all he could offer her was his warmth and protection.

"Madeline," he calmly asserted when she breathed between sobs, "I'm back." And with quiet conviction, he consoled, "I won't leave you again."

And he told her then an embellished tale of his venture into the forest earlier, he told her of the night like this one, when he'd discovered an *engyl* looking for a healer in the forest. How brave and fierce this *engyl*. How she wouldn't listen to reason when he'd tried to tell her he couldn't help her. How he'd thought her dense to defy him, her beauty tormenting him, making him want to do things he knew were forbidden him. How she'd rode in his lap across the stream, every shift of her lush bottom driving a stake of desire through his body. "I told Hywel if he found her," he went on, "not to bring her back here." His voice grew quiet, his tone soothing, his gaze staring into the fire. "Then I saw her face in the light the next morning. Hywel brought her in on a litter. She was soaked through, her lips blue from the cold...." His voice trailed off as he recalled the exact moment he felt the mortal blow to his senses. "I recall, thinking she was beautiful and knowing she was going to give me grief." He smiled at the memory, then looked down to find Madeline quietly peering up at him, her sobs reduced to sniffles. He pressed his lips to her brow and murmured, "On a pallet in the chapel, I peeled her wet shirt and breeches off. I remember bathing her fever. My hands were shaking...."

He breathed in the sweet scent of her; his attention riveted on the slope of her shoulder, the pale perfection of her skin. His thumb skimmed the wound now healed. "And I don't think you knew for some time how badly I wanted to keep you...."

She was quiet in his lap, the tension gone from her body and ready at last, his senses told him, to talk. "Forgive me." He nuzzled his face in her hair. "I never wanted you hurt, *cariad*."

She hid her face against him, her hands twining around his waist to hold tight to him as she started. "I was so afraid you would find me," she murmured into his chest, the words tumbling out in a rush, "all I could think of was getting away from the camp." She sniffled. "I knew I didn't stand a chance against three of them, so I dove into the river. I remember being cold, and when I woke up I was clinging to a rotted tree stump. Then I heard them looking for me"—she shivered, her voice hushed—"and I crawled onto the bank, took off my wet gown and tossed it back in the river so when they found it, it would be far down stream.

"I crawled into the forest," she went on softly, "they were close; I could hear them arguing. I hid in an abandoned burrow and waited there until I couldn't hear them any more. When I woke up it was dawn. I didn't know where I was. But I knew I had to get out of the forest." She dragged in a deep breath. "I remembered being told about keeping the mountains on my right and left, the moon straight ahead. But then I got turned around. Somehow I ended up back at the deserted camp." Her breathing turned shallow, he could feel her desperation, feel her reliving the horror— her body stiffened with remembered panic. "I found the chemise they left behind...."

When she didn't go on, he gathered her more closely, praying to God she hadn't had to watch the woman vilely raped. "The other woman was gone?" he gently supplied into the stretching silence.

She nodded and clutched tighter to him.

Feeling useless, frustrated and wishing he could turn back time, he could only imagine the parts she avoided voicing. "You tried to get away, but they tracked you down?"

She was shivering from shock, her silence answer in itself.

He reached for the blanket that had fallen to the floor. Drew it around her and held her safe.

When he wanted to give vent to the rage he thought contained, instead he very quietly asked, "Did they hurt you, *engyl?*"

She violently shook her head.

Needing to make certain she understood what he was asking, he carefully restated, "You know what I'm asking?"

She nodded fiercely and hid her face. "He...he said you

thought I was dead." She started crying again. "He killed Llwyd—Owain killed them both. He told me if I wanted to see you again...I had to do exactly what he said."

Instantly contrite, he tenderly stroked her hair. "Shhh, *engyl*, it's all right." His mouth brushed her temple. "No more questions, I promise. Rest now." Holding her close, he cupped her head to his chest. "Relax, *cariad*."

Dinner arrived on a tarnished platter. Two bowls of steaming stew, two identical mazers of wine. Water added to one for Madeline as instructed. Hywel wordlessly deposited the tray upon the mahogany night table and turned to Dance for further instruction. A silent exchange of barely decipherable gestures took place—Dance shaking his head to the inquiry of "anything else" and again "no" when Hywel pointed to the bathing tub full of cold water.

Dance paused to glance at the neatly stacked pile of wood, decided there was sufficient fuel to last the night and dismissed Hywel with a nod.

Sheva remained where she was in her usual hapless sprawl near the door, stretched out on the cool stone floor, her lazy gaze following Hywel. Dance gently lifted Madeline as he rose from the chair. She'd cried herself dry; the scars to her soul lanced. He wanted her to have something on her stomach before he put her to bed.

He carried her the short distance—his footsteps muffled over the hand-woven rug—to his empty bed. Sitting on the mattress edge, he settled against the headboard and held her. He reached for the earthenware of venison stew and set it on the blanket between her legs.

"How about trying something solid?" He steadied her. "You hold this...and I'll feed you," he breathed against the softness of her hair. He knew she was trying to compose herself—his distraction working. Tentatively, she placed both hands around the bowl to steady it, while he dipped the spoon in.

"Ummm, this is delicious," she remarked in a soft voice minutes later. "Here, I can do it—" When she reached up, he reflexively evaded her grasp.

"But I like feeding you," he murmured with a smile, her lavender scent surrounding him, her delectable bottom balanced on that part of him painfully erect, while he tried to ignore his instantaneous reaction to her. Wanting to solace her, he prayed fiercely she wasn't repulsed by his obvious desire. "Can I get you a nightdress? Would you be more comfortable—"

"No," she assured him around a mouthful, snuggling closer to him in a way that made him grit his teeth against the sublime attack on his libido. She smiled up at him. "I like it right here."

He smiled back, relieved to see no revulsion in her soft gray eyes. Could she be happy here, he wondered restively, restraining those possessive urges prompting him to bind her to him forever.

When she'd eaten every last bite, he kissed her pert little nose and leaned away, his gaze searching. "How's the stomach feel?"

Licking the spoon, she leaned over to place the bowl back on the tray—and he reached to help her. He offered her the mazer of watered-wine. "Thirsty? We have wine."

She took it from him and sipped—wrinkled her nose. "Rather weak wine…"

He grinned down at her, her color indeed better. "So you noticed? Good. That shows me you can tell the difference." Nothing wrong with her sense of taste—she'd not suffered any permanent paralysis, he thought with vast relief.

She pointed to the night table, the sheaf of parchments

haphazardly crammed into a leather bound volume. "That's what you were reading to me?" she asked, her interest completely diverted from past tragic events.

He looked to where she pointed and gave a negligent shrug, her excitement charming.

"Oh, please," she implored in guileless glee when he said nothing, "read to me."

A dark brow raised speculatively. "If I do, you'll need follow doctors orders and crawl under the covers, first?"

She gave him a slanted smile. "And you'll read to me in bed?" she bargained sweetly, her arms going around his waist to squeeze, her cheek pressed against his chest.

"I think we can manage something," he laughingly conceded, refraining from the need to crawl in bed with her when he'd not had to hold himself in check the last few days. When time was in precious shortage. When it was too soon for more intimate contact even if she was to encourage him. "Only one story." And when she would have protested, he said, "I want you to have a good night's rest so you'll be ready for our outing tomorrow."

That subdued all further protest as he hoped it would.

Giving her head a chaste kiss, he pulled the covers aside and shifted with her in his arms to gently settle her against the pristine pillow before he edged away. For a moment, he stood looking down on her. Tresses the rich color of autumn billowed over the pillow in a brilliant halo making her look chaste and bewitching and incredibly alluring. She stretched in a decidedly wanton fashion. A shimmering heat furled through him, poignant, fierce, unmindful of delicacy. Then her gaze traveled down...settled low. And set off a jolt of spiking lust. The ache throbbing through his groin sought gratification, his body wanting her.

What did she think? Did it revolt her to find he was aroused?

She didn't look revolted.

Would she reject him, he wondered, if he touched her intimately?

He felt time slipping through his fingers, the foreboding waste of it as he bent and tucked her in. Then he grabbed up the volume from the night table and carefully sat on the edge of the bed next to her.

Dance spent the evening at her bedside reading the passages he'd loved as a boy.

"...*Orlando pursued her through thorns and rocks, while the sky gradually became overcast, and at last he was assailed by tempest, lightning, and hail. While he thus pursued, a pale and meagre woman issue from a cave, armed with a whip, and, treading close upon his steps, scourged him with vigorous strokes. Her name was Repentance, and she told him it was her office to punish those who neglected to obey the voice of Prudence and seize the faerie Fortune when he might...*"

When he paused in reading to gaze upon her, it was with undisguised fondness. Beside him, his sleepy beauty listened with a faint smile of a dreaming faerie or *tylwyth teg* on her lips, her fingers resting on his thigh as if she needed him close.

His smile for her was instant, unrepentant, devoid of prudence.

His regard stirred her. Subtle her shift, her lips brushed his thigh in reciprocation.

The sensation left by her mouth curled around inside him to leave him grappling with an insane desire to kiss her back until she was weak with desire.

He reluctantly repressed unruly urges and turned back to the book in his lap.

There was a long interval of silence after the last of the story ended, where he closed his eyes and became the deluded wretch in the story.

It was selfish, he told himself, to seduce her into staying.

His desperation acute, he looked down and found his sleeping *engyl* breathing evenly, restful, her innocence radiating like a nimbus around her. His lungs expanded with her scent. Wishing he could be the one to love her as she deserved to be loved, he silently bent his head and softly pressed his lips to hers.

A vibrant, luminous flux shimmered through him, her essence imprinting his heart. His fiery aura entwined with her fainter lambent corona. He let her delicate life force envelop him for quivering moments more...then he withdrew.

Instinctually, he knew she was meant for him. Yet, as fate brought them together, could he consciously take away her choice?

That night Dance walked the halls of Wolfglyn, his spirit conflicted, his sightless gaze focused inward where he searched for the strength to face whatever came. Too restless for sleep, he visited the chapel. Where he prayed on his knees to the One who listened to the woes of man.

Toward dawn, Dance hitched the litter to ole Bones. He intended they hunt close to Wolfglyn. His longbow and quiver were tied to the litter next. Blankets piled on for warmth.

A pale streak of light brightened the pre-dawn sky. Morning brought with it the promise of mild temperatures and pleasant weather as if the heavens sensed he'd planned to take Madeline out for a few hours. When he went back up to the bedchamber with her breakfast tray, he found her waiting for him.

GOLDEN LIGHT :—
A symbol of the Divine radiance of Truth which
flashes forth from above and illumines the soul.

19.

Madeline was smiling as she was deposited with gentle care upon the litter tied to ole Bones. Breakfast had tasted wonderful. She'd had a bath and Dance had dried her hair for her by the fire, then brushed it until it shone. She felt human again, her spirits buoyant. At peace, she was feeling quite revived.

The damp morning air cooled her skin like a breathy mist, the day gloriously accommodating. With Dance close at hand everything was perfect.

He'd dressed casual in a white lawn shirt, which bared a vee of muscled chest, black leather breeches fitting like a second skin to his long, powerful legs. His hair, too, freshly washed. He looked delightfully heathen. Wildly sensual. All dark beauty chiseled into his features, his full sensual lips, the angular planes of his face. Thick dark lashes shadowing eyes that softened when he looked her way.

Her pagan healer.

She'd also noticed, though inconspicuous, how Dance became pensive when he didn't think she was looking, his thoughts obviously somewhere else.

Though she basked in his attention, she missed his scowl of authority, that impatience that was part of his charm. She hoped to have the Dance back soon, who looked at her with barely restrained hunger. She also realized he needed time and a certain amount of space to workout whatever it was plaguing him.

Hywel had told her Dance hadn't slept.

As she lay back on the litter and closed her eyes against the flush of awareness caused by the proximity of his hard body pressed against her, she silently smiled to herself. Maybe she would require a nap, she mused thoughtfully, in the middle of the afternoon.

He was bent over her, tucking the blanket around her.

Above her head, the soft swish of a tail stirred a light breeze that touched her skin, the buzz of a fly nearby, the heat of Dance's body reaching over hers, all registering on her senses with sublime contentment.

Her plan all settled, she opened her eyes. Dance's face inches from hers, his concentration was on what he was doing. Impulsively, she reached up and cupped his face between her palms. He looked into her with those haunted amber eyes and she felt him searching. For what exactly? she wanted to ask.

Emboldened by the challenge in his gentle restraint, she lifted her mouth to his.

He smelled of clover, a heady scent to her brain. His lips under hers were moist and a heat unfurled inside her. He tasted wicked, his breath hot on her skin.

Then his fingers closed tightly on her shoulders...and he kissed her back.

A chaste kiss. A kiss that contained repressed longing. A kiss that had her near shouting in frustration as she hungrily sucked his bottom lip into her mouth.

The kiss ended with a muted growl as he pulled away.

He stood above her, the cloudless blue sky a silhouette behind him, his expression torn.

She peered up at him, trying to understand what was going through his mind.

Was this his way of distancing himself before he said good-bye?

She felt faint at the thought. Maybe she wasn't well after all, she conveniently decided.

Maybe he'd already sent word to her brothers and they were on their way here. And he was taking her out to meet them under the pretense of hunting.

She swallowed the thickness in her throat and forced a smile. "Shall we be on our way?" she suggested lightly, all while burrowing deeper into the blankets as she chastened herself about wishing he would ask her to stay. *I'll be your leman, your friend, whatever you desire, just tell me.*

His eyes narrowed on her in contemplation for a moment, and he opened his mouth to speak. At that moment Hywel hastened from the castle with a bundle under his arm, and whatever Dance had been about to say was curtailed.

Greeting Hywel with barely a nod, he moved to secure the reins.

Dance's retreat brought her up on her elbows, her gaze swiveling to survey his back with growing apprehension. Something was definitely bedeviling him.

There wasn't time, however, to dwell on it as Hywel placed a bundled wrap next to her on the litter. "There's lunch in there for ye and Ifan." He patted her hand. "Ye have a good time, Maddie *fach*, and mind ye not let him wear ya out."

Smiling when she felt like crying of a sudden, Madeline quietly thanked Hywel for his trouble and watched as he ambled off toward the keep. Her stomach churned nervously.

Above her somewhere, Dance told her to rest and enjoy the sunshine. Then the litter moved beneath her. He walked on foot, leading Bones.

While plagued by doubt, soon Madeline found the gentle jostle of her conveyance dragging through the damp grass, distracting in a soothing way. High in the sky, a speck of color circled and swooped; the call of the eagle sounding far away. A gentle breeze played with her hair; cooled her skin. She was bundled in a peaceful warmth, and truly glad to be out in spite of what she tried to view as premature nerves.

Her handsome guide had taken a path winding north, away from the direction of Llandeglay. Surprisingly, she felt only an unsettling moment of disquiet as they entered the dense forest cover. Then she reminded herself she was with Dance, she was alive and safe, and it passed.

Dappled sunlight filtered through the branches overhead, fell across her face. It was cooler in the forest, the rain-soaked smell of earth prevalent in the dampness.

Smiling, feeling decidedly better for the fresh air, she'd assured him she was fine, though she kept her ear tuned to approaching riders; any little sound that might give her some warning. She didn't know what she'd do if Dance seriously planned on being rid of her, but she wasn't without resources of her own.

Not that much later, he pulled the litter into a clearing that brought her around to a restful pond where the path diverged left and right to follow the mossy perimeter. Overhanging branches draped the water, twinkling sunlight reflecting upon the calm surface.

Dance squatted down at her side in silence. Startled to find him so near, edgy, she hastily flashed him a smile and turned back to the remarkable view.

"Over there," he whispered low, one hand arresting

her as she was about to sit up. He pointed across her to the opposite bank where a thicker glade of underbrush hid from the untrained eye the treasure within. "Watch quietly," he spoke close to her ear.

Madeline's heart was fluttering, her attention held in abeyance, her eyes adjusting to the play of shadows. Then she saw the tiny spotted form.

"A fawn," she mouthed very softly, her gaze riveted on the baby as another form took shape at the fawn's side. His mother was grazing in the cooler shadows. The new fawn stumbled on spindly legs to suckle his mother with greedy little butts of his nose.

Dance's hand moved atop Madeline's, his skin warm, and her fingers reflexively curled around his. They neither spoke aloud, but what passed between them needed no words.

The beauty of the moment, the pulse of life between nature and man and living creature bringing her closer to the irrefutable fact that she'd become a part of his untouched wilderness.

"Are you saying good-bye, today," she whispered at last in breath-held fear, tears blurring her vision of the scene on the opposite bank. "Is that why you brought me here?" She didn't move as she waited for his answer with alarming dread.

His finger rubbed away the tear trailing down her cheek. Then he tenderly cupped her face, brought her focus around.

Flushed with embarrassment, she kept her gaze lowered.

"Madeline, look at me," he coaxed softly, using her given name when he'd always called her his angel.

Reluctantly, she looked up.

He wasn't smiling. In fact he appeared rather serious.

"No, don't tell me," she breathed raggedly, another tear trickling down her face.

"Come here," he said, heedless of disturbing the deer as he pulled her into his arms and rocked her. Into her hair, he spoke, "Is that what you think? That I've brought you here to say good-bye?"

She shrugged against him, sniffling back tears.

"Can *you* say good-bye?" he pressed softly, his hold on her near painful when good-bye was the last thing on his mind. When what he wanted was right here in his arms.

She shook her head—her hair soft on his skin.

"Why would you think this is, good-bye?"

A pained whimper. "I don't know."

Drawing her closer, kneeling next to the litter, he brushed her downy brow with a kiss. "This is where I come when I don't want to be found," he told her. "This is my sanctuary. I don't hunt in this *glyn*. Occasionally I come here to swim, but mostly I come here to be alone."

He could feel the impart of his admission settle some of the insecurity churning around in her mind.

"And you brought me here...because?" she asked very quietly around a sniffle.

"Can you not guess?"

She leaned back to look up at him. "Because I'm special?" she ventured tearfully.

He smiled down at her and hesitated as if pondering over the best way to answer. When she scowled, he laughed and quickly acceded, "Because of that. And because I wanted to be alone with you."

That confused her. "And I wasn't alone with you before? Just the two of us alone in your bedchamber wasn't 'alone' enough?"

Not when her brothers could come and take her away. "I thought you might like to get out for awhile," was all he said.

Greatly appeased by his assurances, she stretched up to nuzzle his ear in a decidedly intimate way.

His breath halting in his lungs, he set her away. For a second held her at arms length before letting her go to get to his feet. "I'll find you a dry place for a nap." He turned away.

To his back she insisted, "I'll only take a nap if you take one with me."

He paused to look over his shoulder at her—started to shake his head.

"—Hywel told me you didn't sleep last night. So unless you have something more pressing to do, I would give in if I were you."

A darkly slanted brow indicated his displeasure in being coerced. "Is that so?"

"Indeed."

Forcing a polite reply, he said, "I definitely hear an order in that tone."

She smiled sweetly and beckoned him with a curled finger. "Order? Request? Whatever? Now come over here. Or I'll have to get up and drag you along," she coerced gently, greatly heartened by his obstinate glower.

"You're deliberately trying to provoke me."

This was much better, the familiar repartee they shared. She slanted him a quizzical look. "Trying?" she teased. "But I thought I had succeeded."

Amused by her game, he shook his head and repressed a chuckle. "Happy now."

"To have you back? Oh, yes."

Yet, he continued to eye her warily. "I suppose you want that nap right now?"

Sublimely happy, she patted the litter in an invitation to join her. "I'll even let you hold me."

To that he sucked in his breath.

Warmed by his reaction, she reflected aloud, "Actually, I'm not sure I'll be able to rest, so perhaps you won't mind reading to me." And from inside the waistband of her breeches, she produced several sheets of velum.

He recognized them instantly—his poems. "You found them."

"Under your bed of all places." A look of dismay registered on her face as he moved toward her.

Before he could snatch them from her, she quickly shoved them under the blanket. "Really, you should bind them and sell them."

"I write them for my own pleasure. So it matters not to me if anyone sees them." He held out his hand. "Now kindly hand them over."

She scowled up at him. "But they are so beautiful—how can you say that?"

"Madeline—"

That imperial tone again. "Why don't you let me read this time? To you."

Closing his eyes, conceding defeat to the soft plea in her voice, he raked his hand through his hair and decided to let her have her way. He bent instead to pick up the bundle next to her on the litter.

Looking up through the trees, he gauged the time and laid out the blanket for their picnic. On it he arranged their meal: wine, cheese, and strips of dried venison. Seeing her happy, her voice teasing was encouraging.

Madeline had been carried to the blanket of which she now lay sprawled upon on her stomach. Dance had removed her boots for her, then removed his.

Propped up by her elbows, chin resting in her palm, she read first a Welsh proverb.

Woe is me that I ever was born and my father and mother reared me, that I did not die with the milk of the breast before reaching the age for love....

When she finished the last rhyme some time later, she handed them over to him with an indulgent smile.

Dance made up a new poem while she ate and drank her fill. The ambient pleasure they took in each other's company watched morning turn into early afternoon.

"Come walk with me," he invited, holding his hand out to help her to her feet as he stood.

Half an hour later he was still holding her hand as she waded along the pond's edge, her smile winsome, her delight contagious as she splashed about, muddy silt squeezing between her toes.

Old Bones grazed contentedly in the shade of a huge oak; Sheva resting out of the way of his hooves on a bed of fallen leaves.

At Madeline's insistence, Dance gave her a lesson in Welsh as they meandered about the pond, his teasing love words recited in a low velvety voice while she repeated after him—faltering over just a few of the more difficult pronunciations. They carried their wine with them, drank the sweet ruby vintage. They were wading now in water up to their calves.

When her foot sank into a hole, she fell against him. Water splashed up; sprayed their clothes. He gathered her close to steady her. The heat from his body felt divine.

He stood completely still, his breathing shallow as he looked down at her. She blushed under his intense regard, water droplets glistening on her cheeks, clinging to her eyelashes.

Relaxed from the wine, impulsively she smiled and lifted her mazer to his mouth, playfully forcing him to drink. Her hand wasn't very steady and most of it ran down his chin.

Laughing up at him, warmed by his solid body, she licked the trail of ruby nectar from his neck. His skin tasted sweet and salty.

When she looked back up at him, wondering why he'd stopped breathing, she found in his amber eyes a stark hunger.

They were both remembering. The incredible lovemaking. The pulsing thickness of his desire penetrating her to her heart as he moved inside her.

Madeline melted against him. "Make love to me," she murmured hoarsely, her eyes shining, her plea quivering in the hushed silence.

He closed his eyes; drew a deep breath. "It's too soon."

She shook her head. "No, I don't think it is."

"Shhh, *engyl,* not today."

"Please," she begged prettily, snuggling into him, the heart of his desire pressed hot against her belly. Was he going to make her seduce him again, against his will?

"I need this more than ever," she moaned adamantly, her mazer dropping from her fingers into the pond with a big splash. Her hand trembling, she slid it between them and shamelessly rubbed her palm down the bulging length of his arousal.

His breath halted as she examined with her fingers the flared head. She smiled knowingly. "You're wanting to put this"—she squeezed—"inside me," she sweetly intoned, feeling him shudder. "Aren't you?"

Shaking his head, his hand trapped hers, held her fingers still as blinding lust vied with control. "No," he growled softly.

Yet his 'no' sounded rather painful and she knew how he felt.

Driven by an ungovernable need, she slid down his body before he could stop her and pressed a kiss to the turgid crown. She was submerged in the pond up to her waist, the water chill, her nipples puckering against the cool linen of her borrowed shirt.

His fingers curled in her hair, his eyes tightly closed, his chest heaving. And she shivered with longing.

Mindful of his weakened resistance, she brazenly nuzzled her face against the soft leather containing his magnificent arousal. His fingers were clenching and unclenching in her hair as she turned her head side to side over his lance, delighting in making him tremble. When he groaned, she felt the first sweet ripples of pleasure streaking through her vitals. Her body half submerged, her urgency shameless and unmanageable and unrelenting.

It was Dance who, with what rational mind he had left, thought for them both. He lifted her out of the water, his brain somehow working independent of lust. Then he dragged her into his arms and waded out of the murky pond.

On the bank he stood her on her feet and quickly started peeling off her wet shirt, one of his own on loan to her, his movements rushed instead of gentle, his attention focused.

Above him, Dance knew the sun was at its zenith, he had to get her wet clothes off of her so they could dry before the temperature dipped. Castigating himself for letting her get wet, he peeled her shirt away—noting as he did, her bruises had a yellowish tinge of those fading, her wound a faint ruddy scar on creamy skin.

When she tried to help him, he brushed her hands aside

in his haste. "You're wet," he offered in explanation—when she'd nearly died not but a few days ago.

"I'm fine," she insisted and when he only glowered more darkly, she restrained his hand and more firmly repeated, "I'm fine. Don't worry."

But he wasn't listening she could see, and nothing was going to dissuade him.

So she stood still while he went to toss the limp linen shirt over a low hanging branch in the sun. Her wet breeches clung to her skin and were harder to remove.

"Hold onto me," he said as he knelt before her. Her hands rested on his broad shoulders as he tugged the waist down over her hips—slid them down her shapely legs. She shivered in the shade of the tree as she stepped out of them. Dance reached for her hand, pulled her into the sunshine. "Stay here," he said with mock sternness as he first wrung the water out then turned to hang her breeches in the sun on another tree limb.

When he turned back to her, she was standing like an obedient maiden exactly as asked, sunlight kissing her skin. A brilliant riot of autumn color tumbled over her shoulders, wavy curls draping her heavy breasts. Dusky nipples peeked through her hair like pearls. She stood there, a lush forest nymph, her waist tiny, slender hips flaring into shapely long legs. Nubile auburn hair damply curled between her legs. His mate, a temptress as pure as a fairy bride, yet delightfully wanton, hot-blooded. He could keep her locked up in his dungeon, he rashly decided. Where he would have her all to himself...if he were capable of such transient disregard for her feelings.

He didn't want her against her will; he wanted her to want to stay of her own choice.

His heartbeat was pounding in his groin, her essence in his blood, and she was shivering.

He held out his hand to her. And she moved toward him, her sultry gray eyes lit with an inner fire, her need unmistakable. Could he simply offer his body warmth, when he wanted to give into his libido?

Her fingers touched his, and a white-hot fission of awareness tingled between them.

"Come, let me warm you," he said, pulling her into his solid muscle heat, wrapping himself around her as they stood there, their breathing the only sound in the highly charged silence.

"Your breeches are wet, too," she reminded him with a raspy moan, "you need to take them off so we can get warm."

He kissed the top of her head with a lingering kiss. "You're determined, aren't you?"

A breathless little "yes" and then her hands moved to the waist of his breeches to untie the laces. He closed his eyes and sucked in his breath; her fingers chill where they touched his skin.

Their first time, they had made love out of desperation. If he took her again, he'd imprint his scent on her, brand her his, his light invading her. It had happened to Aneira and she'd not known, neither had he, until it had been too late.

With Madeline it would be irrevocable—the bond was already stronger, more implicit with her. He knew what it meant this time and it would bind her too him in ways an ordinary man couldn't bind her.

She gripped him with her tiny hand, and his world narrowed to finite sensation.

"We shouldn't," he gasped, his last wavering defense

crumbling as her hand stroked down, his hips canting as sublime desire shot through his body.

"Jesus," he growled through clenched teeth, her hand warm, tight, sliding up...stroking down...his libido screaming.

And his hips set an ageless rhythm, his body shuddering under peaking sensation, thrusting into her strokes...and useless thoughts withered away. She was already his, he rationalized with dazed senses; it was already too late.

He slid his hands down, gripped her bottom. Soft flesh pliant in his hold, he lifted her atop that which she wanted. Her arms went around his neck to hold onto him. Her skin was moist, warm, and he bent his head to the pale hollow of her throat. He smelled her scent, the faint lavender on her damp skin and his tongue flicked the sensitive pulse there.

Her little purrs of pleasure whimpered in his ear— incited his lust to a fevered pitch.

His *engyl's* legs straddled his, her labia wet and pouty, paradise spread wide and encouraging penetration as he gently nipped the tender flesh of her neck. He was wedged against her, her mating heat poignant in his brain.

He could no more stop than he could deny what was destined.

When he penetrated her, her loving sheath wet, tight, sucking him deep...his light exploded inside her. Fierce, intense, radiant and painful, he felt his aura pervading, pulsing, a prickling white heat searing her soul to his, her flesh melding to his. She whimpered choked sobs of pleasure as he held her impaled...let her absorb the full stream of his power, his amorous light streaking though her, curling back, spiking through his nerves, his blood, his brain. Branding her, binding her, bathing her with a rapture not of mortal worlds.

Madeline's eyes shot open, her head rolled back, spine arched in orgasmic bliss as she cried out for the man she loved...her nails scoring his shoulders.

Shuddering, she felt him inside her heart, her mind, her blood, and the pain of pleasure was so exquisite she cried for more...and gave herself willingly to the divine union, her body a vessel for his gift, his light, his virile power. Streaking molten flames licked through her nerve endings, centering in her womb, furling out in shafts of blinding light....

Dance moved a miniscule more...penetrating to a depth that drew a guttural moan from her throat...and orgasm shuddering through her, she screamed a high-pitched, keening sound of rapture.

As she shattered, Dance weakly withdrew from her body in barely enough time...a stream of semen spraying forth over the ground behind her. His legs trembled, lungs laboring for air, his heart pounding fiercely and dazed by the mindless sensations, he experienced a moments disquiet that he was going to collapse. Then he fell to his knees with a jarring thud, his arms just managing to hold her tight enough he didn't drop her.

Both of them gasped for air in the afterglow. Madeline's forehead rested heavy on his chest, her slender body shuddering, her panting breaths hot on his skin. Neither of them capable of movement with the world trembling under them.

It took superhuman effort—his breathing ragged, he murmured, "Are you...all right?"

She faintly shook her head. "No..."

His concern deepened, but he was still fighting for

breath enough to form more than a few words. "Did I...hurt you?"

Again she shook her head. And relief washed over him. Because what they both just shared was beyond human expression and he'd not come inside her. Where her womb was fertile, receptive to his gift.

When he could feel his legs again, when he could manage their combined weight, he staggered to his feet. Madeline was clinging to him, still too overcome by sensation to speak. He got them to the blanket, lowered her down, and followed. She lay on her back, her head turned to him, smiling a sated kind of smile full of wonder. His arm rested atop her stomach, he lay on his side facing her, his nerve endings frayed and tingling.

I'm keeping you, he almost said aloud, feelings of possession gripping him.

Then he closed his eyes and mentally shook himself. He had no right to her other than that of a physical bond exceeding all comprehension.

After a few minutes more, she finally stirred beside him. "What happened just now"—she asked on a soft inhalation—"between us?"

A question with no clear answer, he reflected dryly. "I just ruined you, I believe."

A frown creased her brow. "Ruined me? For what?"

For any other man. "My powers magnify every orgasm."

She turned to snuggle close, nose to nose with him. "Really?" An awed quality hushed her voice. "Each time?"

Only with you, he almost said. "Each time."

She marveled at that, aware he was aroused still, his lance hard against her belly. "Then I've got to be the luckiest woman alive."

He looked at her with an emotion she couldn't fathom. "That would depend on your view."

But her smile was radiant. "I do feel rather faint. Weak, like I've been making love for days." A lambent glow still warmed her skin. "I thought I was dying—I could feel you everywhere inside me...."

"And I, you," he murmured against the corner of her mouth.

"When can we make love again?" Her erratic heartbeat was starting to calm. "Please say soon."

He regarded her with hooded eyes darkened by passion, his lips faintly curled. "Given you're a virgin to this, you might want to pace yourself," he offered softly. "Perhaps if I still have strength enough after our hunt today."

"Hywel *did* tell me not to let you exhaust me," she said, blushing, aware now what he must have thought as he sent her on her way. "He knows, doesn't he?"

His brows slanted. "Knows what?"

"How you're different as well, in bed."

He shrugged. "I think someone mentioned it to him once."

She knew who that someone had to be and felt the stab of green demons. For she envied Aneira her place at his side, even if brief and plagued by certain death. It was no wonder theirs was a bond of extraordinary closeness. "Did she hunt with you, too?" she couldn't help asking.

"She?"

"Your wife."

He held her gaze, his hand reaching up, tucking behind her ear a silky strand. Aneira could never abide blood and killing, her constitution frail. "Fresh kill always left her shaken. And, no, to your other question as well."

She gave him a perplexed look. "Did I ask you another question?"

"You want to know if it was like this between us, between my wife and myself?"

Disquieted by his astuteness, her eyes went round. "You read my mind?"

He smiled. "No, I didn't read your mind, not in the sense you're imagining. But since we are on the subject, I just deduced what was a natural enough curiosity."

She gave him a discerning look. "Very clever of you."

"The bond between us, *engyl*, when we connected just now in orgasm, remember what I said about it being magnified? Well that happens to me on an intuitive level and allows me to feel things deeper," he said gravely. "So if you're worried, it's probably better we don't make things worse."

She frowned. "You mean make love again?"

"Yes, that." Every time his body joined hers now, he was further compounding things, further condemning her to a life of eternal disappointment.

Her lips trailed kisses over his jaw. "I'm not afraid," she whispered in his ear. "Are you?"

Only of losing you. "Of hurting you, yes," he said softly, when her chances of experiencing the same magnitude of pleasure was non-existent in another man's bed.

"I don't know how it could hurt me. When it's harmless...well, maybe not harmless, since I might just expire of the earth-shattering beauty of it. Lord, I still feel faint." But she was smiling smugly and luxuriating in the boundless magnitude of his blessing.

"So you enjoyed it," he ventured with a wicked grin in the silkiness of her hair.

"Modest man," she playfully rejoined, snuggling against

him in a decidedly arousing way that made his erection painful. "Ummm, I think you might just need something I have."

"I've created a habit, I see."

"You're my very own aphrodisiac."

He grinned. "That's something I've not been called before."

"Why, my lord enchanted, don't you know how intoxicating you are? Any cure you can recommend me? Something say…fulfilling…or is that filling."

His attention riveted on her body squirming against him, he captured her ripe bottom lip gently between his teeth. "Keep that up and I'm not going to get any hunting done today."

She shivered at the delicious promise in his voice and heedlessly pressed closer to him.

He groaned into her mouth as he caught her roving hand before she could unearth him. He deftly laced up his breeches and knew in time his erection would cool off. "It's growing late. And I still need to find us dinner."

"Then go…find us dinner." She yawned into her hand. "And I'll stay right here and take a nap."

He rose up on his elbow to scrutinize her carefully. "Are you sure? I can wait another hour."

A second leisurely yawn. "I'm sure."

He had three hours daylight, give or take, the pond private, well secluded and not accessible but by one path. Anyone looking for her would descend on the castle. If he went now, he could be back and have her safely in bed before dark.

"I'll leave Sheva with you." He looked around at the horse, litter, Sheva sleeping in the shade. "Your beast will graze all day like he is." He turned back to her, wondered if she would be warm enough in the blanket? "Do you want anything before I go?"

She flashed him an intimate smile. "You won't let me have what I want, so no."

His hand cupped her cheek, his thumb stroking, his gaze lingering in appreciation of fate's unexpected generosity. "Dream sweet dreams, *engyl*. I'll not be far away." When he'd have normally lit a fire, he knew he couldn't risk smoke being detected from the castle.

Pushing to his feet, he moved to the litter to shuffle through his leather bag. He returned to crouch down at her side, setting the loaded pistol within reach. "You'll rest better, if you have this." When she stared at the weapon with mild alarm, he smiled reassuringly. "No one knows where this place is. Don't worry you'll not need it. You'll be fine—remember I'm not far away. You know which end to point away from you, right?" he added teasingly.

She snorted indignantly, but her eyes were shining with mirth. Gloriously nude, still glowing with an orgasmic pink flush, her ethereal beauty staggering, she hefted the pistol and expertly sighted in on the dangling shirt swaying in the breeze just above his head. "The first button...I think I should be able to manage that."

Quickly arresting her aim, reassembling his estimation of her marksmanship, he graciously deferred to her with subdued amusement. "My mistake, *cariad*, I stand corrected."

Smiling up at him, vastly content, she returned the pistol to its dutiful place and stifled an exaggerated yawn. "Be gone...so you can hurry back to me."

He breathed again, and momentarily brought her fingers to his mouth for a lingering kiss, then he gathered

up his bow and quiver and hurried in search of their
evening meal.

WOLF :—
A symbol of the lower mind attached to desire,
fierce and cunning.

20.

Sheva's throaty growl brought Madeline out of her slumber with a start. Jarred awake, her heart beating hard, she looked around as she pulled the blanket across her. Sheva stood a bare yard away, her teeth bared, and though Madeline couldn't see or hear what had her bristling, she knew at once it wasn't friendly.

The sun was sinking, the forest alive with shadows. Her gaze peering in the direction Sheva was looking, seeing only more shadows, Madeline's fingers slowly hunted around for and closed upon the pistol grip. Dance had told her she'd be fine, no one knew how to find the pond.

One shot would bring him running—but what if she needed it for protection?

Of a sudden Sheva's snarl turned fiercer, her fur standing on end, ears bent flat, her tail kinked. Madeline had seen her like this only once before. She shivered with uncertainty, her breath held. "Sheva," Madeline squeaked out softly. "What is it, girl?"

Sheva heard her. A momentary acknowledgement in her ears as they flickered then just as quickly flattened again, her defending posture unyielding.

Whatever was out there, Sheva was ready. Wasting no more time, Madeline inched herself to a sitting position, while she slowly reached up with her free hand. The tail of her shirt tickled her fingers and she yanked it down. Latching onto the leg of her breeches, she gave a tug.

They fell on top of her. Each movement made Sheva flinch. But she held steady, her teethy growl chilling Madeline's insides. Dare she try to dress? Should she hold her position?

She'd barely moved her pistol into position, pointing in the direction the threat seemed to be coming from, when Dance emerged from the forest.

Her heart leapt with relief then she saw it. The gag to keep him silent, his arms drawn behind him...the cuts and bruises, blood darkening one brow...and then the familiar face forming beyond that.

In a stunned daze, she blinked and couldn't believe it!

"Leroy," she yelped out, her pistol forgotten as it fell—she was pushing to her feet to greet him. Just as instantaneous as her joy, it registered on her mind, that he held Dance captive. Her smile faded as he roughly shoved Dance forward. The action unexpected, he fell to his knees.

Adam emerged, then Theodore, then Wesley...her family spilled from the shadows in an avenging aberration of reality. Their pistols drawn...pointed at the bloodied and battered man kneeling in front of them, their fury silently raging. She heard a barely discernable "Jesus, Maddie." Leroy's offended gaze burned into her, taking in her blanket, her obvious lack of appropriate attire with sneering distaste.

His resounding growl held pain, condemnation, humiliation for his sister and she felt suddenly sick with dread.

"Leroy—don't—"

"Stay quiet," he barked fiercely, "and get yourself out of the way." To Adam he ordered, "Kill the wolf!"

No time to think, Madeline stumbled to put herself between Sheva and danger. "Stop this! Now!"

Snorting with impatience, Adam stepped forward to advance on her. "Sorry, sis, this'll all be behind you in an hour. Then you won't feel a thing, expect the sting that I'm going to put to your backside."

Giving glare for glare, her back stiff with pride she calmed her voice. "Don't come any closer," she warned, not letting herself look at Dance for fear his life would be forfeited instantly. Her bloodthirsty siblings were clearly going to kill him.

"Go get her," Leroy ordered Adam when he hesitated, his pistol jabbing into the back of Welshman's head. "Take her back to the camp."

"No—Adam!" she shot back, then her dramatic move executed with daring gall, she snatched up the pistol she'd dropped and turned it on her brothers.

Her oldest brother's face registered the merest disbelief, before turning menacing again. "She won't shoot."

"Yes, I will, Adam. Trust me, I'll hurt you."

Leroy snarled. "You want him to die right now"—he poked Dance hard—"I can kill him with you watching."

Her aim wavered for a moment as she frantically weighed the seriousness of her brother's threat. "He saved my life," she declared obstinately, "not once, but twice. Is that not worth something?"

"Then he must have put you in peril, not once but twice," Leroy countered sharply, Adam taking the silent signal to advance.

Shaking her head, she watched her brother coming around the pond and fired a shot in the ground at his feet.

Dirt sprayed his breeches. He shot her a fierce glower of retribution.

She'd just used her one advantage. Her last defense short of throwing herself at him and clawing his eyes out.

"If you kill Dance," she railed, "I'll never forgive you." Satisfaction was hers as no one made a move. "And you may get me home, but I won't stay there. You can tie me up, beat me as often as you want, but once I get away from you, you'll never see me again. That I promise you. And papa will be the one to suffer for your pig-headedness." Before he could move, she turned on Adam. "Don't you dare come any closer. Tell him, Leroy. Tell him I'm not joking."

Stopping one brother, she glared at the eldest whose look of contempt broke her heart.

Tears of anger sprang to her eyes as she threw down her weapon. "Damn you, I gave myself to him," she retorted hotly, her pride unflinching, "I seduced him, not the other way around. So there. Chew on that."

A collective breath, they snarled. Helplessly, she looked to Theodore who was scowling darkly—surprisingly saw admiration in his eyes. Admiration for the little sister whom for the first time in her life was standing up to their oldest, most intimidating sibling.

Theo understood. So did Wesley, she noticed as her gaze finished its sweep. "Where's Philip?"

Snorting, Leroy snapped, "With pa. And now I can beat him senseless for letting you go off and get yourself poked by this bastard." Reminded, he looked down on the dark head of the Welshman who'd taken a good beating for accepting full blame for Madeline's denouement. It took guts admitting to what he'd admitted doing to her. Clearing the air when he could have had his head ripped off. "You proud of this, you bastard?" Outraged by the injustice done to his sister, wanting the bastard to pay in blood, he jabbed him with the pistol. "You see her? Take a good look at what you've done. You fucking took away her chances of happiness."

Lowering his voice so it wouldn't carry, Leroy said with lethal clarity, "I ought to slit your goddamned throat." Then he lifted his foot and shoved it into the Welshman's back, sending him face first to the ground. Ignoring his sister's shriek as she let go a stream of curses, he finished with purposeful intent, "but that would make you the injured party here. When I'd rather my sister looked back on this with nothing more than regret." Robbed of his brotherly revenge, he looked upon the once handsome face that no doubt helped blind his sister to rational thought. He took reserved satisfaction in—the blood, bruises, possibly even two cracked ribs. "It's been a pleasure running into you. Now for the next few minutes, I suggest you pretend unconsciousness so we can leave here without her getting hurt."

To Theodore and Wesley standing by, Leroy said under his breath as he stepped over the unmoving body. "Let's get Maddie and go home."

Madeline lay perfectly still in her lavender-scented, plush bed aboard *The Boston Lady*, feeling her stomach lurch with each roll of the deck under her. There wasn't even a sultry breeze to relieve the stifling air below deck. It didn't help being hemmed in on all sides either. Philip's hand rested on her arm affectionately; she recognized the *Jockey Club* he used. He was waiting until the room cleared, she mused, for his chance to pounce. But he hadn't given her away. Bless his disgusting soul, he was the only one Leroy hadn't turned against her. Leastwise, not yet.

Keeping her eyes closed, she fought alternating bouts of overwhelming despair and nausea caused by the constant pitch and roll lumbering. Her father stood behind Philip somewhere, his withered and callused hand on her damp forehead, soothing her hair from her brow, his fatherly gesture reassuring and comforting when nothing gave her comfort in her grief.

"That's my girl," her father's weaker brogue reached her, "my darlin' Maddie. God be blessed you are back with us." She lay there feigning sleep as her father kissed her forehead when she wanted to throw her arms around his neck and hug him close, burrow against his unwavering faith and tell him everything. But Leroy and the others were still in the room, so she couldn't.

They could bloody well stew and brood and pace about all they wanted, she didn't care. She'd not talked to her brothers since they'd bodily tossed her on a horse and escorted her to Llandeglay. She'd refused again, to say one word to them since leaving Llandeglay for Aberystwyth. They'd pay for beating Dance. Indeed, she might not speak to them the rest of her life.

She heard her father turn to those hovering in contemplation of how best to deal with her. "Boys, why don't we go and finish loading the hull. Then we can leave this cursed damp place on the morning tide."

Leroy grumbled something she couldn't catch, but they filed out after her father. Their footsteps fading as the door was shut.

She couldn't help the pressure, the tears choking her. Her brothers' whom she had once loved and obeyed and foolishly prayed would find her, had heartlessly attacked the man she loved. Then they left Dance lying on the ground bleeding, his hands bound, teeth gritted in pain.

Was he still lying there suffering, hours later? Had Sheva known to go find Hywel?

From what she'd remembered as Leroy dragged her away, Dance had been breathing. Although, she was sure his amber eyes had watched her, he hadn't so much as blinked. Had Dance just tried to call out to her...muttered something...growled, fought...anything.

Given any indication that he didn't want her to go.

His utter silence was what haunted her now.

How could he not have made some sound against his gag to give her some hope? Why had he just laid there and watched her be dragged away—

"...Maddie, are you faking?" she heard Philip murmur next to her ear. "You're awake, I know you are," the insistent voice droned. "What's wrong with you? Wake up."

Heartbroken and unwanted and unloved, Madeline wanted only to burrow into her grief and shut the world out. She didn't want to cry. And talking would start her crying.

Philip nudged her none too gently.

Dammit, Philip, go away.

"You fell in love with him, didn't you?" the very astute male voice prodded.

Her eyes flickered open to a blurred outline of her beloved brother, her throat convulsing against emotions she couldn't contain any longer.

He tsked as her chin trembled and swiped at the stream of tears. "I knew it," he said simply.

She tried to shake her head, refute it, but her heart betrayed her. Letting go a suffocated sob, she rolled onto her stomach to bury her face in the pillow and give into self-pity.

Always the more patient one, Philip merely stroked her hair and let her have her cry.

After enough wallowing in heartbreaking pity, she flipped back over. "Stop being nice." She batted his hand away, while tears swam in her eyes. "I don't want your sympathy. I don't want anything from anyone ever again."

"Glad to hear it." He proceeded to grin down at her with infuriating fondness.

She sniffled loudly as he handed her his handkerchief.

"Don't give me that look," she muttered ungraciously, blowing her nose. Getting her mad always worked; her tears curiously abating. "Where were you when I needed you?" she accused unkindly.

"From what I hear, you nearly took Adam's leg off. They've never seen you so all fired up." His brothers had been blustering about the set back to their plans from the moment they carted her aboard. "I thought you handled things just fine all by yerself. Don't you?"

Embarrassing tears flooded her eyes again and he took the handkerchief from her to help her out. "Hey, hey, I'm sorry." Holding the strip of silk to her nose so she could blow, he patted her head like he would a sad child. "You want me to go after that bonny heathen of yours and drag him back here? I shouldn't have much trouble. Seeing as how he'll be favoring his wounds, he'd probably be no trouble at all." He regarded her more seriously. "You'll wanna marry him, though, this time, or there'll be a lynching for sure."

Her brother's teasing wasn't the least bit helpful.

Ill at the thought of forcing Dance into marrying her, she merely turned away from him and hid her face in her hands.

"He doesn't want me," she cried with a teary sob...and her stomach roiled....

Grabbing her mouth, she sprang from bed, nearly toppling Philip over in her dash for the chamber pot.

On the floor at his feet, she emptied her stomach. And heaved some more.

She didn't see Philip's brows drawn together with concern as he held her hair out of the way for her. "Lost your sea legs awful quick there, I'd say."

She moaned. And retched some more.

She had him well and truly worried she saw when she glanced up to catch him peering at her with grave alarm.

"How long you been ill?" he wanted to know, feeling her damp forehead for fever. Though he'd heard no report of scurvy or dysentery, no word of another vessel in the bay quarantined, he knew both of these scourges could overcome an entire ship within hours. And they were a long way from home. "You're not going to agree, but I think we should have the doctor in here just to be sure."

She shook her head. "No. It'll pass, I'm sure it will. In fact," she said, leaving the pot and pushing to her feet, "I feel better already." She held up her hands. "See, almost myself again" and she clasped his arm, held on tight. "Please, Philip," she beseeched, smiling weakly up at him, "no doctor." To show him he was worrying needlessly, she stiffened her spine and turned to the wash stand. Poured herself some water, splashed her face while chastising her growling stomach. She felt weak as a babe. Lovesick and grief stricken. Certainly she was entitled to an emotional outburst, even a bout of dyspepsia. And she was sure she would be over her maldemer by the time they set sail. All she needed was rest.

Philip steadied her with a hand on her shoulder, while he handed her a towel.

"If it comes back," he just as adamantly insisted, "I'll have no choice. No choice, you understand?"

"Yes, ok." And she made it back into bed, pulled the satin coverlet over her head and closed her eyes against a fresh and inexplicable rush of tears. For she'd never felt so empty, so bereft and missing the solid warmth of Dance's body lying next to hers.

❧

When an hour later, Philip edged open the door to her quarters and heard her crying inconsolably his first reaction was primitive. He wanted to hunt the bloody Welshman down and finish him off. His second more rational thought. If someone didn't stop her, she would cry herself sick.

A hand resting on his shoulder had his gaze swinging around.

Harold's worried blue eyes met his son's. He motioned for Philip to come away from the door.

Philip reluctantly retreated and followed his father up the companionway to the main deck where preparations for departure were underway. They were sailing at dawn. The hull was being stocked with provisions for the three-month voyage across the Atlantic. New rigging had been purchased and stored as well against the outcome of a bad storm. They'd commissioned a local merchant to sell the remaining steam-winding engines, the funds forwarded to a bank in London and onto Boston from there.

They would be sailing when the winter seas would be their worst. When they got back to Boston the ground would be covered with snow, the holidays just getting underway. Leroy and Adam had it in their heads that she'd be walking up the isle on the arm of some aging bridegroom by the eve of the new year. They'd break his neck, Leroy assured Philip, if Madeline got wind of it.

Right now, Philip didn't think she could handle anything more or he might have risked a broken neck.

So while Madeline tossed and turned in her bed that night, Philip approached his father with his concern. "She's been puking her innards up and crying since Leroy came back with her—"

His father motioned him to shut the door and take a seat. They were in the stateroom where Harold had been studying the charts for their return trip home. "Has she a fever?"

Taking a chair opposite his father, Philip shook his head. "Not the last time I checked."

Because the doctor ordered it, Harold wore a sling to support the weight of his arm on the side favoring his shoulder wound. "You sure she has no fever?" his father asked, his scrutiny direct, his concern apparent.

Philip shook his head. "Just puking."

The charts were shoved aside as Harold sat. "Check her before you bed down. If there's no change, then we'll let her be tonight. First light of dawn, if things haven't improved, we'll fetch the doctor."

A little surprised by his father's answer, Philip settled on the chair's edge, his elbows on the armrests. "What if it's the auge? Maybe she should have some laudanum to help her sleep?"

Having raised six children by himself after their mother died giving birth to the darling girl, Harold would be the first to send for a doctor if one of his children was in serious danger. Maddie had near died twice in recent weeks; once of exposure and more recently of an arrow that had been poisoned.

She'd been through the worst of hell from the sound, and she'd somehow managed to come away in one piece. A broken heart, though serious, wouldn't kill her. Even if `twas her first broken heart. In his own experience with loss when his wife died, he knew what it was like to mourn love. Unable to eat, to sleep, making oneself ill with grief. It might be a good long time before Maddie got over her loss. She was closest to Philip. Just to be safe, to make sure she didn't languish too long, it didn't hurt to have the boy keep an eye on her. "Laudanum might not hurt," he agreed. "How about we give her some if she's still awake in another couple hours," he decided as he reached for the flask of port and two mugs. "Now what's this I hear Leroy talking to you boys about? Some dadblame wedding?"

Philip snorted. "In Boston. When we get back. They're gonna marry her off to old man Parkinson." His brows slanted ominously. "Whatever she's done, she don't deserve being saddled to a lecherous old coot. I don't care if he is a banker, if he's been after her to accept his damned affections, I can't let them do it, pa...."

Harold poured two drinks and made himself comfortable. "I know, son." He shook his head. "I know."

"We got to put a stop to it," Philip insisted. "She's grown up, she don't have to listen to Leroy."

Mr. Carlton merely smiled and sipped his port. "You know he came to see me one night?"

Blinking in confusion, Philip asked, "*He,* father?"

"That 'bonny heathen' of hers." Harold reflected on the young fool's bold disregard for danger. "I was lying there near dead when he came in and patched me up...that's as much as I can remember." To his son's look of surprise, he raised a bushy brow. "He took a risk doing that. Not the sort of action, I'd say, of a spineless whelp." When you'd lived as long as Harold, one cultivated a gut deep feeling about things. He took a long puff before he smiled again. "I wouldn't fret overmuch about your sister. Boston's three-months away. I'd worry more about the crossing." The winter seas brought gale-force winds that could snap a mainmast clean in two. "This time of year it's goin' to be rough out there."

Dance dreamt the lick of a tongue was bathing his face. A cut above his eye was getting the most attention. Excruciating pain ripping through his body with each breath was slower to register notice.

Tormented by fragmented pieces of some memory, he felt a pressing urgency, but couldn't seem to figure out what to do about it. An *engyl* with haunted gray eyes—she was crying, and he was searching for her. Amidst the mists spraying his face—a fierce wall of water crashing over the bow beneath his feet drowning out his shouts as he struggled against the lashing wind to find her among the shattered debris bobbing up and down in churning waves....

Pain battered his body, dragging at his brain.

At that moment pieces of something started to take shape...bring his senses into better focus...separating reality from dream.

He found what felt like reality. A damp, cold ground beneath his cheek, familiar smells.

He tried lifting his head and pain shot through his temples. Stiffness screamed through the muscles he tried to move next.

No—his mind refused to accept weakness. He had to find her...the *engyl* with haunted gray eyes. Her weeping rang in his ears. Her grief overwhelming, cutting through him....

A brief heartbeat later, Dance came fully awake with a crushing loss settling in his chest, Madeline's name lumping in his throat.

Disoriented for a moment, he stared up at a wavering image of fur. More tongue licks. The roaring sound of peril in his ears receded and he could feel the licking, he was certain because the tongue was wet, raspy on his face. He squinted against the blurring shape and his brain called forth a name.

Sheva.

Someone else was with her. A hazy vision hovering over him with a gaping grin full of spaces. "Hywel," he hoarsely grunted as recognition wavered into place with a face. His tongue felt dry as parched leather in his mouth.

"Lie still, master," came the familiar voice. "You're hurt bad, but you're goin' ta be all right." He'd removed the gag and now with a grunt, cut through the last of the rope binding raw wrists. As Dance's hands fell limp behind him, his teeth gritted as he sucked in his breath against spiking pain.

"What happened?" he bit out weakly as he waited for the pins and needles to go away.

"Ye don't remember?"

Closing his eyes, Dance searched his mind for more images. "Her brothers," he gritted out between his teeth after a moment, the memory not pleasant.

"*Ydw*, they come an' got our Maddie *fach*."

His *engyl* with gray eyes—Dance remembered now the overwhelming feeling of loss. The fleeting images swirled around in his raging brain until they settled on one particular vision.

Madeline being dragged away...and being unable to voice what he needed to say.

Dance had known as he faced the bloodthirsty lot— when they surrounded him they intended to kill him. He hadn't tried to draw his bow to defend himself when they'd rushed him. Crushed him to the ground.

Dance smiled tightly. At one point when he'd told them he'd defiled Madeline, held her against her will, the oldest had drawn his buck knife. Then he'd changed his mind, and taken a better revenge in cracking his ribs.

He'd told them the truth, hoping they'd leave Madeline alone. He didn't want them drilling her for answers. To spare her an interrogation, he'd have let them break both his legs.

He'd taken full responsibility, he had her covered. He should have known she wouldn't keep quiet.

The exact moment he'd have risked taking a bullet in the head, and stopped her, he'd been effectively dissuaded from responding. Then the blow had been delivered. He'd listened to the distorted reasoning spew from the loudest brother. The well-timed assault hitting at his honor, his decency, penetrating with sickening clarity to disarm him with the truth. He'd ruined her.

When Dance was a heartbeat away from dropping her brother to his knees with a well-aimed kick, when he would suffer both his legs broken for his arrogance, he knew he couldn't keep them from taking her away.

He was being given one last chance to make things right. He would yield.

They wouldn't have to kill him and she'd not have to suffer thinking she was responsible.

He felt every bruise, every blow of hours ago vibrating through his body. "What time is it?" he wanted to know, squinting against the glare of lantern light, the forest beyond his vision engulfed in darkness.

Hywel gently tested one arm, slowly lifting it to bring it in front of Dance as he looked down with pity and answered, "Midnight, there about."

He'd been unconscious the good part of eight hours, his brain calculated sluggishly as he let Hywel roll him gently to his stomach to help free the other cramped arm from its unnatural position. Dance sucked in his breath as streaking agony shot through his chest where his injured ribs revolted. Then he was on his back and gulping shallow gasps of air.

"Can you get the litter closer?" Dance asked of his friend as he spotted the dark outline of ole Bones hitched to his transportation home. Hywel brought the beast closer with the litter. Then trying his stiff muscles, Dance gritted his teeth and pushed the pain down inside to roll himself onto it.

They approached Wolfglyn an hour later. Each jarring bump of the litter over the drawbridge brought a grimace of pain to his mouth. But the worst of his pain wasn't from his recent injury, the multiple bruises he bore, it went deeper.

Wolfglyn's mighty stone effigy greeted him with no light, no warmth. It was worse than coming home to a dark keep the hollow emptiness that pervaded his soul. He was free of the shadow that had haunted him for six long years, and yet, he felt more miserable than ever. There was nowhere in the keep he could go and not feel her absence like a great gaping hole in his heart.

She'd come and transformed Wolfglyn from a crumbling sentinel of desolation into a bearable, if drafty cold monument of stone. For a short while she'd made it habitable, filled his thoughts with profound meaning. And when he joined his light to hers, there was nothing else in the world he needed.

How the hell could he live without her?

Hywel stood quiet beside the litter, waiting...ole Bones not twitching a muscle, the heavy dampness oppressive in the early hours before dawn. From the depths of the night, a far away howl came from within the walls of the keep. Sheva raised her nose to the sky and yapped out an answering call as she trotted up the stone stairs to the doors thrown wide to the night.

"How quick can you bind my ribs?" Dance asked his silent friend, knowing the dream he'd been having before he awakened was no ordinary vision. He was feeling her. Inside his soul. Where his light burned with self-recrimination. No other way could he feel what he felt and not recognize the truth.

She belonged to him.

At his side. In his bed. There bodies joined in pulsing accord where he could lose himself to the magnitude of something beyond human expression.

There was going to be bloodshed. Likely his own before he was through with the eldest. They'd not part with her, but then he'd die here without her anyway—he wasn't giving them a choice.

He closed his eyes and willed her what he felt in his heart. He hoped he wasn't too late.

With a great deal of coordinated effort, Dance's ribs were tightly bound while he reclined on the litter in the dark courtyard.

"Bite down on this, master." Hywel handed Dance a strip of clean leather when he couldn't breathe for the pain.

Dance watched the painstaking slow process. Shirts gathered from his bedchamber were torn into wide strips of linen to wrap around his chest and torso.

"Next, I'll need you to saddle Lucifer for me."

To Hywel's credit he only paused in his task to give an amused chuckle. "Ya can't mean to go after her in yer condition. And ye think I'm goin' near that devil of yers, ye cracked more `an a rib. Ye'll be restin' tonight, that's what ye'll be doin'."

Then minutes later, his ribs bandaged and a shirt pulled on, his cloak slung over his shoulders, Dance was headed for the barn, his progress slow, Hywel on his heel and protesting every step of the way. Lucifer as it turned out was as cooperative as a renegade banshee, but finally soothed and subdued enough after half an hour of battling for Dance to drag himself into the saddle. This time the leather medicinal bag thrown across Dance's lap held a king's ransom in gold coin, a holstered pistol strapped to his hip under his cloak. There was just enough moonlight to light his way in the dark. The old man would follow at a slower pace in the cart hitched to Bones. Further instructions for Hywel would be waiting in Llandeglay. But Dance's best guess, he'd find her father's merchant ship anchored in the bay at Aberystwyth.

The moment Dance gave Lucifer his head, the snorting black devil squealed and took off. His hooves clattering over the drawbridge with thundering force that deafened the ear. His powerful long strides carrying his master through the night to his beloved.

HEART:—
Symbol of the casual-body as a centre of
being on the higher mental plane, and the
receptacle of atma-buddhi, the spirit within.
The heart signifies the love principle and the
higher affections.

21.

It was madness riding hell-bent with only moonlight to guide him, but it felt right going after her. In some infinite plan of the God's, she'd been delivered into his keeping. She was meant to reign at his side. Regardless all else—he didn't want to think about living without her.

Driven by an irrational and fierce possessiveness, he wanted her back.

Dance stopped at Llandeglay only long enough to water Lucifer and give him a ten-minute rest then he was on the road again to Aberystwyth. At the toll stops erected by the parishes to improve the roads, he didn't even slow down to toss coins. They scattered the ground as he flew past. He had to stop her from going back to *Tir y Gorllewin*.

If he didn't get to her in time....

Heart pounding with a new kind of fear, he tried not to think about the numerous obstacles he would encounter. He had to consider, after the way he'd hurt her, she might outright refuse to come away with him.

Three hours after leaving Llandeglay—as dawn's light splashed over the horizon and bathed the seaport of

Aberystwyth—Dance hauled Lucifer to a halt and, grasping his ribs, slid from the saddle. A light breeze ruffled his hair. What was left of the morning fog was blessedly clearing. Around Dance the dock bustled with activity—rigging clanging, shouts ringing out from decks as cargoes borne on the broad shoulders of the crew was carted below deck. A pungent fishy dampness hung the air.

Dance stood a minute holding onto the saddle, taking shallow breaths and beating down the agony stabbing his chest. Lathered, sides heaving, hanging his head, Lucifer remained quiet while Dance's gaze scanned the bay. In his quick estimation there were a good three dozen ships out there. Some already underway. Others preparing to haul up anchor. Sails of those farther out, unfurling against the early morning breezes.

By the time he handed Lucifer over to an ostler and managed to find someone who could tell him the name of the Carlton's ship, it was another hour wasted.

Then he had to bribe a reluctant first mate into assisting him in his search for the sister whom he'd told the man had been abducted. The burly seaman's reluctance turned to gaping amazement as Dance offered him a year's ship fare for his time. Bowled over with his sudden wealth, the man fell all over himself to comply with Dance's wishes.

A fine mist sprayed over the deck of the sleek clipper ship where Dance stood bent over and gripping his side with one hand, while his white knuckled hold tightened on the bow's railing. The cold splash of salt water helped keep his head clear as he searched the passing vessels for the painted names on hulls. He searched for a possible glimpse of familiar features among the sea-weathered faces concentrating on their duties.

The captain assured him they would sail back and forth

as long as it took. For his coffer had benefited greatly by Dance's generosity.

"Mus' be the Queen of Sheba, `erself," Captain Wills remarked to his first mate as he brought the ship's nose around for another pass at the Welshy's signal. They neither one believed she was his sister, but who were they to split hairs with a fortune resting in the balance.

The first mate steered from the quarterdeck, while the captain scanned for the woman with his eyeglass. They were hailed with a shout from the handsome Welshman on the lower deck. Aye, the illusive ship was spotted. A roar of cheers went up from the crew watching from their stations.

"Maddie!" Philip yelled as he flung open the door to her berth. It slammed against the bulkhead. He found her bent over retching her innards out. She looked pale as a whale's underbelly. In the doorway, he stood giving her but a second to compose herself before rushing on. "You better get out here," he finished urgently as he went to help her to her feet.

She gave a backward glance at the chamber pot as he steadied her on her feet.

Before she could remark on his intrusion, he guided her ahead of him so swiftly her protest was lost. "He's here!"

Helplessly green around the gills, she looked up numbly as she stumbled along.

"Yer bonny heathen," he clarified as if she'd not heard him. "An' you best hurry. They're going to finish the fool off—damned if they aren't."

That had her heart thundering, her ashen color leeching even further as alarm set in.

"Dear God..." Dance was here? Though his foolhardy

persistence frightened her, she couldn't hide an inward smile of wonder.

That comforting thought all but vanished as she spied the horror that greeted her as she launched herself across the deck in his defense, the scene before her chilling her heart.

"No!" she shouted in earnest.

Her heathen, as her brothers referred to him of late, was favoring his side, but still managing to hold onto the pistol aimed at her brother's heart.

Leroy was furious, his face mottled with contempt. Leroy in full out temper with Adam, Theodore and Wesley, they had Dance surrounded. Their sabers gleaming menacingly in the morning sunlight, and pointed inches from Dance's throat.

He'd come, her heart gratefully noted. Dance was here. Glaring daggers at her eldest brother, his look equally contemptuous and with reason, since they'd tried once already to dismember him.

Stubborn man. Had he signed some kind of death wish?

He had no chance against all five of them at once as well he knew! So why'd he come?

Dance just glowered at her as if *she'd* ordered her brothers to break his ribs. As if she'd had a choice in the matter of her abduction.

Her hand settled on the hilt of Leroy's saber to stay him.

"Stay back, dammit!" he growled, elbowing her aside.

Dance made a move in protest to her brother's unthinking reaction. He got nicked by Leroy's saber for his outrage.

A drop of blood trickled down his neck. Things quickly

escalating out of control, she pinned Dance with a warning. Apology in her gaze, at that moment she wanted to murder her brother for his carelessness. She quickly grasped his arm, stubbornly refusing to be disregarded in the matter of her heathen's life, even should he deserve what he got for getting himself into such a bind.

"*Engyl*, get out of the way," Dance urged, his eyes never leaving hers as he warned her brothers, "If she gets hurt in this foray, I'll rip your heads off."

His protective regard for her was of course wasted on her brothers. They were amassed against him and delighting in their advantage.

"No, I won't get out of the way," she told him softly. "They can't have you this time. I won't let them." And to Leroy she turned and squared her shoulders. "Stop this right now! Haven't you done him injury enough?"

"I say kill 'em right now—"

She turned on Adam with fulminating intent.

"Aye, I agree—"

Her head swung to pin the next brother daring to agree.

"You heard 'im, sis'," Wesley chimed in. "You really shouldn't be here."

That from the more level headed of her siblings now standing united against the man who'd had the unmitigated gall to admit he'd ruined her.

"No, you shouldn't," Dance agreed, capturing her full attention once again. "I don't want you hurt," he insisted in a tight growl while his pistol held level.

That was the wrong thing to say when he'd hurt her by letting her brothers abduct her without one word of protest. "What's gotten into you? You want to die?" she angrily shot back, her emotions as frail as her sensitive stomach, her eyes filling with embarrassing tears.

"String him up—" Adam insisted as he watched his sister crumble.

"Aye—" Theo's nod followed Wesley's in agreement.

"There'll be none of that," a voice of reason joined from the sidelines. No one had noticed Harold Carlton approaching.

Her salvation, thank God! "Father—"

"Relax, child," Harold assuaged, his arm going around her slender shoulders, a wry grin on his crusty face as he looked the Welshman in the eye.

"You would be the rogue who compromised my daughter," he calmly stated, capturing everyone's attention for his surprisingly sedate remark. His gaze took measure of the bonny heathen's marked discomfort, the way he was fighting for breath and making a fine stand in spite of his injuries. When the man could have stayed away and left his daughter to believe he'd not cared enough to bother himself over her.

"You got guts, man, coming after my daughter like this. What with your ribs busted like they are. So you're here for her? You think you want her back, is that how it goes now?"

"Sir," he obstinately declared, "I'm not leaving here without her."

So startled was she, Madeline nearly gasped aloud. Her silly heart leapt in a ridiculous way, a new batch of tears precariously hovering as she tried not to read anything into his surly retort. But it wasn't easy, especially when she needed so very much to make a confession. However, if she spoke up now, she'd never know what it was that brought him looking for her. And she'd rather not complicate things just now.

Then her father took it upon himself to do just

that. "Then, my man, you'd best prepare yourself for a wedding—"

Six collective and varying reactions erupted before the head of the Carlton family was able to finish, "—right here, right now."

Madeline never saw the momentary look exchanged between father and prospective bridegroom. She was shaking her head adamantly, her gaze raised to her father, pleading he not ruin everything. "No. Absolutely not," she insisted breathlessly before Dance could say anything that would break her heart. "You'll not do this to him—"

"Now, darlin'—"

"No, father—"

But he squeezed her shoulder and smiled down into her rush of protests. "Of course he will," he remarked kindly, glancing up at Dance, "won't you?" It wasn't a question, but an order that couldn't be taken any other way.

"I don't care what he says, I won't do it!" She shrugged off her father's arm, affront in her voice. Her world was falling apart before her eyes. And Dance, she couldn't begin to imagine how he felt. Coerced at rapier point into submitting. When he'd never give his heart to her willingly now. When he'd despise her family the rest of his days. Her insides lurched, bringing her thoughts to a halt—and grabbing her mouth she mumbled "Oh, God" and raced for the rail...to promptly empty her stomach.

Afraid she intended to toss herself over the edge, Dance heedlessly threw down his pistol, and started after her, the stabs of the sabers nicking him. His concern for Madeline paramount to pain, he knocked the blades out of the way. Then he followed her.

She was crying and retching, her head hanging over the rail as he clasped a hand on her before she tumbled over the edge, his heart pounding fiercely. Sabers were dropped with a clatter behind him. What brief relief he felt was replaced with newfound concern. She was shaking her head to his soft entreaty of questions.

Her brothers wisely hung back.

The young whelp who hovered protectively, gave a quick shake of his head to Dance's raised brow. "Been doing this since we brought her aboard," the young man muttered as he offered a handkerchief. Ignoring it, Dance turned Madeline into his arms. Her heaves dry now, her paleness acute, distressing, he gritted his teeth against the stab in his side before gently gathering her close.

Her brothers remained where they were, dumbfounded by the obvious tenderness the bonny heathen displayed toward their ailing sister.

Without so much as a look in their direction, Dance asked Philip where her cabin was. Then breath held, he scooped her into his arms to follow the chap.

The rest of the brood poured into her cabin but a few moments behind Philip.

Dance looked up at their entrance and gave a glare of warning. She needed it quiet. He needed her calmed down. Let them glower all they wanted, he didn't give a damn.

The same brother who hastened to offer aide, stood by the bed wringing water out of a cold cloth.

Dance bathed her pale face, his regard once again solely devoted to Madeline. No one said a word about the unusual circumstances that riveted their attention. His familiarity with her. The fact the heathen looked at home in their sister's bed. Whatever argument they might have voiced was curtailed by the sheer gravity of her apparent indisposition.

She was crying so pitifully, no one had the heart to deny her his comfort. Not that the heathen would have stood for it. His expression clearly imposed fatal consequences for the first one to say another word to distress her.

They watched the Welshman bend his head to whisper something to her they couldn't hear. She started crying harder. That did it for Leroy. Unable to contain his brotherly outrage, he turned around and stalked out. Pretty soon the only members of the Carlton clan left behind were her father and the young whelp providing an uninterrupted supply of cool compresses.

While Dance comforted Madeline, Harold Carlton motioned his son over.

The ship's captain was fetched and in short order directed to perform an abbreviated wedding service. All the captain needed to hear, they told him, was one word from both bride and groom.

When it came time for Madeline to verbalize her acceptance of the union, she frantically looked to Dance with a heartfelt apology before she broke down crying again. The question was repeated for her out of courtesy.

At last, to his third patient query, she finally nodded and Dance had to add for her "she will" and then it was over. Mopping his brow, the doubtful captain had no choice but to pronounce them husband and wife. So it was recorded in the ship's log, Lady Madeline Carlton was married to Ifan Gwyalt D'epanier ab Owain, Laird of Wolfglyn, great healer and seer. The fact that there was only one brother standing with Mister Carlton himself as witness to the highly irregular union wasn't questioned.

The unhappy couple were finally given some privacy to themselves below deck.

Madeline maintained her position. She hadn't wanted to consent. Now for better or for worse, he was hers. She was his.

And she couldn't have felt more utterly miserable.

What in heaven's name had gotten into her father? And Dance, how dare he give in so easily, when she'd have gotten him out of it if he'd just given her time to empty her stomach.

His lips were nuzzling her ear in an intimate way meant to divert her attention.

"I knew they were coming for you...." he whispered in the whorl of her ear, his hand soothing, rubbing the tension from her neck. "...and whatever you might think, I didn't want to lose you, *engyl*."

"Well, you didn't have to marry me."

"Yes, *cariad*, I did."

A snort of disbelief. "Indeed."

"Still sore at me, are you?"

She wouldn't answer.

"Has it not occurred to you, I walked right into this willingly?"

"Oh, really. And when did you decide that, pray tell? Before or after they beat you...." her words were choked off by a lump of tears.

"The minute I realized...I wanted you back. The moment I knew I'd never sleep again with your scent in my bed. My every memory haunted by your absence. I couldn't live there without you." He smiled faintly. "I knew it was a mistake letting them drag you off. But, I'd told myself I'd hurt you already enough. I wanted you to have a chance to make your own choice. To do that you'd need time away from me. Your brother helped," he said ruefully, "and I wasn't in a position to argue. But he hadn't counted on me coming to my senses." It mattered not if he told her about the dream — the premonition. There was too much at stake to trust her to arrive at the correct decision. There wasn't time to argue. He couldn't let her jeopardize everything that mattered to him in the world over a misplaced sense of honor.

"Well—it's a fine mess you've gotten into this time."

He smiled at her insistence. "As far as I see it, I've gotten exactly what I want. Haven't you?"

Hateful man was toying with her. "What I want," she declared, tears blurring her vision, "doesn't matter anymore." And to her utter chagrin and mortification, she started crying again.

"What I want, *cariad*," he said softly, kissing away her tears, "is right here. You're in my thoughts constantly. You know my heart is yours. And if you don't then I'll need to make myself clearer." His mouth trailed down her neck...his tongue flicking sensitive skin. A momentary kiss in the hollow of her throat then he moved lower, captured and drew on her tender nipple...and dragged a moan out of her.

Of course, she hadn't benefited from seeing things transpire the way he had. Then again, no one had caught the wink her father had given him as he'd announced a solution to everyone's dilemma. Dance had to admire how the man got around the obstacles to gain his objective. Of course, it wouldn't have worked near as smoothly had Carlton not already surmised Dance's feelings on the matter.

This was once Dance wasn't plagued by his conscience into revealing anything more than his assent in wedlock.

His lips grazed the tender underside of her breast...his mouth nibbling lower. Her taut muscles contracted where he lingered in worshipful devotion, tongue laving, teasing. He closed his eyes...and felt the tiny flutter of his child moving through him. His throat convulsing with overwhelming emotion...with profound joy that laid him wide open. What he felt both humbled him and scared him.

Would she have left without getting word to him? Surely she wasn't ignorant of the fact her menses was late?

Doubt ate at his brain, his senses enflamed by her poignant scent, her body weeping with need, preparing to take him.

Determined to have an admission out of her before the day was over, he put his heart to the task of unearthing her.

He dragged open mouth kisses over damp springy curls, tantalized her nub with his tongue...and slipped a finger into her dripping hot sheath. Streaking pleasure trembled though her...settled in her womb...her hips canted for his lingering stroke—and he felt her unfurling to his touch, seeking the wondrous surcease of the sweetest imaginable pain. He'd soon penetrate her in inexplicable ways, his lambent power surging into her, engulfing, his flux spilling into her wave upon wave of radiant sensation so exquisite he felt his groin gorged with its vibrant heat. When he came in her this time she'd keen sobs of pleasure, and he'd use every fiber of his heart until she no longer questioned the breadth of his love for her.

When he moved between her milky thighs, she stiffened under him, her hand quickly moving to block him as she frantically shook her head. "No, not in me."

His lust held in abeyance, his need fierce and demanding, he felt a moment's death before he gritted out, "Why?"

Her eyes filled with tears at his disparaging look. "Just because," she said fearfully.

In that instant he saw her fear, he understood. "I won't hurt you."

But she wasn't reassured and she protectively deflected

his entry. "But you will," she painfully implored, her tears falling unchecked. His disappointment couldn't be any worse than hers for she was burning for completion, her need so great she had to bite her tongue to keep from uttering a regretful moan.

"I'm truly sorry," she offered in pitiful apology, knowing he couldn't be expected to forego his conjugal rights without benefit of some explanation.

Dance smiled down on her with tenderness instead of contempt and bent to kiss her trembling chin.

"I won't harm the baby," he whispered between feather-soft kisses, and felt her shock. He looked down at her through his lashes, met her unvoiced question. "Yes, *engyl*, I know my seed grows in you." Her hand trembled where she blocked him still. "Our child, *cariad*. The tiny one you keep guarded so valiantly from harm."

A small cry and her arms went around his waist to hold tight, her breath rushing out, "You knew all along...." She rained kisses on his chest. "...and all I could do was hate you and puke my brains out. Oh, please say you're happy."

His mouth descended on hers with poignant emotion. He kissed her fiercely, then tenderly, then stirred by hunger held in thrall, he answered from his heart. "I've no words for the way I feel...."

But he could and did know how to show her...and he indeed set her world aflame with such intense beauty, she wept openly and gratefully. His light thrusting into her, his molten lance stroking her with such infinite pleasure, his riveting power captivating...hypnotic...she knew there would be no one else in all eternity for her. To take away her breath and soul with such beauty streaking through her every thought, every nerve, every corner of her being. When she wept with the splendor of surrender, he drew her cries into his body...and came with her in spirit, in mind and flesh...the purity of their union blinding.

They never heard the gentle rapping on the door until much later when it came again and their senses were returned to earth.

"Welcome to my world, *engyl*," he murmured between gasps of air, his breath cooling her nape while he held her spooned against him. They lay abed in a tangle of limbs, the afternoon light melting into early evening shadow twinkling through the portholes over the bed.

She still couldn't speak, so weak was she from the experience. Inside her though she glowed. Their child curled up in the warmth of her womb. Inside her body she cradled the precious life from her magnificent encounter with Dance's unique brand of passion.

Never could she have left him for long. Never could she have sailed into the harbor in Boston and not turned right around to come back to her healer.

"Your family, I'm sure, will want to see you settled in at Wolfglyn," he said at last, his reasons needing no explanation when it would be natural for them to accompany him home with his bride for the wedding feast.

She looked up in surprise to see he was sincere. "Thank you for being so generous."

"*Ydw*, well I either invite them and get it over with or we get a surprise visit in another few months."

"I think I'll wait to tell them about the baby," she murmured thoughtfully, stretching out along the solid heat at her back.

His kiss lingered at the curve of her shoulder. "Though I'd like nothing better than to rub a few noses in it, this once you have my full support. By all means do as you see best."

She turned her head to smile up at him in blissful contentment. "Indeed—give them time to get used to one shock at a time."

He rewarded her with a winning smile. "Wise woman."

They left that evening after *The Boston Lady* was docked. Horses were found for her father and brothers. Harold Carlton, on his mount, trailed behind the great black beast Dance sat astride with Madeline secure in his lap. Lucifer run the devil out so he behaved himself like a gentleman. Which was more than Madeline could say of her four older brothers. Disgruntled and put out about having their voyage home delayed to escort her and her groom back to Wolfglyn, they said nothing to anyone. Philip on the other hand was enjoying his sibling's discomfort. He cheerfully kept them entertained all the way back to Llandeglay where Hywel was waiting for them.

This time they avoided the tavern of unpleasant memories. Instead they found rooms at the modest hostler that had beds enough for the small nuptial party. That night they ate quietly, for by the time the proprietor served supper it was midnight and they were all exhausted. Tired as she was, Madeline's hunger was fierce and the cawl cennin of bacon, oatmeal, leeks and various other vegetables tasted better than divine. The laver bread they soaked up the broth with was warm and fresh. For dessert they had apple pudding. And blessedly she kept the simple fare down.

Since Hywel was the only one who wasn't dead on his feet, he took it upon himself to draw her brothers into a lively discussion about the trade restrictions. Talk about the new cotton mills from Waltham led to worry about the Welsh iron calamity in the advent of peace—when the long war against Napoleon had stopped the supplies of munitions that Wales was so heavily dependent upon for their mainstay. The one industry, however, that seemed to prosper with the coming peace turned an interest to slate mining. Whether or not Leroy could make a couple of trips a year profitable. Slate was in great demand to roof many of England's finest buildings and he had ships to transport it into port.

By the end of dessert Hywel had put everyone at ease with his stories, capturing interest in solutions to the unusual number of bad harvests Wales was experiencing. Everyone agreed that trade would strengthen report. The corn brought over on *The Boston Lady* was direly appreciated by a struggling and ravaged people. And when ale was passed around the table, a toast for good cheer rose in accord "*Cymru am byth*", Wales Forever.

Another toast was made to the bride and groom, and this time Leroy even managed to look pleased for her. He was turned out in buff nankeen trousers, dark green riding coat and top boots and looking the imperial chaperone.

Similarly dressed and sitting across from Madeline was her father. His wink told her he sanctioned the toast as he also approved of her choice in husbands—he now had a vested interest in a prosperous Wales. Her loyalty to her husband's homeland broadened his business routes. Twice a year, at least, he had good reason to come to see her, bring her a new bonnet—not that she could ever wear all the ones she had already. And if her happiness this night was any indication of the future—he whispered to her later in private—then he could go home and know she'd be well loved.

The next morning found her brothers sullen once more

as they set out for Wolfglyn. Hywel, it appeared, had been busy long before they arose. In the few days he'd been in Llandeglay he'd procured a good number of supplies. He was bringing back with him a small flock of sheep, eleven head of cattle, a dozen chickens and a variety of other such needs. The wagons were to be on their way by day's end to arrive at Wolfglyn shortly after Dance and Madeline got back. Hywel had purchased ole Bones from the hostler for the Mistress Madeline so she would have her own mount to ride. She was just as happy riding in her husband's lap, and just as content holding her, Dance suggested Hywel bring home the beast hitched to the cart.

Hywel said he had one small thing left to do and he would catch up to them.

Madeline had packed a few gowns in a satchel that rode with her father. She preferred casual dress, and Dance liked her breeches, so she'd indulged in her freedom and was quite happy to tantalize her husband in the process.

This time when Madeline looked up at the ribbon of a road winding through the forest toward their destination, she was remembering her first impression. Only today she wasn't imagining a crusade of knights riding in perfect columns through the waist-deep grass, she was with her knight. Her beautiful warrior and healer. Whom she'd seen display a fierce as well as gentle side. She'd found him not in Boston, but here. Amidst the verdant hills of Wales. Amidst a land of bards and lush forests choked with gorse. Where pagan Druids once roamed and fae faeries did mischief and mayhem. While an unholy dark angel spoke in a musical tongue to his four-legged companions.

She imagined a brood of heathens running wild through a castle's keep, the scurry of their tiny feet racing the stairs.

Children with ebony manes and amber eyes gurgling with impish laughter.

She had it all. She had the dream. And it was better than any she could have imagined.

HEAVEN:—
Symbol of the state of consciousness on the
buddhic plane which is above the mental plane.

22.

While Madeline and Dance had journeyed onto Wolfglyn with her siblings as escort—she still couldn't believe her good fortune that Dance was her husband—Hywel, it would seem, had been very busy.

Madeline stood transfixed and wearily leaning against Wolfglyn's open double doors overlooking the courtyard. Peasants of all manner—cotters, carpenters, freemasons—were arriving in droves. The bailey was alive with bustling activity enough to make her head spin. The men were whistling happy tunes, smiles upon their grizzled faces as they celebrated the new master's homecoming. Behind their husbands, the womenfolk carried implements used for castle repairs. It was a busy kind of bustle that was somehow organized. Each man working independent of instruction toward a common goal. That of rebuilding Wolfglyn.

A scaffold was being erected against the worst of the crumbling walls, another going up at the gatehouse, while a crude-fashioned cart loaded with mortar rolled into the bailey behind a shaggy oxen. Another worker stood atop the battlement, replacing the ebony standards of mourning with those of a red dragon on a white and green field. *Ddraig goch ddyry cychwyn. The red dragon leads the way.*

Children scurried about in wild abandon. Squawking chickens raced for cover. It was a good thing Hywel had put Sheva in the master bedchamber where she'd find it quiet and safe. Roannan, Druidh's mate, had surprised them and was expecting a litter soon. Normally the matriarch female and Sheva's sisters had the run of the courtyard, but for today they were given their own bedchamber to destroy as they wished.

Over the clamor of noise, men shouted back and forth to one another. They had work to do and quickly for their beloved Ifan was taking himself a new wife. By nightfall the festivities would commence. They would drink ale with their neighbors and tomorrow more folk would be pouring into the surrounding valley to reclaim their tumbledown cottages—mend fences to hold the livestock in a community pasture until time allowed them to see to their own flocks. The more feeble and elderly rode in on small ponies—which Madeline recognized as the sturdy little mounts of the Welshmen. Large black kettles rolled in after the ponies. Since their lord could hardly be expected to provide an elaborate feast on such short notice, they piled wood upon the fires for the evening meal.

As much as Dance liked her in her breeches, this once she dressed in her finery. Her Agatha robe of soft muslin cut in semi-classical lines was fastened with pearl clasps on the shoulders. With its close-fitting short sleeves it draped open on the left side over a full skirt of a dark bottle green silk. Pearls dangled as well from her ears. With her auburn curls piled atop her head and adorned with a circlet of more pearls, teasing wisps caressing her cheek, she at least felt the part of a regal lady befitting that of their adored master.

Madeline too noticed the number of shier glances

her way. She smiled at each passerby until her face hurt. A small child rushed up to her with his little offering of wildflowers. She smiled back and accepted his gift. Before Madeline could thank him, he turned and fled back down the steps and disappeared into the milling crowd.

She lifted the dried bouquet of heather and daffodils to her nose and sighed. "I do pray with all my heart, I don't disappoint them."

Hywel rested a solacing palm on her slender shoulder. "Them?" He chuckled, gesturing to the throng of revelers. "Na likely, Mistress Maddie. He loves you, 'tis all they care."

While everyone, it would seem, was happy with the young master's choice in wife, she couldn't help but note a few envious looks directed her way. "Them, too," she asked, nodding at the younger clutch of maidens trudging past who's gazes fleeted past her looking for Dance. They were all Welshwomen. The young, ripe and fertile kind. Dance hadn't yet returned from wherever it was he'd gotten off to. It was awful, the path of her thoughts. The momentary twinge of apprehension.

For it was there in their faces, the utter adoration, the eagerness with which they glanced around hoping to spy the recipient of their hearts. Certainly, Madeline had expected to have to share him in many capacities with his people. It was especially critical they be quickly settled into their homes before the first frost.

Dance didn't have to tell her how anxious he was— that he feared his close bond with his people had been permanently strained—but she sensed it just the same. She prayed that he wouldn't be hurt, because he cared far more deeply for his flock than would a lord who held himself distant.

Up to now, she hadn't had to share Dance with anyone but a kind old man, and it suddenly dawned on her how prominent a figure was her husband. His responsibilities to this motley courtyard full of visitors all wishing to bestow upon their beloved master a heartfelt greeting.

The excitement was high. It wasn't quite midday and already the ale was being passed around. Under the shade of the tower wall, a harpist played a lively tune. Young children danced gaily in a circle. The older children clapping and cheering. Soon it would be too dark for work and the congratulatory cheers would break out, and the crowd would feast.

As with all grand celebrations, as the night wore on, the more ale the merrymakers consumed the greater the possibility there would be for an altercation. By tonight the laughter and cheers and general good spirits would be out of control. The crowd would be boisterous and loud and a great deal of boasting would follow. A few fistfights could be expected to break out. And emboldened by enough ale, the women were just as susceptible to uncontrollable urges as were the men.

Madeline's wifely jealousies were uncontainable with regard to Dance, as was a terrifying encroaching sense of inevitability. Her husband was too painfully handsome, too compelling, too accessible. And husband's weren't expected to dote on their wives.

"Na, Maddie *fach*, ye not have ta worry yerself. Ye'll see, Dance will na hurt ye. His heart is lost ta ye. Are ye not certain of it?"

She looked mortally ashamed to have doubted. "But they are in love with him," she objected softly, waving her hand at the crowd. "And there is the memory of Aneira. I can't seem to stop torturing myself with it—thinking he must still love her."

"But his eyes follow *ye*, Maddie *fach*." He lowered his voice. "Ye be his wife now. The wife he chose. Na them."

"I'm sorry, Hywel. You're right and I'm just feeling the jitters. I'm just being oversensitive and silly."

"Mi lady is in a breeding way. It be the babe—"

"I wish—"

"What do you wish, *engyl?*" her husband asked as he joined her from behind, his deep voice velvety warm, his arms encircling her waist to at last join his wife for the festivities.

He felt warm against her, in his arms she felt secure and cherished. Dear sweet Hywel, her confidant, blushed at her husband's wolfish grin and took himself off to join the melee.

How she wished life could stay as simple as it had been before Dance's kingdom had been restored to him.

Before she could respond to his query, a loud cheer broke out. Everyone who hadn't noticed their lord join his darling wife, turned their affectionate gazes to him now. He'd too bathed and changed, Madeline saw, into an elegantly embroidered tunic of a rich reddish brown over a white silk shirt. He looked rakishly debonair with his wild mane tousled the way she liked it best. A pagan satyr came to mind. Devilishly handsome, painfully sensual, and amazingly unconscious of the stares he was receiving from the crowd of budding femininity who looked to be near swooning at the sight of him.

Feeling vulnerable again, she must have leaned into him for she found his hand clasping hers. He couldn't know how thankful she was for his reassuring gesture. Knowing she was being extra sensitive, that she had nothing to worry about, she gave the crowd a nervous smile.

Colorful blossoms were sent sailing into the air to rain down upon Dance and his soon-to-be wife.

"We should have told them," Madeline shouted over the roaring of cheers, her hair pelted with flower petals as they fell to litter the steps at her feet. Sweet rose and heather scented the air.

"And ruin it for them," he said against the shell of her ear. "You can tell them if you want, but I doubt it matters. Look at them." Pride infused his words as if his emotional state hadn't been tested to the limits these past hours, everyone waving and laughing and cheering their lord on, unaware that the vows of marriage were but a formality for everyone else's benefit. No one would ever have to know that Madeline had been forced to rescue Dance from her bloodthirsty brothers. Nor that their hasty marriage had been conducted under less than joyous circumstances aboard *The Boston Lady.* "You see who's watching, back there in the back. Smile, darling, for your brothers—I think they're trying to be genuinely happy for us."

Bless their interfering souls, he suspected they were not going to leave until she chased them off.

She smiled and waved. "Oh, I hope they are happy for us, really I do, Dance."

Philip waved right back, and elbowed the others when her smile faltered. Then they waved as if pained to do so.

Being scrutinized by five pairs of watchful eyes, Dance only hoped her siblings didn't do anything more to upset their sister. Philip was proving to be a likable chap. But the other four had not taken the news of Madeline's pregnancy well at all. To their way of thinking a baby complicated things. Because they still weren't convinced she was completely happy and if she wanted to change her mind and come home she wouldn't be able to do so now until after the baby was born. Dance almost felt pity for the brooding bunch. But he would not tolerate them further distressing her and it would only put more strain on her if he had to escort them off his land. "At least your father is sane."

She laughed. "Papa dearly likes you."

He should, Dance thought, to compensate for all the grief his brood had caused. "I like him, too."

"Philip has warmed up nicely, don't you think? He's getting ribbed for it, you can be certain." She sighed. "Give it time, the others will grow on you, too. It won't take long, and they'll be seeking you out for some sport or wearing your ear out with their bawdy tales. Just don't let them know you play chess or I'll never get you away from them."

"Do you think they'll stay much longer?" he queried, his tone reasonable considering what they put him through. Last night again, they had tried to talk his wife into sailing back with them to Boston for her trunks of gowns.

"Would you like me to talk to them?"

He sighed heavily. "You can if you want, but I imagine you'll be wasting your time."

Loving his surly tone of impatience, imperceptible to those who might be watching, she moved her hips in a sinuous circle, aware that as she did so Dance was needing her in a terrible way. The heady evidence was poking her in the backside.

Soft was the tortured growl deep in his throat. "Keep that up and I'm hieing you off to bed and be damned with the feast."

"You think we could slip away"—a wistful quality in her plea—"for a short while?"

Just thinking about the possibilities had him on the brink of abandoning customary manners. "I'd carry you to bed this instant, if I wasn't certain your brothers would be on my heels."

Her spine arched against his hard body, her eyes closing in sheer wonder of impaling herself on his enormous lance. "I'm sorry, Dance...you have to be subjected to them."

His mouth nuzzling her ear, his erection painfully straining to get at her, he smiled tightly. "As soon as the first toast has been made, I'm sending you up to bed."

"What a splendid idea. I've missed you dreadfully."

His groin was pressed into her so she had no trouble detecting just how dire his own need. "As I have you," he breathed in her ear, his heart pounding fiercely, his desire throbbing.

"Mmmm, I feel every pulsing inch already," she purred deep in her throat.

"Have mercy, *engyl*," he rasped tightly, "I'm close to rupturing."

"Hurry then, please hurry things along."

And because he was as impatient and tormented and consumed by ravenous thoughts, he hurried her inside. Startled by their sudden appearance, Hywel just managed to jump back to keep from colliding with them at the arched entrance to the dining hall.

"We start now," Dance said over his shoulder on his way to the dais with his wife in tow.

Madeline rushed by with a smile of apology for Hywel, her eyes alight with some secret mischief.

Blinking, knowing what his master's command meant if not what was revealed on his Lady's face, Hywel reacted as any obedient minion would and scurried off to fetch the rector from the adjoining room. A few seconds later the jovial soul waddled into the dining hall. Hywel could be heard at the top of the steps shouting for everyone to come in and take their places, everyone who could elbow their way inside, encouraged to come forth now in witnessing this joyous occasion. And for his mistress, Hywel ushered to the front of the crowd those besotted young maidens, so they could see for themselves how impossible were their hopes of snagging the master's attention.

If Hywel's efforts had been for naught, the second the ceremony was over and their lord went down on his knee before his wife a hushed quiet filled the massive hall. A hundred pairs of eyes were focused on the dais, everyone's breath held. For Dance slowly leaned his forehead into her and kissed her belly. He lingered in his kiss, his large hands clasping her hips, her fingers spearing through his hair to hold him as well. When he looked up at her, it was with such love shining in his eyes that it made one's heart weak. The look shared between husband and wife could not be mistaken. He loved his elfin vixen with not only his heart but with his eyes. It was a love that would never cease. No matter the obstacles of family. No matter the looks of besotted maidens. And no matter the evils of jealousy, the wickedness of blood kin, nor the timeless sins of man. Theirs was a love to endure eternity.

And Hywel would sleep this night as he had never thought to sleep again.

His master was safe. Dance never need be alone again.

For the Mistress Madeline had slain the evil dragons for him.

Immediately after the exchange of vows, Hywel joined the head table where a toast was being raised to the Lord of Mists and his lady wife. Up until then Dance had been uncommonly patient while everyone took turns roasting him.

The jugglers and acrobats were filing into the room for the night's entertainment, so again Dance had to be patient and curtail his urgent need of his wife.

Into the hushed expectation of the revelers waiting for the acrobats to begin, Hywel sat his bulk down in the chair between Madeline and her father as he spoke to the table at large. "Good thing yer ship is in the bay," he said into the lull of boisterous cheer, that predictably snagged everyone's attention. Heads swiveled in his direction. "There be a bad storm hit. Same day ye left Llandeglay." And he told them how he just learned from the hostler who'd arrived late for the feast, that his son was on a whaler that came limping into Aberystwyth for repairs. "Several ships were lost at sea `e said."

He shook his head as her father exchanged a disturbed look with her brothers. A look that said they could have gone down in the thick of the storm if not for being delayed.

Madeline shifted her gaze to Dance at her left. He was drinking his ale and being awfully quiet. Then he caught her looking at him and smiled. Under the table her hand sought his. Her fingers clasped his and squeezed as the import of that close call gave her a shiver.

He raised her hand to his lips, his fingers locked in hers, and gave her a profoundly touching look. His love shining brilliantly in his hooded-eyes.

Then a roar of applause drowned out further conversation and the acrobats with their little spotted terriers trotted into the center of the hall. Without a word to his guests, Dance rose and tugged his wife with him, slipping away from the hall. As soon as he rounded the doorway to the foyer, unable to wait a moment longer, he drew her into the shadows. Ticklish, Madeline giggled a soft plea "behave" as her husband's teeth gently nipped her ear, sending shivers down her nerve endings. His hard muscled warmth pressed her to the cold stone at her back. "We can't"—she swallowed as his hand cupped the skirt of her gown against her wet hunger—"do this here...."

"We already are, *engyl*"—his teeth nibbled at her lip—"so no screaming this time," he murmured against her mouth. The noise of applause was frighteningly close. On the other side of the wall the acrobats performing unparalleled feats, distracting the crowd which included her siblings.

"You honestly think anyone will hear me...." and she gasped as his thumb circled over her sensitized nub of passion. She was panting as his finger penetrated, her throat whimpering as sensation streaked through her vitals.

"Would you rather I finish this upstairs...in bed...." and he buried another finger, pressing it deep inside her quivering body.

"Nooo..." she moaned into his mouth, whimpering mindless pleas as her legs trembled. She started to slide to the floor in a boneless heap.

Smiling against her mouth, he lifted her upright, spread her wider. He urged her legs around his hips with the other hand...and lost to passion she opened herself fully to his masterful plunder.

"The trumpets, *engyl*," he commanded softly, "the final act is approaching...we haven't much time...reach down and free him, *cariad*...he's hot and stiff for you."

Delirious with need, on the edge of shattering, Madeline quickly obeyed. In her hand he pulsed with life, hot as a brand and her heart beat with painful yearning where he stroked a blaze of fierce need.

"The trumpets, *cariad*," he breathed tightly in her ear, "scream then...you must wait for them...you must promise to wait...."

"Yes, yes...wait for trumpets...."

"*Ydw, engyl*...." and his lance burned to drive inside her as he nudged his crown into the lush tightness of her wet sheath....

The trumpets blared a long and endless finale...and tucked into the shadows of the foyer Dance filled her with riveting rapture, his legs braced wide as he drove into his new bride. Her screams filling the halls with sweet abandon while the revelers cheered and applauded in boisterous merriment.

"I take thee in the foyer...as my wife," he vowed with laborious breath, his head resting heavy on her shoulder as he righted her skirt. Then he scooped his bewitched and smiling *engyl* into his arms and made for the stairs. Behind them more cheers broke out. The evening festivities officially underway, while he escaped with his bride.

She waited until her husband had her alone, waited until he had her in bed where he could undress her for a more intimate celebration of their own.

She'd seen him talk to Sheva. His gift was extraordinary. His powers seductive, his quiet acceptance of his uniqueness profoundly attractive. He wrote verse and poem. He played the flute, too, rather better than most.

She'd never met a bard before. She'd never met a man, or anyone else for that matter, who healed by touch. Nor had she really believed him a seer.

Indeed, Madeline thought as her gown came off, that storm was a close call. "I don't suppose you knew anything about that storm?" she asked him as she lay in his big bed and let him roll her stockings down.

He gave pause to look up from his task of undressing her. "How would I have known a storm was coming?"

She gave him an arched brow. "Hywel told me once you saw things."

His look told her he knew exactly what she was talking about, while he gave her a dismissing shrug. "You think I had something to do with saving your ship? Darling, your father and Philip excluded of course, I'd have to be a fool to intervene when given a chance to be rid of them. Come, *engyl*, do you really want to talk right now?"

No she didn't, but she couldn't stop thinking about it now that he'd given her a moment to breath. "Did you know about the baby, too?" she softly questioned, her husband's range of uniqueness confounding and unsettling as she tried to comprehend such unexpected notions.

"Your symptoms, *cariad*. A perfectly healthy woman given to bouts of nausea? I'm familiar, remember, with breeding women."

She gave him a baleful snort. "And that should explain everything?"

"Right now I'd like to make love to my bride"—a wolfish smile—"if she's done with today's catechism."

He would be lusting still, she supposed, since his magnificent lance was ever wonderfully aroused and eager to quench the fire he'd started in the foyer. What were a few secrets when he'd just saved her unimaginable heartache? Saved her family?

She recalled the first time she'd laid eyes on him, how she'd felt it then, felt he was different. Indeed, he had gifts beyond healing. He talked to animals. He had dreams and visions and special ways. Here she was worried that he might be holding something back from her, when he'd gone down on his knees in worship to her before the entire hall full of gawking witnesses.

What was that if not devotion?

His *devotion* was what she craved now, his lance glowing like a beacon of love inside her, worshipping her body and soul until she felt faint with passion. What did it matter if he had visions he kept to himself?

"Come, my randy heathen," she whispered up at him, her nipples tingling, her skin flushed anew in readiness, "let me rid you of your breeches...so you may have your way with me...."

Issuing a primal growl of restraint he first divested his breeches. And freeing his pulsing hot beast, his lust for her unquenchable, he entered her without pause and sank to the depths of surcease...where he kept her impaled for a long intense moment...before he slowly slid back, then gripped her hips to thrust deeper. Undone, Madeline sobbed and met him in a frenzied rush of passion, sank her nails into the banded-muscles of his shoulders and rose into his ravaged thrusts...bodies slick and straining, their mating moans piercing the darkness. While outside rain lashed the windows, lightning dancing upon the ground in a maelstrom gathering power. And he took her to the stars, gave her heaven...and filled her with shimmering jolts of light.

"I love you, *engyl*," he growled urgently with eyes shut in climax as he opened his heart to enfold her close for all time.

A keening cry was all she was capable of, yet he felt her love join his where a tiny babe of his flesh tumbled and played in the fertile land of paradise...and a miniature longbow lay forgotten in a rain-soaked marsh.

A weaver of spicy romance, Desirée Lindsey first and foremost enjoys pursing her dream of spinning tales. She admits her greatest joy is giving readers a small window of time to let their imaginations soar, and as an incurable romantic, it's no wonder her talents found a natural home with women's fiction.

She feels that just as important as providing reading entertainment, romance novels advocate literacy among genders of all races and religions, and encourage healthy monogamous relationships while inspiring a sense of well-being. In her opinion, giving readers a happy ending is an admirable pursuit...and loving what she does is the very best of life's rewards.

We hope your journey back in time with Madeline and Dance was ravishing.

Desirée loves to hear from her readers.

You can write to her c/o Lindsey Publications

P.O. Box 1022, Berthoud, CO 80513

Or visit her home page on the Worldwide Web at:

www.desireelindsey.com

Join Desirée in celebrating her long awaited December 2002 release...

LORD OF MISTS

Look for her "HANDSOME HUNK" Contest details at www.desireelindsey.com

Enter contest for a chance to win a woman's gold & diamond wristwatch